THE GARDEN OF EDEN

DEBRA J CLAYTON

ISBN: 978-1-917293-84-6

We Are Not Human Beings
Having A Spiritual Experience

We Are Spiritual Beings
Having A Human Experience

Pierre Teilhard De Chardin

CHAPTER ONE

ONE DAY IN APRIL

'Inheritance,' Gabe stated, 'I'll bet you a monkey.'

Pete raised his eyes above his folded, out-of-date newspaper and ceased pondering what an eight-letter word for 'Thomas isn't sure', ending in G, might be. Pushing himself upward out of his sunbed slouch, he leaned forward to better see the young couple heading toward them. They had towels under their arms and peaked caps over their eyes and they seemed oblivious to the fact that everyone around was staring at them. It was hard not to.

Membership of what had to be the most exclusive nudist resort in Britain had made Pete somewhat inured to the naked form; probably due to the average age there being calculated at fifty-six. His age. These two were half that, being the average age of their live-in staff. But where the staff were always dressed, to save members from developing a complex, these two were stripped, and striking enough to bring on total body dysmorphia. They were what Jake, his favourite barman, had called buff.

Fees being what they were, Pete and Gabe habitually pondered on how The Buffs might afford to be there at such a young age; people having rarely made that sort of money before the age of forty.

'You're on,' said Pete, 'I reckon it's a lottery win.'

They were coming ever nearer so Gabe resorted to a whisper, 'I'll bet you her thre'penny bits are false as well.'

'Morning guys,' Dan offered, in unfettered friendliness.

Phoebe simply smiled, standing at the foot of Pete's sun lounger with legs as lean as a Grand National winner and a stomach as flat as his cap. Not that he noticed, in light of it being her thre'pennies he'd been called upon to assess.

In The Garden — as they liked to call their aptly named resort, The Garden of Eden — breasts, by and large, were overlooked.

But this filly was strung with a pair as high as a jockey's stirrups in a paddock slung with saddlebags. They gave rise to a reaction.

'Can you believe this weather?' she asked, 'In April?'

'Global warming,' said Gabe, 'Long may it last. A fortuitous blessing upon naturists of the northern hemisphere.'

Pete worried that she'd find that non-PC but she just threw back her mane and tittered.

It had been two weeks since Dan and Phoebe had arrived. Two weeks that they'd spent in quarantine, just like the rest of them had endured only three weeks prior. Not that they'd adhered to it. Pete had seen her out jogging around the resort's nine-hole golf course almost every other day. Barefoot in the grass and bra-less. Unusual in itself. The other women always wore bras to jog, but Phoebe – as she'd been soon to introduce herself – had bucked the trend.

Pleasantries exchanged, The Buffs strolled across to the other side of the heated pool to lay out their towels on vacant sunbeds.

As Gabe continued to stare, Pete pulled down the front of his flat cap and returned to his crossword. The sun was only spring warm but he could feel a small bead of sweat run down the side of his face and come to a rest above his Adam's apple.

'Are we on?' Gabe asked him, 'With the bits?'

Pete had reason to be hesitant. Gabe had proved to be as good a judge of women's flesh as he was of horse flesh, but he had to be wrong sometime and it made a change from wagers on the weather.

'On,' he replied, holding out an upturned palm for the customary contractual slap. He grimaced to find it came back to him covered in something strangely oleaginous and he immediately wiped it off on his absent wife's towel.

A steady stream of resort members came by, all making clear their pleasure at the onset of good weather.

'Doubting,' Pete suddenly announced. 'Thomas isn't sure. Doubting.'

Gabe snorted derision. 'Too easy, mate. Even Sal could have got that. How come you struggle with the easy ones and the hard ones you just rattle off? You're wired up back to front. But if ever there was a Doubting Thomas, it's got to be you. Boob jobs, nose jobs, bum lifts, belly tucks, face lifts, I can spot the lot. And your doubting it has just cost you another monkey, I guarantee.'

Pete didn't doubt it.

As the sweat was now running down the inside of his arm, he began to wonder if it was global warming or the chicken jalfrezi he'd had the night before.

'How we going to find out?' he suddenly had a thought to ask.

Gabe was now lying face down and had to lift his head to speak.

'Vic. He might not know about the boob job but I reckon he'll know about the inheritance.'

'Lottery,' Pete amended.

Within the resort, Vic and Gabe were renowned for their gambling habits. Vic, The Garden's esteemed owner, was Gabe's betting partner of choice. Pete being somewhat of an also-ran. Pete didn't get gambling. He never gambled apart from to indulge Gabe; which was turning out to be an expensive indulgence since they'd opted to be locked-in there, safe from the spread of Coronavirus.

Habits were strange things, Pete considered. That feeling of being compelled to do something that you more than likely shouldn't. He'd developed a strange habit of his own since their lock-in. Not so much compelling as entertaining. He'd taken to assigning nicknames to people. People he'd known for years. And they weren't particularly kind names either.

'Do you think they've run off with our money?' Gabe asked, just as he always did when their wives were late to join them.

Pete guessed it was a Freudian thing and that subconsciously, Gabe thought Jude might.

'They've probably hung back to do some cleaning,' he replied.

Gabe burst out laughing. The more their cabins went uncleaned, the funnier it became.

It had been a provision of their being there for the duration of the pandemic, that they accept a shortage of staff. Specifically, cabin cleaning staff. They'd all agreed. Domestic cleaners would have been far too close for comfort. As long as the restaurants, bars and leisure facilities had staff in attendance, they'd considered doing their own cabin cleaning a small inconvenience. Only it wasn't an inconvenience to Sal and Jude, because as yet, they hadn't done any.

Pete thought of his and Sal's house back in Yorkshire. They had two live-in housekeepers, two part-time chefs, three part-time gardeners, and one full-time cleaner. Sal didn't need to lift a finger. And yet prior to them moving indefinitely into The Garden, she'd declared herself thrilled at the prospect of taking care of business again. As if.

'Come on,' said Gabe, 'Let's brave it and do the first swim of the year.'

Pete put down his paper and took off his cap. It wouldn't strictly be true. They had a huge indoor pool on site and he couldn't remember a day that he hadn't swum in it since coming out of quarantine.

The outdoor pool was lane swimming only, so once you were in, you were in to swim, and Gabe was already at the far end by the time Pete was in and acclimatised.

As they swam toward each other in adjacent lanes, passing midway in a leisurely breaststroke, they commented on the arrival of various residents.

'Current bun's bringing them all out today,' said Gabe.

Pete had grown accustomed to Gabe's cockney rhyming slang. Until he'd met him, he'd assumed it was something belonging to a bygone era, rather like his own Yorkshire vernacular; notwithstanding his own greatly rewarded efforts for promoting it.

'What's that name you've given him with the new Aston Martin?' Gabe asked, flicking his eyes right as Pete approached for a fifteenth time.

Pete looked to his left. 'Three Lugs.'

'That's it,' he heard Gabe say as he swam away.

They reached their respective ends and headed back toward each other.

'Why?' Gabe asked, as soon as he was close enough.

'Because if you've got two, he's got three.'

Gabe smirked as he swam by.

Pete couldn't recollect the chap's actual name, which was becoming rather a problem of late. But whatever it was, Three

Lugs suited him better. He'd never known anyone brag as much as he did. It was clearly his compelling little habit.

As Gabe next swam toward him, his eyes were as wide as his grin. The only thing seemingly stopping him from laughing was the risk of swallowing water. He was nodding straight ahead toward something Pete couldn't as yet see.

Pete put a spurt on, hoping to be similarly entertained on his return.

It took him a while to figure out, but it was soon all too evident.

'I had to go onto my back. I just couldn't stare it down,' Gabe confessed, in passing.

As Pete swam ever nearer, he realised he would have to do the same.

It had been quite some time since he'd been confronted with full-frontal undercarriage. Possibly due to it being such a rare thing. Their club code of conduct required that ladies lay on their sunbeds with decorum and dismount from them with even more. Knees together, like female royalty disembarking from state vehicles. Men weren't excluded. Those having dropped something were to squat for its retrieval rather than to bend straight over, thus saving anyone behind from being startled or affronted. Ludicrous, considering that they were all there voluntarily naked.

Pete accepted The Buffs were relatively new to the place, but surely she'd read the booklet on club etiquette? As he swam nearer still, he realised that she'd fallen asleep, with her legs having taken the opportunity to go AWOL either side of the bed. Theirs being an overflow pool, the water level put him almost at eye level, so politeness required that he either close his eyes or flip onto his back. He flipped. Resorting to an ungainly inverted breaststroke until he hit his head, hard, at the lane end, flailing around until he could set himself forward again, front and fast.

As Gabe came toward him, he was laughing and swallowing and spitting.

'You nearly gave yourself a DBT there, old lad.'

Pete wouldn't disagree, the top of his head was throbbing.

His wife's malapropisms — of which there were many; often ludicrous, more often hilarious, but always well remembered —

were reused by them unreservedly. DBT was a Deep Brain Thrombosis, and if his vision didn't sort itself out soon, then he definitely had it.

'I'm out,' he told Gabe, heading straight for the steps.

Pete was once again into his crossword when Gabe returned in an unnecessary rush.

'What's up with you?'

Gabe threw his head sideways as he towel dried it and Pete followed the direction to where Vic was slowly ambling toward his own personal gazebo.

With his silk dressing gown, his tall wooden staff, and the Dunhill pipe clenched permanently between his teeth, Pete considered him a cross between Hugh Hefner and Gandalf. As usual, Rin, his sharp-suited, Japanese personal assistant, wasn't far behind, carrying his laptop and his first Campari soda of the day. Vic didn't do sun. Not since his skin cancer removal. But once under cover, he disrobed with a flourish.

Pete shook his head. 'No flies on you,' he said, realising Gabe's indecent haste was down to their open wager.

As he'd said it, another fly came to mind. The fly Gabe and Vic had once gambled on. They'd bet on how long it would stay on a dish of ice-cream, sitting patient and still while they'd timed it on their phones. It flew off only when Rin came back to eat it. And they'd let her.

'I've no money on me,' Pete informed him.

'Ah, so says the man who foresees himself losing,' said Gabe, rubbing his hands together in readiness of what was about to come into them. 'When do you ever have money on you? When do any of us? Not like we've got pockets sewn into our backsides.'

As Gabe strode fast away, Pete imagined what he'd look like with a pocket sewn on each cheek.

'Need a hand finishing it off?' Pete was asked as another couple walked past.

'No thanks. Already finished,' he lied.

Would he ever cease to be shocked by their leathery, dark mahogany skin? He was always reminded of the tinned prunes he'd been forced to eat as a kid, on account of his mother suffering terrible piles and being advised to consume them, daily. And if she had to eat them, then he and his brother had to. If their mother could have inflicted piles on them, she probably would, seeing as she inflicted pretty much everything else

'What is it you've called them, again?' Gabe asked in a lowered voice, returning just as they'd gone.

It was early days and Pete accepted his names would take a while to stick, especially as very few members were escaping his moniker mission. These two he'd only got to know since they'd begun the Covid lock-in together. They were engaged. Third time around for both of them and they'd each just wasted a fortune on protracted, protective financial agreements.

'The Prunuptials.'

Gabe sniggered, and then to the next passer-by, 'Morning.'

'Afternoon,' he was corrected.

Pete automatically looked to his wrist, forever forgetting that it was without time. Watches and jewellery being banned. But their lunch suddenly arrived, always prompt, so it had to be quarter to one.

Gabe swung off his bed and opened the Starship delivery robot, retrieving the cartons that contained their pre-ordered lunches.

Pete had a great fondness for the small, six-wheeled delivery vehicles that were programmed to go the length and breadth of the resort with unwavering politeness.

'Bye for now. Have a nice day,' it said to them as it went on its way.

'You too,' Gabe replied, as sincerely as if the thing could hear and understand.

Everyone was fond of them and it was all down to Pete that they were there.

He'd first seen them running rife around Milton Keynes, having spent the best part of two years living in nearby Olney, pulling his brother and his ailing business back from the brink.

The Starships had entrepreneurial genius written all over them and Pete only wished he'd come up with the idea himself, but at least he'd had the gumption to propose them to Vic.

‘Go on then. What did he say? Lottery or inheritance?’ Pete asked.

Gabe shrugged. ‘Told me to mind my own business.’

Pete was taken aback. ‘Did you tell him a bet was resting on it?’

Gabe nodded, before biting, savagely, into his salmon and cucumber baguette.

‘Well, I never,’ said Pete, ‘The old goat’s suddenly developed a conscience.’

They ate their lunch, pondering upon it, but Pete could see Gabe was rattled. He wasn’t sure if it was Vic’s denying him insider information or just being denied the possibility of a monkey.

‘What do you think he’s writing?’ Pete asked, to distract him.

‘Who?’

‘Vic. He puts in his AirPods and off he goes. Tap-tapping away on his laptop. It’s all you see him do these days.’

‘Whatever it is, he doesn’t want anyone seeing it. You watch.’

Pete watched.

Gabe was right. Vic closed down his laptop as soon as Ruthless approached him.

Ruthless — on account of his wife being called Ruth but nobody ever seeing him with her — looked like he was about to have an audience with the pope. His head was bowed and his hands were being wrung, obsequiously.

‘I bet he’s been summoned on the back of all the rumours,’ Gabe stated.

Pete had heard the gossip about a possible divorce but he didn’t believe it. He considered they wouldn’t have opted to be locked-in there together if they hadn’t been reasonably happy. But if they possibly weren’t, then they would soon be gone. It was a couples-only club and that was a rule Vic remained resolute to, allowing him to despatch a warring couple on a whiff and a whim, as he’d very recently proved. Not that it had always been like that. Pete himself had joined as a single. But then, Vic had his reasons.

Ruthless was summarily despatched, but with a grin that suggested a favourable outcome.

‘Maybe he’s writing a book about what The Garden is *really* about,’ Gabe speculated.

Pete baulked. ‘Not if he knows what’s good for him. He could end up being the next Ron Hubbard.’

Vic was somewhat of an enigma to the resort’s members. Nobody knew much about him and what they did know, they didn’t know if to believe. He’d been a professor of mathematics for a time, at Oxford. He’d been the owner of a cruise liner, inherited from an eccentric aunt. He’d crashed his car at Le Mans twenty-four-hour race, resulting in his spleen removal. He’d once enlisted in the French Foreign Legion after suffering a broken heart, inflicted by a Soho stripper. The myths made the man and the enigma was wholly enhanced by the vibes he gave off. Vibes which meant you didn’t stick around to chat with him. You asked him something, or you imparted something, but you didn’t chat. Although that didn’t apply to Pete. Pete knew that he was the nearest thing to a mate that Vic had.

A dozen years back, when Vic had failed to surmount the tragic circumstances of his wife’s death and suffered a full-blown nervous breakdown — pretty much the same as Pete himself had had after his first wife, Pippa, had died — it had resulted in his epiphany. And soon thereafter his common or garden naturist resort had gone off grid to become something of an entirely different nature. Only four years after that, Pete’s recently widowed and deeply scarred former self had arrived, with the two of them soon to discover that they had much in common, sharing deep and meaningful conversations lasting well into the night. The only thing they didn’t share was their experience of fatherhood. Vic greatly respected and admired his two step-kids, Eve and Adam, while Pete felt the exact opposite of his own three sons.

‘Where the hell have you been? You were only meant to be going back for your bleeding tennis rackets,’ Gabe grumbled.

‘SOL,’ Sal told him.

Gabe quickly raised, then lowered, his right hand in acknowledgement.

Pete reckoned it was Gabe’s fifth swear word of the day, but where he always chose to ignore them, his wife didn’t.

Swearing within the club was a no-no. Not to the point of punishment but to the point of having it pointed out to you. To which you had a duty to acknowledge. Sal swore more than anyone, even Gabe, but hypocritically, she was always the one most likely to call someone out with a SOL. Acronym for Swearing Out Loud.

They had a lot of acronyms for a lot of misdemeanours and like SOLs, they were to be submitted on a POT form. Acronym for Personally Observed Transgression.

Some people only filled out a POT form for things more noteworthy, but others did it to the letter. Some people considered that if it had been acknowledged then it was enough, others didn't.

Pete rarely pointed out POTs. It was too confrontational. The forms were much better. Sneaky and underhand maybe, but addictively so. Initially, he'd considered POTs as all part of being human, but over time he'd accepted that the small stuff often developed into the more sinister stuff. He imagined it along the lines of smoking weed leading you to snorting coke.

'We got talking to Mo and Carmen,' Gabe's wife replied, 'Much better than being here, talking to you.'

Pete liked Jude. She was snappy and rude, mostly to Gabe.

'We had to wait for them to shut up and walk off,' Sal added, 'We needed to get a good look at her rear-end and see if you were right about her bum lift.'

'And?' Gabe asked.

Sal shook her head. 'We think she just got lucky.'

'Yeh, we want what she's got,' Jude added.

'Now, now, girls. Remember the tenth commandment. Thou shalt not covet thy neighbour's ass,' Gabe told them.

'I wasn't talking about her ass, I was talking about her husband,' Jude countered.

Sal had suddenly leapt forward, shading her eyes to peer across the pool.

'For Pete's sake!' she bellowed, causing Pete to drop the last of his pâté covered crackers, wrong side up, into his naked lap. 'Put the blinking snatch away why don't you!'

Everyone poolside looked to Sal, hand on hip, and then to where her other hand was pointing, accusingly.

Phoebe woke up with a start and realising her faux pas, quickly gathered up her rogue legs to pull her knees tight together.

'SOL,' came a random shout from the midst of their sunbed audience.

'Blinking *is not* a swear word!' Sal returned, springing to her own defence.

'I think they meant *snatch*,' someone shouted across.

'SOL,' the voice repeated.

Yes, they obviously did.

Sal was enraged. 'Snatch is not a sodding swear word!'

'SOL,' came a loud multitudinous chorus.

They were all laughing. It was only offered as a polite prompt for their spiritual advancement but Sal always got apoplectic about being politely prompted.

Pete might have looked like he was laughing but he wasn't. The Garden's members saw themselves as belonging to Britain's elite, while they saw Sal as more belonging to a council estate from the wrong side of Barnsley, which at one point in time she was. Pete didn't see himself as elite and he didn't consider they should either, seeing as most of them were self-made, like he was. Their elocution lessons fooled no one, especially after half a dozen Pimms.

'Snatch does sound a lot like a swear word though, don't you think?' Jude remarked as she perched on the end of her husband's lounger.

'It's probably a Yorkshire swear word,' Gabe agreed, 'One that poured another few million into his bursting coffers.'

Jude smirked. 'A fortune made from swearing, and for your sins, you end up here, where it's banned.'

Pete smiled and then winked at Sal as she sat beside him, scraping the pâté off his hairy thigh with the broken cracker. There was a time when he'd thought snatch a profanity. Albeit a minor, cringeworthy one. But those little handkerchief corners on strings that Sal had called her snatch patches, as opposed to knickers, had made him forget about cringing or even caring. His business brain had had the Snatch-Patch trademarked, manufactured and marketed to give a four million turnover in its first year. Twenty in its second. Not that Pete had ever intended it to, or even needed it to. His first business had sold for one hundred and seventy million and his second, for ninety-five.

'It's just a Sal word, isn't it Sal?' Pete responded, pointing at his own chin, to mirror the fact she had pâté on the end of hers.

'I suppose a lot of words sound like swearing when you say them with a Yorkshire accent. It's just so guttural,' Jude observed.

'No, they don't,' Sal challenged.

'Yes, they do. Just listen to TwatNav.'

'Yes, but TwatNav really is swearing. Yorkshire accent or not,' Gabe chucked in.

They were referring to Pete's first business. The one that had come about on the back of his reading a newspaper poll that put the Yorkshire accent as being the one most people trusted. It also came out top for being the most comedic. People having thought the same joke funniest when delivered by a Yorkshireman. That's what had prompted Pete to create *TwatNav - a Sat Nav with a difference*.

He'd put his own gruff Barnsley accent to good use by delivering all possible directions. Right turns and wrong turns but by turn amusing. A couple immediately sprung to his mind.

'Turn tha sen around yer daft twat, tha's headin' tut tuther side a town b' mistake. Nay the hummer, tha's mekkin a pig's ear a this trip an' reet.'

'Nah then, tha's got junction coming up. Tek thee sen left or tha'll end up in yon allotments wi' a mush full a man-oor.'

And amid the directions, TwatNav gave out something that normal Sat Nav didn't. Random, and more often than not insulting, comments.

'By 'eck tha's med no effort today has tha? Where'd thee get tha shirt from? Mungo and Shoddy yard?'

'Stop picking tha nose, tha'll be going boz-eeyed if thee goes in any deeper.'

There were one thousand 'randoms' in the programme and they were so well distributed that they reached you mostly unexpected and rarely repeated.

People loved it. They'd even stopped using their own in car Sat Nav to install Pete's. They were even using it in countries that didn't speak English, let alone Yorkshire. He had developed a cult following all of his own.

As for swear words, there was only the one, and that had been by mistake. Pete detested swear words. He hated the F word. And the S word. And couldn't bear to hear the C word. Why couldn't people use their imaginations? The F and S were totally oversubscribed as far as he was concerned. Bollocks was the only expletive he'd ever allowed himself, but tame as he considered it to be, The Garden did not, even though declaring yourself stark bollock naked proved admissible. He didn't mind that they were encouraged not to swear, in fact it pleased him no end. Unfortunately, Sal hadn't as yet been encouraged. If he could change one thing in her, it would be to have her stop swearing. As for TwatNav, it did genuinely bother him that people thought of it as nothing but swearing when it was actually nothing but insulting.

'You know, there's only one swear word in it,' he responded. 'Twat. And that's only because I didn't know it was one until we'd gone into production.'

'Bullshit,' said Gabe.

'SOL,' said Sal.

Gabe lifted his right hand in acknowledgement, and then, 'You don't really expect us to believe that, do you?'

'Honest to God. I thought it was related to twit. Like its past tense.'

Gabe shook his head at Jude. 'So now we're supposed to believe that snatch *and* twat aren't swear words.'

'Believe what you like,' Pete told him, 'It doesn't bother me.'

And it didn't. When the novelty of TwatNav had eventually worn off it had already made him a fortune and it was still in production when he'd sold it, for another.

'Did you plan all your businesses around being so ... earthy?' Jude asked him, as she rubbed the blue bunion on the side of her big toe.

Pete smiled. He knew she was now inclusively referring to his second business as well. Another one that he hadn't had a need for starting. Maybe it was a wife thing, since that one had all been down to Pippa. Pip's Skips. It had come into being on the back of her not getting the three skips she'd ordered in time for their change of carpet. Pete had bought a dozen skips on the strength of it and it had gone from there. When it sold it had been the largest privately owned skip hire company in the UK. Pip had loved to see one of her skips on someone's drive, her name emblazoned on the side, full of rubble and old tat. Bless her. Sal was the same. She saw the Snatch-Patch as entirely hers and handed out free packets of them wherever she went, which didn't always go down well at some of the more upmarket events they found themselves invited to.

'As we say in Yorkshire, where there's muck, there's brass,' Pete told her, 'And never a truer phrase has been coined.'

He wasn't going to tell Jude why, but he was casting his mind back to his very first foray into business when he was only twelve. His bedroom window had overlooked the sewage works and it was from there that he'd spied the tomatoes growing around the sewage beds. He'd soon worked out that they came from the undigested seeds of those who had eaten them, which seemed to him rather fortuitous. He'd cut a hole through the wire mesh of the perimeter fence and crept in every night to gather them up. Then using a large Silvercross pram that he'd salvaged from the council tip, he'd set up stall outside the local bingo hall every Tuesday and Saturday night. Earthy indeed.

A mobile began to ring and Sal rooted in her bag, pulling out her own before she went back in to pull out Pete's. Pete never carried his phone with him and not just because he was without pockets, rather that he'd developed an aversion to answering it.

'It's your Jeremy,' she said to him, looking at the caller alert.

'Ignore it.'

Sal put the mobiles back into her bag.

'Look at her,' she suddenly hissed, 'She's at it again.'

She was looking across to where Phoebe's legs had fallen apart, after having once again fallen asleep.

'Don't you go gawping, Peter Hardcastle.'

'For goodness' sake, Sal. What's he going to see from this distance?' Jude admonished.

'Believe me, he can see like bionic man since he's had his eyes tasered.'

Gabe and Jude looked to Pete and Pete immediately screwed up his eyes, then throwing his arms and legs in the air like an upended beetle, shook himself like he was receiving the mother of all electric shocks. Another one to be remembered and reused.

But then one shock followed another as a pack of variously sized dogs suddenly hurtled toward them at an unstoppable speed. The front runner was Adam's collie, with two springer spaniels hot on its heels, followed by an Afghan, Arek's Rottweiler, a couple of Labradors belonging The Shining, Mary's poodle, and a mixed tumult of terriers. The Yorkshire terrier belonging Sasquatch came in last.

Pete was reminded of a Winnalot advert he'd once seen, only this lot weren't heading over the hills for dinner, they were heading straight for the pool, with each and every one of them leaping into it like it was a vat of gravy. The two women that were in there froze in stunned disbelief.

'That's the filters furred up again,' Gabe grumbled, leaning sideways for a frantic scratch, as if two hundred fleas had just found security upon him.

'Sorry! Sorry!' shouted the young woman who arrived after them, shortly followed by another. They were both red faced and breathless. The dog nannies.

'This is getting ridiculous,' Sal huffed, 'They can swim in the lake. They can swim in the river. They even have their own bloody jacuzzi. Why is it they always make a beeline for here?'

They watched as various owners rushed to coax their pets out of the water.

'We never had this many before the lock-in,' Jude observed, 'Do you think Vic specifically selected dog owners?'

'Don't be daft. We wouldn't have got in, would we?' Sal said to her. 'I reckon he selected us based on cabin numbers.'

'What makes you say that?'

'Because Mary says he's into a secret numberillogical thing.'

Numerology even, thought Pete.

'Only numbers Vic's into are next week's score draws,' Gabe retorted, 'But I tell you what, however he selected us, he's certainly managed to piss a few off.'

He'd quickly raised a finger before Sal could SOL him.

‘I got a text from Barry Backhouse yesterday, saying he’s thinking of suing. Says it’s discrimination. But I can’t see on what grounds, seeing as we’ve got blacks, Jews, gays and northerners in here.’

Pete smiled, but he had to admit, it had been an unfathomable selection process.

Just prior to the Covid lock-down, Vic had had the forethought to invite members to stay for the duration of the pandemic, enabling them to be shut off from the outside world. He’d had a huge take-up of the offer. But for some inequitable reason, not everyone had been accepted.

There were one hundred and forty-five cabins within the resort. Cabin number one was Vic’s and the rest were all owned by members. Out of those one hundred and forty-four couples, ninety-one had applied for the lock-in, yet only forty-four had been accepted. Forty-five, if they were to include the most recent couple, The Buffs. A couple who weren’t even previous members. A couple who no one had ever seen before. A couple who had been handed a cabin belonging the couple who Vic had despatched, only a month before, on a whiff and a whim.

Vic had told them that a resident head count of ninety was the maximum capacity to remain compliant with government guidelines, but they all knew it wasn’t true.

Pete had doubts that any of them should be there. Self-contained they might be, but they were mixing without restraint and masks and sanitisers were something they only ever saw on TV. Vic had assured them that what was acceptable for care homes, monasteries and boarding schools was equally acceptable for health resorts. And they’d bought it.

‘Pete! Pete!’ someone was urgently and anxiously shouting.

Everyone thereabouts looked to Pete. Some even pointed at him. Pete held up his hands as if to plead not guilty, then pointed to the pool and the Yorkshire terrier paddling around in it. As everyone looked to the dog in the pool, Pete looked to its owner, Sasquatch. She of the gigantic feet, or plates of meat as Gabe was apt to call them. She and her husband had decided to name their dog after him, and then expected him to be pleased by the honour. He wasn’t. Maybe if it had been a Staffordshire bull terrier, but then he’d have had to be born in Staffordshire, heaven forbid.

It irked him, this latest trend to give pets human names. When he was a lad, dogs were called Rex and Rover and cats were called Tiddles and Tiger. His gran's cat had been called Cockles, on account of it being particularly partial to them.

He remembered his gran with fondness, stood at the back door in her hair curlers and pinny, shouting, 'Cockles! Cockles!' in a voice as gruff as gravel from smoking non-tipped Woodbines since the age of ten, and sounding just like a street market fishmonger. As he recollected, there'd been at least six occasions when people had turned up to buy.

As their wives headed off in the direction of the tennis courts, Pete set off for the charging shed to pick up an electric scooter.

'Don't forget, you still owe me a monkey,' Gabe shouted after him.

Pete couldn't forget because Gabe wouldn't let him.

It was for a bet placed on their first arrival for lock-in. Sheepteeth had turned up in a brand-new Aston Martin and Gabe had wagered that Three Lugs would soon have the same delivered, only higher spec. And as of that very morning, it had come to pass.

Pete purposely dropped his cap to the ground and then he purposely bent over to retrieve it, in a manner contravening club etiquette. He might not be able to say bollocks verbally, but he could always say it gesturally. He could hear Gabe laughing as he scootered on his way.

The Garden of Eden was set in a steep-sided, tree-lined valley that lent itself well to its name. It was certainly Pete's idea of an Eden. The three-tiered waterfall at the valley's head fell into a deep, dark lake and from that came the river Styx. It wasn't its real name. Most people had forgotten what that was, as Vic had long since renamed it. It wasn't a raging rapids sort of river, more a placid, preamble sort, but it ran all the way through the six miles of their valley; around The Dome, past The Pagoda, under The Bridge, past The Hub, around The Tree, and then meandered through their nine-hole golf course before disappearing beyond the perimeter. Thanks to Vic, they had a lot of definite articles in The Garden. So much so, Pete often wondered if he'd one day get around to announcing himself as The Vic, similar to The Donald.

Up until recently, Pete hadn't known that their valley was geologically identified as a blind valley, akin to a blind alley. It was only upon this discovery that he wholly understood the sign that sat at the head of their natural cul-de-sac.

A blind valley for the blind who now see.

An obvious nod to their club anthem, Amazing Grace, and a reminder that they were all singing from the same hymn sheet.

In The Garden, there were signs everywhere. Often intriguing, almost always thought provoking, and occasionally downright baffling. Vic was prone to moving them around or swapping them for something new, having the desired effect of keeping members attentive to them. Pete was more attentive than most.

Taking the riverside track, he headed up the valley at some speed, soon to come to The Bridge. Carved from seasoned oak and made to look rustic and reclaimed even though it hadn't yet seen out a decade. As he walked his scooter across it, he saw that the overhead sign was a new one.

Vibration will do anything. Just ask why it is that soldiers break step when crossing a bridge – Nikola Tesla.

Pete read it twice. Another one he'd have to google.

Vic never gave any reason for using his many adages and aphorisms and nobody had the temerity to ask for explanations, other than Pete. Fortunately, most were self-explanatory.

Once over the other side, Pete pulled back the throttle of his scooter and then just as quickly pulled down his cap to stop it from lifting off. There had been many times that he'd had to go back to retrieve it, but even when lost, it was always soon to be returned. Everyone knew that the flat cap was Pete's.

Gliding over the smooth tarmac, he let go one hand to wave to the two men who were stood knee deep in the slow-moving river, fishing. Vic always made sure it was well stocked as very few trout made it that far up stream by themselves.

Further along was The Pagoda, always reminding Pete of the one by Willen lake, less than three miles from his brother's house. He whistled and waved to the small group that were sat inside it, cross-legged in meditation. Nobody responded and he smiled on seeing the sign there.

Do not let the behaviour of others destroy your inner peace – Dalai Lama.

He was soon to reach the part of the track that disappeared into darkness. It was the one place where the steep woodland stretched down across the meadow to reach the river's edge. Always intensely cold, people were usually numb by the time they came out the other side of the trees. But once there, the sight that met the unwary traveller, or even the wary, was enough to freeze them to the very spot. Even though Pete knew to expect it, he somehow never did.

Vic had never kept secret his love of Centre Parcs. His wife had refused to fly, so for many years the resorts had been their holiday of choice. Knowing this made it easy to see where he'd poached the idea from, only as Sal had once said, he hadn't so much poached it as souffléd it. The Dome, their dome, clearly had aspirations to being more of an O2 arena. If it hadn't been hidden in the deep valley it would never have gotten planning permission, and that was if it even had permission. Pete had his doubts.

Up ahead there was a valley wide fence with a gate to pass through, and as usual, Arek's ponies were just the other side of it. Every week there seemed to be at least one more. They were gathered around the sugar box and when they saw him, they began to shake their heads and whinny.

Pete reached the gate and took time to read the cardboard message that was tied there.

Please shut the gate and keep the ponies from off the golf course. Beneath it, in a different coloured pen, someone had written: *Don't bother. Ponies can swim. Especially gypsy ponies.* There was an arrow pointing to the river.

Pete smirked. Having once visited Appleby Horse Fair, he would agree. The fence ran right down to the river, but not through it, or even into it. The ponies didn't need to swim, they only had to paddle to circumnavigate it.

Once through the gate, Pete reached for the box that was set on top of a waist high pole. It was made from rough timber and had been severely gnawed on all eight corners. The ponies nudged him and pushed him as he struggled to unclip the latch.

'Calm tha sens!' he yelled at them.

Grabbing a handful of sugar-cubes, he scattered them liberally onto the well nibbled grass and they immediately ceased from plaguing him. Pete wasn't sure the sugar box was a good idea. It worked in so much as there were no more nipping incidents — being nipped, when naked, was something that worried them all, especially the men — but now, all they did was loiter around the box like teenage hooligans on a street corner, just waiting to mug you.

The double doors of The Dome were pinned wide open and Pete abandoned his scooter and went on inside.

Right and left of the front foyer were four doors, each leading to other doors, accessing changing rooms, saunas, sand-solarium, massage suites, gym, colonic irrigation, steam rooms, dry bar, and more. Straight ahead stretched the large open shower trough that barred the way like a cattle grid. It came on automatically as soon as you stepped into it, so you had no option but to enter cleanly.

Once through to the other side, there were two routes into their manmade paradise. Directly, through revolving doors, or indirectly. Pete opted for indirectly. It was his preferred route. Suffice it to say it was most peoples.

A cluster of large, inflated rubber rings bobbed around in a holding pen and Pete leapt, bottom first, into the nearest. Using his hands as paddles, he made his way out of the pen and into the adjacent steel, convex canal. This was their rubber-ride. A mechanically induced current provided the gentle flow that took the inflatables on a meandering course throughout the entire dome. It was always an adventure.

Thick, lush, tropical vegetation surrounded him on both sides, with errant, overhanging palm fronds frequently stroking over his head and arms. Three shades of bougainvillea climbed up the inner structural supports with myriad butterflies flitting from flower to flower, while metallic shiny hummingbirds hovered around the golden globes of syrup that hung in-between.

The sounds were of running water, cicadas and parakeets. The scents were of jasmine, frangipani and gardenia. It was a joy to the senses.

Floating gently along, Pete passed through various shell lined grottos, all hidden behind cascades of water that fell like sheets of iridescent glass. Intermittent patches of crawling white mist parted around him as he sailed through, all generated from well-hidden dry-ice machines.

Halfway around, the canal became an aqueduct that rested deep across a large silent pool, brim full of Koi carp. As Pete reached out, their gaping mouths tried to latch onto his trailing fingers. And then he passed beneath another overhead sign.

As a bee gathering nectar does not harm the flower, so do the wise as they move through the world – Buddha.

Pete felt himself sag deeper into his ring as he began to realise that he'd never felt so calm, so happy, or so thoroughly content. All was well with the world. Apart from Covid.

He tilted back his head to stare up at the domed roof; formed from interlocking triangular glass panels that refracted sunlight in a dozen different directions. The only shadow came from the sealed circular slide that spiralled overhead, exiting through a single panel to end in a chute out over the neighbouring lake. The wild-swimmers amongst them — The Eden Lakers as they liked to be known, forever prompting Pete to think of them as a basketball team — were totally enamoured of it, but Pete had tried it once and vowed never again. If the drop didn't kill you the cold water would, he'd once warned Sal.

Eventually, Pete came to where the canal narrowed and where he knew to reach for the overhead lever that would flick him out, like a pinball flipper, into the dome's large central pool. It was an ingenious design and Pete often pondered upon how he might incorporate it into the many conveyors of his Snatch-Patch factory.

The Dome's pool was fashioned just like his rubber ring. One large circular pool with a hole at its centre. Only it wasn't a hole, it was an inner pool, contained and hidden from view by a high circular wall.

With the outer pool being forty-four metres in diameter and the inner, twenty, it left them with a twenty-four-metre-wide ring to swim around. Clockwise. It always had to be clockwise.

The hidden pool was known to them all as The Well and from its centre rose a tall metal cast that stood like a sentinel almost to the roof. Visible only from wall height up, to the staff who worked there it was an enigmatic objet d'art. To the members, it was a gigantic, sometimes operational, tuning fork, but no less enigmatic.

Pete purposely fell out of his ring and swam to reach one of the half-dozen submerged stools at the swim-up bar. He always chose to sit on the same one, and as he spent so much of his time sat upon it, other members were courteous enough to avoid it.

'You not doing your usual laps today?' Jake, the bar-tender, asked him, nodding to the open water behind.

'Nup. Gabe had me doing twenty lengths in the outdoor pool. I'm swum out.'

'Good for you. That's a third of a mile.'

'Is it?'

Jake nodded. 'Sixty-four laps is a mile.'

'Who told you that?'

'Sheepteeth.'

Pete conjured up a mental picture of the person in question. The bloke with all the Hampsteads, as Gabe often referred to him. His teeth were so large and shallow he looked like he'd been chewing the cud since he'd been weaned. Each tooth looked capable of having the ten commandments etched upon it and Pete found them quite scary, although he couldn't ever remember coming face to face with them in the pool.

'Looking forward to tonight then?' Jake asked him, as he passed over the usual gin and tonic.

Pete raised an eyebrow as a lazy way to asking him why.

'Speakers Night. It's back on again.'

Pete had heard, but he wasn't sure he approved. There were still lock-down rules in place on the outside and weren't they breaking enough of those already? But then, he'd really missed their after-dinner speaker nights. So had Sal. They were only once a week but they were often the highlight of it, depending on who was invited.

'I've found out who you've got coming as well.'

Pete raised both eyebrows. Not even the members knew who it was going to be until they were actually being introduced. The anticipation was half the fun.

'How?'

Jake nodded sideways and Pete looked across to where Chloe was aimlessly drifting in her inflatable. Her collagen filled lips floated on top of her face like a miniature version of her rubber ring. Pete knew that it was collagen because Gabe had told him.

'Ah, Blubbermouth. Should have guessed.'

Infamous for being the resort's biggest blabbermouth, she was font of all gossip, personal and otherwise, gathered through stealth, stalking, and the internet.

Jake chuckled, always appreciative of Pete's nicknames. Along with Gabe and their two wives, Jake was the only other person who knew about them. Pete knew it would be unwise to share them with anyone else, so he hadn't. Apart from Father Anthony, but as he was bound by the sacramental seal he could be discounted.

'Well don't tell me who it is, I like the surprise,' Pete told him.

Ruthless waded up and asked for a neat treble scotch. He knocked it straight back and then waded away again. Pete considered it was probably medicinal, seeing as he looked to have the beginnings of a black eye.

'There's some new signs gone up today,' Jake said to him, 'Have you seen them?'

Pete nodded. 'A few.'

'They're all just as loopy as the rest. Have you seen the one that says, *Not all ghosts are dead?* How does that figure? In your cult?'

Pete smirked as he took a sip of his drink. He'd not seen that one as yet.

'I've told you, we're an Holistic Retreat. A Health Spa and Holistic Retreat. Just like it says on the front gates.'

It used to be The Garden of Eden Naturist Resort. But not since Vic's epiphany. The only thing left to suggest that it still was, were the two marble statues set either side of the gates, bought from an auction house in Florence. A naked Adam and Eve complete with fig leaves, but incomplete due to their lack of heads. They'd had them at one time. In fact, they'd had them right up until the week after Pete first joined, but where they were now was a mystery. A mystery that proved an enduring source of scandalous speculation, just as the defiled statues themselves provided an endless source of mockery. As the local vicar always liked to jest about the place, 'First you're confronted by the headless, and then by the topless and the bottomless.'

'That's just a front, for your cult,' said Jake, grinning at him, in defiance.

Pete liked the sound of Holistic Retreat. It sounded healthy and wholesome, which in the main it was, but he also liked the idea of belonging to a cult, because it sounded the exact opposite.

Though Jake and he were good buddies, he had no intention of ever telling him the secrets of The Garden. Jake had signed a confidentiality agreement, as had all the staff, never to speak of what they saw and heard whilst working there. And although Jake never ceased from asking about it, Pete's silence was to keep him from being summoned for legal proceedings; along with the fact that he himself had sworn an oath never to speak of it beyond the company of other members. It used to worry him that anything Blubbermouth let slip to Jake might be seen as having come from him, due to everyone knowing they were buddies, but Jake had assured him that his lips were as sealed as Blubbermouth's were leaky.

'Is it like the Freemasons? Do you have to do a funny handshake?'

Pete sighed. 'Have you ever seen us do a funny handshake?'

'No, but I meant on the outside, when you chanced to meet up.'

'Well if we did, we'd all be pretty screwed right now, seeing as Covid's put paid to that.'

Pete sipped his gin and tonic, wondering if 'screwed' was a SOL.

'Chelsea thinks your mission statement's based on you selling your souls,' Jake persevered.

Bare All: Body and Soul. Hardly a mission statement, but certainly their motto. If it had been *Sell All*, Pete could have understood it, but then Chelsea had a vivid imagination. She had to have, seeing as she believed Covid could be transmitted via flatulence.

'And you believe her?'

'Course not. Though there's definitely some in here that are bordering on soulless.'

Pete smirked as he sipped his gin.

'So, what else has Blubs been telling you?' he asked, once the next customer was served and gone.

Jake grinned but didn't say.

'Go on,' Pete pressed.

'She told me something about you. And I have to admit, Pete, I'd never have guessed.'

'Marvellous. I can't wait.'

Jake leaned across the wet bar, as if he considered distant swimmers might have bat-like hearing.

‘She says, or rather she reckons, that you’re the richest guy in here. Richer even than Vic. Says that it’s common knowledge, too.’

Pete widened his eyes and pursed his lips as if in consideration of it, and then he emptied his glass and slid it across the bar.

‘Better make it a double then, seeing as I can afford it.’

Jake did as he was bid, grinning all the while.

Another customer came and went.

‘I’ve not heard you mention Chelsea for a while. You two still at it?’ Pete asked.

Jake gave a laboured sigh. ‘You need to get on Facebook, mate. Then you’d know me and her are history. I’m with Lillia now.’

Pete was impressed. Lillia was their resident entertainments officer and elegance personified. Although Chelsea wasn’t exactly shabby. The staff there were renowned for how quickly they moved in and out of each other’s apartments, even more so since they’d been locked-in. Sal said they were all in danger of bed-hopping burn-out.

‘How come you can’t do Facebook?’ Jake asked him.

‘I’m sure I could, if I googled how.’

‘No, I mean you lot, being banned. Your cult not allowing it.’

Pete lifted a curious eyebrow to which Jake nodded over his shoulder again. Pete didn’t need to look to know that it was Blubbermouth who had furnished him with the dubious fact.

‘We’re not banned. It just doesn’t fit with our pledge, to *Live in the world, but be not part of the world*. Meaning we don’t engage in social media. Same as we don’t entertain politics or register to vote. It doesn’t serve our purpose.’

‘Which is?’

Pete just grinned at him. It was obviously one of those days when Jake felt compelled to dig and to delve.

‘You know what? It’s all bullshit at the end of the day,’ Jake told him. ‘If you’ve all given up Facebook and voting, to opt out of the world, then why haven’t you given up your country piles and your piles of money? Aren’t they part of this world, then? Or are they just a mirage beamed over from Mars?’

The twins, Tamara and Tabitha, swam up to the bar to order cocktails. No one spoke as Jake concentrated on doing his mixing and shaking routine.

Pete considered the twins old enough to be Jake's mother but that didn't stop them from staring at him in a voracious, non-motherly fashion. There was something not quite right about them. Something creepy. They often sat, both staring at the same random objects, totally vacant. Other times, they whispered to each other when you spoke to them, and then they replied, jointly. He'd named them jointly, as The Shining. The name was Jake's favourite. They scared him too.

'You planning on leaving Dangley Dell once the lock-down's been lifted?' Jake asked, after The Shining had waded away with their Hanky Pankies.

Dangley Dell, Pete understood, was how the local villagers referred to the place. It being one of their more polite names. It was a well-known fact that they weren't approving of the place. To them, opting to live naked amongst strangers meant only one thing, rampant sex and sordid orgies.

'I doubt it. They need to eradicate Covid first.'

'What about the others?'

'No idea. Best ask Blubs,' Pete suggested, and then with a sudden start, 'What day is it?'

'Bloody hell, Pete. Living here's softening your brain. It's Sunday. Speakers Night.'

'What time is it?'

Jake looked up to the ceiling at the incoming sun, as if its alignment alone would give him the answer, then he took a sneaky glance under the bar counter at his mobile phone.

'Quart to four.'

'Bingo.'

'Really?'

'No. Tai Chi.'

'Well good luck with that. After four gin and tonics I bet you fall flat on your arse.'

Pete gave him a farewell salute and then purposely fell backwards off his stool, to swim away.

CHAPTER TWO

NIGHT AFTER DAY

'What did you think to that new woman by the pool, giving us all a bit of vulgar vagina?' Sal asked him.

Pete smirked as he sat himself up to the bedhead, picking up the remote to flick on the TV.

'Like you said, she's new, she needs time to learn the ropes. But I like the way you're thinking. Vulgar Vagina. Vul-Va. Bit crude, but hey-ho, there you go.'

Sal was often the source of his nicknames, which didn't particularly please her.

'Why do you have to come up with all these stupid names for people?' she grumbled, as she struggled to flatten her frizz with the straighteners. 'The number of times I slip up. It's doing my bloody head in. And you know what's worse? I can't even remember their real names half the time. I've known most of these folk for donkey's years and I still end up having to ask Jude. I'm sure she thinks I've got early-onset dementia. Somebody asked me the other day if I thought Dave was suffering from depression. I had to ask them who he was. They looked at me like I'd gone doolally. Told me I'd just been playing tennis with him. I felt a right berk.'

'So who is it? Dave?'

'It's sodding Ruthless.'

'Well, you could have guessed from a question like that. Who else here looks as miserable as him?'

Sal finished her hair, tutted at something on the TV, then went through to their kitchenette to retrieve a half bottle of Chablis from the fridge. For no reason at all, she began to laugh, only it wasn't a laugh, it was a cackle. Pete turned down the volume on the news. Sal didn't cackle often but when she did, he was compelled to listen to it. The only cackle that came anywhere close, belonged to a Sunday afternoon radio presenter who had once interviewed him, brought to her knees by his TwatNav lines.

In the past, he'd always struggled to describe Sal's cackle, but as of today, thanks entirely to Jude, he'd found the exact word. Earthy. And not just her cackle. Sal herself was earthy. Yes, she could cackle like a demon on a daytrip to Dachau, but she also liked to tell dirty jokes and as for swearing, she was unrivalled.

'What's got into you?' he asked, when she came back into their bedroom.

'I took a POT shot at Hannah today. Twice.'

He watched as she began to apply her mascara in the mirror. Not that she was supposed to, make-up being an EVE on the POT form. Excessive Vanity Evidenced.

'Is Hannah one of The —'

'— Swingers, yes.'

'What for? I thought you got on with her?'

'I do, but I reckon it's her that's always having a POT shot at me.'

Pete shook his head. Sal had recently been incensed at the number of Personally Observed Transgression forms that had been submitted against her. Forms that listed everything from a simple SOL right up to a GBH. Only three things were required on it: Offender's name, observer's signature, and a circle around the observed acronym. All surreptitiously posted into one of the many boxes that were spread around the resort.

Saying you'd taken a POT shot at someone had become the norm for meaning you'd posted off a POT form about them. POTs posted about Sal were mainly SOLs but now and again there were others. BABs. Bragging And Boasting. She'd had a flurry of those after she'd bragged about her Cartier watch at the ladies' coffee club. She was inordinately proud of it, but due to its enforced absence, she'd clearly needed to make them all aware of its existence. EVEs. She'd had a dozen of those after she'd been at the hairdressers two days in a row having hair extensions, rules being cut-and-blow only.

Pete always wondered what Vic's stepdaughter, Eve, thought about EVEs. She was resident there but as staff rather than member, so although they might not apply to her, she obviously knew about them.

'And you made something up in retaliation?' Pete asked, realising his wife was becoming obsessed with taking POT shots as a means of retribution.

'No, of course not, it was for real. They were POGs.'

Pete had to think hard to remember what the acronym was for.

'Pointless Overindulgent Greed?'

Sal nodded. 'I saw her eat five Ben and Jerrys.'

'One after the other?'

'Nooo, spread out.'

'What were you doing? Stalking her?'

Sal didn't answer.

'It's been the hottest day of the year so far,' Pete pointed out, 'Everyone probably had five. Maybe more. And chuffin' 'eck Sal, look at her! She's as thin as Vic's staff. She could do with a bit of a POG.'

'I'm going to stop telling you them if you're just going to keep rubbishing them.'

'I'm not rubbishing them. I'm just pointing out how petty they are.'

'Well tell that to whoever keeps taking POT shots at me. I'm fucking sick of being top of the POTS!'

'Oy, less of the swearing,' Pete scolded.

Sal ignored him. 'One of these days I'm going to steal the key to those stinking POT boxes and find out who it is. Then it's going to be payback time.'

Pete shook his head and flicked over the TV channel. In light of Vic always wearing the key around his neck, that would prove difficult.

Five minutes later, Sal was grinning again. Pete could see her in the mirror.

'You've taken a POT shot at someone else, haven't you?'

She nodded, letting out a hint of a cackle.

'Dan,' she told him.

'Dan? What in God's name did he do? Poor lad only came over to apologise for his wife's vulgar vagina.'

'Yes, but then he did a BAB.'

'About what?'

'About him once coming eleventh at Toronto marathon.'

Pete had to think to recall it. It was on the back of Gabe asking him if he also jogged, along with his wife.

'Sal, it was just conversation. It was just stating a fact.'

'No, it wasn't. I say stuff like that all the time and I always get POT shotted for it.'

'No. You say stuff like, "I've got a Cartier Baignoire watch at home, paved in diamonds and worth forty-five grand". There's a difference.'

'Well I don't think there's a difference. It still falls under boasting.'

Pete gave up, got up, and went for a pee.

'Any more?' he asked when he came back out of their en-suite.

'No.'

'You sure?'

'Just the one.'

Pete sighed. 'Who?'

'Jude.'

'She's your best friend? What would you take a POT shot at her for?'

'Because she always thinks she's betterer than me.'

'Stop saying betterer. You can't make better any better.'

Pete appreciated his wife hadn't had the benefit of an education beyond the age of fourteen, but surely, just speaking to people, watching telly, and reading Hello magazines, would have cured some of her ignorance by now. Not that it had been her choice for quitting school. Her single-parent mother had died at the age of thirty-five, leaving her with two younger siblings to look after.

'Go on. Better in what way?' he asked.

'She thinks I'm common because I call it my snatch,' she told him, nodding south to her undercarriage.

'No, she doesn't.'

'Yes, she does. She winces every time I say it. But who the hell calls it their twinkle? And his, his tinkle? It's like she's six. It's like they only use them for playing tiddly winks.'

Due to the mental picture that instantly conjured up, Pete couldn't help but laugh.

'So what POT did you shot her with?' he asked.

'A JOE. Obviously.'

Not so obvious. Pete had to think on it again, but soon recollected it was Jealousy Or Envy.

'No way,' he told her.

Sal didn't respond.

'Okay, what is it you reckon she's jealous of?'

'Over Gabe only making millions, whereas you've made squillions. And over me, having a Cartier Baignoire watch, plastered in diamonds and worth forty-five fucking grand.'

She delivered it deadpan, but as soon as she had, she began to cackle. As much as he didn't want to, so did Pete.

They were finally dressed. Speakers' nights being the only time that they actually did, other than for inclement weather.

In the early days, the speakers had proved incapable of speaking — certainly with any authority — while subjected to a seated sea of bare bodies. A few had been so disconcerted that they'd actually fled. Initially, Vic had provided them all with long, black cloaks for the occasion but that had unnerved their speakers even more. So now, they just dressed as they would for any after-dinner speaking event, although they'd frequently been asked to tone it down, or at least the women had. Not that it had prevailed. Not even when Vic had seen fit to add the TIT acronym — Too Immoderately Togged — to the POT form. Pete often found himself broadsided by a barrage of silk, chiffon and sequins, with Sunday nights becoming a POT fest of EVEs and TITs. And yet it seemed to be an unwritten rule that nobody submitted any. Rather, it would seem, the women were all quite happy to make complete TITs of themselves.

Sal had brought enough evening attire to never be seen in the same outfit twice for at least half the year, which was madness seeing as their three room, two-bathroom cabins had such limited closet space. It was a nudist colony after all. Good job that all the men were happy to wear the same black-tie tux, week in, week out.

'What d'you think to the frock?' Sal asked him.

‘Smashing. Where’s it from?’

‘T K Maxx.’

Pete smiled but shook his head. The only clothes and accessories of any value that Sal had, were the ones that Pete had bought for her. Try as she might, she couldn’t break the shopping habits of a lifetime.

The still evening air was unseasonably warm as they made their way down the lantern lit paths that led to The Hub.

The great, circular, stone building sat beneath a high conical roof that tapered as sharp as a church spire, surrounded by an off-set ring of mini spired hubs, all branching out from the central station like adjoining satellites. From above, Pete imagined it looked a lot like the sputnik chandelier that they had back home in their vaulted hallway.

The Hub was the centre of everything. Reception, restaurants, staff apartments, snooker room, art studio, library, confessional, medical, and needlework-cum-craft room. They even had a ballroom, but not that they ever balled. Its only use was for their well-attended disco on Friday nights where Jake doubled as a DJ. Since lock-in, they’d also had an on-site hairdressing salon, which doubled as a dog-groomers on Mondays.

Sal was humming happily as she swung on Pete’s hand, while Pete was pondering on the likely topic of their speaker.

His ponder didn’t last long, as arriving at the front doors, there was a placard outside: *Tonight – Nirvana is nearer than you think.* Buddhism then.

Inside, they were met with a hubbub of noise. People were mingling around the lobby, helping themselves to the hors d’oeuvres and aperitifs that were being offered around by their formally dressed staff.

Pete weaved his way through to a drinks trolley to make himself a proper drink and on his way back he bumped into Gabe.

‘You alright, mate?’ Pete asked, seeing the pained expression on Gabe’s face.

‘No. It’s the Farmers again. I can feel my heart pulsating in my arse. It’s purgatory.’

Pete smiled. He appreciated Gabe's cockney as much as Gabe appreciated his tyke. Farmers, he knew of old, was short for Farmer Giles, rhyming slang for piles.

'First rule of Buddhism. We are all here to suffer,' Pete informed him, 'Take it as a minor trial.'

'Too late. I've taken a major suppository,' Gabe quipped.

Pete nodded in sympathy. 'It could be worse. It could be Covid.'

'Agreed. Which kinda makes you wonder why we're all here, letting in an outsider. I can't believe Vic caved in to the pressure.'

Gabe was right. People on the outside were dying from the rampant virus while people on the inside seemed oblivious, blissfully cocooned as they all were. Didn't they ever watch the news? He put a hand on Gabe's shoulder and squeezed it.

'Here yer go, this'll cheer you up.'

Pete withdrew a small metal disc from his jacket pocket and slipped it into Gabe's. It was similar to a gambling chip in that it had a recognised value of five hundred pounds. A monkey.

'Oh, cheers mate. I'd forgotten.'

'Like chuff.'

Sal and Jude had joined them, glasses of Aperol in hands and Sal with flaky pastry on her chin.

'Where's the speaker from?' Pete asked Gabe, 'I'm guessing it's not Tibet.'

Gabe smirked. 'Believe it or not, he's from your neck of the woods. Yorkshire.'

'He a physicist at Leeds Uni,' Jude expanded, 'Apparently, his talks are very interactive.'

'Great. That's all I flippin' need. Please don't let it be hypnosis again,' said Pete.

Gabe began to snigger and it proved contagious as Sal and Jude were soon to join in.

Pete was still trying to live down the night their speaker had focussed on reincarnation, inviting half a dozen of them up on stage to demonstrate past-life regression.

He'd been good. Too good. Pete had been the last of those he'd selected. The first five regressions had brought them a World War Two soldier; a Victorian London prostitute; a sixties plumber; a surgeon from Seattle; and a turn of the century aborigine. But Pete? He had to go and embarrass himself by being a chicken. No specific time or place, just a chicken. All he could put it down to was that prior to going on stage he'd been thinking how nice his Chicken Chasseur dinner had been.

'Clurrrrck, cluck, cluck, cluck,' Gabe clucked, his bent arms flapping like wings and his head bobbing as he circled on the spot.

'Oh, give it a rest,' Pete told him.

But it was funny. Gabe had videoed it on his phone and when Pete had watched it, he'd been hysterical. Two of the other five victims had been convinced of seeing a card flashed before them, telling them who they were to be, leading Pete to think he'd been subliminally flashed the word chicken. If the speaker had thought to end his act on a high note, it had worked. The place had been in uproar.

Blubbermouth had suddenly inserted herself into their group.

'Sal, pleeeease, you've got to tell me where you got that dress from. It's fabulous. Whose is it?'

Sal practically preened.

'Dior. But it's a one-off, I'm afraid. I had it specially made.'

As Blubs disappeared, disappointed, Pete raised an eyebrow at his wife. And then Jude took a backward step and made clear she was looking Sal up and down, as if she hadn't noticed her dress before.

'Hmmm,' she agreed, 'it is rather striking. But it wouldn't do a thing for me.'

'Oh, piss off, yer bitch. It's better than that bloody post box you've got on,' Sal responded, nodding to Jude's scarlet, full length, tunic dress with black epaulettes. 'Who designed that? The Royal Mail?'

The two of them glared at each other before bursting out laughing.

James had joined them and with him he'd brought a short, squat man with large, protruding ears.

Pete considered the wingnut lugs were due to the industrial sized, glass and rubber, all-encompassing face mask he was wearing. Its straps not having been lengthened correctly.

'Evening all. Just thought I'd introduce you to Toby,' James said to them.

Pete resisted an urge to laugh, as a double handled Toby Jug immediately sprang to mind.

Toby thrust his hand out to him but then retracted it immediately. Covid caught out the best of them.

'I understand you're from Yorkshire?' Pete asked, convivially.

'Oh God, no. I only have to work there. I actually hail from Surrey,' Toby Jug imparted, his voice sounding overly shrill as it came out through the breathing filter.

Pete gave a thump to his chest and threw out a Roman salute.

'All hail Surrey,' he responded.

Gabe sniggered but Toby Jug chose to ignore it.

'And you?' he asked of Pete.

'Place called Cawthorne. Just outside of Barnsley.'

'Barnsley? Oh dear, well I suppose somebody has to.'

Pete sighed. It was always the same. Why did people adhere to age old stereotypes? It peeved him. But right now, what concerned him more, was Sal's usual reaction to their home town belittling. He was hoping that she hadn't heard, but from the sudden jutting out her chin, he knew that she had.

'Have you ever fucking been there?' she demanded to know, as she squared up to him.

Toby Jug's mask had suddenly fogged-up. He shook his head, too meek to speak.

'Well how d'yer fucking dare? There's parts of Surrey that are right bloody shitholes,' Sal continued.

Pete and Gabe half turned into each other to hide the fact that they were both trying very hard not to laugh.

'Last time I was there,' Sal raged, 'they were fishing a dead dog out of the river. But we weren't sure it was a dog, seeing as the rats down there are just as fucking big. I wouldn't live in sodding Surrey if you paid me.'

Toby Jug finally drew in a deep whistling breath. 'Well, that's told me.'

'Yes. And don't you damn well forget it.'

There was an uncomfortable silence and Pete suddenly realised there was a small enthralled audience gathered around them.

'I think there must have been at least six SOLS in there, Sal,' Hannah pointed out to her.

'Oh, go shove your SOLs up your skinny little arse!' Sal retaliated, gathering up the hem of her one-off Dior dress and barging her way out through the throng.

Once they'd stopped laughing, Gabe asked, 'Aren't you going after her?'

'No chance,' Pete replied, 'There's Chicken Chasseur on the menu tonight.'

They were ushered into the dining room where they took up their usual table for four. Only now they were just the three.

After-dinner speaking at The Garden was never entirely true. Most of the speakers began before the dessert arrived. Toby was no exception.

'Earth,' he began, after spending a few minutes tapping the microphone, 'What are the chances of its existence?'

Nobody replied, so Pete had a thought to.

'We're still eating, mate. Ask the questions after the coffee comes out.'

Toby thumped his chest and threw out a Roman salute to him, causing Pete to grin.

'If the Earth was just a fraction further away from the Sun, we would freeze,' Toby continued. 'A fraction nearer and we would fry. The distance … is absolutely perfect. And as we rotate around it, the entire surface of our Earth is warmed and cooled every single day, so as to perfectly sustain life.'

Pete suddenly appreciated the clarity of which a Surrey accent enabled you to be understood through a mini-muffler, but even so it was a bizarre experience having a talk delivered to you by Darth Vader.

'Gravity,' Toby continued, 'The Earth's gravity holds a thin, fifty-mile layer of gases — mostly nitrogen and oxygen — around its surface. If the Earth was any smaller, this layer would be impossible. If the Earth was any larger, its atmosphere would contain deadly hydrogen.'

Pete was unexpectedly envious of the mask. If the earth suddenly grew, he might need it.

'Earth. Its size … is absolutely perfect. It's the only planet we know that has the right mixture of gases to support life as we know it. Plant, animal and human.'

Gabe gave Pete a nudge. 'Haven't we had this talk before?'

Pete shrugged. 'If we have, I don't remember. But what the hell has it got to do with getting nearer to Nirvana? I was expecting a Buddhist monk.'

'Rin put out the wrong sign,' Jude told him, 'Nirvana is in July. Tonight is God and The Scientist.'

'The Universe,' Toby put to them, 'is ruled by mathematics.'

Gabe nudged Pete again. 'I bet Vic knows this gent from his Oxford professor days.'

Pete considered it might be true, although the age difference meant that Toby would likely have been his student.

'Yes, our entire Universe is governed by immutable, indisputable, mathematical laws, that can be measured with total precision. All our sciences — chemistry, physics, biology, astronomy — are all based on these well-ordered laws. Reliable laws. Logical laws. But the chance of all this precision, this perfectly balanced order, is now appearing —' Toby paused for effect, 'To more and more scientists —' Another pause. 'As something absolutely impossible to put down to random chance.'

'Yep, we've definitely heard this before,' Gabe said to Pete.

'Will you be quiet,' Jude hissed at him, 'I'm trying to listen.'

Pete smiled He was glad Sal wasn't with them. She'd have been bored and randomly texting by now.

'One thing that scientists don't refute and that's The Big Bang. That one cosmic explosion that brought everything into being at one single point in time. A time we now know to be around fourteen billion years ago. That's a length of time that's almost impossible to comprehend for most people. And as to what came before it, well, that's even more impenetrable. But what we do know, is that the universe hasn't always existed. It had a beginning. And yet we have no answers and no explanations for what was there before that beginning.'

Toby looked like he'd reached the end of a very short performance. He was pulling down his shirt sleeves and putting on his jacket.

Pete felt anxious. He needed to know what came before, even if it was only hypothesised. Thankfully, Toby went straight back to the microphone.

'And here's the rub,' he told them, 'We scientists and physicists — some, but not all — are now starting to look for answers in other places. And we're starting to accept that such order and precision could only have come about by the direct influence of a supreme, all-knowing intelligence. And not an AI type either. An intelligence that has emotions. Not just to know them but to actually feel them as we do, because that's something that even the most advanced form of AI could never be programmed to do. Then we must presume, that we are actually made in its image. And that it knows us. Entirely, profoundly, emotionally.'

Pete suddenly found himself sat forwards, and not just for the stirring of his coffee. Toby was turning out to be a jug and a half.

CHAPTER THREE

ONE DAY IN MAY

Pete slid his putter into his golf bag and then slung its heavy weight over his bare shoulder. Another hole birdied. He was playing as part of a foursome but two of the players he hardly knew. Phil and Joel. He'd seen them. Plenty of times. But never to talk to, not properly. Phil's bristly back had always fascinated him. He'd never seen a bloke so hairy. Every time he saw him, he wanted to comb him. And Joel. You heard him before you saw him. His laugh was like a braying donkey. It was like he held his breath and then let it out in long, protracted gasps. It was as startling as it was entertaining. Great blokes, the pair of them, and Pete felt a little contrite at having previously named them The Boar and Eeyore.

Between the fifth and sixth holes there was a coffee caravan and that was where they'd stopped for an expresso and a doughnut. Sitting down at the riverside picnic bench, they'd struggled to avoid the deposits of green and white goose poo. It was bad enough getting it on their golf balls but rather them than their own balls.

'Room for a little one?' Mary asked, squeezing herself between Eeyore and The Boar.

Seeing as there wasn't, they had to make some.

'Do you mind if we play through, ladies?' Adam asked of the women's foursome.

Adam, being Vic's stepson, had by default some accorded influence.

Pete was delighted that he'd asked. He hated having to wait while the women hacked and sliced their way around the course. Playing a round right behind them was the bane of his life and he would never deny that he was the typical golfing chauvinist pig.

‘It’ll cost you,’ Blubbermouth said to him, playfully, while The Shining just stared.

‘Okay, doughnuts are on us,’ Adam offered.

It was the standard club joke to offer up food or a round of drinks when everything was all-inclusive.

There was a strong wind suddenly blowing its way down the valley and Pete put his hand up to hold onto his flat cap. He was sat opposite Mary, who, at seventy-three, was their oldest lady member. Her aging breasts were hanging low and flat like spaniels’ ears and Pete wondered if at any minute a sharp gust might propel them into giving The Boar and Eeyore a slap around the face.

‘You going to art class this afternoon, Peter?’ Mary asked him.

Pete was immediately plucked out of his reverie.

‘Aye, why not. It’s been a while.’

He found the class engagingly unconventional. For starters, they always asked their volunteer models to pose fully clothed, as opposed to the norm. But more often than not, they decided to do something entirely different, like amateur dramatics.

They teed off on the sixth without any concern for hitting one of the four ponies that were grazing mid fairway. Adam had been straight on his mobile to Arek, apoplectic that they were there once again, but Pete preferred the ponies to the geese and it was always one or the other.

As soon as they’d fanned out toward their individual balls, the ponies split up to follow them, so that they might be individually mugged. Due to Pete having a box of sugar lumps in his bag, he was the only one able to throw a distraction and play on. Fortunately, Arek was soon to arrive with his cattle prod and the ponies only had to see him waving it, to kick up their heels and run.

‘I’m not sure how we’re ever going to put a stop to them,’ Adam ventured when they all met up again on the green.

‘Have you thought about glue?’ Pete suggested.

Eeyore began to bray.

When they reached the final, ninth green, Pete went to remove the flagstick from the hole. The flag had a message written on it which came as no surprise. A lot of Vic's signs were ingeniously placed.

We're an improbability in an improbable universe – Ray Bradbury.

Pete didn't like to think of himself as improbable. He liked to think he was intentional.

'Shall we have another round, same time tomorrow? Eeyore asked.

'Suits me,' said Pete, 'It's been a cracking game. Nice and tight. Right to the wire.'

He liked it when it wasn't clear that he'd won by the third hole. He was a scratch player but even with handicaps the others rarely tested his metal. These three were worthy opponents.

'Won't Gabe be wanting a game?' The Boar asked him.

'Probably. But I can go out with him later on.'

That was the thing with a nine-hole golf course, you could easily play two or three rounds in one day.

'We refuse to play with him anymore,' Eeyore divulged.

'Because he always wants to play for money?'

'No, because he always cheats. Especially in winter, when he's got pants on.'

Pete grinned. Gabe was an expert at dropping a spare ball down his trouser leg when his shot had taken him into the rough. Vic had been guilty of the same thing, up until his bad hip had curtailed his game and reduced him to the bowling green. There, the same trick wasn't viable, unless you wanted people thinking you'd suddenly given birth.

Pete met up with Sal, Gabe and Jude by the outdoor pool, just in time for their lunch delivery and just in time to say Hi and Bye to James.

'Do you think you could tell him and Joe apart?' Sal asked Jude, as soon as he was out of earshot.

Jude shook her head. 'Maybe, if I ever saw them together, like The Shining.'

'Strange,' Gabe mused, 'how identical twins, marry identical twins. Happens a lot.'

Pete didn't dispute it, he'd somewhere read the same. He could definitely tell the difference between Tamara and Tabitha but no way their respective husbands, James and Joe. Mainly because Jude had it right, the two men were never seen together. Their family business was apparently very hands on, with one of them needing to be there at all times. So even though they'd both been selected, they'd still had to toss a coin to see who would be coming. It had been James who was in, and Joe who was out. Though rumour had it they were actually swapping over every other week, against all their lock-in rules. James was Tamara's husband, leaving Tabitha alone in the nearby cabin, which in itself proved contentious, considering it flew in the face of their strict couples-only policy.

'I've seen them together,' Sal suddenly announced.

'When?' Jude immediately quizzed.

'In their cabins. They've got the same framed photos above their fireplace. It's of the four of them, posing by some old banger at Salon Privé. I've looked long and hard at those photos every chance I've had and I can't see any difference. I reckon their own mother couldn't tell them apart.'

They all pondered on it. Wondering whether she could, or she couldn't.

'The wives were out playing golf,' said Pete. 'One of 'em got pulled up by Adam for forgetting her golf shoes.'

'Huh, I wouldn't have stood for that,' Sal huffed.

'It wasn't a public flogging. He just asked her to remember in future, in case of complaints.'

'Complaints? The only complaints he's likely to be getting are about those damn ponies sinking their feet into it. At least she's not got bloody hooves.'

'I wouldn't be too sure,' Pete sniffed, 'The pair of 'em seem pretty cloven hoofed to me.'

Gabe sniggered.

'Why are the sodding things here, anyway?' Sal asked, 'They weren't here at Christmas. Where've they all come from?'

'He inherited them,' Pete informed her.

'Who? Vic?'

'Arek, yer mugwump.'

‘That says it all, doesn’t it. You can’t refuse minority groups anything these days.’

‘I didn’t think gypsies were a minority group,’ Jude queried.

‘They’re not,’ said Gabe, ‘they’re a marginalised group.’

‘And what’s that supposed to mean?’ Sal asked.

‘It means they live on margins of grass by the side of the road.’

Pete grinned.

Rosa and Arek were bona fide Romany gypsies, but if they’d ever had Romanian accents, they’d become well camouflaged by their Cumbrian ones, due to having lived there for twenty plus years.

Rosa had *the gift* and Vic had discovered her on a weekend away in the Lake District. Through her, he’d received messages from his dead wife and on the back of it he’d invited her and her husband, Arek, to live in The Garden as non-paying guests.

While Rosa was there to be at the disposal of residents, Arek was there to dispose of any unwanted residents. Rats, wasps, pigeons, moles, all of them despatched within an hour of causing a nuisance and what he couldn’t despatch, his loyal and trusty Rottweiler could. A dog that loved people and other dogs, but would readily rip apart anything else it was prompted to. Pete called it Hellmutt.

Their caravan was up beside the lake, along with their ponies, when they stayed put. And Vic was generous. They had all the resort’s facilities available to them for relatively little work and Pete didn’t begrudge them it one bit. He loved Rosa. Arek he could take or leave, but Rosa was something special. Through her, he’d been able to communicate with his long-departed grandmother, showing herself to Rosa with Cockles on her lap. But the most precious thing of all was being put in touch with Pippa. She had come through to him just as she was in life. Her same sense of humour. Her figure of speech. Even the little clap she did when she was excited, or rather the little clap she had Rosa do on her behalf. And the messages had been about things only she and he knew, which had simply astounded him. Before he’d arrived there, he’d never believed in *The Beyond*, but Rosa had given him that belief.

'You know why it's so busy here today, don't you?' Jude was asking.

'It's sunny,' Sal replied, snidely.

Jude shook her head. 'Rosa's let it be known she's coming up.'

Rosa didn't come up often, but when she did, they were always ready and waiting. You didn't select a time with Rosa, Rosa selected a time with you. Similar to Vic. And just like Vic, she wandered around the place in a dressing gown, no matter the weather, puffing on her pot filled pipe. If she came to you, she would simply give you a time, and at that time, you were expected to visit her in her lakeside caravan. Nobody refused. Nobody even thought to refuse. Her messages were usually so astounding and profound that they were often life changing, and at the very least they were life after death confirming, which at their age was reassuring.

Vic had granted Rosa a sign. It was on the edge of the lake.

Notice the signs. Not just the physical but the metaphysical. Allow the world of spirit to come closer to you — Rosa.

As much as Pete had allowed, he still hadn't noticed any signs, physical or otherwise.

Vic was heading toward them, with Rin not far behind.

Sal immediately wiped her chin with the back of her hand and sat upright, while Jude put down the sandwich she was about to bite into. Vic had that effect on people.

'Gabriel. Judith. Peter. Salome,' he acknowledged, one at a time, giving them each a bow of his head.

They each returned various greetings and he moved on to the next couple, and then the next, clearly in a solicitous mood.

'It's like we're all in bloody school, getting ticked off the register,' Sal remarked, 'And why does he always have to call me Salome? Nobody's ever called me that.'

'Apart from your dad,' Pete reminded her.

Sal's dad was German. Not that she'd clapped eyes on him since the age of nine. Yorkshire mother; Rhineland father. The name Salome was apparently as common as salami in Germany.

'It could have been worse,' Gabe told her, 'You could have been a boy and been called Adolf.'

As Jude burst out laughing, Pete could see Sal bristle.

'You're not far off a nasty name, yourself,' Sal spat at her. 'Jude. Short for Judas.'

Jude's nostrils flared ever so slightly.

'Judith. You heard the man,' she said, flicking her head sideways toward Vic.

'I bet it's been you that's been pot shotting me all along,' Sal told her. 'Got to be you, with a name like Judas.'

'Oh, sod off,' Jude told her.

'SOL,' said Sal.

A mobile was ringing and Sal reached into her bag to pull out Pete's.

'Guess who?'

'Jeremy?'

'No. It's Kyle.'

'Ignore it,' Pete told her.

Gabe suddenly leaned closer in, to whisper.

'Don't all look at once. But you need to take a butcher's at Vulva's eating habits.'

The three of them immediately looked at once.

'You'd think it was her last meal,' Jude observed, 'The way she's gulping it down like a seaside gannet.'

Phoebe was eating her lunch as if she hadn't eaten for days and Pete felt a painful stab inside, remembering days in his childhood when he'd eaten like that.

'You've got to stop calling her that,' said Sal, 'I can cope with all his other names, but not that.'

Jude was nodding in agreement, so Gabe looked to Pete. Pete just shrugged. It would have to remain boys only.

'I don't think they really fit in here,' said Jude, 'Look at them. They're like refugees in a foreign land.'

'More like paupers in paradise,' Gabe remarked.

The sun had risen high in the sky and the few remaining clouds began to evaporate.

'Just feel that heat,' said Jude, closing her eyes and putting her face to it. 'So nice after all that rain we've had. I thought it was never going to stop.'

‘Hmmm, we’ve hardly seen you lately,’ said Sal. ‘What you two been doing, locked away in your cabin all the time? Playing tiddly winks?’ She’d looked to Pete and he had to look away so as not to laugh.

‘It’s going to get even warmer,’ Gabe stated, ignoring the question, ‘It’s going to be over twenty-five tomorrow. I’m planning on laying out in it, all day.’

‘Me too,’ Jude agreed, eyes still closed.

Pete was gathering up their empty lunch cartons for the waiting Starship.

‘You want to be careful. You could end up like them,’ he warned, nodding over to The Prunuptials.

Jude opened her eyes to see who ‘them’ were.

‘Or worse, him,’ Pete added, nodding toward Vic.

Vic’s skin cancer hadn’t exactly been a good advertisement for naturism.

They all sat staring at Vic for a while.

‘You seen your invite from him?’ Gabe asked Pete.

‘Vic?’

Gabe shook his head. ‘Prunie.’

Pete smiled. Without his assistance, The Prunuptials had individually evolved into Prunie and Pruness.

‘Invite to what?’

‘His stag-night. He says there’s twenty of us invited.’

‘Where’s he having it?’

‘It’s to be announced. All dependent on Covid restrictions, I should imagine. Are we going?’

‘Of course we’re chuffin’ going. When else would we get chance to do mean, despicable things to him?’

Another Starship arrived, but it was lost and needed some assistance. Gabe told it not to worry and used his phone app to send it back to base.

‘I see you’re top of the POTs again, Salome,’ Jude said to her, casually delivering two barbs on one hook.

Sal pushed down her bottom lip with the tip of her tongue, but didn’t bite.

‘And they’re all SOLs again,’ Jude continued, ‘We just happened to be in reception when Vic was putting up the results.’

Vic counted the POT submissions once per week and transmitted the scores via the vast screen in The Hub's reception. All members names were on the spreadsheet. Listed in alphabetical order, they had columns to the right of them, showing the total under each acronym-headed transgression. A final column showed the full total, with the one receiving the most POTs having their name flashing in neon.

'Oh, so you just happened to be there, did you?' Sal challenged. 'My arse you did. I bet you'd been sat there waiting since the bloody sun came up.'

'Now, now, Sal. Don't go getting disheartened,' Gabe cajoled, reaching out to pat her leg, 'It's only week seven. You might get a trophy if you make it to week ten. In fact, I think we should suggest that SOL be changed to SAL in your honour. It could stand for ... Swearing Absolutely Limitless.'

'Oh, fuck off,' she told him.

'SAL,' he returned.

Sal picked up her half glass of iced tonic and threw it across Gabe's bare belly causing him to jolt forward with a yelp. Then picking up Pete's glass of coke, she turned to Jude.

'As for you, Judas, don't you dare call me Salome ever again,' she threatened, glass raised and ready.

Jude put up her hands, surrendering, blocking, and shaking, with laughter.

Pete lay back on his lounger, scanning around the poolside. There had to be half their current residents there, including The Mushrooms, which was rare, seeing as they preferred deep shade.

Pete liked The Mushrooms, but boy were they boring. He would have named them The Bores but as he already had The Boar, he considered it would be too confusing, and besides, The Mushrooms suited them better. Another name that could be credited to Sal. All because her nosiness knew no bounds.

Since coming out of quarantine, she'd made it her business to visit each and every occupied cabin. All cabins being equal, to avoid a litany of complaints, Sal had needed to make sure of it. Each cabin had only five rooms, albeit large ones. The lounge was their largest, incorporating a kitchenette and a study area, and then two bedrooms, each with an en-suite. The second bedroom being for those who liked to sleep separately, usually due to insomnia or snoring.

Sal had weaselled her way into The Mushrooms cabin with one of her many fabricated, yet feasible, excuses, returning to report that their choice of décor was appalling, describing it as a complete *mish, mash, mush.* Hence providing Pete with their name, The Mushrooms. Singularly, they had become known as Mush and Mushette.

'Haven't you got a confessional to go to?' Sal was suddenly asking him.

'Oh, bollywollocks!'

Pete instantly leapt off his bed. He'd totally forgotten.

It was a dash, but he made it over to the confessional mini-hub just in time for his allotted time slot.

Father Anthony was their confessor. There had never been anyone else since the confessional's inception, so they were totally familiar and at ease with him. Only he wasn't a Father at all. Pete had discovered this on his very first visit:

"I'm not sure about doing this," he'd told him, "I mean, I'm not even Catholic."

"Well, that's alright because neither am I," Father Anthony had replied, "I'm not even a priest."

"But you're qualified to take confessions, right?" he'd queried.

"Vic obviously thinks so," was the response. "Seeing as he knows I can keep secrets. Seeing as I've kept his for long enough. But I swore an oath on The Bible, never to break the sacramental seal, just like a real priest, which we figured to be good enough.'

And that had been that. Their confessional was clearly just intended as a cathartic exercise. Which is what it proved to be.

Pete climbed into the confessional box and pulled on the curtain. The box was the real deal, even if the rest wasn't. It was Italian and over four hundred years old and Vic had paid a fortune for it at an auction house in Florence. The same auction house he'd bought his Adam and Eve statues from.

Looking through the mesh, Pete could see Father Anthony perched on a stool. Prior to Covid he'd been perched in person but now he was perched inside a laptop, visible to him only on its screen.

'Bless me father for I have sinned,' Pete began, in time honoured fashion.

'Tell me my son,' Father Anthony invited.

Pete leaned back in his pew, wondering, as always, if anyone else knew that Father Anthony was really a retired chartered accountant from Bexley Heath. It had always seemed too impolite to ask them. He would have asked Sal, but she had never attended any confessionals. On their steady climb toward enlightenment, it was the only rung that she refused to step on, resolutely declaring that she had no *skellingtons* in her cupboard.

'I'm still averaging forty-four gin and tonics a week.'

'And you've not been able to cut down?'

'No, Father.'

'Okay, you can do a penance.'

'I've also let a few swear words slip out.'

'Let Vic have those,' Father Anthony told him.

Father Anthony knew all about their Personally Observed Transgressions and Pete presumed that he and Vic had previously called judgement on which sins came under confessional and which came under POTs.

'Anything else, my son?'

Pete leaned nearer to the mesh. 'I had a right old ogle at another woman.'

'And did you have lustful thoughts?'

'No. It was more of an anatomical ogle. It was down to accepting a bet on whether her boobs were false or not.'

'With Gabe?'

'Who else?'

'And were they?'

'I don't know. We haven't managed to find out yet.'

'Okay, you can do a penance. For the bet, not the ogle. Go on, my son.'

'Last Friday, I kicked my opponent's golf ball into the rough when he wasn't looking.'

'Someone you don't like?'

'Tugger. Tugger's alright.'

‘Was it because of his masturbation? In front of Sal? It is him, isn’t it?’

Father Anthony knew all of Pete’s names because he’d confessed them, but not always their origins. Pete had forgotten he’d told Father Anthony about the origin of Tugger. Another one chalked up to Sal’s nosiness.

She’d gone around to try view their cabin when she knew Tugger’s wife, Ali – short for Alligator, on account of her overlong body and short stumpy legs – had left for her bridge club; it being common knowledge that she never let anyone over her threshold. But before Sal got to knocking on the door, she’d seen him through the venetian blinds, having a good old tug. She’d also seen the stimulus on his computer screen. A glaringly graphic porn performance.

She’d come back red in the face and flustered, saying she’d been so shocked she’d been rooted to the spot, which Pete had found hilarious. Her being rooted and him being up-rooted. He’d initially named him Wanking Webster, but as ‘wanking’ was a SOL, he’d opted for Tugger.

‘Yes, it’s him,’ Pete confirmed to Father Anthony, ‘But nothing to do with his masturbation.’

‘So why did you do it? Was he winning?’

‘No. He was playing like a woman. Which is why I did it.’

‘Okay, you can do a penance. Go on, my son.’

‘I’m still doing the thing that I shouldn’t. And the guilt’s getting worse.’

‘I’d agree, considering you can’t even say it outright anymore. But it’s not got you so bad that it’s made you want to stop, has it?’

‘No. So can I just do another penance?’

‘Okay, my son. Anything else?’

‘I hit two more vehicles on purpose.’

‘Driving through the golf course?’

‘Yes. I thought the lock-in would cure me of it. But we’re still getting deliveries. Food. Post. That sort of thing. It’s become a habit that I can’t resist. Pathetic, really.’

‘I agree. Another penance. Anything else, my son?’

‘I peed in the pool.’

‘Another one for Vic.’

As there wasn't a POT for it, Pete considered the pee was for free.

'Is that it?'

'No. One last one. I put Fiery Jack in The Swinger's hot tub.'

Pete thought he heard stifled laughter.

'Why would you do that, my son?'

'Because of all the racket they make when they're in it. One of their cabins is nearest to ours and the other two couples are always around there.'

'And the racket is their lovemaking?'

'Nooooo. It's their singing. They're always singing. All warbling away like they're in a giant birdbath.'

'Strange mix. Singing and swinging.'

'Tell me about it,' Pete agreed.

'Are you sure that they do wife swapping?'

'Absolutely. They've forever sneaking in and out of each other's cabins. And at dinner, there'll be just one half of each couple, or one couple out of three. They're an unassuming little bunch, but we all know what they're up to.'

'Okay, another penance,' Father Anthony told him. 'Are we finished?'

'Yep, that's me, all up-to-date,' Pete replied, 'How much do I owe you?'

There was a pause and Pete peered through the mesh to the laptop screen, to see his confessor had put on his glasses and was holding out his notebook to tally-up.

'Six,' Father Anthony told him. 'How do you want to pay them?'

'Same as always.'

'Hmm, don't you think it's time you stepped away from the easy option?'

Easy? Shelling out a monkey for each and every penance wasn't easy, not even for him.

'What do other people do?'

'They usually pay with random acts of kindness,' Father Anthony shared with him.

'Okay. I'll do some of that. Beats giving another three grand to charity.'

There was a few seconds of silence.

'Pete. Can I ask you something?'

'Sure.'

'These sins of yours. They're not very .... sinful. You're not just doing them so you have something to confess to, are you? Just because others come to confession, doesn't mean to say you have to.'

Pete leaned forward. 'Now you've got me intrigued. What sort of sins do other people get up to?'

'You know I can't divulge that. But I have to confess, they're certainly more substantial than yours.'

Pete immediately wondered what, who, and how. Nobody in The Garden seemed capable of anything more substantial. But then, The Swingers looked like they belonged to the church choir, so who was he to say.

'Bless you, my son. May your God go with you,' Father Anthony said to him.

That was Pete's cue to leave. He pulled back the curtain and hopped out.

When Father Anthony said 'your God', it always made him wonder if Vic had told him something of what they were about. But then if he had, he'd just say TC, rather than 'your God'.

In The Garden, they believed in TC. But they had a choice of which TC. The Creator or The Cosmos. Although, if you were unsure, or were simply having a bad day, you could opt for both. Once they had passed through their initiation, they were encouraged to interact with TC on a regular basis. Not that Pete could remember the last time he'd interacted.

'Let's hope I'm there in person next time!' Father Anthony shouted out to him.

Pete hoped so, he missed their usual post-confessional round of golf.

As he walked down the link-corridor from the confessional hub to the main hub, he read the new sign that was now facing him.

Fear is a natural reaction to moving closer to death – Prema Chodron.

It made him feel slightly depressed. The thought of death always did that to him. Thankfully, above the end door, there remained an existing sign.

Love the skin you're in - Salome Hardcastle.

It always brought a smile to his face. They were all encouraged to submit suggestions for signs. Not many were accepted, but this one of Sal's, was. Pete had been so proud of her for coming up with it, until he'd seen it on a skin care poster on the London Underground.

Sal had fumed over her sign being attributed to Salome, rather than Sal, so Vic had moved it into the confessional corridor, knowing that she never went.

The central hub had a circular corridor that ran all around its outer edge, from which all other corridors branched out into each satellite hub. Pete walked a third of the way around until he found the one leading to the art studio.

'Have I missed it?' he asked as soon as he walked in, seeing them all packing up.

'No, we're having today's class outside,' Mary told him, 'It's Andy's choice of tableau and he wants us all out under The Tree.'

Pete looked around. Which one was Andy? He spotted the bloke being most officious.

Ah, Ginnel – because he couldn't stop a pig in one; his bowed, bandy legs being his most name-worthy feature.

'Could you carry two easels, Peter?' Mary was asking.

Pete nodded and obliged.

The Tree wasn't far away, just ten minutes to where the road curved in a broad camber to circumnavigate it. It was a huge oak. The largest tree in the entire resort and by far the oldest. When, after his epiphany, Vic had repurposed The Garden, he had named it The Tree of Knowledge, so as to be situationally appropriate. But everyone just called it The Tree.

As their class of fourteen spread themselves evenly around it, Ginnel was soon to usher them all to one side. The reason soon became clear when Gabe arrived, dressed in loose white shirt and baggy trousers, proceeding to kick off his flipflops and sit with his back to it.

With him in the picture, they all spread themselves out again, some near, some far.

'What's our title?' Tamara asked.

It was customary for them to be given a title before they began. It apparently helped with the theme - subject or abstract. Pete had previously decided upon subject, but now Gabe was going to be in it, it was definitely going to be abstract.

'I'm not going to say,' Ginnel told them. 'I'm going to ask *you* what the title is, once you're finished. A bit of a brain teaser, to liven up your day.'

Gabe had pulled up his knees on which to rest his book. He'd opened it in the middle and upside down so Pete knew he'd no intention of reading it. He strained to see what it was and then he smiled to himself. It was out of the library and he'd only recently read it.

Pete set out his watercolours and then went to fill his water pot from the communal jug.

'You needn't include the ribbons,' Ginnel was instructing them, 'Just pretend they're invisible.'

'What if I want to include them?' somebody asked.

'Okay, if you want them, paint them. Your choice.'

Pete went back to his easel and studied The Tree. Did he want them? Or not? He quite liked the red and white ribbons that were tied up in its branches; the ribbons that had prompted Gabe to name it The Man United Tree.

The red ribbons had written upon them their most fervent wishes and prayers. The white ones, their greatest pain or regret. Once they were up, they were up, never to be taken down, but new ones could be added at any time if they were meaningful enough. You gave them to Vic and Vic tied them onto the tree, with the help of Arek and the scissor lift.

Pete was thoroughly enjoying himself. He'd forgotten how much he liked the art class. It hadn't taken him long to paint The Tree and now he was concentrating on painting Gabe, out of proportion, with a giant face that was split into two halves, Picasso like.

'Not sure you've got the right balance there, Pete,' Ginnel advised him over his shoulder.

What the 'eck did Ginnel know? He was no more an artist than the rest of them. Bestow a modicum of authority on some people and it went straight to their heads.

'It'll come good. I'm going to put some abstract birds on the top branches.'

'Ah, of course, that should balance it,' their maestro offered, moving on to his next critique.

Pete had been wondering if he should incorporate into his composition the two signs that were pitched left and right.

To the left:

Sorrow is knowledge. They who know the most must mourn the deepest over the fatal truth. The Tree of Knowledge is not that of Life - Byron.

To the right:

For God knows that when you eat from The Tree of Knowledge your eyes will be opened and you will be like God, knowing good and *evil - Genesis.*

Pete pondered on it. Far too many words to incorporate. He'd leave them out, same as the ribbons. Dipping his brush, he was suddenly aware of a white transit van hurtling up the road toward them. They all were.

It should have turned off at the deliveries entrance, but it hadn't. It kept on coming until it was at the far side of The Tree and then it slammed on its brakes. They'd all stopped painting and were now watching and waiting.

The door flung open and out jumped a man who looked like he was on a mission. Pete guessed him to be in his mid-thirties and slightly unhinged. He was scruffy and unshaven and he was frantically looking around, as if he'd reached the end of a rainbow and was desperate to find the pot of gold.

As he headed straight toward them, Pete worried for Gabe, him being the nearest and the most likely to be dealt something unpleasant. But the madman walked right past Gabe, and headed towards … him.

Pete had a sudden realisation as to why. There was a dint in the side of the transit van. In fact, there were three.

He gripped his longest paint brush and readied himself, but regardless, the madman rushed at him, stopping up close and personal.

'You got a Daniel Saunders staying here?' he demanded to know.

Pete nodded, but immediately wished he hadn't, realising he'd been caught off guard.

'Where is he?' the man growled

'He's away. He's gone to the coast. For a few weeks. Maybe a month.'

The man glared at him. 'You certain of that?'

Pete nodded. 'Definitely. Dan's the young, good-looking fella, isn't he?'

Madman presented something akin to a snarl.

'When's he going to be back?'

'I couldn't say, but if you want to leave me your —'

'Oy! You, you fucking cretin! Give me back my van!' came a furious shout.

They all looked to see another man racing up the road toward them, red faced and furious. It was the seafood delivery man and it was instantly clear that the madman had stolen his van. Pete guessed it was probably when he'd left it to go to the entrance gate intercom, asking to be let in.

'Get away from my van! Do you hear me? Stay away from it!' the seafood man shouted.

Madman immediately sprinted back toward it and leapt in, driving up over the verge and onto the grass, taking a direct line back toward the front gates.

They watched as seafood man turned and ran back down the road, not having a hope in hell of catching him. It was a bizarre occurrence in an otherwise calm and tranquil day.

They all came to gather around Pete, keen to know what was said.

'He just wanted to know if there was another way out. When I told him there wasn't, he turned nasty.'

Pete didn't know why he hadn't told them the truth, all he knew was that he wasn't going to tell anyone, not even Dan.

'He looked desperate,' said Mary.

'He look deranged,' said another.

'Got to be,' Gabe agreed, 'Hoping to flog off a tonne of wet fish in weather like this.'

'Any of you care to guess what today's tableau is called?' Ginnel asked them as they started to pack up, 'I'll give you a clue. It's a name for the tree.'

Mushette immediately put up her hand.

'Tree of Knowledge. He was sat there reading and learning.'

'Sorry, Sarah.'

Mushette looked crushed.

'Shady Arbor?' someone shouted.

Ginnel shook his head.

A few others tried, without luck.

Pete waited a while before he put his hand up.

'Yes, Pete?'

'Gabriel Oak.'

'Well done,' Ginnel said to him, beginning small applause to prompt the others to do the same.

'I don't get it?' Ruthless shouted out.

'Me neither,' shouted Tabitha.

'Go on, Pete,' Ginnel invited.

Pete pointed to the book. 'He was reading Far from the Madding Crowd. In it, there's a character called Gabriel Oak.'

Even Gabe looked surprised.

'Well fancy you knowing that, Peter,' Mary said to him.

Pete sighed. Why did wearing a flat cap always mark him out as an illiterate cloth-head?

He reached The Dome later than usual so skipped through the obligatory shower and set straight off on his tropical ring-ride.

'Afternoon TC,' he began, 'It's been a while, so many apologies. How've you been keeping? I can imagine you've been pretty busy, what with all this Covid nonsense. I bet you're glad you're up there and not down here.

'One of the trio phoned again this morning and I still didn't answer, but I guess you already know that. I knew he'd just be after money. Like they always are.'

His three sons only ever rang him to ask for money. Good job Pip wasn't still alive, she'd have been disgusted with them. Her darling boys. His greedy, ungrateful trio.

'I honestly know how narked you must feel when people never say thank you,' Pete went on. 'I bet most folk only ever get in touch when they're wanting something off you. Pain relief. Or an end to their grief. But I reckon there's just as many constantly tapping you up for brass, like mine. And I might have three to contend with, but what do you have? Seven or eight billion? Maybe more if you've got beings on other planets.'

Pete liked to talk to TC as if it were a two-way conversation, but then he believed that it was, it was just that the response wasn't audible.

'I figure there was a reason you made us able to have our own kids. It's so we know what it's like. Having to take care of them. Worry about them. Get angry with them. Ignore them. Love them. Want them to love us. Want them to show some gratitude. Want them to make us proud. You couldn't have left us with a better example of what it's like for you. Pure genius.

'Anyroad, I just wanted to let you know that I'm extremely grateful. Life's just champion. Been a bit rough at times, but all in all, you've given me a cracker.'

Just then, a palm frond poked him in the eye and he tried not to interpret it as his gratitude being ill-received.

'You know that Sal has asked me to *learn* her how to play golf? Well, I'd just like to ask for a bit of moral support. And tolerance. Aye, a hefty dose of tolerance. Better still, put her off the idea completely.'

The people sat on the terrace by the koi pool stared at him as he floated by mid-sentence and he abruptly ended his conversation.

He began his usual ten laps of the circular pool, keeping himself tight up against the high inner wall so as to make the laps shorter. Jake waved to him from the swim-up bar, holding up a bottle of gin, and Pete returned the wave and motioned for him to pour. It tickled him that Jake knew nothing of what lay behind the wall. None of the staff did. They were all under the illusion that it was just a tall, solid platform for the massive metal sculpture.

What they also didn't know, was that on the wall's quieter side, there was an entrance hole at base level, not readily seen beneath the water. Through it, attached to the floor, ran a steel bar for you to pull yourself through with, and tonight, they would all be pulling.

Pete perched on his usual stool and Jake immediately pushed over his gin and tonic.

'What do you think of Dan?' Pete asked.

Jake didn't answer as a customer had arrived. It was Secret Squirrel. So named because he'd told everyone he used to work for MI5 and because he had the smallest nuts Pete had ever seen. Ironically, he only wanted a bag of dry roasted, so he was soon gone.

'Is Dan the guy who's married to Vulv —' Jake pulled himself up short. 'You know, I'm not too sure about that one, Pete. It's a bit crude. Don't you think?'

Pete shook his head in dismay. The name would obviously have to remain between him and Gabe.

'Don't think of it as crude, think of it as a little bit cheeky. Like TwatNav.'

Jake grinned at him and leaned over the bar, conspiratorially.

'I sneaked out, early yesterday morning. Drove fifty miles going absolutely nowhere, just so I could listen to it.'

Pete smiled. He'd forgotten that he'd given one to Jake as a Christmas present. But due to Covid, the lad hadn't had the opportunity to use it much, him being one of the staff that had volunteered to be locked-in, for double shifts and treble pay.

'Do people in Yorkshire really speak like that?'

'Not really. Not anymore,' said Pete, 'Though some places are still doing their best.'

'I finally heard the famous growler line,' Jake told him. 'Tell me the truth. Did you honestly not know?'

'I honestly did not,' Pete assured him.

Jake was referring to the: *Nay the 'ummer, why's thee had to come out at dinner time? Well tha's gunna 'av to cope wi out mi while I get mi gob around a couple of growlers.*

And like Jake said, it had unwittingly become one of the more famous of TwatNav's random interruptions. Pete hadn't known that the Yorkshire name for a pork pie had meant something entirely different in Scotland, being the equivalent of what Sal called her snatch. Hence, it had sparked a lot more merriment than ever intended and it had also added to his ever-increasing fame. Pete hadn't liked being famous. Especially when it brought him the tag of being *Yorkshire's second most famous Peter*, bearing in mind who the first was.

Pete and Jake fell silent as another customer came to the bar.

'Afternoon Becky. The usual?' Jake asked.

Becky nodded, then watched while Jake popped a cork and filled two flutes.

Pete turned and nodded a small hello. He didn't think much to Beck-and-call. Mainly because she always was, at her husband's. He liked a woman to have more spirit. He didn't care much for her husband either. He was the biggest hypochondriac imaginable, always having something wrong with him. Pete had aptly named him ShamPain. One of Pete's better ones, in light of him only ever drinking champagne. Their Border terrier he'd named ShamPoo on account of its chronic constipation. So many of its daily squats were sham poos.

'Go on then? Dan? What do you make of him? Other than him being a pillock?' Pete asked.

Jake smirked. 'I quite like him to be honest. I gather you don't?'

'I didn't say I didn't. He seems alright to me.'

'So why'd you call him a pillock?'

'Because he is. I don't mean pillock as in plonker, like you lot mean it. I meant it as in having only one gonad, which is what my generation mean by it.'

Jake looked genuinely surprised.

'So he's only got one plum?'

'Correct,'

'Poor bloke. I've never noticed. Not that I make a habit of looking.'

'I don't think I'd have noticed, if he wasn't in the habit of sitting with his legs spread.'

'Same as his wife then, eh?' said Jake.

They both sniggered.

'Actually seems like a nice guy,' Jake decided to add, 'Says he's got his own kayak and he'll take me out and teach me if I want.'

Pete knew that he had, he'd seen him out on the river with Yakky. Yakky being thus named due to having once kayaked for her county, and ever since, talking for England.

'Works as a fireman,' Jake continued, 'so I've no idea how he can afford to be in here, the most expensive club in the world. Maybe his brother shared his ill-gotten gains with him, seeing as he's just got out of the nick for armed robbery.'

Pete was faintly shocked. 'Did he tell you that himself?'

Jake shook his head. 'Vulv — Phoebe told me. He's a right nutter, apparently. She says he's one of the reasons they're hiding away in here.'

One of the reasons? What were the others, Pete wondered. And what were the chances that the madman in the stolen fish van had been his brother?

'But people don't hide from their own family for no reason, so I reckon they robbed him while he was still inside,' Jake postulated.

Pete nodded. He had a strange feeling that things were going to get interesting from thereon.

Above The Dome the sky was growing dark from a sudden gathering of clouds, prompting the lights to automatically spring into life. There were lights in the steelwork frame and lights hidden amongst the tropical vegetation, and together, they gave the place a whole different ambience. An ambience Pete particularly liked.

'Don't you think it strange,' Jake put to him, 'how Vic has the staff living totally separate from you, in The Hub, but lets us park our cars right alongside yours?'

Pete nodded, he always felt guilty that the staff apartments were so closely compacted. But then he knew they quite liked living cheek by jowl, although if what he heard was true, it was more like twinkle by tinkle.

'You know which car gets the most attention?' Jake asked him.

Pete thought about it. 'Gabe's Bugati?'

Jake shook his head. 'Your rusty old Ford Escort.'

Pete grinned. He loved his old Escort. It was the first car he'd ever owned.

'I bet there's more Bentleys out there than there is in Mayfair. And you know what? Most of them have got dints in them,' Jake informed him.

Pete was only too well aware. That's why his Bentley was still back at home. He wasn't about to get his pranged by some nutter out on the golf course.

'But I think it's about to change,' said Jake.

'What?'

'Us. Being allowed to park in the same place. Blub's Nine Eleven has just been scratched all the way around, like on purpose. And seeing as there's no cameras, Vic thinks it's one of us being envious and doing it out of spite.'

'That's utter rubbish. For starters, there's better cars to scratch than hers. And why just one? Why not do a few while you were at it? More likely it's something personal. Somebody with a grudge against her.'

'That's exactly what I said,' Jake agreed, 'So will you tell Vic?'

'Too right I will,' Pete assured him.

Adam came in through the back of the bar with a box of gin. Bobby's. Pete's favourite brand and Adam knew it.

'Don't drink it all at once,' he warned Pete, making room for the six bottles on the back shelves, amongst the many others.

As soon as Adam left, Pete nodded to Jake, and Jake knew exactly what he was expected to do. The six bottles were immediately withdrawn and hidden under the counter. As far as Pete was concerned, they were his.

'Swingerdy-do, swingerdy-dah,' he intoned, dryly, as three out of the six swingers swam by.

'They're going to hear you one of these days,' Jake warned him, while mixing himself a cocktail.

Pete knew to say that it was his, if anyone were to ask.

'What's that?'

'A Witch's Brew,' said Jake, passing it across for him to try. 'Not long to go before you're back in here, doing some witchcraft of your own, eh?'

Pete just smiled and took a sip of the cocktail.

'We know, you know. That you all come traipsing down here once a month,' Jake informed him. 'It's why Vic gets Zane to make sure all the scooters are charged up. But what I've finally figured out, is that it's not every month, it's every full moon. And is it any wonder that I think you're all part of some crackpot crazy cult?'

Pete just kept on smiling, and then, 'I'm amazed you've not sneaked in for a look.'

'And I'm amazed you don't know Arek and Hellmutt are always sat outside, guarding the door.'

Pete wasn't aware, but he wasn't amazed.

'Does that mean you've tried?'

Jake nodded. 'Several times.'

CHAPTER FOUR

NIGHT AFTER DAY

Back at the cabin, Pete warmed up his waiting dinner as quietly as possible, knowing Sal would already be in bed. There was a time when they could stay up all night without sleep, but not anymore. Now they had to forgo their restaurant dinner and get their heads down for a few hours. Be-twitched nights might only be once a month, but they stayed with you for days.

Kicking off his slippers, he slid under the quilt, absorbed by thoughts of the night ahead. There was a rumour that it was going to be rather special, and as the source of the rumour had been Adam, rather than Blubs, it was highly likely.

'You're cold,' Sal grumbled, as he spooned into her.

'And you're warm. So give some of it here.'

Sal dug her elbow into his ribs and he immediately un-spooned.

'I see you've been busy,' he told her, having seen all the wallpaper and fabric samples spread around the lounge. 'Must be nearly finished if you're lining up the decorators.'

'It was. Until Derek rang this afternoon. You'll never guess what's happened now.'

'Go on.'

'They've only gone and dropped half the balustrade onto the marble floor. I had to get straight on the bloody phone to Bologna and get some more slabs shipped over. It's been a right shit show.'

Sal had spent the last three years of her life planning, designing, and managing, the build of her dream home. Pete might have paid for it, but she had too in her own way, with blood, sweat and tears; possibly not the blood, but the other two had compensated for it.

Sal took in a deep breath and sighed.

‘Sometimes I wish we were back in your skanky flat. Stress free and happy.’

Before Pete could comment she began to laugh, and rightly so. It had been the lowest point of their lives.

He and Sal had met at therapy sessions. He’d had a delayed nervous breakdown after losing Pippa two years before, stricken with crippling anxiety and panic attacks. Sal had been suffering the same, but hers had been due to the catastrophic drops in oestrogen caused by the menopause. They always joked about how they’d shared their first panic attack before they’d shared their first orgasm. Only Sal got over hers when she’d given in to HRT, having previously resisted due to her mother dying of breast cancer. Pete had only gotten over his when he’d given in to gin.

After one particular therapy session, she’d asked if he’d like her to do the dance of the seven veils for him, seeing as she was, after all, called Salome. And what bloke wouldn’t? He’d been a member of The Garden for just over a year by that time and nudity no longer aroused him, or so he’d thought. And of course, he’d lost his head, and they were married ten months later.

Not that she’d had an easy time of it. There had been a lot of snide remarks thrown her way. Most memorably, ‘*And what first attracted you to the millionaire, Peter Hardcastle*?’ she’d been asked, Mrs Merton style. Quick as her wink, she’d replied, ‘*Cos he’s got a dick the size of a tractor exhaust pipe*.’ Fortunately, they’d been on the outside rather than the inside. In The Garden, one glance would have told them that wasn’t true.

And yet, if folks had known how it had all begun for the pair of them, they might never have made those remarks. When he’d first taken Sal out, he’d picked her up in his rusty old Ford Escort, careful never to use his TwatNav. And when he’d first taken her back to his place, it had been one of his rental properties; one that he’d never got around to fixing up. It was so bad he wouldn’t have leased it out to an incontinent hoarder and yet Sal hadn’t batted an eyelid. She’d cleaned it up, then spruced it up, and then, after three months of dating, she’d taken pity on him and suggested he move into her place. That was when he’d popped the question. And when she’d said yes, he’d finally taken her to his actual home.

He remembered the day, vividly. Unlocking the front door of his enormous country manor and showing her in. Two hours later, when he'd finally managed to convince her that it was his, she'd thrown up on the floor of his crystal chandeliered kitchen. He'd immediately summoned his Filipino housekeeper to come and clean it up but Sal had insisted on doing it herself. But within two months it was like she owned the place, telling him off for riding his trials bike up the sweeping, oak staircase and having him take down the Barnsley Rovers football shirts that had been strung across the dining room like long forgotten laundry.

The alarm woke them at eleven thirty and they quickly turned themselves around and headed out into the night. The light rain was intermittent as they scootered up to The Dome and they were glad they'd thrown on their monogrammed, resort issue raincoats. Everyone had. They were all in one big heap in the foyer. Sal and Pete added theirs to the pile and joined the others who were entering in through the shower trough.

On Be-twitched nights, everyone entered through the revolving doors that led onto the first of many staggered terraces surrounding the circular pool. The underwater LEDs were lighting it Caribbean blue, while up above, through one of the glass panels, the full moon peered in on them as if drawn to watch proceedings.

Everyone was stood in silence, listening to the cicadas while watching the giant clock that would herald the moment for the music to begin. At the stroke of midnight, it did.

It was music to accompany their anthem; their sacred hymn, Amazing Grace. And just as they were expected, they began to sing.

'*Amazing Grace, how sweet the sound, that saved a wretch like me. I once was lost, but now am found, was blind, but now I see.*'

Those were the only words they sang from it and those were repeated, nine times over, as they all filed down into the pool. Then the music stopped as suddenly as it had begun.

Vic remained behind, enrobed on the poolside, flanked by his two stepchildren, standing in the shadows left and right of him.

‘Tonight, brothers and sisters, we welcome into The Fold our two newcomers,’ Vic announced. ‘Would you please give a warm welcome to Daniel and Phoebe Saunders.’

Everyone applauded as the newcomers were prompted to come in through the changing room doors.

It had been a long time since they’d had an initiation ceremony. Pete remembered that the last one had been for The Mushrooms, five years before. Initiation didn’t come easy. It normally took a year to reach, which in real terms equated to much more than that as couples rarely stayed beyond two months at a time. The Buffs hadn’t undergone a quarter of that time so there was definitely something special about them. At least in Vic’s eyes.

Stood chest high in the water were eighty-seven members. Forty-four couples, minus the absent Joe, all intently staring at the clearly very nervous couple who were about to undertake their rite of passage.

Phoebe was invited to come forward first, to stand solemnly before them all.

Placing her right hand on her heart, she cleared her throat.

‘I vow to The Fold my allegiance. I vow to bare all, body and soul. I vow to dedicate my life to seeking truth and enlightenment. I vow, as much as I am able, to live in this world while not being part of this world. Do you accept my allegiance?’

‘We accept your allegiance,’ they all chanted as one.

Phoebe stepped back and Dan took her place, stating his vows, hand on heart.

‘Do you accept my allegiance?’ he then asked.

‘We accept your allegiance,’ they all chanted once again.

Pete was watching them with interest. If they were there to avoid the nutcase brother, then they must be desperate if they were prepared to go through with this.

Vic lifted the two handled silver chalice from the stone table behind him and passed it to Phoebe. Pete knew of old that it was filled with a strong port wine.

The couple each took a sip, and then so did Vic, and Eve, and Adam. From there, it was passed down to the pool, and in turn they each took a sip and passed it on. If any of them had Covid, they were screwed, thought Pete.

Eve passed to Vic a golden box and after pushing back its lid, he took it and held it out for the couple to help themselves. They each took out a small wafer and ate it, and then in a queue that had formed like a conga, the witnesses in the water all trooped by the poolside, where the box had been placed for them to take a wafer for themselves.

Next, Vic took the sword that Adam was holding, and as Phoebe knelt before him on a folded towel, he used it to tap onto each of her shoulders.

'Arise,' he said to her, 'From this day forward, may everything you seek be found, and may all of your trials become truths.'

Phoebe stood up and stepped back, so that Dan could take her place, with Vic repeating the ritual for him.

Pete considered the ceremony to be an amalgamation of a Christian communion and the bestowing of a knighthood. He wasn't sure what else an initiation might consist of but he liked to think that he'd have come up with something more original. Even so, it was only done for entertainment value. Nobody took it seriously apart from Vic. Or at least he didn't think they did.

Eve, Adam, Phoebe and Dan were descending the steps into the pool to join them all. Vic came last, tossing his silk robe across the stone table and confronting them all with a mop of white pubic hair and a map of purple varicose veins.

Once they were in, they slowly waded through the water to reach that part of the high inner wall where they knew to be the entrance hole. Then they parted themselves like the red sea, to leave a passage for the newly initiated, being led forward by Vic.

'Entry into The Well symbolises your new birth,' Vic told the couple, 'Once you pass through, you have entered into The Fold. We stand here to witness your entry and look forward to being one with you on the other side.'

Dan had placed a supportive arm around his wife's shoulders and was guiding her forward, but those nearest could see her reluctance.

'You can do it,' he was telling her, 'Just take a deep breath.'

His words had the opposite effect of what he'd wanted and Phoebe immediately retreated. Dan cast an anxious glance toward Vic but Vic just motioned them forward, causing Phoebe to stiffen, panic stricken. She refused to move. It was an unexpected impasse and nobody knew what to do.

'You don't know how to swim, do you?' Sal asked, pushing her way out of the crowd.

Phoebe turned around to her voice. 'How did you know?'

'Because you never go in the pool. Like me. I can't swim either,' Sal told her, 'But if I can do this, month in, month out, then so can you.'

Phoebe looked unsure.

'Here, put these on,' Sal instructed, unwinding the elasticated swim goggles from around her wrist.

Pete had wondered why she'd asked where they were that morning. She'd heard the rumour and obviously guessed the rest.

Sal helped tighten them around Phoebe's head.

'Right. Stick your head under and have a look to see where that hole is,' she directed her.

Phoebe put her face into the water and looked. Slowly, face still under, she edged nearer to the dreaded hole.

'See,' said Sal, once Phoebe had come up for air, 'It's big enough for even Jude to get through. Did you see that metal rod with the balls on?'

Phoebe nodded.

'Those balls are there for you to grab hold of and yank yourself through,' Sal told her, 'You don't need to be able to swim. Three yanks is all it takes.'

'Now, watch. The pair of you. And listen. Because when you hear me shout, you'll see just how quick it is.'

Sal nodded to Pete, just as he'd been expecting her to. This was what they did, and hopefully, Dan and Phoebe would be able to do the same.

Pete took a deep breath and plunged down toward the hole and the metal bar. Once he had hold of it with his left hand, he threw out his right, to Sal. Her hand grabbed his in an instant and with it, he pulled her down until she had hold of the first ball. Seconds later, she was through, with Pete only seconds behind her.

‘I’m here, Phoebe!’ Sal shouted out.

They heard a loud ripple of applause.

‘Well if you like me that much, stop taking bloody POT shots at me,’ she shouted in response.

There was a ripple of laughter and not one SOL.

Phoebe reached them with a rush of exhilaration.

‘I’m here! I’m through!’ she shouted ecstatically, ‘Woohoo! I made it!’

There was cheering from the other side of the wall and Phoebe suddenly threw her arms around Sal’s neck. Sal was stunned. She didn’t do outward shows of emotion and Pete rightly anticipated her immediate recoil, to which Phoebe looked instantly apologetic. But then it was Pete’s turn to be stunned as his buttoned-up wife suddenly threw her arms around Phoebe and hugged her right off the ground. Dan had emerged in time to witness the embrace and he immediately joined in as a threesome. On a whim, Pete made it a foursome.

The others were starting to emerge, one after the other, all effusively congratulating their newest members. Pete and Sal waded out of the way, knowing it would take a while for them all to arrive.

At the centre of The Well there was a huge metal orb which Pete knew to be six foot in diameter, but only because he was level with the top of it. It was magnetic, which he only knew because his wedding band — their one permissible piece of jewellery — repeatedly flung itself upon it. Same with the huge circular coil that was fastened securely around The Well’s outer rim. None of them had any idea what the huge magnets were there for as Vic never cared to explain, just as they had no idea as to the purpose of The Fork, other than it played some part in The Vibration and Sound.

In The Hub’s reception stood a stone replica of an Egyptian statue, complete with etched hieroglyphs. The hieroglyphs included two tuning forks connected by wires and Pete had once googled it, finding lots of theories on how tuning forks had been used for the building of the pyramids; theories that would have you believe vibration alone was capable of cutting and moving their heavy, integral blocks of stone. That being the case, he didn't care to think what it could do to the human body.

The Fork's stem was set into the centre of the orb and where it intersected, cables came out, like the hair of Medusa, snaking over the orb's crown. Pete knew that Vic had constructed it because he'd once told him so. He'd said he was a follower of Tesla and that he'd continued his life's work for their transcendental advantage, but to Pete, it all looked more Heath Robinson than Nikola Tesla.

Leaning back, with his elbows on the hard outer coil that also served as a hand rail, Pete cast his eyes up the full length of The Fork's two tines. He'd heard that it was taller than the one in the Guinness book of World Records, but he'd had his doubts, seeing as he'd heard it from Blubbermouth. It was stainless steel at a guess, having never had the slightest patch of rust on it, but that didn't stop the impressive staghorn fern from growing in the crook of its tines.

They moved further around as The Well was filling up fast, although it would never be as full as in pre-Covid times when May meant most members were in attendance.

As Sal stopped to talk with Yakky, Pete stopped to look at the three signs that hung, evenly spaced, at the top of the high curved wall. These three signs had never been removed or replaced but Pete always had to check to make sure.

To his left:

If you want to find the secrets of the universe, think in terms of energy, frequency and vibration - Nikola Tesla.

To his right:

Three things cannot be long hidden: The Sun, The Moon and The Truth - Buddha.

Above and behind:

It is during our darkest moments that we must focus to see the light - Aristotle Onassis.

Yep, same three.

'Ready to steady,' Adam was shouting to them, stood as he was, beside the operating panel. People who couldn't take hold of the circular bar took hold of someone who could and Adam put into motion the raising of the floor.

Huge, hidden hydraulics leapt into action and the ground slowly began to rise beneath their feet. They were all careful to stand well back of the orb, knowing that the floor had a central hole, wide enough to accommodate its girth, and knowing that to be caught between the two would result in a possible dissection.

Once the operation came to a halt, they were all half exposed, and the operating panel had gone from being level with Adams's face to being level with his crotch.

Letting go of whatever, or whoever, they had hold of, they spread themselves out to sit down, submerging themselves back to their shoulders.

The exit hole was now beneath the raised floor and inaccessible, giving Pete his usual moment of panic.

And then it began. The Vibration and Sound. Initiations might be once in a blue moon, but this they could rely on each and every full moon.

Pete could feel the tremor in his backside as it started to rise up though his spine and into the back of his head. His hair stood on end, but it would settle, it always did. And then the tics and the twitches began. Tics above his eyes and below his cheeks. Twitches in his calves and then his glutes and then his biceps. But they would stop, they always did. This was why it had become known to them as Be-twitched night. The first time was always an unnerving experience and Pete could only imagine what Dan and Phoebe were thinking right now.

As The Vibration took over his entire body, Pete compared it to being sat on a giant subwoofer. The resonating hum seemed to come from everywhere, reaching his brain through his skull as much as his ears. He put his head back into the water and listened, wondering if what he'd recently heard was true, about sound travelling four times faster underwater. If anything, it sounded slower. When he lifted back up, the surface of the water was rippling all around him in pulse waves, and he looked across to see the subtle smile on Sal's face. She liked that the vibration toned her ass, or so she said, but Pete wasn't sure if it was something else.

He suddenly needed to pee. With all the distraction of the initiation he'd forgotten to let it go while he was out in the main pool. He could never pee in The Well. It was sacrosanct. Even though he knew the water was one and the same.

Half an hour later, Pete was growing warm, but best of all, he was growing calm. The calmness always seemed to come from nowhere. He'd asked some of the others about it. Those who were regarded as boffins. They'd spoken to him of cymatics and diamagnetism and other words he neither understood nor cared to. But Pete had a theory of his own.

When he'd suffered his nervous-breakdown, he'd sought the help of a therapist. One of Harley Street's best. Harry Gascoigne. Before his treatment began, Harry had made him watch a video. It was a horrible video, bearing in mind he was then in the habit of crying over roadkill.

The video was of a gazelle, hanging limp in the mouth of a lioness. When the lioness had been chased away, presumably by the cameraman, the gazelle had just laid there for what seemed an eternity. And then, it had begun to shake. Pete hadn't known what to make of it. The gazelle just kept on shaking and shaking until it suddenly stopped. And then it had stood up, looked around, and trotted on its away as if nothing had ever happened.

Harry had explained to him that this was nature's way of dealing with trauma, allowing animals to live unhindered by PTSD. This was how it was meant to be for humans, Harry had told him, only we'd conditioned our brains to overrule it. Stupid humans.

Harry had proceeded to teach him TRE. Trauma Release Exercises. And that had been the start of Pete's recovery. The tremor that he was feeling now was something akin to the self-induced tremor brought on by TRE. And that, he reasoned, was why it was so calming. And yet, TRE came from the inside out, while this came from the outside in, and wasn't remotely similar, so who was he to say.

As the resonating hum became deeper, the vibration became stronger, and Pete would have been serenely calm if it hadn't been for his bursting bladder. A few of them had begun to float, a sign that they were well over halfway. Sal too was on the rise. Pete watched her with envy. She said it was never intentional and that the intense relaxation was probably the cause, but Pete had never floated, intentional or otherwise.

And then it was over. The Vibration and Sound ceased. And as Adam lowered the floor, they quickly found their feet.

It always struck Pete as strange that nobody had anything to say afterwards. They all made a patient, polite exit, before towelling, dressing, and scootering off home without a word being said. None of them would sleep. Some of them wouldn't sleep the following night either. For all The Well's calming effects, they were afterwards as energized as having had eighteen expressos.

When Sal and Pete got back to their cabin, they sat out on their veranda and waited for the sun to rise.

CHAPTER FIVE

ONE DAY IN JUNE

'Do you mind if we team up with you?' Phoebe asked, catching Pete and Sal unawares as they readied themselves for the weekly coffee morning quiz.

'Not at all,' said Pete, nodding to the two vacant restaurant chairs normally belonging Gabe and Jude.

Gabe was currently occupied on stage as resident quizmaster and Jude was banned for risk of having insider information. She went to Stitch and Bitch instead, which irked Sal somewhat. Not because Sal liked embroidery class, but because those not present were usually subject of the bitching.

'You do know we play individually, not as a team?' Sal asked them.

'No. No, we didn't,' Dan replied, slightly embarrassed by their ignorance to the fact.

'That's shit,' said Phoebe.

'SOL,' Sal was quick to respond.

Phoebe immediately acknowledged it with a raised finger.

'We picked you because you looked the cleverest as well.'

This girl was shrewd, thought Pete, seeing as Sal immediately pulled out Jude's chair and patted it for Phoebe to sit down next to her.

'We used to do it in teams,' Sal told them, 'But we could never agree on which of us had the right answer.'

Pete grinned. It was shamefully true.

'I'll warn you now,' he added, 'They take it deadly serious. It's like sitting an exam. Your nerves will be frayed by the end of it.'

'Don't much like the sound of that,' said Phoebe, 'We thought it was going to be a fun thing.'

'Oh, it is,' said Sal, 'You'll get totally addicted.'

'Aye, it's only half serious,' Pete added. 'Gabe and Eve set all the questions and you can tell straight away whose question it is.'

Sal was nodding. 'Eve has a PhD. She's really clever.'

'And Gabe hasn't. And isn't,' Pete tagged on.

Pete wasn't keen on Eve's questions. Give him Gabe's every time. But Eve's were always worth a guess.

'Eve takes after Vic then,' Dan remarked, 'They say the apple never falls far from the tree.'

Sal was shaking her head. 'Vic isn't her tree. He's her step-tree.'

Coffee was delivered courtesy of Lottie, their usual waitress. A tray of cups, cream and sugar and a large pressurised dispenser.

'How are you settling in?' Sal asked them, as she stood to pump out a cup.

'Great. This place is totally awesome,' Dan replied.

'And we're having such good weather,' his wife added, 'All this sun we're having, it's like it was just made for taking your clothes off.'

Pete smiled. He had an inkling she'd never done the 'taking your clothes off' thing before.

'Oh, frigging hell!' Sal swore, startling their companions.

Pete waited for one of them to say SOL, but they didn't, bless them.

'Shar Pei's here,' Sal said to Pete, and then to the others, 'When she comes, we've got no chance.'

'Which one is she?' Dan asked.

Sal pointed across to the woman in question.

'Isn't she called Joanna?' he queried.

'She is. But Pete calls her Shar Pei.'

Phoebe immediately began to giggle and then seemed unable to stop.

'What?' Dan asked, smiling.

Phoebe had thrust her hand between her legs, holding onto her undercarriage, making it obvious she was in danger of leaking.

'The dog,' she finally managed to tell him, 'Shar Pei. She's like the dog with all the folds of skin.'

Dan looked back at Joanna and a wide grin developed across his face.

'She's lost a lot of weight, due to her gastric band,' Sal explained.

'Does she know?' Dan asked.

'That she looks like a Shar Pei?'

Dan began to laugh, 'That you *call* her Shar Pei?'

'Does she 'eck,' Pete quickly responded, 'If she did, she'd probably give me a right biff.'

'Or bite,' Phoebe quipped, giggling again.

'Morning all,' Gabe suddenly began, while adjusting his mic. 'Have you all had plenty of the old brain boost?' he asked, holding up his cup of coffee.

They all shouted some form of affirmative.

'Good. Then are we all sharp and snappy?'

'No, one of us is Shar Pei and snappy,' Phoebe wisecracked.

She and Sal were in fits of giggles.

Eve was working her way amongst them, passing out lined paper, pencils and erasers.

'Remember,' Gabe continued, 'From the minute we kick off, not a word, not a signal, not a facial expression, not nothing. Or you're out. And no trips to the bathroom to any hidden phones.'

'What?' Phoebe exclaimed, 'I'm going to need to go after having all this coffee.'

Pete considered she needed to go before the coffee.

'You'll have to hold it, girl.'

'But if you don't, don't worry about it,' Sal added, 'Mary wets herself all the time. They're forever reupholstering her chair.'

Phoebe began to giggle again but then quickly stood up.

'Have I got time to go for a quick one?' she shouted out to Gabe.

Gabe threw his hands up in the air, as if it were an outrageous request.

'At your age? Blimey O'Riley. At your age I had a bladder like a bleeding camel.'

A few titters erupted, along with a few SOLs, but Phoebe had pushed back her chair and set off at a trot.

'Okay. Have your papers all got your names on?' Gabe asked.

Those who hadn't written them, quickly wrote them top right. Dan wrote his and then he wrote Phoebe's.

Pete lined up his paper, square to the table, and then took a shield from top of the centrally placed stack. They were simple pieces of cardboard, folded to form a steep wedge. High enough for you to get your hand and your eyes under, but low enough to hide what your hand was writing.

'To hide your answers,' Pete told him, as Dan's eyes begged the question, 'I told you it was serious.'

There was a minor panic as some people realised there were no shields on their table and a mad scramble ensued to source those going spare. Phoebe returned just as things were getting settled.

'Are we ready?' Gabe called out.

'Ready,' they all shouted in response.

'Right then. Time to zip it and hit it.'

Phoebe was about to ask Sal a question, when Sal's hand flew out to cover her mouth. Phoebe coughed instead and the four of them tried not to laugh.

'Number one. What is the name for a baby goose?'

Everyone was eyes down scribbling. There was always an easy one to begin with.

'Number two. Ganymede is a moon of which planet?'

Phoebe looked to Dan but he was giving nothing away and Pete immediately knew he was going to become one of the addicted.

'Number three. What is the correct name for a woman's genitalia?'

Pete had been chewing the end of his pencil but on hearing that, he almost bit right through it. He looked to Gabe and Gabe looked to him, with a grin as wide and wicked as a Halloween pumpkin.

'Number four. What is a tetrahedron?'

An Eve question if ever there was one. They had ten seconds to write down each answer but Pete failed on that one. He jotted down the question, so as to revisit it later.

'Number five. What is the most popular car in Brazil?'

A Gabe question for sure, but Pete still hadn't a clue.

'Number six. Who lived for nine hundred and sixty-nine years?'

Pete grinned smugly at Sal, as she looked at him, blankly.

Between questions, everyone was quickly taking a turn to pump out another coffee. Their tables were always splattered by the end of the quiz, such was their urgency. By question seventeen, Pete was on his third cup.

'As a haircut, what is a Brazilian short for?'

Pete wasn't doing too well. This was the third in a row he couldn't answer. He looked to Sal. She obviously knew it as she just smiled at him and winked. Dan and Phoebe had been equally quick to put down their answers. Phoebe caught Pete's eye and put her hand up under her nose, as if about to sneeze, but then she subtly brought it down in a steep swoop. She did it again, while Sal just shook her head at the unnecessary pity being shown to him. As Pete jotted down an answer, he wondered at the reason for all the Brazil questions. Was Gabe winding him up? Knowing that his three errant sons were all living out there?

'Number eighteen. What is the approximate circumference of the sun?'

Pete was stumped. He couldn't even hazard a guess. It was an Eve question for sure. If it had been Gabe's, it would have been: *What was the average circumference of The Sun's page three thre'pennies?* And he'd have been able to guess at forty-four double D.

'Number nineteen. Who is currently top of the POTS leader board, and has been for some time?'

Everyone looked to Sal, and Sal, uncharacteristically, went ketchup red. She immediately gave the finger to Gabe, who just grinned at her.

'And I need their full and correct name, not just a shortened version,' Gabe told them all.

Pete realised this had been a gift to him and Sal, seeing as they would be the only two likely to get it right.

Before Gabe could ask his next question, there came a clattering and commotion from behind the double doors leading into the kitchen, soon to be followed by acrimonious shouting.

'Oh, for Pete's sake,' said Gabe, coming off stage to go and investigate.

In his absence, everyone was keeping a close eye on everyone else, making sure there was no conferring.

Whatever had happened in the kitchen, Gabe hadn't managed to resolve it, and the shouting continued unabated throughout the next dozen questions. Then it abruptly stopped.

'Question thirty-one. What does the sign say that's currently hung on the back of our entrance gates?'

Everyone looked at each other, blankly.

There was always one 'sign' question in their quiz. It was Vic's prerogative. Meaning the more serious quizzers amongst them could often been seen out and about with their notepads and pens. But this one was a sneaky one. Due to Covid, most of them hadn't been anywhere near the front gates, for months.

'Question thirty-two. What is the most repeated phrase in The Bible? And I'll give you a clue, it's only four words.'

Pete chewed on his pencil as he tried to think, but ran out of time.

'Question thirty-three. What is Easter Island famous for?'

Phoebe looked to Dan, but Dan shrugged her off.

Eggs, Sal mouthed to her.

Phoebe was about to write it down until she saw Pete, chuckling. He tapped the side of his head to give her a clue and she resumed writing. What were the chances she'd written down balding men, he wondered.

'Number thirty-four. What nationality was Rin Tin Tin?'

Another one for Gabe to grin at him with, touching on the fact Pete called Rin, Rin-Ting-Tong.

Mush shot his hand up, and everyone ceased writing and waited. Sometimes Gabe allowed queries but more often than not he just gave the questioner two fingers, mainly because their avowed silence guaranteed him no immediate SOLs.

'Go on then. What's your question?' Gabe asked, surprising them all.

'Do you mean as in birth place? Or as in breed place?'

'Well then, now you've thrown that one up, I'll think we'll have to have both. Half a point for each.'

Everyone scribbled another answer.

As soon as the forty questions had been answered, papers were immediately gathered in.

'Got to dash,' Pete said to them as soon as Eve had taken theirs, 'I've got a visitor down at the golf house.'

'Aren't you waiting to see if you've won?' Phoebe asked him.

'You must be joking. It takes them forever to add them all up. The only thing this lot are still sat here waiting for, is lunch,' he told them. 'Results'll come up in reception, around half two. Good luck. If you win, you get a monkey.'

The Buffs looked at him, blankly, but Sal would no doubt explain.

He had eleven minutes to get to his buggy and then down to the front gates, which would mean beating his previous record. Needless to say, he did.

He reached the resort's entrance just in time to see a lorry pull up. Only the top half of it was visible above the high gates, but its green and yellow livery made it instantly recognisable. Pete keyed in the code to open the gates, reading the sign that was fixed to the back of them as they rolled out of the way.

No one ever leaves for good. Like leaves on a tree, they always make a return – VD

A Vic Dawson original by the look of it.

'Do any of you ever get arrested?' his brother asked, grinning at him through the open window of his lorry.

'Arrested?'

'Yeh, for standing out here by the side of the road, stark bloody naked.'

Pete laughed but then quickly leapt out of the way as three flatback lorries peeled past them, all with tracked excavators loaded on their backs. Government lock-down had obviously been eased enough to allow construction to resume on their new river-fed swimming pond.

‘What’s brought you over into this neck of the woods, then?’ Pete asked, once they were in the golf house lounge, sharing a pot of tea.

‘I’ve bought a new quadbike for our lass. Just picked it up. It was only twenty miles away, so I thought I’d drop by and see you, now that we’re being allowed.’

‘Ah, that’s why you’re in the truck,’ said Pete, and then, ‘I thought she’d packed it in, since her accident?’

His brother shook his head. ‘It was only a thumb. That’s what she sez. It’s only a thumb, Andrew, I’ve got another one. Honest to God, she’ll be driving it like she’s stolen it, again. I don’t know why I let her talk me into it.’

Pete laughed. She was a woman after his own heart.

‘How is she? Apart from the missing thumb?’

‘She’s good. She sends her regards.’

‘Still wanting to move back home?’

‘Of course. Talks about it all the time. Still looking on Rightmove every night.’

‘You should sell up and retire back there. Make her happy.’

His brother shook his head. ‘If I had a house like yours to move back to, then maybe I would.’

‘You can have it,’ Pete told him, ‘Once we’ve flit to the new one.’

‘It was the new one I was on about,’ Andy replied, grinning.

It was a mutual joke. His brother and his wife were enraptured with Sal’s creation. It was the perfect house in the perfect setting, they said. It should be on Grand Designs, they said. Sal said, just because she watched it didn’t mean she wanted to be on it. She also said, they should stop dropping by to see it as they were seeing it more than she was, but she didn’t say that to them, only to Pete.

‘Once Covid’s over, you should come and stay with us for the weekend,’ Andy suggested. ‘It would be like old times. A lot of the customers still ask after you, you know.’

Pete nodded. He’d liked living in Olney, and the weather had always been better than in Barnsley.

‘Sal’s not keen to go anywhere as yet,’ Pete told him, ‘That being said, she’s ventured out for Botox and fillers readily enough. You’d think those places would be the last to open their doors, wouldn't you? How d'you pump somebody's chops full of botulism when they're bagged up in a mask?'

Andy shrugged and dunked his digestive into his tea.

Plucky sauntered by. 'You up for a round tomorrow, Pete?' he asked.

'Aye, why not. Give me a shout first thing and we'll weigh up the weather.'

Plucky didn't leave. He obviously wanted an introduction.

'Andy, this is —' Pete panicked, he couldn't think of Plucky's real name, ' — the luckiest chap we've got in here. Goes from being chicken farmer one day to Euromillions winner the next. How's that for a turnaround?'

'Phil Matthews,' said Plucky, offering out a hand, before quickly changing it to a wave. 'I'm guessing you're Pete's brother?'

'Yep. I'm the good looking one, he's the stinking rich one. But he's learned to live with it.'

Phil smiled and nodded and then wandered away.

'Still looks more like a chicken farmer than a Euro-millionaire,' Andy observed.

'That's why I call him Plucky. Lucky that he's not still plucking chickens for a living.'

Andy smirked, he knew his brother of old.

'You know, I still don't get why you want to do all this nudity stuff. I can't take anyone seriously. It just makes me want to laugh all the time.'

'It's a nervous reaction.'

'Is it?'

'So they reckon. Especially with the British. It stems from when the Victorians used to cover up their table legs. It left us all congenitally repressed.'

Andy shook his head, not sure if his brother was pulling his leg, covered or not.

'What's with the statues outside the front gates?' Andy asked, 'I get that they're meant to be Adam and Eve, with the fig leaves, but why headless?'

Pete shrugged. 'We never got around to putting new heads on them.'

'You mean they were bought like that?'

'Course they weren't. Their heads were knocked off and nicked not long after I joined up. But finding those heads might mean resolving the biggest mystery in The Garden's history.'

Andy leaned over the coffee table. 'Pray do tell.'

Pete leaned in to join him, covertly looking around so as to add gravitas to what he was about to impart, seeing as his brother was clearly expecting it.

'There were two couples. Here from the very beginning. The wife of one, and the husband of the other, ran off together. Disappeared overnight. Never to be seen or heard of again. The statues' heads disappeared that very same night.'

Andy looked suitably intrigued, so Pete ploughed on.

'The two left behind were totally distraught. I'd often come across them, crying on each other. That's how it was at first, the two of them leaning on each other for comfort and support. But then it wasn't long before they'd moved in together, which for some members, wasn't long enough. It was deemed to be *unseemly*.'

Pete paused for a few sips of his tea, adding to the suspense.

'Six months later, plod arrives, saying that the absconded couple had failed to get in touch with any of their relatives. Which in turn, led to the newly moved-in-together couple being interviewed, and on more than one occasion. It left everyone highly suspicious of them, and you know how it is with people, one suspicion got heaped upon another until it was actually them that had had the affair, and then murdered their partners to be free of them, without having to part from any of their brass.'

'Were they eventually arrested?' Andy asked.

'No, never. They stayed on here pretty much permanently. And then, when it was legally allowed, they got married. They're here now. Along with the lingering suspicion.'

'So where do the missing heads fit in?'

Pete grinned. 'You're gunna love this,' he told him. 'The pair that ran off with each other, were called Adam and Eve.'

'No way?'

Pete nodded. 'The original sinners. And, believe it or not, they might have left, but we've still got another Adam and Eve living here. The owner's step-kids. Brother and sister. And their partners ran off with club members, too.'

'Well, it's tempting fate, isn't it? Being in here, with names like that,' Andy surmised. 'But what about the heads?'

Pete realised he'd been remiss.

'Souvenirs. That's as the rumours have it. When Adam and Eve ran off together, they took their heads with them, as souvenirs.'

'Bit bizarre. Stopping to knock their blocks off before making a speedy getaway. It's not like it's normal to carry a hammer and chisel around in your car. Not unless your name's Peter Sutcliffe, of course.'

Pete smirked. 'Exactly. That's why so many here believe the souvenir rumour was one put about by the remaining couple, so as to convince everyone their spouses had left. Ironic that you should mention Sutcliffe, though, because that's what their name is. The remaining couple. Dave and Lydia Sutcliffe.'

It was why he'd named them The Rippers, only too happy to comply with the general consensus of them having murdered their previous partners, before burying them somewhere in The Garden.

Pete poured more tea.

'Why don't you stop for a round?' he asked, 'We've got plenty of spare clubs. But you'd have to strip off, mind you.'

'No thanks,' Andy laughed, 'I haven't got time. And you've whupped my arse enough without you whupping my bare arse as well.'

Pete grinned at him.

'Do you remember when we used to sneak out onto the course up Royston road, as soon as the sun came up?'

Andy nodded. 'When we couldn't even afford to play on a municipal, never mind private.'

Pete chuckled. 'Aye, and with only the one nine-iron between us. One shared club. To be driver, putter and wedge. How sad is that.'

'I've still got it,' Andy admitted.

'Seriously?'

‘Seriously. I keep it under the bed to whack any possible intruders.’

‘I think I’d opt for an AK47 myself.’

‘Yeh, but you wouldn’t need to. You’ve got that much security around your place, they’d never reach your front porch, never mind your bedroom.’

Pete wouldn’t disagree. He had that many cameras, he had cameras just to look at other cameras, and all of them linked through to somebody sat somewhere he hadn’t a clue, being paid to watch. It made him suddenly realise how liberating it was living at the resort, never thinking to lock the door, never worrying about what might get stolen. A five roomed cabin didn’t lend itself to being filled with wall to wall valuables.

‘Everything okay back at base?’ Pete asked, knowing his brother could just as easily have sent one of his men to collect the quad.

‘Yeh, fine. Just annoying that we’re in danger of another full lock-down. I’m going to have to start drawing up a list of redundancies. What about you? How you getting on at the factory?’

Pete shrugged. ‘Not a problem. We’re not at the factory. I had all the sewing machines taken out and set up on folks’ kitchen tables. They’re all working from home.’

Andy shook his head. ‘I might have known Covid wouldn’t set you back.’

‘Set me back? It’s sending profits through the roof. They’re stitching up more masks than they are knickers. Same satin. Same lace. There’s hardly any difference between them. Just a patch of cloth on strings at the end of the day. Just covering different orifices.’

As Andy burst out laughing, Pete laughed with him, but not for long.

‘It’s not bothering you, is it? Having to make folk redundant?’

‘No, not at all. It’s not nice, but I think we’re carrying too many as it is. We’ll ride it out, same as everyone else.’

‘That’s the spirit,’ Pete said to him.

‘I was more worried about you.’

‘Me?’ Pete asked, surprised, ‘Why?’

'Well, your mobile's always turned off, for starters.'

'And I always ring you back when I see that you've rung.'

'Yes, but you're not ringing back your lads.'

'Ah, the trio in Rio. It's them that's got you onto me.'

'I'm not onto you. But while you're not onto them, they're onto me all the flaming time. Are they living out there permanently now, or what?'

'Nup. It'll only be until the money runs out and the women lose interest.'

'It been nearly three years. They must have had plenty of brass to last them that long.'

'You can bet your Barnsley boots they did. My brass. But please don't tell me you've let them squeeze any out of you?'

Andy shook his head. 'They've never asked, not outright, but I guess they've hinted once or twice, suggesting I might like to put my hand in my pocket to help with their latest venture.'

'Then let me give you some advice,' Pete told him, 'When you see that it's one of them that's calling. Ignore it.'

Andy nodded. 'I'm glad I never had kids.'

As Pete took a ginger biscuit from off the tray, he dropped it, and from out of nowhere, ShamPoo was on it and eating it. Pete gave him another while ShamPain wasn't looking.

'You still going up north to see the in-laws once a fortnight?' he asked.

'Not since Covid, no. We've been really worried about them. Ron caught it you know? He was in hospital for a week.'

'Aye, you told me. We were worried too. Smashing fella, Ron. Both of them are. Your lass was blessed being born to them.'

'Unlike us, eh?'

'Aye, unlike us,' Pete agreed. 'Do you ever drop by and visit they're graves when you're up there?'

Andy immediately shook his head.

'I once did. But it was only to piss on them.'

Pete nodded. 'It was tough r'kid, it was tough.'

'Maybe it's a cyclical thing? Bad parents, good kids. Good parents, bad kids.'

Pete pursed his lips as he nodded, considering it a fair point.

‘Maybe we should be grateful to them,’ Andy suggested, ‘Maybe it’s them that drove us onwards and upwards. Drove us away from a likely life down the pit.’

‘And maybe it’s them that made us both susceptible to nervous breakdowns, years later,’ Pete responded.

Andy nodded. ‘I’m still on the pills,’ he divulged.

‘Well you need to get off them, and soon. Or you never will.’

‘What? So I can swap them for the booze? Like you did?’

Ouch, thought Pete. Only your brother could hit you with that.

‘Want another pot of tea?’

‘No, I’d best get off. Don’t want to hang about too long, this nudity thing might be catching.’

Pete went out for a look at the quad bike and then jumped into a buggy to head for The Dome.

‘Who won?’ were his first words to Jake, as he reached his usual stool at the swim-up-bar.

‘Who’d you think?’

‘Shar Pei?’

‘Correct.’

‘I’m sure she cheats.’

‘How? You can’t take your phones in. You can’t even take bags in to sneak your phones in. It’s impossible,’ Jake told him. ‘Unless she keeps one squat under all those folds of flesh?’

Pete grimaced. ‘If it were that easy, we’d all be sneaking one in between our arse cheeks.’

Prunie and Mush swam up and took the stools either side of Pete.

‘Joanna won the quiz, again,’ Prunie announced.

‘I know, Jake’s just told me. She needs a handicap setting up for her, like we have in golf.’

‘That’s a great idea. Do you think she’d go for it?’

‘No,’ said Pete, in a word.

Jake lined up their drinks and they toasted commiserations to each other.

‘What did you put for the Angel of Death?’ Mush asked them.

‘Josef Mengele,’ said Pete.

‘I put Satan,’ said Prunie.

‘Me too,’ said Mush, ‘But I think Pete might be right.’

Pete didn't think, he knew. He'd named his high school biology teacher after him, due to his fondness for dissections.

'Did you get the most common biblical phrase?' Mush asked.

The other two shook their heads.

'Me neither. I googled it. It's, *Do not be afraid.*'

'And ain't that a joke,' Prunie scoffed, 'God throws Satan down to walk the earth amongst us. He makes death an inevitability. He gives us pestilence and plagues. And then he has the gall to tell us not to be afraid? It's a wonder any of us keep our sanity. What did you put for the haircut? The Brazilian thing?'

'Brazilian Bob,' said Mush, 'What did you put?'

'I didn't.'

'I put Brazilian Bomber,' said Pete, thinking of Phoebe's dive-bombing hand gesture.

Jake was suddenly laughing.

'Go on then smart arse, what is it?' Mush asked him.

'It's a Brazilian Landing Strip.'

The three men stared at him.

'Like a tramline shaved over your head?' Prunie asked.

Jake was still laughing. 'It's not for the head. It's for a woman's pubes. And it's everything shaved off apart from a narrow strip down the middle.'

'Like a muff Mohican?' Prunie quizzed.

'No. It's neater. Flatter. Like it says, a landing strip,' Jake explained, 'Christ Almighty, I can't believe that three jet setting men of the world didn't know that.'

Pete had always considered Jake to have a very glossy view of how they all lived.

'If it had been a Barnsley Landing Strip then maybe I'd have known,' he reasoned.

Jake shook his head as he grimaced and Pete could well understand how that might appear less exotic, or erotic. He began to wonder how many times his sons had touched down on a Brazilian landing strip.

'I knew the symbol for gold,' Mush told them. 'I was swotting up on the periodic table till midnight. I knew we were due for one.'

These boys were keen, thought Pete, the only thing he'd been swotting were the bluebottles on the remains of his supper.

'Come on, fellas, you need to be drinking up. I'm shutting up shop in ten minutes,' Jake suddenly announced.

'How d'yer mean? We've only just got here?' Pete was incredulous.

'We're having a hog roast tonight. Haven't you heard? Staff are invited, too. And I've been roped in to help get it up and running.'

'News to me,' said Prunie.

'And me,' Mush agreed.

'It's going to be wicked,' Jake enthused, 'We've still got to serve you all, but with a bit of luck, you won't drag it out, so we get to enjoy ourselves for a while.'

'You better not start playing that garage garbage music again,' Mush warned him, 'Last time we let you join in, we were all in bed by ten with migraines.'

Pete remembered it well. It hadn't been that long ago. It was a party thrown to celebrate their release from the initial two weeks of cabin quarantine.

Jake ignored him. 'Vic's letting us use the pool as well, but only after you lot have demolished the roast and we've cleaned up your mess.'

'Demolished isn't what *we lot* do,' Pete returned, 'It's what *you lot* do. Remember Bonfire Night? *You lot* were shifting racks of ribs faster than hyenas with worms. And as for mess, we're still finding the bones even now. Window boxes. Car exhausts. Golf course bunkers. You stuffed them everywhere. No wonder we had a sudden scourge of rats. Poor Hellmutt was run ragged.'

'Who's Helmut?' Prunie asked.

'Arek's rottweiler,' Pete told him.

'I thought it was called Daisy?'

'A dog that can break the necks of a dozen rats in five minutes flat, should not be called Daisy.'

Prunie laughed. 'No, it should be called Hell mutt.'

'Tell you what,' Pete said to Jake, 'When you're setting up the barbeque, get Arek to wheel out one of the incinerator bins, so that it's nearby. Then get *your lot* to hand out paper plates and plastic cups instead of the glass and china.'

Jake leaned forward, attentively.

'You go get yourself into the stores,' Pete continued, 'and gather up what bottles you need to mix up a vat of Sangria. Use that really big vat that we got for the mulled wine at Christmas. Then hang a couple of ladles over the side of it, for self-service.'

Pete was on a roll, 'And just put out baskets of crusty bread. And bowls of salad. Then you can tell everyone it's a help-yourself hog roast. You won't have to serve a thing. No food. No drink. And no tidying up. We'll just chuck everything into the incinerator bin for Arek to burn, tomorrow.'

'Wow, Pete, that's totally awesome. You think everyone will go for that?'

'Sure they will. You'll be in that pool, stoned out of your minds, before I'm on my third gin and tonic, and I'm on my second now.'

Jake held up his palm and Pete gave it a high five.

'Right, I'm outta here,' he said to them, gathering up their glasses while they still had an inch left in them, 'Me and Mitch have promised to give Eve some spit roasting.'

Mush exploded with mirth, falling back off his stool into the water like he'd been shot.

Jake grinned. 'At least one of you is a man of the world, then?'

CHAPTER SIX

NIGHT AFTER DAY

Pete homed in on the sound of music to locate where the hog roast was at. He found it situated between the sputnik spires belonging the snooker room and the library. The grand piano had been wheeled out and Lillia was sat to it, playing as she sang. It was something tasteful and semi-operatic and Pete had an inkling it was from a Westend show that Sal had once forced him to go to. The candelabra on top was possibly there to give it a flavour of Glyndebourne, but as the incinerator skip was parked only five yards away, it had more an essence of back-alley busking.

As Pete headed across to where Sal was talking with Shar Pei, he caught sight of Jake and Mitch stood either side of the roasting hog, turning the long-handled spit with their over-sized oven mitts. Jake waved a mitt at him, and on seeing he'd caught Pete's eye, waved it toward the large open vat that had ladles hanging over its rim. Pete gave him a thumbs up.

Apart from Jake and Mitch, none of the other staff were working, they were already in their bathing suits; some suits so infinitesimal they might as well have been in their birthday suits, like the rest of them.

'Where was Tin Tin from?' Sal was asking.

'Belgium,' Shar Pei told her, 'But the question wasn't about Tin Tin. It was about Rin Tin Tin.'

'His Japanese sister?' Sal asked.

Shar Pei stared at her, trying to work out if she was being witty, winsome or just plain thick.

'Hi Joanna. Congratulations, once again,' Pete said to her. 'You must be holding the quiz record by now. Bit like Sal, with the POTs.'

Shar Pei didn't comment.

‘Was the goose babies, gobblings?’ Sal asked.

Pete cringed. ‘Goslings,’ he told her. ‘You make them sound like little snacks,’ he joked, hoping to raise a smile on Shar Pei’s saggy chops. It didn’t.

‘And you make them sound like little spits,’ Sal snapped, before strutting away.

Pete mingled. He liked mingling. He always seemed to be welcomed into any given conversation. Unlike Gabe. Gabe had a habit of throwing out verbal grenades. That’s why the POTs he received were always SICs. Acronym for Sarcastically Intrusive Conversation — which basically meant butting in with cynical comments and snide remarks. Pete considered himself more Hello magazine and Gabe more National Enquirer.

‘I’ve stopped watching it. It’s just doom and gloom, every night,’ Pruness was telling Ruthless. ‘Unless they come up with a vaccine, we could be in here for years.’

‘I’m not sure I’d want one. If they rush it through, we could end up with things that are a lot worse,’ Ruthless responded.

‘I think if those in government all have it. And then the royal family. Then I’d be willing to have it,’ said Pete, adding his two-penneth.

‘What if they just say they’ve had it, and then they wait to see what happens when we’ve all had it? We could be guinea pigs, and then —’

‘Have you seen what we’re being expected to eat off?’ Mary interrupted, crossly, ‘Paper plates. With plastic cups to go with them. And to say this place prides itself on being high end. It’s an absolute disgrace.’

Pete quickly sidled off to latch on to Gabe.

Three Lugs was remonstrating with him, animatedly.

‘I only used it to go to the hospital for my hernia pushing back in. The thing was spewing out more smoke than Rosa’s caravan chimney.’

‘Did you put diesel in it, instead of petrol?’ Gabe asked.

‘What do you take me for? A flipping idiot? The tank was full on delivery and it was the first time I’d used it. I’m telling you, that car has been clocked. There’s no way it’s only done ninety miles. Ninety thousand more like. There's hardly any rubber left on the accelerator pedal.'

'And what do you expect me to do about it?'

'I expect you to take it back and reimburse me,' Three Lugs demanded, 'And if you don't, you'll be hearing from my lawyer.' With that, he stormed off, spewing smoke of his own.

'So,' said Pete, 'you sold him the Aston?'

Gabe nodded.

'And did you sell him it before you laid your bet on me, predicting that he'd buy one? Or after?'

Gabe set off for the option that let him off the hook, but then realised neither did, so he stalled.

'I expect you to reimburse me,' Pete demanded, 'And if you don't, you'll be hearing from my lawyer.'

The pair of them burst out laughing.

As Gabe headed off to find his phone, Pete homed in on Yakky who was stood talking to The Boar and his wife, Mac; Mac, on account of her name being Beth and her birthplace Scotland.

'There's a really tricky bit just after The Bridge,' Yakky was explaining, 'You have to lean tight into the bend otherwise you get grounded. It's only happened to me the once but you really have to keep your wits about you. There's another tricky bit where it winds through the golf course. You can see where it's changed its course over the years because of the ox-bow lakes it's left behind. Have you seen them?'

Pete guessed she wasn't going to wait for an answer, and he was correct.

'It's in the winter when the water level is at its highest that it becomes most dangerous,' Yakky flowed on, 'That's why I always wear a life-jacket, October through to March. Even then, it probably wouldn't save me if I got carried out under the road toward the sluice gate.'

One could only hope, thought Pete. He hadn't named her Yakky without good reason. When it came to SACs — Self-Absorbed Conversation — she was unbeatable. SICs and SACs caught a lot of people out, mainly due to the amount of time they spent talking to each other. Yet no matter how many SAC POTs

Yakky got, it never prompted her to curtail them. But then the same applied to Sal and her SOLs, unfortunately.

Pete moved swiftly on, returning to Sal, who was now stood with Eeyore and Jude.

'You don't look happy,' Jude said to him as he joined them.

Pete shook his head and then nodded toward Yakky.

'That woman can talk the back leg off a donkey.'

Jude smiled and nodded.

'You better be careful to avoid her then, eh?' Sal said to Eeyore, with a wink.

Pete coughed from a sudden constriction of the throat and waved himself away toward the nearest water dispenser.

'There's no way I'm sitting down to eat without proper cutlery,' Carmen was saying to The Shining.

Pete kept moving.

'We lost our neighbour at the weekend,' Sheepteeth was telling The Mushrooms. 'He'd only just bought himself a new Lamborghini as well. Covid really doesn't care who it takes, does it?'

'Obviously doesn't care what car you've got, either,' said Gabe, having slipped in to join them.

Sheepteeth looked instantly piqued, so Pete pulled Gabe away.

'Where did you beetle off to?' he asked him.

'I had calls to make. It's called work. Not everyone in here is retired, you know,' Gabe was quick to respond.

'You think looking on the internet at cars all day constitutes work?' Pete scoffed.

'Aw, here we go. When I were a lad, I were up at three in't morning picking turnips for five hours. Then down't pit for another six. Then once I gor'ome, I'd have to clean all't clogs belonging everyone in't street. And then —'

Gabe stopped as soon as Pete doubled over.

Pete couldn't help himself. Gabe's Yorkshire always cracked him up.

Carmen and Mo came to join them.

'Come on, something that funny has to be shared,' Mo said to Gabe.

Gabe raised an eyebrow at him as if it were none of his business, but then relented.

'I was just telling Pete that my nan's died. Of food poisoning. They've put it down to all the jellied eels that she'd fished out of Lambeth sewer.'

Pete laughed all the more, giving proof it was an untruth, so Carmen and Mo simply shook their heads and smiled.

'If we're going to be eating with our hands, and drinking out of the same tank, I bet we'll all have food poisoning by tomorrow,' said Carmen.

Quick as a flash, Gabe came back, 'You're on. And I'd say the odds are fifty-fifty. So what d'you reckon? A pony? No, let's make it a bullseye. A nice, round fifty quid?'

As Carmen tried to withdraw her throw-away wager, Pete simply withdrew.

Gabe was incorrigible. Why was it they didn't have a POT for gambling? But then he supposed he knew. Vic created them, and Vic was their biggest gambler of all.

'Jake. Come here a minute,' Pete beckoned.

Jake gave a low, fluted, distinctive whistle and from out of nowhere, Lewis turned up. Jake immediately passed over his oven mitts and came to join him.

'The women are having a right old bleat over the dumbed-down dining,' Pete told him. 'I need you to back me up with what I'm about to tell them all.'

'I don't have to say anything, do I?'

'Nothing. Just follow me and nod when required.'

At that, Pete strode through the middle of the throng toward the large metal vat of sangria. Taking one of the ladles, he banged it hard on the side, three times. Everyone went quiet as they turned to look.

'Evening folks. Nice to see everyone having such a good time,' he said to them. 'And great that the rain's held off for us, eh? We'd not be getting any pork scratchings off that baby if it got soaked through the skin,' he added, nodding over to their roasting hog.

They were all clearly wondering where he was going with this.

'I just wanted to get you all onboard with something, because we're going to be needing your help,' Pete continued.

Everyone was suddenly spreading out and pushing forward so they might see and hear better.

'Jake here, has kindly tipped me off that we could be in for a visit from the dreaded Health and Safety brigade later this evening. Don't ask him how he knows. Let's just say he knows somebody who knows somebody, like we all do. And he thinks they'll be coming mob handed.'

Pete looked to Jake and Jake nodded vigorously.

'So I'm afraid we've had to lower our usual refined standards, to make things more likely to pass muster, just like it is out there in the real world, where you can't take glasses and knives out into the beer garden.

'And what we need from you, if you wouldn't mind, is for you to start by lifting your tables further away from each other. We need to be more spread out, cos they'll no doubt be looking at our Covid compliances an' all.'

They'd all turned around to where the tables had been placed, seeing them within reaching distance of each other.

'And Lottie's going to be putting out some masks. So if you hear this whistle —'

Pete gave Jake a firm nudge and Jake gave his low, fluted, distinctive whistle.

'That's when you need to go grab one and put it on, sharpish,' he told them.

He could see their reaction was positive. If they'd had sleeves, they'd have been rolling them up, ready for action.

'Come on, then. Let's get cracking. Let's get them tables pulled apart like we've just had the mother of all scraps with each another.'

Everyone was chatting and laughing as they hurried to make things compliant.

'I don't know how you come up with this stuff,' Jake said to him, 'but I think they should give you an OBE for it.'

Pete smirked. 'If Eve asks why you din't go tell her first, about the Health and Safety visit, tell her you thought she had enough on her plate.'

'Her paper plate?' Jake asked.

Pete grinned at him and nodded. 'And if anyone asks you what's in this vat, don't tell 'em it's Sangria. Tell 'em it's a special type of Pimms that's normally reserved for Argentinian polo clubs.'

He passed Jake the ladle and then began handing out a stack of plastic cups to those who were now eagerly arriving to take one.

Vic was sat by himself, his head slowly rotating like a wise old owl, taking in the gathering.

'What made you decide on a hog roast?' Pete asked him, as he arrived with two full plates of bread and meat.

Vic took one, gratefully.

'I just like to see everyone having a good time. The news is so full of death and disaster these days. At least in here we can forget about it.'

'I'm not sure that we should,' said Pete. 'Isn't enlightenment all about empathy? I think we should be watching the news each and every night. I actually feel guilty that I'm in here, oblivious to it all. Don't you?'

'No,' said Vic, 'Whatever happens in this world, TC has his reasons for it. When your time comes, it comes. Whether it's from Covid or cancer, it's out of our hands. Would you mind getting me a glass of water, Peter?'

Pete went to the water dispenser to fetch one.

'Where's Rin?' he asked, as he watched Vic drink it all in one glug.

'She can't be doing with it,' Vic replied, nodding toward the hog.

Pete had forgotten she was a vegetarian.

'Couldn't we have had a nut roast option?'

Vic shook his head. 'She still wouldn't have come. It's the sight and the smell of it. You'd think we were roasting the thing alive the way she carries on.'

Pete thought the sight and the smell, fabulous. The taste, even better.

'There isn't any visit from the Health and Safety department, is there?' said Vic.

Pete gave him a grease covered grin.

'Course there isn't. But if the staff are invited, then they're invited. No half measures.'

Vic nodded in agreement.

Pete wiped himself down with his paper napkin and then took their empty plates to the incinerator bin.

There was a large group gathering outside the library's French doors and he sensed some excitement. Going in to investigate, he saw that there were sizeable pieces of paper laid out on the two library tables, currently being studied by one and all.

'If we all wrote letters of complaint, I'm sure that would do it,' Sheepteeth was saying, his top lip stretched tight over his teeth.

'I rather think it won't,' Ginnel told him. 'This isn't our permanent address, so our comments would be null and void.'

Pete went to take a look. They were detailed drawings. Building plans. For the fields opposite the entrance to The Garden.

'Aren't the villagers up in arms?' Mo asked.

'Of course they are. Prior to this, the only permissible building was for extensions and renovations. It's going to change the character of the village, completely,' said Mushette.

'What about the vicar? Can't he throw any weight behind quashing it?' someone asked from the back.

'Do you honestly think he's got any influence?' Ginnel asked, derisively, 'He's a vicar. He might preach the word of God, but he isn't God, and God is probably the only one who would be able to put a stop to it. If you ask me, developers and town planners are as corrupt as each other. That's why planning officers always live in houses twice the size of any other council officers.'

Pete wondered if it were true. He'd bought a lot of houses in his time but he'd never built any, apart from the one Sal was currently on with. If Barnsley council hadn't passed their plans, would he have been prepared to bribe somebody? No, he wouldn't, but then Sal would.

'Maybe we send Rosa into town? Have her read some palms, find out which ones have been greased,' he suggested.

They might not have found that useful, but at least they'd found it amusing.

Pete decided to have his lawyers look into it. It would give them something to do, to warrant their massive retainer.

There was suddenly a voice he recognised. It was Sal's. Shouting.

'Pete! You need to come. Dan's gone missing and Phoebe's got herself in a right old tizz.'

People parted as Pete sprang into action. Mo and Sheepteeth following close behind him.

Phoebe was sat at one of the tables, head in hands, with Eve, Carmen and Mary crouched beside her.

'How long's he been gone?' Pete asked, as soon as he reached them.

'Since the quiz results came up,' Phoebe told him, 'We thought they'd include all the answers, but they didn't. He was going back to our cabin to get his phone, so we could google them.'

'Have you been to your cabin?' Mo asked.

'Yes. And he's not there. And the door was wide open.'

'Your door's always wide open, Phoebe. We pass it, breakfast, lunch and dinner,' Mary reminded her.

Phoebe looked surprised, but then realised it was true, and nodded.

Gabe and Jude arrived on the scene, both looking intrigued.

'Where's he likely to have gone?' Sheepteeth asked. 'Golf? The Dome? Kayaking?'

Phoebe shook her head.

'Have you tried ringing him?' Sal thought to ask.

'Yes. It's just going straight to voice mail.'

'Look. Stop panicking. It won't help,' Carmen told her, rubbing Phoebe's quivering knees, 'There's absolutely no way anything bad has happened to him, do you hear?'

'Carmen's right,' said Sal, 'And he wouldn't leave the resort without telling you, so he's got to be here somewhere. All we have to do is look for him.'

‘That’s right. We’ll look for him,’ Sheepteeth told her, ‘I’ll get off down to the golf course.’

‘And I’ll go see if he’s at the lake,’ said Pete, ‘Seeing as he’s a fan of the wild swimming.’

‘Ooh, I hope he’s alright,’ Sal suddenly fussed, ‘They say there’s some nasty spikes in there.’

As Phoebe burst into tears, Pete glared at his wife.

‘They say there’s pikes in there. There’s a difference,’ Pete told her, ‘And I can assure you, Phoebe, there’s no spikes and there’s no pikes, either. If there were pikes, you’d never see all those ducklings that we have.’

‘Ah, but we don’t see any gobblings, do we, Sal?’ Gabe said to her.

Pete realised Gabe was playing on Sal’s quiz answer, and now Sal was solemnly shaking her head in agreement, clearly reassured that her answer had been right all along.

‘Mo, how about you come with me in the buggy?’ Pete suggested, ‘You can take a look around The Dome while I’m round the back, checking on the lake.’

Mo gave Pete a thumbs up.

‘I’ll go up to their cabin and see if he’s come back,’ Eve volunteered.

‘Good idea. While you’re up there, collect something of his from the laundry basket and we’ll get Arek’s dog on his scent,’ Pete told her.

‘It’s a rottweiler,’ said Gabe, ‘Not a bleeding bloodhound.’

‘SOL,’ Sal told him, with Mary adding another.

‘Okay, so where are *you* going to go and look?’ Pete turned on him.

Gabe’s nostrils flared, until he suddenly realised that he’d been elevated into the team.

‘I’ll go check The Hub,’ he offered, ‘And then I’ll go check the terrace and the pool.’

The search team all high-fived each other and set off. It was a touch boys’own, but Pete found it irresistible.

Swinging the golf buggy sideways onto two wheels, Pete juddered to a halt outside the front doors of The Dome, with Mo’s knees juddering against the front dash.

Mo grumbled as he got out.

'Don't wait for me, I'll take a scooter back. I value my life.'

Around by the lake, Pete climbed out of the buggy and peered across the water. It would have been flat calm if not for the ripples caused by the tiered falls at the far side and the draw of the river from the near. Dan was nowhere to be seen. If he had been swimming, then the spikes and the pikes had definitely got him.

Catching sight of Arek coming out of their caravan, Pete immediately set off toward him.

'We've lost Dan. You haven't seen him, have you?'

'Which one is Dan?'

'He's the young one. Flat belly. Full head of hair.'

Arek flicked back his head in instant recognition.

'So have you seen him?' Pete persevered.

'Maybe.'

'Oh, come on, Arek. He's gone missing and the lad's wife is getting her knickers in a twist over it.'

Arek raised an eyebrow at him.

'Alright, no knickers, but you know what I mean.'

Arek sighed. 'If I tell you. It hasn't come from me.'

Pete was instantly intrigued. 'On my wife's life. I promise never to tell.'

'He's in cabin number eighty-five,' Arek told him, pointing across the meadow to the edge of the rising woodland.

'Whose is that?' Pete asked.

'The Browns. Tina and Tony.'

'But they weren't selected for the lock-in. It's empty?'

'Empty, except for Rin,' said Arek, grinning.

'Rin?'

Arek nodded.

'How long have they been in there?'

'Long enough.'

Pete was puzzled. 'Do they meet up often?'

Arek shrugged. 'Maybe once a week. Maybe more. I probably don't always see them. They used to meet up in cabin forty-four, up over there.' Arek was pointing to the opposite side of the valley. 'But the bed's broken.'

'Bed?' Pete exclaimed, 'Is that what you think they're doing?'

'Who knows. Maybe he's doing her some favours?'

Pete found it hard to believe. Everyone knew that Rin was more than Vic's personal assistant, they'd shared a cabin for the past four years, and the cleaners — when they'd had them — hadn't kept secret that they shared the same bed.

'It's maybe a favour for Vic, too,' Arek added, as if he'd read his mind. 'Saves him having to use Viagra.'

Pete pondered on it. Rin was half Vic's age. Maybe Arek was right. Maybe Dan was there in The Garden for the sole purpose of keeping Rin entertained. To do what Vic couldn't. But Dan was a married man, and to all intents and purposes, a happy one. So why would he? Unless they considered it a small price to pay for their all-inclusive, out-of-the-way, stay.

'Maybe she just likes the type of sex that Vic doesn't?'

'Oh, chuffin' 'ell, Arek, don't go there, mate. It's enough to make me hurl my hog.'

'Okay, what do you think they're doing?'

'I've no idea. But not that. Maybe she's teaching him Japanese.'

Arek shook his head at Pete's apparent innocence.

'Do they know that you've seen them, meeting up?' Pete asked.

Arek nodded.

'Marvellous. Then you can go and interrupt them. Tell Dan that his wife wants him back.'

'No chance,' Arek replied, bluntly.

'Alright then, I'll go pull him out,' Pete declared.

Arek's face immediately broke into a broad grin.

'I meant out of the cabin. Not her.'

Arek gave a sigh of resignation.

'Okay, I'll go. I'll say I met you on The Bridge and you told me you were out looking for him.'

'Good man,' said Pete, giving him a grateful slap on the shoulder. 'And not a word to anyone else, eh? Let's just keep this between you and me. Nobody needs to know we've got sinners in The Garden.'

Arek raised his bushy, joined-together eyebrows.

'You think they're the only ones?'

Pete had a moment of surprise, until The Swingers sprung to mind.

Pete parked up outside The Dome's front doors. He guessed Mo had already gone as a single scooter was missing from the rack. While he waited, he turned on the radio. It was tuned to Radio Four. More often than not, he found that all the buggies were. What was wrong with these people? Listening to Radio Four didn't prove they were highbrow or high-born. He knew the majority of them were from humble beginnings, the same as he was, but he didn't feel the need to distance himself from it, like they did. In fact, he was proud of it. Proud of making it, against the odds. Proud of having vowels as flat as his cap.

He'd been sat waiting for just over fifteen minutes when he saw Rin coming around the left-hand side of The Dome on Vic's personalised scooter. The vivid red of her summer dress was already painting her the scarlet woman. Pete waved to her but she was staring straight ahead, her long black hair billowing out behind her like a witch's cloak.

Five minutes later, Dan came around from the opposite side on his pushbike. On seeing Pete, he headed straight toward him.

'Really sorry, Pete. I forgot to tell Phoebe where I was going. I hear she's sent you out looking for me?'

'Arek told you then?'

'Yeh, he came to find me.'

'Where were you?'

'I was swimming. In the lake.'

Pete looked him up and down. 'You've dried off quick?'

'I would, wouldn't I? In this heat,' he replied, innocently.

'Was Rin swimming, too?' Pete asked.

'Rin?'

'Yes. I've just seen her come around from the other side.'

Dan shrugged. 'She must have been visiting Rosa.'

Interesting, thought Pete, that Dan was prepared to lie to that extent. Whatever he and Rin were up to, it was obviously something he wanted to keep secret.

'I best get off,' Dan told him, 'Put Phoebe's mind at rest.'

As Pete waved him on his way, he had a thought to go take a look inside cabin number eighty-five, and put his own mind at rest. But if he did, and it didn't, then what?

When Pete arrived back at the hog-roast, he felt like Moses returning from Mount Sinai, finding his people given over to anarchy. They might not have been bowing down to a golden calf, but they were certainly bending over backwards to help each other desecrate the place.

The Shining were pulling up the flowerbeds, egged on by others. Eeyore was stamping on their plastic glasses with his bare feet, while others passed him more. Yakky was helping Mac waterboard somebody under the water dispenser. The skip was alight. The chairs were all gone. The hog was on top of the piano. And Mush was sat in the vat of sangria, with Tugger and Plucky ladling the grog over his head like a pair of cannibals. Pete struggled to take it all in.

As he wandered amongst them, wondering what had gotten into them, he suddenly guessed. He headed straight to where the thump, thud, thump of music was emanating from. The pool.

'What the hell did you put in that Sangria?' he asked Jake, finding him poolside, throwing in a rubber ring belonging of The Dome.

'You mean the Argentinian Pimms?' Jake asked, innocently.

Pete smirked. 'Have you seen them all? If they weren't already naked, they'd be ripping their clothes off right now. You didn't put any of your weed in it, did you?'

'Weed wouldn't mix.' Jake assured him, 'It would have to be something like Crystal Meth.'

'What?' Pete screeched.

'Don't be ridiculous. Course I haven't. Not when we're expecting the Health and Safety brigade to drop by any minute.'

With that, Jake took three steps back to take a running jump at the rubber ring, landing bullseye into its middle. He paddled it around to wave and grin at Pete.

Pete stared at him and shook his head, but just then, there was a hoop and a holler and all six of The Swingers hurtled past him to cannonball into the pool, either side of Jake.

As Jake looked aghast, Pete gave him a wave and a grin. Swingerdy-do, swingerdy-dah.

CHAPTER SEVEN

ONE DAY IN JULY

'Well would you Adam and Eve it?' said Gabe, as they sat huddled under the poolside parasol, sheltering from the rain.

Pete knew before he even looked that it would actually be Adam and Eve, rather than something you might not believe.

The two siblings were wearing hooded club raincoats, same as the four of them were, which was a pity as Pete loved to see Eve's tattoo.

Most people loathed it but he was mesmerised by it. A serpent. The tip of its tail down by her left ankle and its body snaking around her leg, across her bum cheek, around across her belly, and finishing between the shoulder blades of her back with its forked tongue at full angry extent. It had to be the most ironic tattoo possible for a woman called Eve.

Being family to the owner seemed to trap the two siblings in a position of ambiguity. Part staff, part member. Sometimes naked but more often, not. Sharp-suited Rin was seen the same way. Although she had never been seen naked. Not even in a swim suit.

'Do you think they're going to tell us what's going on?' Jude asked.

'Somebody has to. It's not like we can't what's going on,' Gabe responded. 'Look at us all. It's chucking it down and the place has never been so bleeding busy.'

'SOL,' said Sal, just as someone else arrived on the scene.

That someone was heading straight toward them, headphones on, whistling, and clearly unaware of the intrigue and speculation in the air.

'Good morning. How are we all today?' ShamPain asked, brightly, removing the headphones and tilting back his umbrella so he could see them.

'We're good,' Pete replied, 'And you?'

As soon as he'd asked, he realised his mistake.

'Not good, I'm afraid. Too much stomach acid. I think it's maybe from all the vitamins I've been taking. Can't be too careful at our age, what with Covid killing us off like it is. And I think I've got an ear infection from the pool. It's not that well chlorinated, you know.'

To say he was so afflicted, he looked remarkably happy. ShamPoo had trotted up behind him, coming to sit in front of Pete, clearly remembering he was in the habit of dropping biscuits.

'You probably have,' Sal informed him, 'Seeing as people pee in it all the time.'

As ShamPain immediately looked to the water, horrified, Pete kicked Sal's foot.

'Have you seen that the police are here?' Jude asked, as a distraction.

'Are they?'

Jude pointed him down the valley toward the construction site of their new swimming pond.

The pool terrace being ideally perched to take in the majestic view of the river as it wound its way south, was now also the ideal place to view a possible crime scene.

'Good grief!' exclaimed ShamPain, 'There must be five police cars down there.'

'Six,' said Gabe, passing him his horse racing binoculars.

'What do you think they're here for?' ShamPain asked, as he focused to see.

'Not a Scooby. There's been nothing over the Tannoy, and there's nothing on the screens in reception, either. That's why everyone's sat out here. Watching.'

Adam and Eve had separated and were moving from couple to couple, one after the other.

'But I guess we're going to be finding out, soon enough,' Gabe added.

ShamPain suddenly gripped his stomach.

'I think I best be heading back to my cabin. Slightest bit of stress has my diverticulitis playing up. I'm not sure I want to know. It must be something dreadful to have so many police here.'

'You picked a good name for that one,' Gabe said to Pete, as ShamPain and ShamPoo shambled away.

Pete nodded, but of late he was thinking he should have called him Dandy. Short for Dandelion. The man's head was cocooned in an ever-expanding globe of white fluff. Very soon he wouldn't need a haircut, a huff and a puff would do it.

'You better not have come up with any names for us,' Jude warned him, as she stuck a hand out from under the brolly to test for rain.

Pete smiled and shook his head, but that wasn't to say he hadn't tried.

'He hasn't. But I know somebody who has,' Sal informed her.

'Oh, yeh? Who?'

Gabe equally rose to it. 'Go on. What they named us?'

Sal leaned back, holding on to it for a few seconds.

'The Cockney Spivs.'

'You're making it up,' Jude told her.

'No, I'm not. Sasquatch called you it when Mush asked her what line of business you were in.'

'And car sales makes me a spiv?' Gabe asked, affronted.

'Don't tek it out on me. It's not me who said it. I don't even know what a spiv is.'

'It's an acronym,' Pete told her, 'It stands for, Sells People Incontinent Vehicles.'

Gabe gave Pete the finger and Sal gave Gabe a SOL.

'Morning all,' Adam said to them, when their turn finally arrived, 'I guess you're aware we've got the police here on site?'

Nobody spoke, they just nodded, which in itself forced Adam to expand.

'Campbells called them in, first thing this morning. One of their diggers uncovered something rather gruesome, I'm afraid.'

Campbells were their ever-present, mud and noise generating, construction company. They alone were gruesome enough for Pete, without adding anything else into the mix.

'What do you mean by gruesome?' Jude asked.

‘Sorry, but I can’t say. The police have asked me not to. All I can tell you is that nobody is allowed to leave the resort. Not until we’ve all been interviewed.’

‘Interviewed?’ Gabe queried.

‘That’s what they’ve said.’

‘But I’ve got a Botox appointment this afternoon,’ Sal squawked.

‘Sorry,’ Adam told her as he moved toward the next group.

‘You can’t just leave us like that!’ Gabe shouted after him.

Adam shrugged, but then pointed to Eve, two couples further down, heading up the rear.

‘What do you think it is?’ Sal asked, excitedly, ‘It must be something really bad if it’s *gruesome*.’

Nobody replied. They were pondering on it. They continued to ponder up until Eve arrived.

‘Adam’s told you?’ she asked them.

‘No,’ said Gabe, ‘He told us he couldn’t tell us.’

Eve nodded and then grinned. ‘That’s what the police have told him, yes. But I’ve spoken with Campbells and they didn’t tell me that I couldn’t tell anybody.’

The four of them instantly brightened.

Eve leaned in under their umbrella.

‘They unearthed two bodies. Laying side by side. One is shorter than the other, so they guessed male and female.’

‘Oh my fucking God,’ Sal exclaimed. ‘It’s the couple that ran off, isn’t it? Did they find the marble heads, too?’

Eve raised a quizzical eyebrow.

‘She means the heads off our front statues,’ Jude explained, ‘The rumours. You know. After them disappearing at the same time.’

Eve shook her head.

‘Why do we all need to be interviewed?’ Sal asked, ‘They should just be concentrating on interviewing The Rippers.’

‘The who?’

‘She means Dave and Lydia Sutcliffe,’ Jude explained.

Eve immediately put her hands up to stop them.

‘Look. Please. Can we just drop all this nonsense? Dave and Lydia went through enough, I can assure you. I know how it feels to have your partner run off with another member. They really don't need any finger pointing right now and certainly no speculation that it's their exes buried down there.'

'Of course,' said Pete, 'Absolutely. There'll be no finger pointing from any of us.'

'Thank you,' Eve told them. 'It's enough with Chloe kicking off, without anyone else jumping on board. What doesn't help, is that this being The Garden of Eden, the police are referring to the two bodies as Adam and Eve. You couldn't make it up, could you?'

'I wonder why Blubs is kicking off?' Sal speculated, once Eve had moved on.

'Probably because she and Eve Sutcliffe used to be best buddies,' Jude told her, 'And when she failed to get in touch, she got suspicious. It was her that called in the police to have Dave and Lydia interrogated.'

'How come you know all this?'

'Because we were here back then and you weren't.'

Sal thought about it. 'Did you know about the affair?'

'I don't think anyone knew, not even Dave and Lydia. Not until Adam and Eve actually ran off with each other.'

'Yes, but they didn't run off with each other, did they? They got murdered and buried. Down there.' Sal was pointing south to the crime scene.

'Stop it,' Pete snapped, 'Until we get some answers, we're not going to speculate or pass judgement.'

'Oh, you're a fine one to talk,' Sal turned on him, 'You obviously speculated and passed judgement, otherwise you wouldn't have named them the bloody Rippers.'

It had stopped raining, and as was often the case, the sun was straight out of the blocks and baking hot in minutes. The paving tiles began to steam around them and they all shrugged off their coats and readied their sun loungers.

'Who do you think's putting all the POTs in against you?' Jude turned to ask Sal, minutes later.

Pete had seen the latest POTs chart. He knew his wife was at the top of it, yet again.

'Ruthless,' Sal replied, 'I'm certain of it.'

'Why?'

'Because I keep winning him at tennis.'

'No,' said Pete, 'You keep *beating* him at tennis. If you'd won him, you'd be carrying him home and sticking him on the mantelpiece.'

Sal stuck her hands on her hips. 'Don't you dare point out my fur-paws in front of other people!'

'They're not other people. They're our friends. And *they* should be pointing them out.'

'No, we bleeding well shouldn't,' Gabe pointed out.

'SOL,' said Sal.

'Hey you, give me a break, I'm trying to defend you here,' Gabe said to her, and then to Pete, 'Incorrect grammar isn't listed as a POT. Speaking proper's not going to save her mortal soul, is it? If it was, you'd be damned for hell quicker than a nit on Jesus, considering everything you've said on TwatNav.'

Pete couldn't argue it, he was too busy chuckling about it.

'I still think it's Ruthless taking POT shots at me,' Sal declared, 'He's a ruthless POT shotter, that's what he is.'

Gabe snorted. 'He's about as ruthless as a Frenchman on the frontline. He can't even go to Be-twitchings unless somebody goes with him.'

It was true. His wife always went on her moped, leaving him to tag on to anyone who'd let him, seeing as he didn't like scootering alone, in the dark.

'Well who the fuck do you think it is, then?' Sal raged.

'Stop the swearing! I can't be doing with it!' Pete snapped.

'Oh, sod off. You're too indoctrinated, that's what you are.'

'Turned out nice again,' DoLittle said to them as he walked past carrying their Yorkshire terrier, Pete Junior as he was now known, so as to avoid confusion.

His wife came ten yards behind, carrying two coffees.

'Did you know she was a nurse?' Jude asked, once they were out of earshot.

'Sasquatch? A nurse?' Sal mocked.

Jude nodded. 'Blubs told me.'

'Often the case. Nurses marrying doctors,' Gabe remarked.

Pete would agree, he'd somewhere read the same. But his name? He couldn't remember why he'd called him DoLittle. Obviously on account of him being a doctor. And? There had to be an and. Then it came to him. It was due to him doing so little. No sport. No hobbies. No reading. No exercise. No meditation. He didn't even walk his own dog.

'I don't like her,' Sal openly admitted.

'Me neither,' said Jude, 'Cheeky cow. Calling us spivs. She thinks she's something special just because she married a consultant. But would you be happy with your husband peering at women's twinkles all day? I certainly wouldn't.'

Gabe was about to say something, but Jude hit him before he could.

Pete had forgotten he was an obstetrician. Maybe he should have named him Twinky-Winky?

Dan and Phoebe came to join them.

'Have you heard about the two dead bodies?' Phoebe asked, excitedly, unfolding the cushions that they'd collected from the nearby cabana.

'Dreadful, isn't it?' said Jude.

'Everyone's saying it's that couple who were having an affair,' said Phoebe, dragging her lounger to directly face the sun, 'Do you think it is?'

'No,' said Pete.

'If it is, then they got their comeuppance,' Phoebe blithely carried on, 'I think it's a despicable thing to do. Leave your partner if you must, but don't do the dirty on them beforehand.'

At that, Pete looked straight to Dan. Maybe he was imagining it, but the colour looked to have drained right out of his increasingly tanned face.

The Prunuptials were up and leaving, but stopped to talk as they came by.

'Are we all set for the big night then?' Prunie asked.

'We are John. Really looking forward to it,' Dan told him.

Pete looked to Gabe and they shared a joint gratitude for Dan providing them his real name.

'Any decisions on where we're going?'

'London. Covid permitting.'

'Excellent,' Gabe enthused, 'Home territory. And how are we aiming to get there with all the restrictions?'

'Oh, don't you worry about that. He's sorted that one out good and proper,' Pruness responded, somewhat scathingly.

'You not having a hen do then?' Sal asked her.

Pruness took a breath and sighed, as if sick and tired of being asked.

'I am. But it's for close friends and family only.'

As Sal nodded, Pete knew what his wife was thinking. *Miserable bitch.* No. *Miserable fucking bitch.*

'Have you got any boots?' Phoebe abruptly asked her.

'What kind of boots? You mean like wellingtons?' Pruness queried, warily.

'Any. But wellingtons would do. It's for pony trekking. I'm trying to put a group together, if you're interested? Arek says we can use his ponies.'

'Yes, I wouldn't mind joining you on that,' Pruness agreed. 'They are tame, aren't they?'

'Placid as pit ponies,' Pete was quick to assure her, knowing he would have to confess the lie to Father Anthony a week on Friday.

'You'll be fine,' Phoebe told her. 'I'm a riding instructor. You'll be an expert by the time I've finished with you. Let me take your number so I can put you in my WhatsApp group.'

Pruness handed over a calling card from out of a clip purse.

'And you're certain it's going to be safe?'

'Absolutely. They'll all be tied together in one long chain, with me leading.'

'Just like the donkeys on Filey beach,' Pete joked.

Sal swotted him with the back of her hand.

'Phoebe knows what she's doing. She's got them eating right out of her hand.'

'That's cos it's got sugar lumps in it,' Gabe retorted.

Just lately, it had been, Phoebe this, Phoebe that, I'm off to meet Phoebe to chew the fat. Pete realised Jude was in danger of having bestie title wrested from her.

As The Prunuptials went on their way, Sal shouted after them.

'And wear some jeans! Unless you want a snatch full of horse fleas!'

Tugger's wife walked past wearing a bra and trainers and Pete wondered what sport she was heading for.

'Hi Ali. You going jogging?' Sal asked her, clearly wondering the same.

The woman turned to her, her face suddenly fierce and furrowed.

'Look, I've told you before. I'm not an *Ali.* I'm not even an *Alison*. What is wrong with you, you ignoramus?'

Sal reeled back, and then glared at Pete, and then at *Not even Alison*.

'Nothing's wrong with me. It's not short for Alison. It's short for Alligator. A snappy, crappy, beady-eyed, long-in-the-tooth alligator. So slither off back to your fucking swamp, why don't you.'

From the large poolside gathering, there came at least two ROYs and more than half a dozen SOLs.

'You're going to get us thrown out of here,' Pete warned his wife.

'No, Pete. It's your stupid fucking names that's going to get us thrown out.'

'What's a ROY again?' Gabe asked, once the uncomfortable incident had turned into something more amusing.

'Rude Or Yobbish,' Pete replied.

Gabe began to laugh. 'It's going to be top of the POTs again for you next week, young lady,' he said to Sal.

Sal huffed.

'All you need to do, is acknowledge it,' Jude advised her. 'Put your hand up. Claim them. Say sorry.'

'But I'm not sorry. So they can just keep on POT shotting me.'

Pete let out an exasperated sigh.

They all took a turn with the binoculars.

Gabe had spotted a gazebo being erected and a transit van arriving, with *FORENSIC SERVICES - CRIME SCENE INVESTIGATION* written on its side.

'They'll be exhuming them soon,' Gabe announced, 'Bet you a —'

'No,' snapped Pete. In his mind, there were certain things that should never be bet on.

'I wonder how much skin they've got left on them?' Phoebe speculated.

'Oh, pleeeease,' said Jude.

Phoebe laughed.

'Talking of skin. Have you seen Shar Pei's belly? It's hanging that low, it's hiding her monkey's forehead,' Gabe observed, as the woman in question exited the pool.

They all turned to take a look, and then immediately looked away as Shar Pei caught them.

'I should have hidden mine,' Sal suddenly had a thought to tell them, 'Instead of leaving it lying around for somebody to help themselves to.'

Gabe and Pete immediately cracked up laughing.

'What you on about? Jude asked her.

'The monkey's for'head, that I won at the tennis championship. Five hundred quid. Gone.'

'Ah, you mean one of Gabe's coins.'

Gabe's gambling had led to him having dozens of metal alloy discs created. Making it easier for him to lay his bets on everyone. Over time, they had become a form of resort currency, cashable on reception. The monkey's head imprinted on them made clear they only had one value.

'What else would I mean?'

'Nothing Sal, you're right. I'd be pretty peeved if I lost one too,' Jude agreed.

A mobile was ringing and Sal began rooting in her bag.

'It's yours,' she told Pete. 'It's your Jeremy.'

'Ignore it. He'll only be after more money.'

'Ah, but you don't know that for sure,' Gabe told him, 'He could just be ringing for some fatherly advice. Like wanting to know why his car keeps conking out on him.'

'Unlikely. He's knows I know diddly squat about them.'

'My horse is called Jeremy,' Phoebe suddenly announced, 'But he hates cars. He always does his best to avoid them.'

'So does Pete. Since he lost his licence,' Gabe re-joined.

Phoebe looked shocked.

Pete pointed at Gabe. 'His fault. Sold me too many horses that did like them. All of them under the bonnet of a McClaren.'

Within seconds another mobile was ringing and this time Sal retrieved her own.

'Ey up, Derek. How's it going?'

From his wife's ever-narrowing eyes, Pete could see that it wasn't well. There followed a lengthy diatribe where she ripped poor Derek a new one and then cut him off.

'This house is going to be the death of you,' Jude told her, 'It's been nothing but grief and frustration the whole time you've been in here.'

Sal's phone pinged, twice, in quick succession.

'Is that him, again?' Pete asked her, as he rolled over to lay face down on his lounger.

'No. It's Eve. She says she wants me to call in and see her. Says she's got something important to discuss.'

'How intriguing,' said Jude, 'Maybe she's going to divulge who's been Pot-shotting you?'

Sal shook her head. 'I already asked her.'

'And we're to assume she didn't tell you?' Pete probed.

Sal gave a sneer of a smile. 'She said she didn't know. Nobody knows apart from Vic. It's like he's God. All knowing and all seeing, while we're left in the dark like mushrooms.'

She and Jude grinned at each other as just at that moment The Mushrooms walked by.

Pete was just about to roll back over when he felt the thrust of something wet and warm into the crevice between his bum and thighs. He let out an unmanly squawk, which had the others laughing.

Twisting his head around, he saw the Yorkshire terrier stood on the back of his legs.

'You shouldn't have given him half that fillet steak you had delivered, last night,' Sal chided, lifting the small dog so that Pete could turn over and take it from her.

'Don't exaggerate, I gave him a few pieces,' he replied. 'And after he'd walked nigh on a mile, from their cabin to ours, I reckon he deserved it.'

'You're never going to get rid of him now,' Jude laughed.

'Sorry, again,' said DoLittle, arriving to collect him.

'Not a problem,' Pete replied, passing him over.

'I think he must know you're from Yorkshire, like him. Maybe he considers you're his kin.'

'Aye, I reckon he must,' Pete agreed.

Lunch arrived, courtesy of two Starships, and Jude passed around the named food cartons.

'What's wrong, don't you like it?' Sal asked Phoebe, seeing her staring dolefully at her tray.

'Not really. It's not what I ordered.'

'What did you order?'

'Same as Pete, burger and chips.'

'And you got what? Salmon and salad?'

Phoebe prodded it, like it was shit and salad. 'Looks like it.'

Sal suddenly reached out, one hand left, one hand right, and picking up both their cartons, she deftly swapped them over.

'He could do to lose a few pounds,' she said.

Pete feigned disbelief at what had just happened to him.

'Aww, Pete, it's yours. I couldn't,' Phoebe said to him, offering it back.

He smiled and shook his head. 'All yours. Fill your boots. Just be careful you don't end up looking like this.'

He had pushed out his paunch and was patting it proudly.

'If your husband decides he like's little skinny ones, you'll be scuppered.'

Why had he said that? Phoebe was perfect. She wasn't little. Or skinny. But Rin was.

'I'll risk it,' Phoebe told him, taking a huge bite out of the burger.

‘Where you two sneaking off to?’ Gabe asked, surprised by Pete and Sal getting to their feet as soon as they’d finished their lunch.

‘We’ve got massages booked,’ Sal replied, ‘We need something relaxing. Pete’s not slept since Be-twitching. It’s left him with inzombia.’

They all looked to Pete who immediately stretched out his arms, and with stiffened legs, walked like a zombie behind his wife’s back.

‘Me too,’ Dan was quick to agree, ‘I’ve been waking up every morning at the crack of dawn.’

‘Lucky Dawn,’ said Sal, to everyone’s amusement.

‘You know, I think we’ll come with you,’ said Phoebe, quickly gathering up their belongings.

‘Oh, here we go,’ Dan groaned, ‘She’s addicted to that rubber-ride.’

‘What if I am?’ Phoebe snapped, and then turning to Gabe and Jude, ‘Are you two coming?’

‘No thanks. It’s a bit too juvenile for us,’ Jude told her.

‘How about coming for the scooter ride, then?’

‘No can do,’ said Gabe, ‘I’m off for a gypsy’s and then I’ve got some calls to make.’

‘Jude?’

‘I’m fine here,’ she replied, and then as they turned away, ‘I wouldn’t want to play gooseberry.’

Sal swung back to her. ‘Why not? You’re pretty good at playing sour grape.’

They took four scooters from out of the shed and headed off at a pace. Up past The Hub, out around The Tree, then off along the tarmac track that led to The Bridge, and ultimately, The Dome. The speed limit was five mph but they were all hitting twenty as they got into an impromptu race.

A new sign had gone up en route.

For what is it to die but to stand naked in the wind and melt into the sun – Kahil Gibran

Naked and windswept as he was, Pete felt fortunate for only being blinded by the sun.

The Buffs parted from them as soon as they'd all stepped out of the barrier shower.

'Do you want to go with them?' Pete asked Sal, 'We've forty minutes to kill.'

Sal thought about it. 'No, let's do the sandpit. And let's have a mocktail while we're at it.'

As Sal headed for the sand, Pete headed for the bar; the 'dry bar' as opposed to the 'wet bar' in the pool.

'What you doing here?' he asked Jake.

'I might well ask you the same thing?' he replied, reaching for the Bobbys bottle.

'No gin. I'm here with Sal. Just knock us up a couple of Virgin Mojitos, ta very much.'

Jake began to knock.

'You heard about the two dead bodies?'

'I've heard of nothing else,' Pete replied.

'You don't think it's the —'

'No.'

Jake stared at him. 'You don't know what I was going to ask.'

'Yes, I do.'

'How?'

'Because I'm psychic.'

'I see. You'll soon be giving Rosa a run for her money then. You do know she's been looking for you, don't you?'

'No.'

'Ah, so not as psychic as you thought.'

As Pete grinned, he suddenly found Owt-for-Nowt stood beside him.

'I hear you've got some new clubs?' he asked.

Pete nodded, guessing what was to come next.

'I can take your old ones off your hands if they're going spare?'

'Sorry, mate. Jake here is having them.'

Pete looked to Jake and Jake immediately nodded.

'Since when have you played golf?' Owt-for-Nowt threw at Jake.

'I'm learning. Pete's teaching me,' Jake tossed back.

Owt-for-Nowt glowered and walked off.

Pete shook his head. 'If you told him your pee was for free he'd probably bottle it.'

'Am I really having your old clubs?'

'Aye, if yer want them.'

'And you'll teach me?'

'Definitely. Especially now Sal's no longer wanting me to. Thank heavens above.'

As he made his way to the solarium, Pete pondered on why Rosa might want to see him. It was a sand solarium. A room full of powder white sand that was heated sub-thermally, into which Sal was already deep and dusty.

Pete placed the high sided tray down beside her and then put some effort into finding his mobile in her bag.

'Has she a message for you?' Sal asked, as soon as he'd finished his call to Rosa.

Pete nodded. He would have to forgo his late afternoon dunk and drunk session — as Jake was prone to call them — and head straight out the back to her caravan.

'It's been a long while since you've had one,' Sal told him, clearly excited by the prospect.

Pete would agree. He'd only been thinking the same thing the other day.

'How come Gabe gets so many messages?' Sal asked.

'Does he?'

'Yes, you know he does. He's always saying he's off to go see her.'

Pete had to think about it. Really think about it.

'Yer daft apeth. When he says he's off for a gypsy's, it's not for a message. He's off for a gypsy's kiss. A piss.'

Sal stared at him. And then she began to cackle. Earthy and deep, just like the sand.

'I'm glad you've stopped calling Phoebe, Vulva,' Sal said to him, minutes later, 'It was too crude. And she's such a nice kid.'

'She is,' Pete agreed, instantly feeling guilty that he was still using it, with Gabe.

'So why did you have to go and say what you did?'

'What did I say?'

‘About Dan going off her if she didn’t stay skinny? Can’t you see how much weight she’s piled on?’

‘Has she?’

‘Yes. If you stopped looking at her chest once in a while, you might notice. And if you can quit calling her Vulva, why can’t you quit all the other naff names? They’re ridiculous. I often think there’s part of you that’s still stuck in the playground.’

Pete couldn’t deny it. He’d always had a schoolboy’s sense of humour. Even in the Snatch-Patch factory, he couldn’t resist playing pranks. He once had Gabe ring up on their graveyard shift.

“Go on,” he’d told him, “When the night security answers, ask him to put a call out over the Tannoy for Bobby Tupper”.

They weren’t allowed mobiles on the factory floor, but they were allowed to take calls at the front desk.

“Why can’t you?” Gabe had asked him.

He’d then explained how Bobby Tupper, in a southern accent, sounded like Bobby Tupper, but in a Yorkshire accent, like that of himself and the security guard, it sounded like ‘bob it up her’. He knew they would appreciate the levity and know that it was him, thinking of them. But as for giving up his names, no way, naff or not.

‘Let me think about it,’ he told her.

There were two separate massage suites in The Dome but if you went as a couple, the two masseuses would set their beds up in the same room. Pete and Sal often went together. They were both fond of the two young women who set about tenderising them like a pair of old stewing steaks.

For some reason, Pete was feeling unusually ticklish. He wriggled and writhed as Chelsea ran her thumbs up the soles of his skin toughened feet.

‘Just ignore him,’ Sal advised, ‘He’s got himself all giddy cos he’s been invited to see our fortune teller.’

‘Rosa not a fortune teller,’ Karina told her.

‘So what is she, then?’

‘She’s clairvoyant. She brings words from the dead to prove they not.’

'Yes, but these dead people, they can tell her things about the future,' Sal argued.

'Sometimes, very rare, they warn of something bad coming. But mostly, they just share secrets from the past that only you and they know. Giving proof.'

'How do you know?'

'Because Rosa is my aunt.'

In all the time they'd been coming for a massage, Karina had never told them that.

'You never said,' said Pete.

'You never ask,' Karina replied.

'Have either of you had messages?' Sal asked, wincing, while her calves were being stripped.

'Yes, when we not busy we give each other, sometimes,' Karina replied.

'Noooo. *Messages*. From Rosa. From the other side.'

'I have,' Chelsea was quick to respond, 'She told me I kept my nan's jewellery in the back of my fridge. And she told me that I'd once caught herpes when I went to Ibiza and that my nan was saying, "Tell her to keep her bleeding knickers on." Which is what my nan always used to say when she was alive. I only had to go up the off-licence and she'd be saying it. How spooky is that?'

Very, thought Pete, if it were true. Chelsea was known to embellish. She told everyone that she was Chelsea from Chelsea, but Gabe had told him that she was pure East End, same as him. She certainly had the same cockney twang.

'But she's never told you anything about your future?' Sal probed.

'Nothing. Other than my nan, telling me to keep my bleeding – '

' – knickers on,' Sal finished. 'What about you, Karina?'

'Nothing since I'm here.'

Pete had forgotten that she'd only arrived there prior to their Covid lock-in, but for the life of him, he couldn't remember where she'd said she was from.

'Nothing about your future?'

'No. It's impossible for future to be told. Unless it's for warnings, like I had.'

'Warnings about what?' Sal immediately asked.

'That I must go west of Ukraine. Better still, Europe.'

That was it, thought Pete, she'd come straight from Ukraine.

'Rosa said something bad will happen in the east, in Mariupol, where I live with my family.'

'And has it?' Pete asked.

'Not yet. We think it will be earthquake. I'm here for saving money to move family west to Ivano-Frankivsk. They need land, for animals.'

'What made you decide to come to The Garden?' Pete asked.

'Because Victor said okay for me to come. Because Rosa ask him.'

Good old Vic, thought Pete. He might be an oddball but he was obviously a softball, too.

Sal and Pete were by the door, ready to leave, when Chelsea let out a shriek.

'Oh my God! What if your message is from the two dead bodies? Telling you who murdered them?'

Pete shook his head. 'About as likely as getting one from your nan. Telling me to keep my bleeding knickers on.'

Leaving The Dome, Pete headed one way and Sal the other, but in less than an hour, he was back with her in their cabin.

'Go on then? What did she have to say?' Sal asked, as soon as he came through the door.

Pete didn't answer, he went straight to pour himself a whisky; the whisky that was only ever poured for Gabe when they dropped by for a visit. Gin suddenly wasn't strong enough.

'I see Junior's with us again,' he said, pointing at the Yorkshire terrier who was sat in front of the woodstove, even though it wasn't lit.

'He was sat out on the porch when I got back,' said Sal. 'They obviously don't care about him. If they did, they wouldn't let him wander off all the time.'

She perched on the end of the chair arm. Waiting.

'Was it from Pippa?' she eventually asked. 'You know it doesn't bother me, Pete. I know you loved her. Probably still do. It doesn't mean that you don't love me.'

Sal was always magnanimous when it came to her predecessor and Pete loved her for it.

'It wasn't a message for me, it was a message for Phoebe. It was to tell her not to let anyone ride the piebald pony with the white socks, because someone is already riding it.'

'How d'you mean?'

'Mushroom's daughter. The one that died when she came off her horse at Burghley. She's hanging around here, to be near them. And she likes riding that pony because it isn't spooked by her.'

'Sodding hell. That's awful.'

'Is it? I think it's awesome.'

'Do The Mushrooms know?'

Pete nodded.

'Did Rosa say anything else?'

Pete shook his head, but it was a lie. A lie that he didn't intend to admit, not even at his next confession.

'Why don't you go get a shower?' Sal suggested, taking his empty glass, 'Get all that sand out of your arse.'

As Pete worked up a lather, he thought about what Rosa had told him. About him being in for 'a rough ride'. The message for Phoebe had been just an aside. He'd wanted more detail but Rosa didn't have it to give, other than the ride would eventually come to an end. He'd asked her why she would want to tell him, knowing that it would only serve to unnerve him. But she said it was important that he knew. That by knowing, he would also know he was going to ride it out.

As he shaved his chin, he cut himself from an unsteady hand. He had to pull himself together. He had to believe it wasn't true. She might have been uncannily correct in the past, but today, she was definitely wrong. Of course she was wrong. If mediums really could communicate with the dead, then they'd be making the news headlines every night of the week, wouldn't they?

CHAPTER EIGHT

NIGHT AFTER DAY

With rain being due, Pete had thought to leave a hooded golf buggy parked outside their cabin. And with the rain now pouring, Sal praised him mightily for it.

'Come on then, let's be having yer,' Pete said to Junior, after the terrier had followed them out onto the front porch.

The small dog leapt straight into his lap and off they sped toward The Hub, careering around every bend like it was Silverstone.

On arrival, they found Arek and Hellmutt stood either side of the front doors like a pair of nightclub bouncers.

'Are we expecting trouble?' Pete asked.

Arek grinned and then held open a door for them, only it wasn't for them, it was for a man pushing a wheelbarrow full of white pebbles. Another man followed behind him with the same, all coming from a wagon that was parked out on the forecourt.

Pete put out his hands, palms up, begging the question to Arek, but Arek shrugged and returned an expression of not having a clue.

Junior wasn't interested in the unusual traffic; he was straight up to sniff the rottweiler's bum.

'Nay lad, you might have amorous intentions, but I doubt you'll manage to tackle that,' Pete told him.

Arek grinned as he shook his head.

'Aw, fucking hell!' Sal exclaimed, stopping dead in her tracks as soon as they entered the reception.

'Stop swearing!' Pete yelled at her, before looking to see what she was swearing at.

Tonight - Nirvana is nearer than you think, was on the welcome placard.

‘Come on, we’re leaving. I’m not suffering that cocky little prat again,’ Sal told him, turning on her heel.

Pete threw out a hand to grab hold of her.

‘It’s not him. I told you before, Rin put out the wrong sign. This sign is right, for tonight.’

Sal was instantly placated.

The main restaurant was on the furthest off-shoot of The Hub’s outer circular corridor and there wasn’t a night went by without Sal complaining about the distance involved. Pete often wondered if a Starship would be able to handle her weight.

As they went in, the first thing Pete noticed was that one of their permanent wall signs had been covered over. Odd. It was a Buddhist sign, and as they were obviously having a Buddhist speaker, he’d expect it to take pride of place. The second thing he noticed were the white stones, uniformly sized, like Waitrose baking potatoes, and tipped into heaps at the side of each table.

Pete followed Sal across the dining room toward their own table, picking up a stone along the way. Beach pebbles. They still smelt of the sea.

‘What’s with all the rocks?’ Sal asked Dan.

He and Phoebe were already sat waiting, always first to arrive since they’d moved up from a four-seat table to a six, to accommodate them.

‘We’ve no idea,’ Dan replied, ‘Maybe we’re going to stone somebody?’

‘If we are, they must be expecting us to be pretty poor shots with all this lot,’ Pete remarked.

Sal had now picked up the tabard that was hung on the back of her chair and was holding it up to inspect.

‘We’ve all got one,’ Phoebe pointed out. ‘What do you think we’re going to be doing? Pottery or baking?’

‘I think I’ll opt for the stoning,’ Pete quipped, as he sat himself down.

Dinner began with a frisson of excitement, not just for the gruesome discovery within the grounds of their hallowed resort, but also for the possible purpose of the tabards and the stones. More excitement was soon to follow when a sudden, shrill screech rang out. Gabe looked to Pete, Pete looked to Sal, and Sal stood up and looked to see who it was.

‘Sasquatch. Lovely red stain across her white silk blouse. Looks like Lottie’s dropped a dish of tomato soup over her.’

They all craned their necks to see.

‘Why’s she dabbing at it? She’s making it worse,’ said Jude.

‘I’m glad I opted for the pâté,’ said Sal, pronouncing it the same as fate, ‘Lottie’s obviously been on the wacky-baccie, again.’

Phoebe was nodding in agreement.

‘Have you ever walked across the end of The Squat? If you hang around too long, you come away as high as a kite.’

Pete smirked. They called it The Squat because Eve had told them that was how their staff all lived. Like squatters. Both Eve and Adam had their private apartments nearby and were always bemoaning the fact, but Pete considered that that was how all young people lived when left to their own devices, in premises they didn’t have to pay for.

As soon as dessert came out, so did their speaker. He had the shaven head and saffron robes of a Tibetan monk but as soon as he began to speak, it was obvious he wasn’t Tibetan.

He told them all he was from Lincolnshire. Pete could live with that. At least it wasn’t Lancashire. But he did at least have a Tibetan name. His Dharma name. Genji.

‘Last time I was here we talked about Buddha and his life,’ Genji began, after giving them a polite Buddhist bow, ‘And since then, I understand you’ve received further instruction on karma and rebirth.’

‘Clurrrk, cluck, cluck, cluck,’ clucked Gabe, imperceptibly, like a ventriloquist’s dummy.

Pete kicked him under the table.

‘So, tonight, we’re going to look at Zen breathing and then following on from that, we have some interactive meditation to do.’

‘Not in these trousers, we won’t,’ Gabe hissed.

‘I know you’re already familiar with The Three Universal Truths, seeing as they’ve been right here for you to think upon every day,’ Genji went on, pointing to the covered sign.

‘Oh, shit,’ whispered Sal, ‘He’s going to test us on them, I know he is. And I’ve not thunk upon them enough.’

‘Don’t worry,’ Pete told her, ‘If he picks anybody on this table, he’ll pick me. I bet yer.’

‘A monkey?’ asked Gabe.

‘Oh, shut up.’

Genji was now centre front of stage.

‘Knowing as we do that Buddha was not a God, and that Buddhism does not follow a God, these truths are solely for liberating us. Liberating us from Samsara, that endless wheel of suffering.

‘Let me see … the man with the cravat. Could you give me one of the Three Universal Truths?’

Yep, they were going to be tested. He could have at least waited until the coffees had come out.

‘In the universe, nothing is lost,’ DoLittle threw out, confidently.

‘Excellent. And a second? The lady with the sequinned dress?’

Tabitha looked dumbstruck but Pete could see her twin quickly whispering to her.

‘Everything changes,’ Tabitha then announced.

‘Yes, it does. It certainly does. And the last one? The gentleman with the small dog on his knee?’

Pete immediately wished he’d accepted Gabe’s bet.

‘We are governed by the laws of cause and effect,’ he answered.

‘Yes, we are. Karma. For every event that occurs, there is another that is caused by it. Karma teaches us that our actions, good and bad, have on-going consequences, good and bad. So, we much practice to make sure our actions are always good and we must conduct ourselves with the best of intentions. Do unto others as you would have them do unto you. A precept of all major religions.’

Genji had given a thumbs up to Eve, and she went to yank away the sign’s cover. And there they were. The Three Universal Truths.

‘You need to stop crying over it,’ Sal said to their waitress as she came to gather up their dessert dishes, wiping her nose on the back of her hand.

Lottie looked at her, surprised.

'Crying? You've got to be joking. Crying laughing, more like. I've not laughed this much since I first started here and saw all you lot, strutting around in the nuddy.'

'You wicked little mare,' Sal scolded her.

'Aww, don't go telling on me, Mrs Hardcastle. I said sorry to her but she just kept saying I'd done it on purpose.'

'Did she now? I tell you what, if you go do it again, I'll give you a monkey's for'head for it.'

As Lottie looked perturbed, all the others could do was laugh.

Pouring himself a glass of water, their speaker took a sip before going back to his mic.

'Just out of interest, can anyone give me The Four Noble Truths?'

A dozen hands went up in the air.

'Clever bastards,' Gabe hissed. 'Is there a POT for being a clever bastard?'

Genji looked around and then picked. 'The lady with the red lipstick.'

'He's being overly polite,' said Gabe, 'He should just say the lady with the lips like a baboon's arse.'

Blubbermouth had immediately withdrawn her upright arm.

'Sorry, I was just trying to get the attention of our waitress,' she shouted out.

There was an audible tittering, but then Mo was suddenly on his feet, without invitation.

'One, suffering exists. Two, there is a cause to it. Three, there is an end to it. And four, for it to end, you must follow The Eightfold Path,' he announced.

'See. I told you they'd gone Buddhist,' Sal turned to tell her husband. 'They've got a huge Buddha sat on their veranda.'

Everyone had gone Buddhist at one time or another, Mo might just as likely have gone Hindu by the time Diwali came around.

Pete liked Mo and his wife. They were the only black couple at the resort, which by default made them stand out, but they had other attributes that stood out more. They were getting on a bit but she was still stunning. Endless legs, perfect figure, and a face that you just kept wanting to stare at. She reminded Pete of a dancer on a ballroom dancing programme that Sal watched. Mo was similarly blessed with good looks, no doubt about it, but it was his oversized penis that mostly grabbed your attention. Pete had always thought it just a fallacy, put about by black men themselves, about their being genetically well endowed. But judging by this one, the only black one he'd ever seen, it would appear to be true. Pete had named him Mo Big Dick. Mobi'dick for short. Which had soon been shortened to Mobi, and then even further, to Mo. Rather defeating its purpose.

Genji gave Mo a quick bow.

'Life is suffering,' he concurred. 'We can't avoid it. We get sick. We have accidents. We lose loved ones. And we live out every single day of our lives knowing that we're eventually going to die. And the cause of this suffering? Our attachment to things. Our desire to have, and to own, and to control. And how do we end it? By letting go of that attachment. Only when we let go, do we find liberation. Then, and only then, does the suffering cease and we reach Nirvana.'

'He makes it sound so simple,' Gabe grumbled, 'Like we sign everything over to the cats' home and we could all be there by next Friday.'

'Could you be Buddhist?' Dan suddenly asked him.

Gabe shook his head. 'Too much meditation. All that emptying your mind. No thanks. That sign in the snooker room says it all. *A mind at rest is a mind distressed.* That's why half of people crack up when they retire.'

'What about you, Pete?' Dan asked.

Pete shook his head. 'Too much reincarnation. All those deaths. Chances are, you're going to get burned to death, drowned to death, stabbed to death, and eaten, at least once. Scares me to death just thinking about it.'

Genji had removed the mic from its stand and had come to wander between their tables.

'Okay. I want you to close your eyes. And I want you to take in a deep breath. In through your nose, and down, down, into your belly. Belly breathe. We strive to get rid of our bellies, but we've got it all wrong. Think of Buddha figures, they're as good a sign as any of how our bellies should be.

'The medical professionals are now telling us about the vagus nerve. The gut-brain axis. Tranquillity can be brought about by the stimulation of our vagus nerve. And we stimulate it by breathing deep down into our belly, pushing it out to achieve vagal tone. It's all we need do. It slows our heart rate and it keeps us from shallow, over breathing.'

Pete pushed out, suddenly pleased with his vagally toned Buddha belly.

'Keep belly breathing. That's it. Purse your lips to slow it right down. I'm going to count to six, and you're going to slowly inhale. One, two, three, four, five, six. Hold. And out. One, two, three, four, five, six.'

They were all breathing, deep and slow.

'Bloody hell, my Spanx won't let me get past four,' Sal gasped.

'That's it, keep going, keep going,' Genji urged them. 'Exhale until you can't possibly exhale any more. We all breath much too shallow and it leaves us with air trapped in the bottom of our lungs. This is how viruses take hold. Imagine Covid is in here with us, floating around in the air, waiting for you to breath it in so it can catch hold. You can't avoid breathing. But you can avoid contracting the virus by breathing it all the way out.'

They inhaled and then exhaled, and exhaled, until they all began to cough.

'Now for the interactive part,' Genji told them. 'You're going to take part in something I call Lightening Enlightenment. See the marker pens in the middle of the table? And the stones at the side of you? I want you to take up one of those stones, and with a pen, I want you to write on it something that you have, or have experienced, that is an extravagance.'

The all looked at each other, in complete denial.

'If you have a box on your table. Open it,' Genji instructed them.

They had a box, so they opened it.

'Inside will be a pink ribbon, maybe two. It will have somebody's name on it. Somebody who sits at your table.'

They had one ribbon, with Phoebe's name on it.

‘These people need to pin their ribbon to their tabard, and they need to use the sheets of paper at the bottom of the box to write their extravagances on. From your medical records, it’s been decided that you’ll be exempt from lifting stones.’

Pete could see ShamPain, pinning on his pink ribbon. No surprises there.

‘What’s wrong with you?’ Sal asked Phoebe, so blunt it made Pete cringe.

Phoebe looked too pained to say.

‘It’s none of our business, Phoebe,’ Pete told her, ‘Forget she even asked.’

Dan leaned in to his wife. ‘Tell them.’

Phoebe grinned, then started, then hesitated, and then, ‘I’m pregnant.’

‘Congratulations,’ they all offered at once. Apart from Pete, who looked straight to Dan. How could he? How could he be tup-scuttling Rin while Phoebe was expecting his child?

‘I wasn’t sure you’d be able to have any,’ Sal told her, ‘With Dan only having one bollock.’

Pete squirmed with embarrassment. If only his wife had an off-button. Fortunately, The Buffs were both laughing.

‘Yes,’ said Dan, ‘but that one bollock has proved so potent, I figure it could supply a dozen fertility clinics all on its own.’

A seed of a thought instantly fertilised Pete’s mind. Perhaps that was what Dan was doing with Rin. Fertilising her. Maybe she’d failed to get pregnant by Vic, assuming she wanted to? Maybe Dan had put himself out to stud? For a fee? Or a free holiday?

‘I thought you were filling out a bit,’ Sal was saying to Phoebe.

‘I certainly am,’ Phoebe was quick to agree, ‘My boobs are absolutely killing me. They’ve turned into a pair of watermelons.’

‘They’re not false then?’ Sal asked.

‘No way. Why anyone would want to put a load of silicone inside of themselves, beats me.’

Pete raised an eyebrow at Gabe. A monkey’s for’head was soon to be headed his way.

‘Come on people. Your extravagances. You know what they are. All the things over and above that which is necessary for a decent, humble life. Give me your indulgencies. And no false modesty, I want them all. One after the other.’

People began picking up stones, or paper, and writing on them.

‘That’s it, keep them piling up around you,’ Genji encouraged. ‘Normally when I set this up, I tell people to write down additional rooms in their houses, rooms that are more than they actually need, but judging by the cars I’ve seen in your car park, I think you skip that and go for additional houses. And yes, those cars. Most of them would equate to five times the average family saloon. So, get writing. They’re an extravagance. You can’t deny it. Palatial houses that are simply temples to your own egos. Status symbol cars that drive you only to smug, self-satisfaction. You might not want to walk away from your wealth, like Buddha did, but tonight, you can do it symbolically to see how it might feel.’

Their table was filling up with stones. Pete glanced to his right to see Sal writing: Cartier watch with Full Pave of diamonds. To his left, Gabe was writing: Ferrari Testarosa. He felt compelled to tell him that Testarossa had two S’s, but he refrained.

So where did he begin? Additional houses? They had the one they lived in. The one Sal had just finished building. And thirty-seven rentals. Would they have enough stones?

As his stones began piling up, Pete suddenly felt stricken with shame. The table was groaning with them, and it was in danger of tipping over because all the stones were to one side. Dan had so few in front of him that it was tragic, and he looked to be struggling to add any more, while Phoebe, although using pieces of paper, looked to have written on only three.

‘Okay everybody, time to put down your pens and put on your tabards,’ Genji told them. ‘I want you to start packing the pockets, front and back, with your stones. They’re heavy duty, they’ll take quite a lot, but you’ll need to be able to walk so don’t overdo it. You can always come back for a refill.’

‘Is he joking, or what?’ Sal asked.

'Nup,' said Pete, 'So put on your pinny and get packing.'

'You're going to be doing a walking meditation along the Eightfold Path,' Genji told them. 'Each step, with purpose. Each breath, with purpose. A weighted, walking meditation. You're going to go out to the central circular corridor, and when you get there, half of you are going to go clockwise, and half of you, anti-clockwise. See the emblem on your tabards? You're either a Lotus Flower or a Karmic Wheel. Lotus flowers, clockwise. Karmic Wheels, anti.'

Pete fell in with everyone else as they headed for the double doors. The weight was ridiculous. No wonder they'd had to check their medical records before allowing them to do it. His heart was beating so hard he could hear it. He held up the stone filled pocket on the front of his tabard, like a pregnant woman holding up a nine-month bump. What if this was going to be the start of his rough ride? What if it was going to induce a stroke, leaving him dribbling and incontinent?

'One more thing you need to know,' Genji called out to them, 'This exercise is done in silence. Golden silence. Please resist the urge to speak to one another. The only voice you should be hearing is mine, when I'm next speaking to you over your PA system.'

They abided by the rules. They walked. They breathed. And they tried not to pass out. Midway around their second lap, Genji's voice came over, loud and clear.

'Keep breathing everyone. In through the nose, out through the mouth. In through the nose, out through the mouth. Now, pay careful attention. After every six breaths, I want you to stop the very next person who's coming toward you. You're going to take out one of their stones and place it to the outside of the corridor. And please, make sure it's well out of the way, we don't want any tripping hazards. Six breaths. Deep breaths. And then stop someone again. If it's someone having paper, take just the one sheet and leave it on the windowsill.'

Every time Pete tried to take a deep breath, he couldn't. The strain on his respiratory system allowed him only short, sharp, gasps. He took six gasps and then stopped Mary. She looked like she was about to have a seizure.

‘Oh, thank goodness, thank you, Peter. Pick a big one. And from the back, my back’s killing me,’ she told him.

Pete looked in her rear pocket. No big ones. Just similar sized ones. He took one out and read it as she went on her way. *Grandson’s private education*. Bless her. He tried to bend to put it to the edge of the corridor, but he couldn’t, his knees were in danger of buckling. He saw that others were just dropping them and kicking them aside, so he did the same.

As soon as he set off, he was immediately stopped and divested of a stone, and then stopped again. People were obviously taking pity on him, seeing him red in the face and sweating.

After six breaths, he stopped Tamara. *Villa in Tuscany,* was written on her stone. He dropped it and kicked it.

The corridor seemed to be lengthening, with each lap taking him longer. He could see Sal coming toward him for the third time and they took a stone from each other irrespective of breaths.

‘Why are you only stopping women?’ he whispered to ask.

‘Because I want to see what they’ve got,’ she admitted, unashamedly.

Pete decided he best even things up by only stopping men.

Sheepteeth was heading toward him so he put up his hand to stop him and take out a stone.

Helicopter, was written on it. Pete was impressed, assuming Sheepteeth had his pilot’s licence to go with it. Next, he chose to stop Mo. His stone had written on it, *Fender Stratocaster*. Again, impressed, assuming Mo could play it. Then he was stopped, and then stopped again, but if his load was getting lighter, it was imperceptibly lighter.

Genji’s voice jumped out over the PA system again.

‘As you lighten the load of others, so they lighten yours. Feel the burden of materialism lifting. Feel the lightness that comes from letting go of your possessions.’

Pete next stopped Prunie. *Divorce*, was writ on his stone. Ouch. No wonder he was covering himself this time around.

He next stopped The Boar. *Hair transplant*. No way. How utterly crushing to have all that hair, but only on your back.

Maybe that was where his transplanted hair had been harvested from?

Pete was trying to put himself in front of on-coming traffic, so as to be chosen, but everyone else was doing the same, so there were endless bottlenecks. They were all breathing, and counting, breathing and counting. He decided to take a break, leaning against the wall to recover, and then suddenly, they were queuing up to take his stones. He pointed some of them to the rear as he was becoming unbalanced.

Setting off once again, Blubbermouth came straight at him, stone in hand, to thrust it directly into his. Was that allowed? He read it. *~~Facelift.~~ Sutcliffes killed them.* He turned around to watch her, walking away along the corridor, thrusting her stones on everyone. All her stones obviously had the same message written on them. She must have gone back for a marker pen as soon as she'd seen an opportunity to champion her cause. Good job the Sutcliffes were walking in the same direction.

'I'll be glad to get this over with,' Gabe whispered to him, as they stopped each other for the sixth time.

Pete nodded, although he was discovering he quite liked it. He didn't bother to look at Gabe's stone. It would only have been another car.

Coming toward him was Dan. Pete took a stone from him. *An en-suite.* It wasn't *Seventh en-suite*, or even *Third en-suite.* It was, *An en-suite*. And this was an extravagance?

Next, he stopped Three Lugs. *Racehorse number five*. Highly unlikely. Somebody had probably told him they owned four.

DoLittle had a *Rolex Submariner*, but then so did Pete, and he'd not even considered doing a stone for it.

Now their loads were a little lighter, everyone was suddenly enjoying themselves. Weren't they supposed to be suffering for this enlightenment?

Pete had followed Sal in going back to their restaurant table for a refill. As soon as he re-joined the circular flow, ShamPain stopped him. He took out a stone and then pulled open his own pocket, clearly expecting Pete to reciprocate. *Chateau in the Dordogne*. Pete wasn't impressed. He'd heard they could be picked up for the equivalent of a Barnsley back-to-back.

Ruthless was stood right behind ShamPain, and Pete assumed he was queuing to take one of his stones, but he just stood, waiting for Pete to take one of his. *Around the World Cruise*. Pete kicked the stone into a door corner, wondering how his wife managed to avoid him on that.

Oh-oh. Swingerdy-do, swingerdy-dah. A male swinger was heading straight for him. He was decidedly smiley but Pete decided to remain stone faced. Any show of familiarity on his part might lead to him and Sal being propositioned. Pete took a reciprocal stone. *McClaren*, was written on it. Pete wondered if it had similarly led to the losing of his licence.

He was stopped eight times in quick succession and was suddenly able to walk without looking like he had the Farmers. As there was a sudden run on woman, he was duty bound to stop one. Beck-and-call. *Therapy*, was writ large on her stone, unsurprisingly. And then Prunie was in front of him, again. Pete lifted a stone from him. *Double-decker bus*. Seriously? Why would anyone want to own a double-decker bus?

Owt-for-Nowt stopped him and helped himself to two of his stones, which figured.

Eeyore had spotted him and was dodging everyone to get to him. Taking a small hip flask out of his trouser pocket, he passed it over. Pete unscrewed it and took a slug. He couldn't decide if it was Tequila or Meths. He gave it back and with a mutual downward nod, they took a stone from each other.

They stared at what was written on them and then they stared at each other.

'Snap!' Eeyore shouted.

'Ssshhhh,' passers-by hissed.

They put their stones together. One said, *Solid gold testicles*, the other said, simply, *Golden Balls*. It immediately prompted a heightened respect for each other.

This was a trophy that very few people would ever receive, or even want to. It was achieved by undertaking the most outrageously expensive — not to mention ridiculously dangerous — round of golf that existed on the planet. Not just to finish it, but to survive it. Few golfers had heard of it and those that had, considered it a myth. But with enough money and the right contacts it was anything but.

Somewhere in the deep south of the USA, in a place you were taken to blindfolded, there was a half decent golf course. Well-manicured and maintained, but surrounded by swamp. Alligators roamed across its fairways by the dozen and in-between them, venomous snakes slithered from mangrove to mangrove. If you came out the other side and reached the clubhouse, you were immediately welcomed into the hall of fame and awarded the 'Golden Balls' trophy. Dimpled like golf balls and hung from a small golden tripod, an unmistakable sculpture of a pair of testicles. Twenty-four karat gold. As solid as you can get.

'Would you ever do it again?' Pete asked him.

'Never,' Eeyore replied.

Pete nodded to agree. 'I heard they've put a half course together. Nine holes like ours,' he told him. 'If you get through it, you just get the one ball. It's called the Golden Pillock trophy.'

As Eeyore began to bray, Pete went on his way.

After seventy minutes, there were very few people left in the corridor, going either way, so those that remained just emptied each other's tabards and headed back to base camp. Pete was one of them. He was feeling dizzy and light limbed. Flopping into his chair, he fell face down into his remaining white stones. The smell of the sea salt being just the tonic to revive him.

'So, do you feel lighter?' Genji rallied them, like a gameshow host.

'Yes!' they responded.

'Yes, of course you do. But let me tell you, you don't need to walk away from it all, like Buddha, you just need to see what you have, for what it is. A weight. One that's dragging you back from your spiritual progression. Less is more. More is less.

'And as you walked around The Eightfold Path, reading each of the eight as you crossed over them, time and time again, they will have become ingrained. So now you have the knowledge to end your wheel of suffering. And reach Nirvana.'

Pete suddenly realised that the hand-written, evenly spaced rubber mats he'd been walking across, had been there to be read. Eight, in each direction. He'd been so busy breathing, and counting, that he hadn't even thought to consider them.

'At Vic's suggestion, the stones will be remaining where they are in perpetuity. Let them be a reminder to you, of how you Lightened and Enlightened yourselves this evening,' Genji told them, before taking his final bow.

'Christ, it's going to be like walking around a bleeding riverbed from now on,' said Gabe.

The evening over, Pete and Sal jumped into the golf buggy and headed back to their cabin, yawning incessantly from all the overextended breathing.

'Find out anything interesting?' Pete asked.

Sal thought about it.

'Nearly all the women drive Porsche nine-elevens.'

'Oh, here we go. I suppose you'll be wanting one, now?'

'You've got to be joking. They're as common as muck,' Sal retorted. 'What about you?'

'Not really. Usual stuff. Apart from Prunie. Bought himself a double-decker bus.'

Sal thought about it.

'Has he got a ton of grandkids?'

'Must have.'

'Can't see how Pruness likes having that parked outside her mock-Tudor mansion,' Sal scoffed.

'What about Blubs? Handing out her stones?' Pete asked, 'I assume you got given one?'

'I got two,' Sal replied, 'Seeing as I changed direction, like she did. The only people who didn't get one were probably the two that would have brained her with them.'

CHAPTER NINE

ONE DAY IN AUGUST

'I dun't know where thee 'ell tha's gone, cos 'av got nowt on mi radar forrit. Get tha sen back ont' main road, sharpish, yer great steaming mugwump.'

Pete was sick of hearing himself, but having entered through the gates of The Garden of Eden, he knew that TwatNav would soon cease to function, the place being off its grid.

Dan drove the double-decker bus up toward The Hub, weaving his way through the golf course and around The Tree. That's when they saw the three police cars parked outside the front doors.

Once they came to a standstill, Pete was first off, staggering forward to throw up in one of the newly planted borders. He sat down on the front steps, face skyward, letting the morning rain cool his throbbing brain.

'You okay, mate?'

Pete could see Jake had wasted no time in taking back his TwatNav, loaned only for the duration of their stag-night excursion. Pete didn't reply, he just stared at him, the same way The Shining stared. Vacantly.

Dan came to join them. Having a licence to drive a fire engine had proved parity with driving a bus, so he'd volunteered for the job, having temporarily sworn off alcohol in solidarity with his pregnant wife.

'Want us to go find Sal?' Jake asked him.

'No need. She's here,' Pete heard Sal saying, as she came up from behind to sit down beside him on the steps.

Dan and Jake immediately headed off toward the restaurant, and breakfast.

'Is that yours?' Sal asked him, nodding to the vomit in the flower bed.

Pete nodded, and then closed his eyes in prayer.

'Please TC, I'm begging. Please take away this evilness. I promise I'll never drink again.'

He could hear Sal, cackling.

They sat and watched the other stags disembarking from the bus. Some by themselves and some being escorted, roughly, by their wives.

'Well at least we know why Prunie bought himself a double-decker bus,' Sal observed, and then, 'What happened to Tugger's trousers?'

'In the Thames.'

'What happened to Plucky's?'

'Gabe's wearing them.'

'What happened to Gabe's?'

'In the Thames.'

Sal began to cackle.

'Ssshhhhh!' he demanded, the noise ringing in his ears like timpani.

'What do you remember?' Sal asked him, after he'd finished wiping another trail of bile from off his chin with the leaves of a geranium.

'We mooched around London for a while. Then we got on the boat that Prunie had hired. We did some sightseeing on it. Then we moored up and they served us some dinner. After that there was a drag queen comedian. And a stripper who started out naked and put things on.' The joke hadn't been lost on them.

'Then the two barmaids quit because we weren't observing social distancing. And then Jake took over behind the bar.'

And ruination had been their destiny.

'He mixed us some Zombies. And after the third, we were.'

'What happened to Eeyore?' Sal asked.

Pete looked up to see him limping past, his eye socket purple and shiny.

'He got into a fight with Sheepteeth.'

'Oh dear. What was that about?'

'At a guess, his trousers going into the Thames.'

'So where's Sheepteeth?' she asked, after he hadn't been seen to exit the bus.

Pete wished she'd stop asking so many questions and just sit quiet.

'We dropped him at the village dentist. He needs some temporary teeth.'

Sal began to cackle.

'Ssshhhh!' he hissed at her.

'Think you could get back to the cabin without throwing up on me?' Sal asked him, once the bus was empty and the show was over.

'I can try.'

She helped him into the golf buggy and floored it back to their cabin. Pete threw up twice, but only on himself, so Sal stripped him off on the porch and then hosed him down in the shower.

As he crawled into bed, Junior came scampering in from the lounge and leapt onto the pillow beside him.

'He's come to give you the lick of life,' Sal told him, 'Cos you won't be getting a kiss anytime soon.'

Pete took the glass of Alka-Saltzer she was offering.

'So have the police found them?' he asked.

'The burglars?'

'No. Vic and Gabe.'

'What do you mean?'

'What do *you* mean?' Pete returned.

'We've had a break-in. Last night. Burglars broke into the main office,' Sal told him, and then, 'What's happened to Vic and Gabe?'

'We lost them.'

'How d'you mean you lost them? How could you lose them?'

'We could because we did.'

There was a knock on the door and Sal went to answer it.

'I've brought over Pete's toys,' Pete could hear DoLittle saying.

Toys? He tried to think what toys he might have. Golf clubs? Snooker cue? Darts? And what was DoLittle doing with them?

Sal had invited DoLittle in and obviously pointed him to the bedroom door as he was soon to wander through it. He stood at the foot of the bed.

'I brought Pete Junior's things.'

'Is he staying?' Pete asked.

'Well, yes, that was what we agreed. Last night.'

'Did we?'

'Yes, in view of the fact he's practically living with you already.'

'And you're okay with that?'

'I told you. We're fine with it. I don't think we're actually dog people. It was just a Covid thing. I'll get his vaccine cards next time we're back home. He's all up-to-date.'

'What about that little jacket he wears when it's raining?' Sal came in to ask, an eye on the accessories at all times.

'It's in the bottom of his bed. A Starship's bringing it.'

Sal went back into the lounge to check out the toys.

'Thanks for defending me, Pete. Last night.'

'Did I?'

'Yes, with a chair, when they were trying to de-bag me.'

'Right. I'm sure it'll all come back to me, eventually.'

DoLittle smiled at him, looking doubtful of it, and then left.

Five minutes later, there was another knock on the door.

'Can I come in, Sal and have a word with Pete?'

'Sure. Go on through.'

'Have you heard from Vic?' Adam asked him, as soon as he was at the end of his bed.

'Nup.'

'What about Gabe?'

'Nup.'

'Do you remember where you last saw them?'

Pete thought about it.

'On the embankment.'

'And how did they look?'

'Pissed.'

'You don't think they might have got on another boat? Or fallen in?'

'Not that pissed.'

'Are you alright, Pete?'

'Do I look alright?'

'No.'

'Well hey-ho, there you go.'

Sal came into the room.

‘Where were you?’ she asked Adam. ‘How come you don’t know where they went?”

‘I was one of the last to get off the boat. I was helping John sort out all the trouble.’

Sal perched on the end of the bed.

‘Oh aye, and what trouble would that be?’

‘Damage trouble. They wouldn’t let him get off until he’d paid for it.’

‘Bloody hell. What got into you all?’

‘Zombies,’ said Pete, with a groan.

‘I better head back,’ Adam told them, retreating to the door, ‘I’ve got the police to deal with, and without Vic, I’ve absolutely no idea what’s actually been stolen. I can’t believe the same cops are back again, so soon. I thought we’d seen the last of them once they’d handed over to the Shovelbums.’

Pete winced at the mere mention of the name, even though the only good thing about them was that name. Shovelbums. The accepted, self-styled title of all archaeologists, apparently. It suited them well.

The furore over Adam and Eve — the supposedly buried Adam and Eve, as opposed to the living – had lasted less than a week. Police forensics had departed almost as soon as they’d arrived, due to the bodies proving to be over one thousand years old. Not old enough to be the first man and woman on the planet, but old enough to be Anglo-Saxon. Hence, they now had half a dozen anorak clad, uncombed, unshaven, bohemian types, shacked up in a portacabin on the edge of the ninth hole, spending their days scraping, sifting and sieving. Worst of it was, Vic had granted them permission to do ground penetrating radar surveys and trial trenching, all over the entire course.

Ten minutes after Adam had left, there was another knock on the door.

‘Chuff me. It’s like Piccadilly blummin’ Circus in here,’ Pete complained.

‘Well you’d know. I bet you went and demolished that, too, didn’t yer?’ Sal said to him, cackling all the way to the front door.

‘Hello Father, what a pleasant surprise,’ she greeted.

Pete sighed and pulled the duvet up under his chin.

'How are you doing, my son?' Father Anthony asked, as soon he appeared before him.

Why did he persist with calling him his son? He might be wearing a dog collar but even if he'd worn a papal mitre, Pete still wouldn't accept him as a priest.

'Bad. I'm doing bad.'

'Yes, that's what I'd heard, so I thought I'd come and give you the last rites.'

'Too kind,' Pete replied.

Sal came in and put a small dish of dog biscuits under the terrier's nose, causing Pete to gip.

'You missed your confession this morning. And our golf.'

'Sorry Father.'

'Is there anything pressing that you'd like to confess?'

'There's probably lots. Just a shame I can't remember.'

'Apart from the partaking of too much alcohol,' said Father Anthony, clearly enjoying his current penance for it.

Another knock on the door.

Pete groaned, loudly, and then leaned sideways to peer out through the open bedroom door.

A man in a black uniform had stepped into their cabin. Plod. With a mask on. As Sal began talking with him, Pete and Father Anthony fell silent through some unstated agreement, so that they might listen.

'And you didn't see anything? Or hear anything?'

'Nothing. I was in here. And our cabin's probably one of the furthest away,' Sal was saying.

'What about anyone new around the place? Acting suspiciously?'

'No. It's always the same old people. The postman. The delivery drivers. The scruffy buggers digging up the golf course,' she replied, and then, 'Do you want me to put some clothes on?'

'No, not at all.'

'Then would you mind looking at my face, rather than my feet?'

There was a sharp clearing of the throat.

'I understand you were one of the first on the scene?'

'The first was Eve. But yes, I was there not long after, amongst others. We were up early for breakfast because our husbands were away doing some demolition work in London.'

'I see. And Miss Mitford, Eve, she came to tell you what had happened?'

'No. She just took us to see it. A right old ransacking. Drawers out. Glass all over the place. Papers all over the place. It was like poltergeese had got in there.'

'Miss Mitford says the door to the office was locked. So would you say the point of entry was through the window?'

'Flamin' 'ell. Are you a trainee? I'd have thought it was bloody obvious. It was hanging off its hinges.'

'Did you touch anything, madam?'

Plod's tone of voice had changed, he was clearly rattled.

'No. But I took a photograph on my phone, so I could show it my husband.'

Pete realised he had yet to see it.

'What do you know about a man by the name of Arek?'

'Arek? Hmmm, what do I know about Arek? He keeps ponies. He has a dog that likes to see off rats. He's got one long joined-up eyebrow instead of two.'

Another clearing of the throat.

'You've not seen him receiving any visitors, lately?'

'Ah,' said Sal, 'You mean his thieving gypsy relatives who might be here to ring our cars and swipe our fine silverware?'

Pete and Father Anthony grinned at each other.

'There's no need to take that attitude, madam.'

'Well, what do you expect? You're just looking for a quick culprit, aren't you?'

'We most certainly are not. We've just been pointed in that direction by many of your neighbours.'

'Well shame on them,' said Sal. 'Now, if you don't mind, I've got some vomit to clean up.'

They heard the door slam shut and assumed plod was on the far side of it.

Sal immediately came in to them, to vent her spleen, but just then, there was another knock on the door and then a shrill call from someone who had let themselves in.

'Oh, for goodness' sake!' Pete exclaimed.

He just wanted to be ill on his own. Misery might like company but hangover's definitely preferred solitude.

'You're going to thank me for this one,' his wife told him.

When she came back to them, she had the resort's once-a-week nurse in tow.

'She's come in off duty. So be grateful,' Sal cautioned.

The nurse dumped her large carpet bag at the bottom of the bed, just missing Pete's feet, and then lost no time at all in setting up her stall.

'Will yer look at the state of yer,' she said to Pete, her Irish lilt oddly comforting.

Pete suddenly wanted to cry, but being seen crying by a nurse had to be worse than being seen erect.

'Father, can you go get me that there coat stand from by the door, if you will. Minus the coats.'

Father Anthony did as he was bid and in the meantime the nurse shone a small torch light into each of Pete's eyes.

'Oh jeez, leave it out, that's given me an instant migraine,' Pete whined.

'And you, at your age,' the nurse admonished, 'What on earth were you thinking?'

'I was thinking, let's have another one, probably.'

The nurse manoeuvred the coat stand nearer to the bed and then hooked onto it a bag of saline. She roughly took hold of Pete's arm and began to slap it to the inside of his elbow.

'You're dehydrated and that's a fact.'

She'd made two holes in him before the needle found a willing vein.

'Right, it's in yer. Now you just sit tight and soon enough you'll be feeling less shite.'

Pete managed a weak smile.

'I'll be back in an hour,' the nurse said to Sal.

'Where you going?' Sal asked.

The nurse opened her large bag and tilted it forward. The three of them could see more saline bags.

'Makes a change from my normal round,' she told them. 'All the piles, the hernias and the imaginary ear infections.'

'Shall I come along to help?' Father Anthony immediately offered.

'And why not indeed,' the nurse replied, instantly passing him her bag.

'And what part of Ireland are you from?' Father Anthony was asking her on their way out, 'I'm originally from Kilkenny myself.'

Sal closed the door behind them and went back to her drip-fed husband.

Forty minutes later, there was another knock on the door.

'Have you heard from him?' Pete heard Sal asking.

He raised his head from the pillow, so as to better hear.

'No. But I've heard from his Aunt Agnes in Bethnal Green. She says he's asleep on her sofa. And his mate's in her bed.'

It was Jude.

'Thank heavens for that. At least we know they're safe,' said Sal, 'Have you told Adam?'

'An hour ago. He's already on his way to pick them up.'

'Shall I put the kettle on?'

'No. Got to dash. Eve's asked me to find Phoebe. Vic's donkey is in the scooter shed again and nobody dare go in.'

'Where's Arek?' he heard Sal ask.

'Nobody knows. Rin's out looking for him.'

The donkey might be in the scooter shed, but for sure, Arek was in his potting shed. Not that he'd tell them. Pete guessed he was probably the only one who knew that Arek was growing pot, in his shed, having a nice steady trade going on with The Squatters. He'd previously asked Pete to water them for him when he and Rosa had taken a trip back to Cumbria to look at another caravan. Pete had been honoured to be trusted not to grass on his grass. As for the donkey, Vic had obviously watched the girls out pony trekking and decided to give it a go himself, on something milder and meeker. Only it wasn't. Vic, it actually liked, Arek and Phoebe, it obeyed, but everyone else, it tried to kill.

As soon as Jude left, the nurse returned with Father Anthony in tow.

'Feeling better?' she asked Pete.

Pete nodded. 'Can I have another one?'

'No. You've had enough,' she told him, plonking herself down in one of their bedroom chairs.

In the space of an hour, Father Anthony had become proficient enough to remove needles, plaster-up resulting flesh wounds, dismantle saline bags and tubes, and take the patient's temperature. While his mentor put her feet up with the offered cup of tea. Also, within the hour, the pair of them had become so familiar with each other that it wouldn't have surprised Pete if they'd had a minor skirmish somewhere on route.

There was yet another knock on the door and as Sal was still trying to get the vomit stain out of the bedroom carpet, it fell to Father Anthony to answer it.

It was Prunie.

'We're off now, Pete. I just thought I'd drop in to say goodbye.'

'Aye, crikey, I'd forgot. Wedding on Wednesday, eh?'

Prunie nodded and smiled.

'Sorry I couldn't invite any of you. It's a small private jet. And the villa's only big enough for the both of our families.'

'No worries. You enjoy yourselves and just send plenty of photos.'

'We will. You do know we're not coming back? That we're letting go of our cabin?'

'Aye, you said, but I'm sure you'll be dropping in now and then to see us. Covid permitting.'

'We most certainly will,' Prunie assured him, and then, 'I'll send you the paperwork and whatnot as soon as we get back, but here's the keys. And thanks again for buying it. It's the best wedding present you could have given us. I've had so much earache about it being parked up outside the house. She's been calling it the double-decker marriage-wrecker ever since we got engaged.'

Pete took the keys, but he was speechless. What had he done?

'A bus? A sodding double-decker bus?' Sal shouted, as she came back into the room after seeing Prunie out. 'You don't even get your licence back for another bloody year. So why? Tell me? Why?'

'I've no idea. I must have taken pity on him.'

‘Oh, that’s alright then. So Pruness doesn’t want it parked outside her mock-Tudor mansion, wrecking her marriage, but it’s okay to have it parked outside my new mock-Georgian one, wrecking mine?’

Sal had her hands on her hips. It was serious.

‘It can stay here. There’s plenty of room for it. We can use it for day trips,’ Pete told her.

‘Oh, I can see it now. A bus full of old nudes trundling off to the seaside. Frightening the kids and ending up in the nick for indecent exposure.’

Father Anthony and the nurse were laughing fit to burst.

‘You two. Hop it,’ Sal told them, jerking her thumb over her shoulder.

As soon as the two of them had hopped it, Gabe arrived.

‘Christ Almighty, you’re that green, you look like bleeding Shrek. I knew you’d be laid up bad when I saw Moby in the golf buggy outside,’ he said to Pete.

‘SOL,’ Sal shouted from the lounge.

‘You’ve no idea. I’ve been on a saline drip for an hour,’ Pete lamented.

Gabe shook his head. ‘To say how much gin you can put away, I’d have thought you could handle it better.’

Sal came in to them.

‘Did he say he was going to come in? I looked out and he’s gone?’

Gabe looked to Pete, and then back to Sal.

‘Who you on about?’

‘Mobi. You said he was in the buggy, outside?’

Gabe looked at Pete and they both cracked out laughing.

Sal’s nostrils immediately flared and she turned and stormed out. Pete would have to explain to her, later, that Moby was short for Moby Dick. Sick.

‘Go on then? What happened to the both of you?’ Pete asked.

‘Nothing happened. We just decided on a visit to the Hippodrome.’

‘A nightclub? At your age?’

‘Casino,’ Gabe corrected.

Pete rolled his eyes back, making clear he should have known.

‘It was closed,’ Gabe told him, ‘Due to Covid. But the taxi driver knew of this other place. A gentleman’s club with a gaming room. Where I gently trousered a couple of grand.’

‘But not in your own trousers.’

‘No,’ Gabe sniggered, pulling out a roll of notes from the pocket of the pants that were at least one size too big for him.

‘You heard about the break-in?’ Pete asked.

Gabe nodded. ‘Adam told us on the way back. Someone who obviously knew most of the blokes would be out of the way. Or at least knew that Vic would.’

‘How’s the old boy taken it?’

‘Not that bad, to be honest. He says they’ve nicked loads of rare stuff that he’s collected. But on top of what he lost last night, on the Rats and Mice, it’s probably crucifying him.’

‘Rats and Mice?’

‘Dice.’

‘Terrible habit,’ said Sal, tutting as she came into the bedroom.

‘It’s not a habit. It’s a hobby,’ Gabe informed her, ‘Habits are what crackheads have. And as far as hobbies go, it’s the best. It enhances all other hobbies. Golf, snooker, football, horse racing. They’d all be as boring as Bovril without a bet on them.’

Just then, Jude and Phoebe walked in, soon to be followed by Dan. Sal immediately picked up her phone to put in an order for a small buffet to be delivered.

‘Woohoo! You guys just missed all of the action!’ Phoebe exclaimed, excitedly,

Jude was stood beside her, grinning and nodding.

‘So, we’re in the middle of lunch, and a couple of the wives began having a right old hissy fit,’ Phoebe forged on, ‘And before we knew it, they were full on fisty cuffs, knocking seven bells out of each other. Eve couldn’t split them up, so she’d to go ask one of the policemen to get involved. And he cautioned them. Can you believe it? The place was full too. You should have heard all the ROYs being shouted out. Plus some GBHs. I don’t think we’ve ever had a GBH on the POTs board before. You’ll be knocked off the top for sure next week, Sal.’

‘Hang on, hang on,’ Sal said to her, using her hands to conduct a slowing down, ‘Which wives?’

'Noose and Lucifer. They were like a pair of wild cats. It was awesome,' Phoebe trilled.

'What was it about?' Pete asked.

'Their men. Because they'd thrown each other's pants into the river.'

'No, it was Sheepteeth's pants and Eeyore's jacket,' Jude corrected her.

'But the blokes made up about it. They shook hands and put it to bed,' said Pete.

'Yes, but that was before Eeyore remembered the Harrods necklace he'd collected for Luci, was still in his pocket. She'd only ordered it the day before.'

'And she expected you all to trail to Harrods with him? Just so he could pick the damn thing up?' Sal asked, caustically.

'We went as part of a game,' Gabe explained. 'As soon as we got off the bus, it was the first one to get there.'

'Who won?' Phoebe immediately asked.

Gabe and Dan both pointed at Pete.

'Did you run?' Phoebe asked.

Gabe answered for him. 'No, he flagged down a passing police car. Had a word. And next minute he's in the back and on his way.'

Sal looked at her husband and raised an eyebrow. It was the eyebrow that must be obeyed.

'I told them I'd got dementia and left my grandson there by accident.'

Phoebe giggled as Sal tutted, while Gabe leaned forward, clearly with intent.

'Want to hear about another fight?' he asked them.

They all nodded.

'Adam and Vic. On the way back here. Having a right old ding-dong, they were. Adam pulled the car over at one point. I actually thought he was going to drag Vic out the back and give him a good hiding.'

'What was it about?' Pete asked, both shocked and surprised.

'Your favourite thing. The golf course. Adam's fuming that Vic's given the Shovelbums permission to dig it up. He wants them gone. But Vic said it wasn't his place to tell him what he could and couldn't do. They weren't half giving it some.'

'That's not very nice, is it?' said Phoebe, 'Having a big fall-out with him, just after telling him he's been robbed blind.'

They all nodded to agree.

'Am I to presume your trousers are now floating in the Thames?' Jude asked her husband.

'You are,' Gabe replied, 'But probably sunk, seeing as I had Pete's wallet in my back pocket.'

They all looked to Pete, who gave them a smile and a shake of his head to indicate it wasn't the case.

'So those trousers aren't your trousers?' Phoebe asked him.

Gabe shook his head and lifted up his jumper to show they were held around his waist with the aid of a tie.

'Whose tie is it?' Jude asked.

'Prunie's.'

There was sudden shouting from outside.

'Anybody home? We're here! We're outside!'

Pete smiled. He'd had a hand in programming the Starships. Vic had refused to have Yorkshire accented, semi-offensive versions, so he'd kept it friendly and polite.

Sal and Phoebe immediately responded to them.

As everyone was already perched around the edge of the bed, Sal threw a tartan picnic blanket over Pete's legs and they ate where they sat.

Junior kept doing the rounds to see what he could scrounge, while Gabe's mobile went around in the opposite direction, showing them a time-line of events through photos and videos.

'What the hell were you all playing at?' Sal asked.

'Truth or Dare,' Gabe replied, literally.

There was a video of Adam, peeing on a potted plant. One of Three Lugs eating what looked like a candle. Someone with their head in an ice bucket, brim full of ice. And Dan, stripping off and diving into the river from the side of the boat.

'Are you mad? You could have given yourself a DBT doing that,' Sal said to him.

Dan looked puzzled.

'Deep Brain Thrombosis,' Pete explained, relieved when Dan just nodded and smiled.

He was clearly learning never to contradict Sal's malapropisms; probably for the sake of not wanting to witness her going off at the deep end. Fortunately for Dan, he had gone off at the deep end, thus avoiding a DBT.

'So did any of you do truths or was it all dares?' Phoebe asked.

'Truths? Truths? What do you take us for? Wussies and pussies?' Gabe railed at her, comically, 'No winky-wanky truths for us.'

'SOL,' said Sal.

'What?'

'Winky-wanky.'

'No way that's a SOL. If that's a SOL, then I'm going to SOL you every time you say willy-nilly.'

'No, I do not!'

'Oh, come off it. You're always giving it, *Gabe, stop leaving the towels all willy-nilly. Gabe, stop leaving your shoes willy-nilly for me to go arse over tit and get a DBT.'*

Sal remained quiet, quietly amused.

Dan was passing on his phone, showing them another video. It was of Pete, climbing up the Eros statue.

'If I hadn't seen that for myself, I wouldn't have believed it,' Pete told them. 'Did I get to the top?'

'No,' Gabe told him, 'Pieces kept coming away in your hand, so we made you get down.'

Pete shook his head. Sal had been right. They had demolished Piccadilly Circus, or at least he had.

'I still can't believe we've had someone breaking in here,' Phoebe reflected. 'In a place as peaceful as this, it's a pretty poo thing to have happened. Am I allowed to say poo?'

'Yeh, poo's okay,' Gabe assured her, 'It's shit you've got to worry about.'

'SOL,' said Sal.

Gabe threw a half-eaten growler at her.

'Talking of which, I bet Shar Pei's shitting herself right now. Waiting to go under the knife for half her body amputating.'

Pete had forgotten that she was currently in a private hospital somewhere, having her excess skin removed.

‘Yes, but when she gets back, she’ll no longer be a Shar Pei,’ Phoebe stated. ‘You know, Pete, I’m so grateful you never gave me and Dan names.’

Gabe immediately brought his hand down to grab Pete’s quilt covered leg.

‘You’d never have dreamt of such a thing, would you, Pete?’

‘Never,’ Pete replied, his eyes fixed firmly on Gabe’s over-tight hand, while wishing he had an over-tight hand around Gabe’s neck.

Rather fortuitously, Junior provided a timely distraction by throwing up a huge glob of vol-au-vent vomit across the tartan landscape.

Sal immediately sprang to parcel it up inside the blanket.

‘Like father, like son,’ she chuntered.

‘Well, he did warn you,’ Gabe said to Pete.

‘Who did?’

‘DoLittle. Last night. He said every time he came back from yours, they always knew what shite you’d been feeding him, cos he’d puke it up as soon as he got through the door. And on that note, we’re off. It reeks to high heaven of Moby in here.’

Pete considered the haste at which they all left to be quite distasteful. Even Sal deserted him with the feeble excuse of visiting Eve.

Rather bizarrely, after a constant stream of visitors throughout the day, Pete found himself wanting for company. He had himself another shower and decided upon making a visit.

CHAPTER TEN

NIGHT AFTER DAY

Vic's cabin was halfway up the valley side. All the necessary trees had been removed to allow for an uninterrupted view of the entire valley. From the waterfalls and lake at one end, to the golf course at the other, with The Dome, The Pagoda, The Bridge, The Hub and The Tree, stretching in-between. Nobody else had a view like Vic's and Sal would have happily given a big toe to have possession of it. Or so she'd once said.

All the cabins in The Garden had a small porch to the front and a full-length veranda to the rear. Vic's was the reverse, with the veranda at the front to make the most of the view. But just like all the others, it had a glass canopy all the way across it, with a state of the art hot-tub at one end. Only Vic never used his on account of him keeping koi carp in it. This was where Pete found him, feeding his fish.

'Now then, how you doing after your long night out on the tiles?'

'I'm doing fine, Peter. But all the better for seeing you. This is an unexpected pleasure. You never come to visit like you used to,' Vic told him, motioning him across toward the rattan sofas.

'Don't go blaming me. I'd come all the way up here, only to find you on the phone to your bookies. I never got a look in,' Pete replied, as they went to sit, facing each other.

'Was I? Well, I'm sorry for that, Peter, because I really miss the chats we used to have.'

'Me too.'

Rin came out with rice tea.

'Good for hangover,' she told Pete.

Pete realised he must still be looking green.

As she walked away, he had a good long look at her. She was skinny, androgenous and plain. What did Vic see in her? And more to the point, what did Dan? Especially when he had a stunner like Phoebe.

'How's the break-in hit you? Have you lost a lot?'

Vic shrugged. 'A fair bit.'

'It's only stuff, Vic. I bet if you wrote it all on those white stones and dropped it out in The Hub corridor, you'll have forgotten about it by next week.'

Vic shook his head. 'It's not the stuff that bothers me, it's my laptop. Why did they have to take my laptop? It had my book on it and I was only ten pages off finishing.'

'A book you were reading? Or writing?'

'Writing. It was all about The Garden and The Fold. I only had the final summary left to do.'

'Did you not save it onto a USB stick?' Pete asked him.

'A what?'

No, obviously not.

'Well, maybe it's not such a bad thing. A book like that – books like that, tend to get cult followings. We'd have all sorts of weirdos turning up on our doorstep. Not to mention the media, labelling *us* as weirdos. I'd hate that, wouldn't you?'

Vic stared at him and furrowed his brow.

'It wasn't going to be for sale. To the ignorant masses. It was only for in here,' he responded, indignantly, 'Something to pass down to future custodians of the place. To explain how The Garden came about and what it actually means, to be in The Fold.'

'Ah, then that would be interesting, bearing in mind most people in here aren't exactly sure.'

Vic grinned at him.

'But you know what?' Pete continued, 'Maybe it works best that we all come to our own conclusions. Nobody can enlighten us better than ourselves.'

Vic nodded and pointed to the sign at the far side of his veranda.

You have to grow from the inside out. None can teach you. None can make you spiritual. There is no other teacher but your own soul – Swami Vivekananda

'Well hey-ho, there you go,' said Pete.

He picked up the teapot and poured.

‘Maybe you should start writing it again?’

Vic looked off into the distance, wistfully.

‘I think I’m past it now.’

He might be the oldest in there but Pete didn’t consider him past it.

‘Don’t be daft. You just need to get cracking. If you start now, you’ll remember most of it. Dictate it to Rin, so she can type it up for you.’

It might keep her from wandering off to cabin number eighty-five, Pete had a thought to add, but didn’t.

Vic was shaking his head.

‘You don’t think it was stolen on purpose?’ he asked, ‘Because members thought I was writing a book for popular consumption? Maybe they were worried about the bad publicity, like you obviously were.’

Pete shook his head.

‘I think they’d have confronted you about it first. These people aren’t shy about coming forward, Vic, it’s how they all got where they got.’

Vic nodded and eased back into his chair, then they sat, quietly deliberating, while sipping their tea.

‘So, you don’t want to know more about The Well? And The Vibration and Sound?’ Vic asked.

Pete shook his head.

‘You already told me as much as I needed to know. About you having used some of Tesla’s vibration theories, when you constructed it. About it being able to impact our nervous system and brainwaves on some sort of transcendental level. But if it does anything more than that, I think I’d prefer not to know.’

Vic nodded. ‘What about The Signs? You used to question me about them all the time.’

Pete shrugged. ‘The Signs I now mostly get. They’re out there to send us down unexplored avenues. To keep us thinking and questioning. And that’s what it’s all about, isn’t it?’

Vic nodded and smiled.

‘I see you’ve become very friendly with our latest recruits?’

‘Yes, I suppose we have. They’re injecting us with some youthful exuberance. Phoebe reminds me a lot of Sal. Full of it, but not always on it, if you know what I mean.’

Vic smiled. ‘She’s pregnant. Did she tell you?’

‘Well if she hadn’t, I think I’d have guessed by now.’

‘She needs to stop the pony trekking sessions but she refuses now that it’s become so popular. Maybe you and Sal could have a word with her?’

‘We could, but I doubt she’d take any notice,’ Pete quipped. ‘Is that why you got the donkey? To go out trekking with them?’

He’d seen the donkey on his way up to the cabin, tethered to a post and grazing on a mound of hay. Phoebe had obviously managed to coax it out of the scooter shed.

Vic pulled a disagreeable face as he shook his head.

‘I like to go off on my own. Up into the woods. He’s ideal now I’m not too steady on my feet. But they gave me the idea, I’ll admit to that. I’ve been trying to think of a name for him. What do you think to Eeyore?’

Vic was looking at him, straight-faced, but with a twinkle in his eye that caused Pete to wonder.

‘Too obvious,’ he told him.

They sat quiet for a few minutes.

‘Do you get on alright with being naked all the time?’ Vic randomly asked him.

Pete snorted a laugh. ‘It’s a bit late to be asking me that, isn’t it?’

Vic shrugged.

‘I don’t really think about it,’ Pete told him, realising an answer was expected. ‘I suppose I’ve just got used to it. At least it lets you ditch the vitamin D tablets. But it has to be said, it ruins your sex life to some extent.’

‘Does it?’

Pete nodded. ‘You no longer see yourself as naked. Naughty naked. Sexually arousing naked. Before I came here, a Pirelli calendar could get me going, but now, not even porn does it.’

‘You don’t think that’s your age?’

‘No. I think it’s just how it is. Maybe Eve eating that apple was the plan all along. For us to suddenly see the sexual allure of nudity. It’s what set us all on the horny path, so we’d be rattling each other's bones and creating offspring for ourselves. Saved him upstairs a job. Having to do it with endless rib borrowing. But other than that, it's got a lot of plusses. I guess the thing I like about it most, is that it strips us all down to being equal. There's no designer clothes to define us. No old school ties. No country squire attire. No stacked heels to lift us up and no Spanx pants to hold us in.'

'Except for Sunday nights,' said Vic.

'Except for Sunday nights, ' Pete agreed.

They both took a sip of their tea.

'Your flat cap defines you,' Vic told him, nodding at it.

'Maybe it does. But seeing as I don't want to get what you got, on top of my bonce, it's staying put. And besides, it's so old and tatty it gives folk the impression that I'm on my uppers.'

'Is that why you wear it? To counteract the fact that you're anything but?'

'Jeez, Vic, it's just a cap, not sackcloth and ashes. I'm attached to, like you are to your shepherd's crook thing.'

Pete was pointing to where it was leant against the hot-tub.

'It was a gift,' Vic told him, 'From Lilith. Not long before she died.'

Strange gift, thought Pete. Not like he had a flock of sheep. But then again, maybe he had.

They sat quiet for a couple of minutes.

'Does it ever bother you, being so wealthy?' Vic asked him.

'Are you having a laugh?'

'No, actually, I'm not. It would bother me, if I were in your shoes.'

'That's a bit rich. You're not short of a bob or two, yourself. What you getting at?'

Vic shrugged. '*It's easier for a camel to pass through the eye of a needle, than for a rich man to enter the kingdom of God.*'

Pete smirked. 'Then how come God made Solomon and Abraham so stinking rich? You quote from a load of contradictory old tosh.'

Vic smiled and poured more tea.

'You've not joined up with the church, have you? Like Tugs?' Pete questioned.

'Tugs?'

Pete had to think quick. 'Tim Tugster.'

'You mean Tim Webster?'

Of course he meant Tim Webster. 'Yes, that's him.'

Vic smiled and shook his head.

'No. I went a few times. But it wasn't for me. I'm still sticking to the Three B's.'

Vic's religion was what he called his Three Bs. Bible, Buddhism, and Beyond. Beyond being spiritualism. It always struck Pete as rather contrary, considering The Bible forbid belief in the other two.

'Mick the Vic keeps trying to get me down there,' Vic added, 'Or he did up until Covid, when it shut.'

Their local vicar had been thus named prior to Pete's arrival; it being the one name he couldn't put claim to. It made the hapless vicar sound like a gangster, and on first meeting him, one Speakers night, Pete had laughed to see that he looked less gangster and more ging gang goolie scout master. It had been Vic himself who had named him, but what Vic didn't know, was that due to his Irish ancestry, he in turn had been named Vic the Mick.

As for Mick the Vic, he might not be a gangster, but he had somehow managed to press gang Tugger into church going. That was the thing with inviting speakers. Over the years it had led to a loss of members. One couple had even left to join the Jehovah's Witnesses after Vic had allowed a dozen of them to go around the resort, knocking on doors.

'And you've never been tempted to go back for another visit?' Pete asked.

Vic shook his head. 'Nowhere in The Bible does it tell me I need a church. Especially one that's worth billions and counting.'

Pete nodded. 'My grandad used to tell us that we were born with a moral compass. And going to listen to a fella in a frock every Sunday wouldn't alter magnetic north.'

Pete was pointing skyward.

Vic weighed it up. 'Can I make a sign of that?'

'Course you can. Just don't let Mick the Vic clap eyes on it. I know he's only invited once or twice a year, but he'll never come again if he sees that.'

Vic gave him a thumbs up and they carried on sipping their tea, watching a barn owl as it swept low across the open meadow, scouting for unsuspecting prey.

'Have you never thought to add any other beliefs to your Three Bs?' Pete asked.

'Of course. I think about it all the time. Most religious teachings hold some truth. But not all religions are open to us, are they?'

'Aren't they?'

'No. They tell you as much. If you aren't born into them, then they aren't for you. Consider that sign, above the restaurant bar. *We are open to everything, except that which is not open to us.*'

Pete considered it. He'd thought the sign was to do with the bar's reduced opening hours, aimed at curbing people's alcohol intake, especially his own, seeing as his POTs were always EACs. Excessive Alcohol Consumption. Folk obviously thought he had a problem. Although, by rights, he should now be receiving multitudinous PIPs. Personal Imperfections Parodied. When the PIP acronym had been added to the POT form, back in April, Pete had been paranoid, thinking that Vic had somehow cottoned on to his defamatory name calling, creating it entirely for him, bearing in mind it was also the name of his first wife. But the paranoia had gradually abated, seeing as he'd yet to receive a single PIP POT.

A green woodpecker was laughing, somewhere nearby, and Pete wondered if it was the same one that had flashed across in front of him on his way up.

'Do you ever look back and think about your Amazing Grace Moment?' Vic asked him.

'No, I prefer not to. I know it's what brought us all here, but I think if you asked them, the majority of members would say they preferred to forget. What about you?'

'I think about it all the time. I think the minute we forget will be the minute we lose sight of what our life is intended for. It's the one thing that actually opened our eyes to it all.'

Pete and Vic had talked about this before. Lots of times.

How, after their wives had died, it had seemed like a veil had been pulled back, giving them a panoramic view of the dark side of the world. A view that had left them both suicidal. Like the eating of the apple had enabled Adam and Eve to be like God, seeing good and evil, when previously they'd seen only the good, they had been blind until they saw. And how, after they had both prayed on their bended knees to have that veil returned, it was. And it had been like a rebirth. Like a second chance. And they'd vowed, just as John Newton had, to use their second chance for living a more meaningful, spiritual life.

'Do you still go visit the place he wrote it?' Vic asked.

'Before Covid I did, yes. You know my brother lives there?'

Vic nodded. 'Olney.'

Olney indeed. Home of Newton and his hymn.

'*Amazing Grace,*' Vic began to sing, deep and low, '*How sweet the sound ...*'

Pete joined in. '*That saved a wretch like me. I once was lost, but now am found. Was blind but now I see.*'

They smiled at each other.

'It still haunts me. That I let her down,' Vic told him, his smile instantly giving way to teary eyed emotion.

'You didn't let her down,' Pete told him, firmly, 'You did what you thought was right.'

They'd had this conversation before, many times, and would probably have it many more before they were through. Pete never knew what to say to convince him. Lilith had had cancer, the same as Pip, but hers had spread to such an extent that she was wracked with an ever-increasing pain. She'd begged Vic to help her end it. And he had. He'd left her with boxes of tablets and a bottle of whisky. But as he'd waited in another room, he'd panicked and rung for an ambulance.

When Lilith came around in the hospital, having had her stomach pumped, she'd told him she would never forgive him for it. It was that, and her lonely unassisted suicide only weeks later, that had left him so anguished and self-vilifying. Vic must have relived that fateful night a thousand times, playing it out like a horror film in his mind. How she'd driven to her favourite beach, right to the waves edge, before leaving her car to walk into the sea and let the riptide take her, and her pain, away. The police had managed to provide Vic with periodic camera footage of her journey there, clearly seen, wearing her best hat and coat for the event. And it had destroyed him. At least there had been letters left for Eve and Adam, written prior to her first failed attempt, giving them some closure. But for Vic, there had been no letter. His only consolation had been in receiving messages, via Rosa, confirming she had survived death. But there hád never been a message to say he was forgiven.

Down in the meadow, Pete could see two people walking along the riverside. It was The Rippers. He recognised them from the mass of red, curly hair on Lydia's head.

'I'm glad they're out and about again. It must have been a huge relief to find out the two bodies weren't their exes.'

Vic leaned forward to see who Pete was talking about.

'Won't stop people speculating though, will it?'

Pete shook his head. He guessed not.

'Any idea how long the Shovelbums are going to be with us, digging up the fairways?'

Vic shrugged but stayed tight-lipped.

'It's your land, you know. You don't have to have them here, if you don't want,' Pete told him.

Other than looking away, Vic gave no response at all.

'I know it was some sort of leader and his wife, but if they've found the chief, all they're likely to find now are a few Indians,' Pete stated.

Still no response from Vic.

'If that course stays shut for much flamin' longer, my chuffin' handicap is going to go up,' Pete declared in frustration.

Vic finally made eye contact.

'There was more than just the bodies,' he divulged, 'There was grave goods. Swords, helmets, buckles, brooches. Silver *and* gold. It was quite a hoard. All of which has been turned over to The Crown. But when The Crown has assessed it, I'm likely to get a share of it, with it was being found on my land.'

Pete stared at him. How had that remained a secret?

'And you're hoping they find more, if they keep digging?'

As Vic nodded, Pete shook his head.

'What was it you were saying earlier? About being too rich to get into heaven? For a man who likes to quote from The Bible, you surprise me. Think on what the sign in the golf house says.

Do not store up for yourselves treasures on earth, where they can decay and be stolen, but store them up in heaven, where they are everlasting.'

Vic smiled. 'Touché,' he responded.

'But you're not going to reconsider?'

As Vic shook his head, Pete shrugged.

'So be it. But I can't see why you and me couldn't get a couple of metal detectors and go out looking ourselves, early doors. If we found another hoard, you wouldn't need to even tell The Crown. And you'd get to keep it all for yourself.'

Vic's eyes were suddenly wide at the prospect.

'Why on earth didn't I think of that? You're right, Peter, you're right. Tomorrow, I need to give them all the heave-ho. I've to give two months as a notice period, but they'll be gone before you know it. And let's just hope they don't find anything, beforehand.'

Rin came out with the biscuits that Pete had smelt baking for the past half hour. They were well received.

'Do you know what Gabe does for a living?' Vic asked him.

Pete smirked. 'Course I do. Some days he's on his phone from dawn till dusk. Wheeling and dealing.'

'In what?'

'Surely you know?' Pete countered.

Vic shrugged.

'He's a second-hand car salesman,' Pete told him, 'At least that's what I call him. But he's actually got a chain of garages right across Greater London. Vast garages, selling vast numbers of cars. Why d'you ask?'

'I heard someone calling him a cockney spiv. I thought it sounded a bit dodgy.'

Pete grinned. 'I don't think you're too far wrong. I think he might go in for clocking a few of them.'

Pete helped himself to another biscuit.

'I hear Dan's a fireman?'

'He was,' Vic replied, 'But I don't think he'll be going back to it, somehow. Not after the baby's been born.'

'Do you mind me asking how he can afford to be here? On a fireman's salary?'

'I've no idea.'

Pete knew Vic well enough to know that he was lying, but not enough to know why.

Darkness was falling and the nightlights in the canopy were prompted to come on.

'Are you still leaving your leaflets in the Harley Street clinics?' Pete asked.

'Not done that for a long time. Once we were full, I didn't see the point. It only meant turning people away.'

Pete had been passed the details of The Garden by his therapist, Harry Gascoigne. The perfect retreat for people recovering from traumatic breakdowns. Wealthy people, seeing as he only canvassed Harley Street. They had to be, if they were to meet The Garden's annual membership fees, and ultimately, buy their own cabin. Rest and recuperation had been what they'd expected, but they'd soon found out it wasn't the only thing on offer.

'Rin! Rin!' Vic was suddenly shouting, causing Pete to drop his biscuit in his tea.

Rin came rushing out onto the deck.

'Pee bag's full,' he snapped, as if it was her fault.

As she came and pulled open his dressing gown, Pete could see the bag hanging between his legs. It was hooked onto a band around his waist and it wasn't dissimilar to the one Pete had recently had attached into his arm, only Vic's was catheterised into his penis. And whereas Pete's had been putting fluid in, Vic's was clearly taking fluid out.

'Water infection,' Vic said to him, seeing Pete somewhat disconcerted. 'Antibiotics. Making me piss myself.'

Pete nodded, as if he was only too familiar with the problem. Thankfully, he wasn't.

Rin attached a new bag and scurried away with the old.

'I feel more like ninety-six than seventy-six,' Vic murmured, either to himself or to Pete, Pete wasn't sure.

'You didn't have it on last week when we were in The Well?'

'No. I just peed in the pool. Same as you do,' Vic told him.

'What makes you think I do that?'

'You told everybody. Last night, when we played truth or dare.'

'I don't remember giving a truth? I must have been absolutely ratted.'

'And some.'

Rin brought out a fresh pot of tea; her flour dusted apron making her look homely and wholesome.

'Has she never fancied joining in with the naturist thing?' Pete asked, once she was gone.

Vic shook his head. 'Even if she did, I wouldn't let her. Somethings are best kept for yourself.'

Pete felt inclined to tell him that things weren't being kept for himself, they were being shared, with Dan.

'Do you love her?' he asked.

Vic looked surprised by the question.

'Of course. What makes you ask that?'

Pete felt sad. He'd have preferred it if he hadn't.

'No reason, really. Just there's such a big age difference between you.'

Vic shuffled in his seat, clearly uncomfortable.

'I dare say she'd be better off with someone nearer her own age, but then I'm not stopping her. We're not married. She could easily leave me for somebody younger if she wanted.'

Pete nodded. She might already have. And who would change his pee bag then?

They sat, silent for a while, watching the barn owl in the fading light.

'Any ideas as to who might have robbed you?' Pete eventually asked.

'None. Not even a suspicion.'

'Who else has been into your office? Who might have seen what you had there and taken a fancy to it?'

Vic thought about it.

'A couple of the speakers we've had. Those who wanted paying in pound notes.'

'And you opened the safe right in front of them?'

'I don't have a safe. I keep the cash in a tin, in my bottom drawer.'

'Well hey-ho, there you go.'

Vic shook his head. 'The tin was untouched. Along with the cash.'

Pete was surprised. What kind of thieves would leave the readies behind?

'Did these speakers show an interest in anything?'

Vic nodded. 'My Airfix spitfires, hanging from the ceiling. And no, before you ask, they're still hanging. But neither of them are capable of breaking and entering. Too fat for a start. Toby something or other. Remember him? And that recent Buddhist I really liked. Ganja man.'

'Genji,' Pete corrected. Ganja man was what The Squatters called Arek.

It was getting late and Pete knew Sal would be wondering where he was. He stood to go.

'I'd like you to take over as custodian of The Fold, Peter. Lead everyone on Be-twitching nights and select our speakers. Take care of the signs and the spiritual stuff. I'm getting too old for it now.'

'Why me?'

'Because I believe you're the one who's the most enlightened.'

'Vic, I can assure you, I'm not. Not at all. I'm not your man.'

Vic smiled at him, like Jesus to a child.

'Come back next Saturday,' he told him, 'We can talk about it some more. And I'll tell you just why you are.'

CHAPTER ELEVEN

ONE DAY IN SEPTEMBER

'Thanks for coming, Pete,' Dan said to him, as they met at The Bridge.

'My pleasure. It's months since I've been on a good walk. Where we heading?'

'I've no idea. I was hoping you'd know a route.'

Pete thought about it, but not for long.

'Have you got time to do about seven miles?'

'Lead the way,' said Dan, rubbing his hands together in a show of eagerness.

They cut across the open meadow where the last of the wild flowers were throwing a riotous leaving party.

Pete had taken off his shirt, but otherwise the two of them were dressed. The weather had been changeable of late and when the temperature dropped, it dropped so sudden that it left you with what Sal called the *plucked look.*

The path that led them up through the wooded valley side was steep and uneven and their hiking boots were put to good use as they clambered over exposed roots and rocky outcrops.

Pete loved the smell of the Scots pine first thing on a morning and he picked up a windblown branch and sniffed at its bleeding resin.

It took them the best part of an hour to reach the high rim, although they would have reached it sooner if not for the many signs they stopped to read along the way; Dan asking for Pete's interpretation of each and every one. The topmost sign read:

The true miracle is not walking on water or air but simply walking on the earth – TNH.

No interpretation being needed.

Following the sand and grit path, they came to a clearing in the trees, providing them a view of the valley below. A bench had been placed there since Pete's last visit and on the back of it was a plaque which read: *For Lilith.*

'I never knew this place existed,' Dan remarked, opening his backpack to retrieve drinks and snacks.

'Well shame on me, because I did, and I'd forgotten just how amazing it was,' Pete confessed.

They sat in silence, giving reverence to the serenity of the sunlit valley.

'Are you all geared up for fatherhood, then?' Pete finally asked, helping himself to a bag of nuts.

'I've been trying not to think about it. Which is proving difficult now that Phoebs' bump has expanded so much. It's kind of there, every time I look,' Dan replied. 'You've got kids, haven't you?'

Pete nodded. 'Three boys. To the first wife.'

'Care to share any fatherly advice?'

'Don't overindulge them. Nurture them. Guide them. But don't ruin them by giving it all on a plate, like I did.'

'Yours not turn out too well, then?'

'Lousy. You've heard of the prodigal son? Well I have three. They're out to spend their inheritance before I die and then come back afterwards for another shake of the tree.'

'Did they not want to go into business, like you?'

Pete snorted derision. 'They had companies, but they were companies that I set up for them. Companies that all went bust. They were under the impression that having your own firm meant leaving it in the hands of feckless friends while jetting off on endless holidays.'

Dan rolled his eyes, to sympathise.

'All three of them have been married,' Pete cared to go on, 'One of them, twice. And not one of those marriages lasted longer than a year. And I paid for all of them.'

'Shit, Pete, that's really bad luck.'

'Luck? Luck has nothing to do with it. The women they married, married them for their money. Glamour models who marry men who look like they do, don't do it for love,' he scoffed. 'I paid for their divorces too.'

Dan shuffled, uneasily. 'Any grandkids?'

'Thankfully, no. I can only imagine what type of fathers they'd be. Absent ones more than likely. I couldn't be more ashamed of them if they roasted small children and ate them.'

'That's how I feel about my brother, Scott,' he divulged. 'The black sheep in our family. He's just got out of the nick, for the third time.'

Pete acted surprised, careful not to show that he already knew, courtesy of Jake.

'How long was he in for?' he asked.

'Five and a half years. I knew he was a coke head. What I didn't know, was that while I was breaking into people's houses to rescue them, he was breaking in to rob them, to fund his habit.'

'And is he clean, now?'

Dan shrugged. 'So he says.'

They sat, listening to the birdsong and watching the squirrels gathering in their winter larder.

'Can I ask you something, Pete?'

'Sure. Fire away.'

'Do you think people are okay with us, with me and Phoebs, being here?'

'Sure they are. What makes you think they might not?'

'I don't know, but we haven't been invited to your AGM for starters.'

Pete looked at him. 'We don't have an AGM?'

'Yes, you do. We missed it. And people are talking about it.'

'Whoa there, fella. Just a minute. Who exactly is talking?'

'The twins. The Shining. They said we were too young and that we shouldn't be here because we haven't had an AGM. But we didn't know when it was.'

Pete lifted an eyebrow and grinned.

'Well you are young, compared to the rest of us, aren't you?'

'Yes. Obviously. But is that a problem?'

'Not in itself, no. It's just that at your age, it's unlikely that you've had what we call an Amazing Grace Moment. Some call it an AGM, for short. It's something that most people here have had. It's what brought us all here in the first place. But I'm guessing it's not what brought you.'

Dan looked at him, blankly.

'You've heard the hymn?' Pete asked.

'Yes. It's what we sing before we go into The Well.'

'And do you know how that hymn came about?'

Dan shook his head.

'The chap who wrote it was a successful slave trader back in the day. But on one of those days, his boat got shipwrecked and he cried out to God to save him. And saved he was. After that, he realised he'd previously been blind to what the true purpose of life was. Hence the words, *Was blind but now I see.*'

Pete had always thought it a God-given coincidence that it should be The Garden's anthem, after having spent nigh on two years living in its town of origin. Two years, spent pulling his brother from the clutches of despair and depression, just like his brother had done for him not so many years before. And in rescuing his brother, he'd also rescued his ailing garden centre business, rescuing it to the point of one garden centre becoming three. And not just centred on the garden either. They were veritable cornucopias of delight for the ladies who lunched. They had restaurants, pet shops, up-market clothing, al-fresco cafes, delicatessens, home furnishings and art galleries. And as the business had thrived, so had his brother.

'So, you've all been shipwrecked?' Dan asked.

Pete immediately burst out laughing.

'Course we haven't, yer chump. But I dare say something not dissimilar. Something that brought us all to our knees, calling out to God, to the universe, to our departed relatives, to anyone we thought might listen. So desperate were we for help.'

'Has everyone here had an AGM?' Dan asked, intrigued.

'Not everyone, but certainly one half of each couple that's in here. And in more than a few cases, both of them. Two couples here have lost a child, in dreadful circumstances. Another couple survived a helicopter crash. If I thought about it, I could probably tell you all their AGMs. We're not shy about them. We've bared our souls.'

'Have you had an AGM?'

'I certainly have.'

'And Sal?'

'Of a sort, yes.'

'So you came here together?'

Pete shook his head. 'I was already here and initiated before Sal arrived. And then of course she had to do her year, before she could be initiated. That's what it normally takes, a year.'

'To reach initiation?'

As Pete nodded, he could see Dan now realising their welcome into The Fold hadn't been the norm, at only two months. But he didn't look unduly bothered by it.

'What about Gabe and Jude? Did they have an AGM?'

'Jude did. Gabe just came here on the back of hers. Thing is, about Jude and Gabe, it was him that wanted to join, when it finally came to it, and her that didn't.'

'What happens if you've done your year and you don't want to join?'

'You leave. End of.'

Pete was beginning to realise that Dan and Phoebe hadn't been given the choice, because it was an answer Dan would have already known.

'How come you were first here on your own, when it's a couples only club?'

'Not to begin with it wasn't. That only came about after Adam and Eve's partners ran off with single guests. I think Vic decided it was safer to restrict it after that.'

Dan looked at him, confused.

'I thought Adam and Eve ran off with each other?'

'Not that Adam and Eve. I meant Vic's step-kids.'

Dan chewed it over.

'Okay, then what about Tabitha? How come she's allowed to be here on her own?'

'Because half the time, she isn't. It's just that James and Joe have to take it in turns. They don't trust their staff to run their business without one of them being there. The exact opposite of my sons.'

Dan had another chew.

'Were you the only single person back then?'

'Not the only one, no, but there weren't many of us. I remember ShamPain being single.'

'What about his wife, Becky? Was she single? Is this where they met?'

'She was here, but she was married to Prunie back then.'

‘No way?’

Pete nodded and smiled. He realised they all had so much history that just went unsaid.

‘But Prunie invited ShamPain on his stag-night?’ Dan pointed out.

‘Why wouldn’t he? He doesn’t hold it against him. And besides, once your ex remarries, you no longer have to pay them maintenance. He owes the guy.’

Pete could see Dan was fascinated by it all.

‘Anyroad, now you know why people are saying you shouldn’t be here.’

‘And maybe we shouldn’t.’

‘Yes, but you are. And there’s obviously a reason that you are.’

Dan stood up and slung his pack onto his back.

‘There is, but I can’t tell you, Pete.’

‘And I’m not asking you to, so leave it be.’

They walked toward the valley head, passing an abundance of fig trees. In the midst of them was a staked sign:

Then the eyes of Adam and Eve were opened and they realised they were naked, so they sewed together fig leaves to make coverings for themselves – Genesis.

‘I can’t believe how easily I took to going naked,’ Dan shared with him, ‘What about you? How long did it take you to adjust?’

‘About five seconds. It never bothered me in the slightest. What did bother me, was other men, looking at Sal. When I first brought her here, I was watching them all the time. Looking for the slightest glint of lust in their eyes.’

Dan was laughing. ‘Believe it or not, that’s how Phoebs has been over me. Crazy, eh? When she looks like she does, it should be the other way around.’

‘Maybe she thinks some wealthy old bird’s going to tempt you away to a life of luxury. Same as what happened with Eve’s fella.’ He was tempted to add, ‘Or maybe you’ve got a habit of straying and she simply doesn’t trust you.’ But he didn’t.

‘That would never happen,’ Dan declared, ‘I couldn’t give a shit about being rich. It’s Phoebs that hankers after all that. She’s not greedy or anything. She just doesn't want us to spend our whole lives struggling, like our parents have.'

Pete smiled and nodded but he considered the struggle served people well, he only had to look at his three sons to appreciate that.

They followed the well-worn path, circumnavigating the briar-rose and the buckthorn that frequently tumbled into it. On a whim, Pete took them off at a tangent along a new track that had sprung up as an off-shoot. It led them around thickets of holly, rhododendron and gorse, until they reached the high wire perimeter fence that kept them all corralled in The Garden. A narrow deer path lay adjacent to it and Dan didn't hesitate to follow along it. It took them to where a neatly cut hole had been snipped through the wire mesh.

'I bet this is the work of our burglar,' said Dan.

Pete wasn't so sure. It was a long way to come, carrying a bag of swag.

'Come on, let's check it out,' Dan suggested, already through to the other side.

Pete quickly threw on the shirt that had been tied around his waist and tucked it into his pants.

Up ahead, on a path overhung with birch, Dan had stopped and turned to him. He was holding up a stone. A white stone. A potato sized stone.

Pete caught up and took it from him. There was black writing on one side. *Aston Martin Vantage*. It was Gabe's. Pete had watched him write it.

'There's more. Come and see,' Dan told him.

The white stones lay central to the path, all placed approximately five yards apart. Pete picked up another one. *Catamaran in Portofino*.

'Who do you think put them here?' Dan asked.

'Why. Is the more pressing question,' said Pete, picking up another. *Birkin*. Whatever the hell that was.

These were the surfeit stones. The ones left behind on their tables. The ones they'd failed to shed on their pilgrimage of Lightening Enlightenment.

The trail took them on a convoluted route through dips and hollows, with Pete likening it to the trail of bread in Hansel and Gretel. At least with these they could be confident of finding their way back, stones being inedible.

'Here, Pete, come and take a look at this,' Dan yelled to him from further ahead.

The stone trail came to a halt on the edge of a small clearing in the trees, at the centre of which lay a perfectly hemispherical, ominously black, miniature version of The Dome. But smooth metal rather than glass panel.

Pete guessed it to be about five metres in diameter, putting its height at two and a half. It had a very discreet door, which Dan immediately went to try, clearly disappointed to find it locked.

'What do you think it is?' he asked.

'Beats me.'

Pete had taken his mobile out of his back pocket and was searching for Vic in his contacts. He called him, twice, but it failed both times due to lack of signal. So much for Sal insisting on him bringing it, for emergencies.

They wandered around the mound, drawn to running their hands across its matt black surface. At the rear, they found a sign stuck upon it.

He determines the number of the stars and calls them each by name – Psalms.

'Vic's got a hand in this, whatever it is,' Pete observed.

They retreated back to where they'd first branched off, finding themselves suddenly surrounded by fallow deer. They were everywhere. Lifting their grazing heads to stare at them as they went past.

'Is it normal for them to be this tame?' Dan asked.

'It is when there's a fella laying out a line of deer-nuts for you every day. It's probably as addictive as a line of coke,' Pete replied, and then, 'Sorry, mate. Forgot about your brother.'

'Hey, coke, deer-nuts, gambling, rubber-rides, we've all got our addictions.'

Further along, they came to a sign lying on the path, clearly blown there by the wind. Pete went to hang it back on its nearby tree hook.

Religion is for people who are afraid of going to hell. Spirituality is for those who've already been there – Vine Deloria Jr.

Dan reacted in an instant. 'That one's for you, Pete. For all of you who've had an AGM.'

Pete slapped him on the back. The lad was learning.

'What do you think to organised religions?' Dan asked, as they walked alongside.

Pete gave it some thought.

'I reckon there's a lot that we can take from them. But to believe in any one of them, blindly, exclusively, every single word, is a mistake. It means closing yourself off to all other sources of enlightenment.'

'What about evolution?'

'Nah, never. We're born with a conscience. We feel guilt. We feel grief. We feel love. We feel joy. None of those things can be put down to evolution, because none of them are needed for our long-term survival. And there's not enough evidence of transitional species. The complexity of a cell means it could never just cut a piece of itself away, which is what would be needed to make the significant jumps. One of our regular speakers is an evolution debunker. Hopefully you'll be here long enough to hear him.'

As they walked on, Pete's phone pinged as it picked up a signal and a message. He took it out of his back pocket and read the text.

The Squatters have got the clap. It was from Gabe.

Pete thought about it for a second and then sent a text to Jake, asking if it were true.

'Are those eagles?' Dan asked.

Pete put a hand over his eyes to peer up into the clear blue sky. There were six or seven of them, circling on the rising thermals.

'Kites. Red Kites.'

'Makes me glad I'm not a squirrel,' said Dan.

'You'd have to be a dead squirrel. They only want you when you're slightly ripe.'

Ahead was a staked sign at the side of the path and they stopped to read it.

You only live twice. Once when you are born. And once when you look death in the face – Ian Fleming.

'Another one you can attach to our Amazing Grace Moments,' Pete remarked of it.

Dan nodded with enthusiasm.

'I really wish we'd done this sooner, Pete.'

'Me too. We should maybe do it every week. It'll help to keep my weight down.'

'I wasn't meaning the walk. I was meaning the talk. I know we're meant to find our own way and all that, but me and Phoeb, we're not that clever. I'm not sure we think deep enough to find any sort of enlightenment.'

'Don't talk daft. Some of the world's greatest intellectuals are some of the most stupid people on the planet. They're blinded by their own brains. They don't see. And they don't seek. All you have to do, is look up at the sky. Every morning. Look up at it and ask yourself, where does it end? We're all here in the middle of infinity and yet day after day, we never give it a second thought. But it's mind-blowing. So go on, every morning, do it. And ask for guidance, while you're at it. It'll come, soon enough. Don't need to be clever to do that.'

'No, I guess not,' said Dan. 'You know, I've learnt more in one morning with you, than I have the whole time I've been here. You should be a teacher. You're like one of those wise men who sit meditating on top of a mountain. There's a name for them?'

'Yogis.'

'That's it. That's what I'm going to call you from now on. Yogi.'

Karma had been delivered. The namer had been named. Pete knew it had to happen, eventually.

A narrow bridge spanned the river at the head of their three-tiered waterfall and they stood upon it, watching the water curve into its descent. Pete closed his eyes and let the rising mist settle upon his face. Life had never felt so good.

At the far side, a warning sign certified the danger of an overhanging rock ledge, but with total disregard, Pete climbed up onto it and began to strip. He took off everything barring his underpants and then he set his mobile phone to camera and passed it to Dan.

'Snap it,' he shouted, sitting himself down, crossed legged, and pushing his palms together in a recognised pose of meditation.

Dan snapped.

'Sal will go mad when she sees that one,' Dan said to him, passing it back once Pete had dressed.

'After the ones she saw of the stag-do, I doubt it.'

Pete chose the best of the three shots and then sent it directly to Vic, with the caption: *Yogi*.

The signal was now at full strength and he instantly received a call back.

'Does that mean you're accepting?' Vic asked him.

Pete didn't hesitate. 'Yes. I reckon it does.'

Vic was overjoyed and didn't hide it.

'Did you know we've got a hole in our perimeter fence, up at the top of the valley?' Pete asked, 'It's probably where our intruders came through.'

'It's my hole. Nothing to do with any intruders. And that's not the perimeter. There's another fence further out. We're double skinned.'

'The hole's Vic's,' Pete said to Dan, as an aside.

'Who's there with you?' Vic immediately asked.

'Dan. We're out on a hike.'

Dan was eagerly hovering. 'Ask him about the stones and the domed thing?' he prompted.

Pete didn't need to, Vic had heard.

'The stones are there for me to follow with my torch, in the dark. And the domed thing is an observatory.'

Pete had put his phone onto speaker so Dan could hear.

'Are you into astrology?' Dan asked.

'Astronomy. Yes,' Vic replied.

Dan shook his head, realising his mistake.

'Why don't you drop by to see me, Peter, tomorrow morning?' Vic suggested.

'Aye, alright. We'll get some breakfast delivered in, like we used to.'

Pete rang off and he and Dan began their steep descent into the valley bottom.

There was a canvas sign, midway down, strung high across the path.

Remember to look up at the stars and not down at your feet. Try to make sense of what you see and wonder about what makes the universe exist – Stephen Hawking

'On a path like this, you've got to look down at our feet, otherwise you'd definitely end up seeing stars,' Dan quipped.

Pete wasn't listening. He was thinking about the observatory. Wondering why Vic had taken to star gazing. He'd never mentioned it before.

When they finally came out of the trees, onto the valley floor, Dan immediately set off back toward the lake with Pete feeling obliged to follow.

The huge, water riven rocks that sat in a heap on its near side, mirrored the rocks on its far side, brought down by the unceasing torrent. As they clambered up onto the highest of the heap, Pete realised that the waterfall would at one time have been right there. How many years lay between the two was impossible for him to guess.

They sat to watch the swallows as they skimmed across the lake's surface, ultimately to land on Rosa's washing line. They were gathering for their journey south and Pete knew they would be gone in a matter of weeks, heading for warmer climes, just as they themselves retreated into The Dome, October through to March.

Dan nudged him, prompting him to look down upon a group of fish, biting at the surface. The clear water magnified their brown speckled backs and Pete was reminded of the liver spots on the back of Sal's legs, the ones she was constantly going off-site to have 'tasered'.

A sudden raucous screech had them both looking up to see someone shoot out of The Dome's chute, falling into the lake with an enormous kaploosh. Another soon followed. A man. And then a woman, doing an unintentional back flip and landing with arms and legs flailing.

'Why do you call her Noose?' Dan asked.

Pete had to think about it. 'Because she's highly strung.'

The woman emerged, arms in the air, woohooing.

'Doesn't strike me as highly strung.'

'That's because Sal fixed her. But you're right, I should rename her.'

'What do you mean by fixed?'

Pete took a long breath.

'Sal's AGM was on the back of a menopause from hell. The catastrophic drops in her oestrogen levels took her to a really bad place. They wouldn't let her take HRT because her mother had died of breast cancer, so she was forced to try everything else. CBT. Acupuncture. Antidepressants. She even tried knicker magnets at one point.'

'Knicker magnets?'

Pete nodded. 'You shove them down the front of your knickers and they're supposed to empower your ovaries. But with Sal, they just empowered everything else. She once found herself stuck to a supermarket trolley and couldn't get off.'

Dan thought it hilarious.

'And she advised Noose to try the knicker magnets?'

'No, she advised her to use HRT, because in the end, that's what she did. The risks just became worth it.'

They watched the three Eden Lakers as they swam to the shore and scampered back toward The Dome.

'Fancy a swim?' Dan suggested, suddenly pulling off his shirt.

'No thanks. But you go right ahead. I'll take your clothes and leave them in the changing room.'

He was already gathering them up. If Dan had any ideas about following his swim with a visit to cabin eighty-five, he'd have to go cold, wet and barefoot.

The enormous steel and glass dome sat like an alien outpost hidden in their blind valley, and as Pete walked toward it, he saw Rosa beckoning him from the steps of her caravan. She was far enough away for him to pretend he hadn't seen her. The last thing he wanted was any more messages of impending doom.

'No laps today, Pete?' Jake asked him as he swum up to the bar.

'Nup. Been on a long hike with Dan. No point overdoing it.'

There were already three stools taken out of the six that curved around the bar and the three men that were sat upon them were huddled in deep conversation. Mo was in the middle with Sugar and Spice sat either side of him. Pete liked Mo, but he liked Sugar and Spice more. They were famous TV chefs and their apt stage names meant Pete hadn't felt inclined to appoint them with any others. One did the spicy cooking, while the other did the sugary. Main course followed by dessert. They played perfectly to stereotypes. Spice being saucy and suggestive, outrageous and rude, with Sugar being all flambé and flamboyance, hysterical and camp. Neither were the people they portrayed. They were both street corner tough and rugby hardened rough and Pete considered they were more like a couple of old lags than designer handbag fags.

Pete used his thumb and forefinger to squeeze the water out of his eyes, and then swivelled his stool so as to eavesdrop on the clustered conversation.

'Can I buy you gents a drink?' he interrupted.

It always raised a laugh.

'Yeh, we'll have whatever you're having,' Mo replied, but to Jake.

Jake set about producing four G and Ts.

'Somebody been upsetting you?' Pete asked them.

'No, sweetheart, we're just swapping notes on our questions for tonight. You know it's Mick the Vic?' said Sugar.

Pete nodded. The only speaker they ever got a heads-up about prior to arrival was the local vicar. He always held a question-and-answer session after his talk, which meant giving them fair warning to come up with some.

'Crack on. Don't mind me.'

'No, we're done, Pete. We're just heading off to the sandpit,' Spice told him.

Jake immediately produced a deep sided tray to put their drinks into, he was nothing if not efficient. Sugar took the tray and he and Spice waded away, only for one of The Swingers to swim up.

'Six Porn Star martinis, if you will, young man.'

Jake grinned as he set out his stall to making them, while Mo pulled Pete to one side.

'Can I ask you a favour?'

'Sure. Fire away.'

'It's not for me, it's for the missus. And it's actually for your missus.'

Pete could see he was finding it difficult to ask.

'Go on?' he told him.

'Could you ask Sal if she wouldn't mind knocking off the Carmen thing? It's starting to wear a bit thin.'

Pete was baffled, but not for long.

'Ah, Mo, that's my fault. I'm truly sorry. Please, can you tell Oprah that we're sorry. That it's all my fault, not Sal's. I know just how it's happened. Some months back, we were all talking about her name, Oprah. About it being unusual, like Sal's, being Salome. And then it prompted me to talk about opera, showing off like, saying my favourite was Carmen. I think Sal's just managed to get herself confused and been left with the impression that Oprah's actually called Carmen.'

'Aha, I get you,' Mo said to him, slapping him heartily on his wet back, 'Yeh, I can see how that's come about. But glad we got it sorted.'

'That was quick thinking,' Jake said to him, once Mo and the six Porn Star martinis were well out of the way.

'Tell me about it.'

Jake smirked. 'I'd love to see you get out of MoBigDick.'

Pete had never felt more relieved that one of his names had, over time, become shortened back to its original.

'I thought for a minute he was going to get on your case about the mystery tour.'

'How d'you mean?' asked Pete.

'Well, you conned them, didn't you? Telling them all they were going on a pilgrimage to the holiest peak in England, to sing its dedicated hymn.'

Pete thought back to the previous week, to their whistle-stop, rules-bent, blinds-down, double-decker bus trip.

'And that's what we did.'

'Yes, but they all thought they were going up Glastonbury Tor, to sing Jerusalem. Not to Yorkshire, to sing on Ilkley Moor Baht 'at.'

Pete shrugged. It was holy enough for him.

Another customer came and went.

'What type is it?' Pete asked, nodding down at Jake's undercarriage.

'Chlamydia.'

'And have they put you all on antibiotics?'

'It's not all of us. Just a dozen of us. But I'm the one being blamed for it.'

'Why's that?'

Jake sighed. 'They think it was me that brought it in because I'm the only one who's been off site since the restrictions were lifted. But why wouldn't I? I only live in the village. It's not my fault the others live so bloody far away.'

'And am I to assume you had a bit of a skirmish, while you were in the village?'

'Just a couple,' Jake admitted.

'Oh dear. And now you're in the doghouse.'

'Worse. I'm in the golf house. On a bunk in the back room.'

Pete began to chuckle.

'It's not funny. I could be infertile after this. And it'll be on my medical records. Which means if I'm ever in an accident, my mum and dad will find out.'

Pete pointed to the sign at the back of the bar.

You don't have to believe everything you think – Erykah Badu.

'Pointless worrying about things that might not happen,' Pete told him, realising it applied as much to himself as to Jake.

Jake just shook his head and looked forlorn.

'Do you want me to get a specialist doctor to come in and see you?'

Jake looked uncharacteristically emotional.

'Would you do that?'

'Yes. If the antibiotics haven't nuked it by this time next week.'

Jake held up the flat of his hand and Pete gave him a high five. Then ShamPain arrived, to give Jake another, without any question as to why. Was high fiving contagious? Clearly not as contagious as Chlamydia. If ShamPain had known about that, Pete doubted he'd have come within swimming distance.

'I'm thinking of off-loading some of my shares,' Jake said to Pete, as he passed over a second gin and tonic, 'The ones Ginnel gave me for saving his wife.'

Pete had forgotten about Mary's seizure in the middle of the pool. He had been sat on that very stool, explaining to Jake what a mugwump was, when Jake had leapt onto the bar and dived right over his shoulder, resurfacing with a spasming Mary. Ginnel had bestowed on him some shares from his company, in heartfelt gratitude.

'Any reason why?' Pete asked, intuitively aware that Jake wanted him to.

'We're worried that the rent's going to go up on our cottages. The whole row of us.'

Pete showed some concern. Over the years, he'd learnt all about Jake and his family. They lived in a terraced row of six, in their entirety. Grandma and Grandad at one end; mum, dad, sisters and brothers in the middle; and Jake, with a steady stream of girlfriends, at the other end.

'Somebody in the village says their rent's just gone up by double and they've got the same landlord.'

Pete shook his head. 'The government needs to be putting a block on rent increases through the pandemic.'

'It wouldn't matter if they did. He'd pay no attention to it. He's a right arrogant arsehole. Which means I've got to get ahead of the game. I'm the only one of us with a job right now. So, what do you know about shares? You must be an expert in them.'

'Not a clue. Never had any. I'm too risk averse. My brass is in things I can actually see. Gold. Property. Land.'

'Barnsley Rovers.'

Pete smiled as he nodded. 'Aye, Barnsley Rovers. But let me have a word with a mate of mine and get him to give you a call.'

'Thanks, Pete.'

Just then, high-pitched feedback whistled over the PA system, having them all reaching to cover their ears. And then Vic's voice arrived, loud and clear.

'Hello. Good afternoon. Just to inform you that this evening there will be a Congregational Court. Six o'clock prompt, before the start of dinner. Please be aware that you are all required to attend. Our after-dinner speaker will go ahead as planned. Thank you.'

That was it.

Jake stared at Pete. 'That's two in two months,' he remarked.

Pete was as surprised as he was. Looking around, he could see that they all were. They had stopped swimming, to stand and listen, and they were still standing. Jake was right, they'd only just had one the month before, albeit a double one, while the one before that had been so far back, he couldn't even remember.

'Tell me how it works again?' Jake asked.

'You're not supposed to know.'

'Yes, but I do know because Blubs — Hi Chloe, what can I get you?'

The chance of her appearing, just at that moment, startled the pair of them.

'Nothing,' she said.

'Make it two,' said Three Lugs, her adoring husband, as he swam up from the opposite side, clearly not having heard her properly.

'I just thought I'd come and let you know who it is, who's drawn the Court,' Blubbermouth told them.

'What makes you think we want to know?' Pete asked, staring straight ahead, dismissively.

'Oh, stop being such a prig,' she told him, 'Everyone wants to know.'

'Yes, I want to know,' Jake agreed.

'So do I,' said Three Lugs, leaning forward, all ears.

'See,' she said to Pete, and then to Jake, 'It's Susanna Sutton. She's drawn it, but I've yet to find out who she's putting on the stand. I've got a bit of a suspicion, but when I know for sure, I'll let you know.'

She swam off toward the people sat on the terrace, with her husband following in her wake.

'Is Susanna Sutton —'

'Sasquatch, yes,' Pete confirmed.

Jake served a customer and then came back to him.

'Can anyone draw a court? If they get pissed off enough?'

Pete knew it was pointless evading, if he didn't tell him, Blubs would.

'Yes, if they consider they've received a Personal Injury, Injustice or Insult. What we call a PI.'

‘And it goes to a jury?’

‘Of a sort. First you present your gripe to Vic. Vic then decides if you can draw a Congregational Court for it. At the court, you state your PI, and the person you’ve called it against has to stand to deny it or admit it. Either way, it comes down to the jury. The Congregation. If twelve people or more stand to support the PI, the accused is immediately asked to leave The Garden.’

Jake stared at him with a look of unbridled excitement.

‘Don’t get too giddy. Last month, only one person stood to support either of them and that was their best friends. It was a total waste of time.’

The wives of Sheepteeth and Eeyore had each drawn a court, one against the other, for Personal Injury received on the back of their cat fight. It had been a fiasco. Vic should have dismissed them both out-of-hand, but for some reason, he hadn’t.

‘Yes, but what if—’

‘What time is it? Pete suddenly asked, cutting Jake off.

Jake was about to do his usual routine of consulting the position of the sun through The Dome’s roof, but Pete threw him a look that said, ‘Skip it’.

‘Half three,’ Jake told him, directly consulting his mobile, hidden under the bar counter.

‘Oh dear. She’s not going to be pleased.’

‘Sal?’

Pete nodded. ‘I promised her I’d be back for three.’

He knocked back his G and T, and with a goodbye salute, he flung himself off his stool and straight into a front crawl toward the pool’s exit.

‘I know I’m late, but I got talking to Mo and you know what it’s like, I just didn’t —’

‘Shut up and come and sit down,’ Sal said to him, pointing at the chair that had the whisky decanter beside it. It didn’t normally.

‘I’ve something I need to tell you,’ she told him, turning over a glass to pour him a measure.

Pete guessed it to be a quadruple.

‘Let me guess. It’s gone way over budget again?’ he sighed. ‘That house is turning into a chuffin’ money pit. What have you had fitted now? A gold plated jacuzzi?’

Sal pulled up a chair and sat down opposite him. She had some papers in her hand.

'I'm going to do the talking and you're going to do the listening, and you won't question, and you won't argue, and you'll agree with everything that I tell you.'

Pete stared at her. This wasn't the Sal he knew who was talking to him. He suddenly felt light-headed and far away. He nodded.

She reached and took his hand. 'I've got cancer. And it's terminal.'

It hit him like a bullet to the back of his brain.

'I don't want chemo. I don't want to lose my hair and look and feel like shit for weeks on end. I just want to go out with dignity.'

She put three letters into his hand. They were from the nearby hospital. Department of Oncology – Consultant Mr Singh.

Pete began to read. What was this? How was this? When was this? They were about options. Life expectancy. End of life care. And they were about Sal. His wife. Salome Hardcastle. Not somebody else. Her. He read them all. And then he stared at her, and as he stared, he realised tears were falling off the end of his chin.

'Nobody else knows,' she told him, 'Apart from Eve. And that's only because I asked her to intercept them in the post, to stop you from finding them in our mail box.'

Pete couldn't speak.

'I don't want anyone else to know. Nobody. Not one single person. Do you hear me?'

Pete stared at her. And then he threw up on the floor.

'Now don't go getting all maudlin on me, Peter Hardcastle. You're not going to blub. Tha's from Yorkshire, remember. You're going to pull yourself together and get on with it.'

Pete knew that no amount of pulling would keep him together. This was going to be the hardest thing he'd had to do, since doing it the last time, with his first wife.

He suddenly found his voice.

'We can beat this, Sal. We can find the best surgeons and the best treatment in the world.'

Sal put her hand up to stop him.

'It's too late. It's too advanced. And there's no way I'm having chemo and going bald. We're just going to carry on as normal, because that's how I want it. No fuss. No misery. Just doing all the things we normally do.'

Pete stared at her. Why wasn't she sobbing and shaking and screaming?

'I've had time to get my head around it, you haven't,' she told him, as if she were psychic, 'But you will. You'll see.'

'When?' he asked her. 'When did you find out? And why didn't you tell me? I could have been there for you?'

Sal shook her head. 'I didn't want you there. There's nothing you could have done. When I told you I was going for my beauty treatments, I was actually going to the hospital. It was probably the HRT that caused it. But I've no regrets. If it wasn't for that, I'd probably have jumped off a tower block by now.'

Pete flung his arms around her and wept. And then he wept some more. And then Sal pushed him away.

'I need to get this Moby cleaned up. Junior's eating it.'

What a remarkable woman she was. Pete would never have imagined her capable of such stoicism and bravery. Did it help that she now had faith in something? Had The Garden at least given her that? They used to discuss their slowly burgeoning spirituality, but since Covid, they rarely had. Was she convinced that she was headed for a better place? Was that the reason for her serene acceptance?

Later, when Pete looked up to see Sal stood before him, her hair in a chignon and her body in another one-off designer dress from TK Maxx, he realised he hadn't moved from where he'd been sat for near on two hours.

'Come on,' she told him, 'Or we'll be late. And I'm not missing this Congregational Court for anything, not even if it means going without you.'

Pete shook his head. It was like he'd lost the ability to function. Sal tutted at him and went to the wardrobe to pull out his suit, shirt and tie.

He dressed on automatic pilot, his internal conversation with TC still raging. Begging for help, for strength, for hope, for anything at all that might take this sudden nightmare away from them. His rough ride had begun.

CHAPTER TWELVE

NIGHT AFTER DAY

Pete and Sal were the last to take their seats in the capacity full restaurant. Their four friends already there and waiting. Very few people were talking, and when they did, it was in whispers. The drawing of a court was a serious matter and as no one had any idea what lay behind it, there was an air of nervous tension as they speculated who the claim would be against. Pete found himself wishing Blubs had actually known, and told them. It would have saved him the additional angst. Since Sal had delivered her news, his escalating anxiety had caused a tic to develop above his right eye, along with an unrelenting spasm in his lower bowel.

Vic was soon to rise to his feet, solemnly rattling off the order of proceedings, before inviting Sasquatch to stand, and with one hand on a bible, state her PI. She looked a little unsteady, but Pete considered her oversized feet would help keep her firmly planted.

'Rumours have been put about that my husband has been having an affair,' she began, 'Rumours that are totally unfounded and untrue. Rumours that are hurtful and spiteful and have resulted in making me feel humiliated and undermined. And for that, I wish to bring a Personal Injustice claim against the person responsible for those rumours. Chloe Hughes.'

They all looked to Blubbermouth to see that she was just as stunned as they were. She was clutching her chest like her heart was about to fail. Pete knew the feeling well, having had it himself not so many hours before.

There was a flurry of hushed, horrified conversation. Some were surprised, some weren't. Pete's table were, or at least the three men were. The three women seemed more concerned that the rumour of the alleged affair had previously passed them by.

Vic got to his feet again. 'Before I invite you to stand, Chloe, we have an unusual turn of events in that there are two claims being made against you. So I now invite David and Lydia Sutcliffe to stand.'

The Rippers stood, each with a hand on a bible.

'We wish to bring a Personal Injustice claim against Chloe Hughes,' Dave stated. 'Not just for spreading rumours, but for blatantly implying that we're guilty of murdering our previous partners. It's been excruciatingly traumatic. People have been going out of their way to avoid us, or eyeing us up from a distance with suspicion and mistrust.'

As The Rippers sat down, Vic stood up, and waved for Blubbermouth to do the same.

'I don't have anything to add to these claims,' Vic told them all, 'So it only remains for me to ask you, Chloe, do you admit them or deny them?'

Blubs, for once, was absolutely lost for words.

'Do you admit them? Or deny them?' Vic repeated.

She immediately burst into tears.

'I admit them,' she eventually responded, through racking sobs.

Vic held out both his arms like Jesus on the cross.

'The Congregation must now decide,' he said to them all. 'If twelve of you should rise, then the verdict will be an immediate expulsion.'

It was now up to them. Up to everyone barring the three accusers.

At first, nobody stood. But then, as soon as one stood, so did another, and another, and then it wasn't long before there were twelve and then thirteen, and fourteen, and fifteen, and then it stalled, and stopped.

'Fifteen people support the claims,' Vic announced, 'I thereby ask that you, Chloe Hughes, make necessary arrangements to leave The Garden of Eden, forthwith.'

Blubs had turned to her husband, Three Lugs, who had stood to bear her head while she blubbed, profusely, onto his shoulder.

There was a sudden loud, repeated, banging of a hand on a table.

They all looked to see that it was Pete.

'Let's just hang on here a minute. Let's just stop and think about this, shall we?' he said to them, standing away from the table so that they could all see him.

'Aren't we being a little harsh? Yes, slander is a dreadful thing to contend with. And I understand the need for its punishment. But does it have to be so brutal? We're a Congregational Court, not a Kangaroo Court. Surely we can come up with something else? Chloe's clearly full of remorse.'

Everyone went back to looking at Blubs, to weigh up just how full.

'Dave, you've just said it yourself, *people* have been avoiding you. That's all of us. We're all guilty of having been suspicious and mistrusting of you. All those years ago, it only took one visit to your cabin from the police to set tongues wagging, and they've been wagging ever since, I can assure you. *People* didn't need Chloe to set them off. Okay, so she handed out a rather blunt statement on The Bedrock Telegraph, but it didn't particularly alter what any of us were already thinking. Those bibles in your hands, what do they say? *Let he who is without sin, cast the first stone.* So Chloe cast out quite a few stones, but are any of us fit to add to that by stoning her?

'And let me tell you, I've been as guilty as the next person. So, for the record, I publicly offer you my sincerest apologies.'

Pete looked to Sal and she immediately leapt to her feet.

'And I want to offer my apologies, too. I'm very sorry.'

And then Jude was up, followed by Gabe. Then Phoebe and Dan. And then there was a scraping of chairs as everyone began to stand to state the same in a cascade of apologies, all speaking one on top of the other.

The Rippers looked stunned.

'As for Susanna's claim,' Pete continued, as they all began to sit back down, 'It's as I said. Slander is a terrible thing and I'm sure it's caused a lot of pain. But aren't we all here to learn how to be more forgiving, more humble, more enlightened? Chloe clearly has some way to go on her path to enlightenment, but that's not to say the rest of us are that much further ahead. Look to those bibles again. *For if you forgive others when they sin against you, your heavenly Father will also forgive you.* So, I ask the three of you, can you not find it in your hearts to forgive her?'

'I can forgive plenty,' Susanna shouted, 'But I still think a crime deserves a punishment. There's plenty of that in The Bible as well.'

Everyone went from looking at her, back to looking at Pete.

Pete looked to Blubbermouth.

'If you were allowed to stay, Chloe. If Susanna, Dave, and Lydia, allowed you to stay, would you be willing to demonstrate how grateful you were for their forgiveness?'

They all went quiet so they could hear the response. There was a small squeak of yes from Chloe.

'And if I were to suggest, that for atonement, you spend an hour a day cleaning each of their cabins. For a month. Would you be willing?'

Again, another squeak of yes, but this time clearer as Chloe had now lifted her head.

'Susanna. In view of us all now having to do our own cleaning, would this be an acceptable punishment, bearing in mind it would save you the job?'

Sasquatch was looking down at DoLittle, the maligned husband. He looked as if to say it wasn't his problem, which struck Pete as odd. In fact, why wasn't he the one making the claim? It was him who was actually being slandered.

'Yes,' Sasquatch replied, 'It would be acceptable. But only if it's for two months, not one.'

Pete looked to Blubs, who nodded.

'Dave? Lydia? What about you?'

'Just one month will do,' Lydia responded.

'Right then, I think we have a more reasonable outcome. Is there anything you would like to say, Chloe?'

Chloe looked down at the floor as she spoke.

'I'm sorry, and I apologise. I promise not to say anything about anyone ever again. I know I gossip, but it's only because I want everyone to like me, and I thought that – well, I thought wrong. And I'm really, really sorry.'

Some of the women were dabbing at their eyes and Pete, in his present emotional state, had to fight the urge to leak, himself.

He suddenly decided, from that point on, on the back of Chloe's pledge, he would no longer call her Blubbermouth.

He turned to Vic.

'I'm asking for you to grant that Chloe be allowed to stay in The Garden of Eden.'

'It's not down to me. It's down to them,' Vic returned, serving around his open hand.

'Alright folks, if twelve of you now stand, then it's decided. Chloe can stay.'

Pete raised his hand, seeing as he was already stood. Sal immediately stood, and then Phoebe, and Jude, and then one after the other they got to their feet, until all of them were standing, including Sasquatch, DoLittle and The Rippers.

Chloe was crying like she might never stop and everyone began to clap. It was like she'd gone from zero to hero in less than fifteen minutes.

As soon as they were all sat back down, their starters were being served and dinner went ahead through a clamour of conversation.

'Well that was all pretty ridiculous,' Sal observed. 'Everyone in here gossips. The place is rife with it. Why single out poor Blubs? I can understand The Rippers, after the stone thing, but the thing with DoLittle is complete crap, if you ask me. We've never heard no flamin' rumours. And who's to say it is a rumour? There's never smoke without fire.'

'Too right,' said Jude. 'You know, I've a good mind to put in a slander PI myself. For her calling us cockney spivs. It's a pity Lottie isn't here to drop some soup on her again.'

'Yes, where is she?' Sal asked, looking around for their usual waitress.

'She's got the clap,' said Gabe, 'Probably gone to ground for a couple of weeks.'

Sal raised an eyebrow, and then the other.

'And to think she was worried about catching Covid.'

As soon as their dessert was served, so was their speaker.

'Evening, everyone. I must say, it's a pleasure to be back here amongst you all,' he began, taking the mic out of its stand.

'I recognise most of the faces out there, but just in case we've anyone new here, I'm Mike, and I'm the vicar from the local church.'

Mick the Vic was back and Pete was pleased. He was a laid back, affable kind of chap, albeit with an air of divine superiority that Pete recognised as common within the clergy, and plod.

'Folks in the village refer to me as The Rector, but I have it on good authority that the kids in the school prefer to call me The Rectum.'

A titter ran through his audience. He'd used that line before, Pete remembered, but it was a few years back, so it was on a lengthy recycle.

'I was actually hoping to see you all sat there naked. I know I've said it time and time again, but I personally wouldn't mind in the slightest.'

He'd be hoping for a long time, thought Pete. The women would never forego their weekly opportunity to dress-up.

'Last time I was here, I made a note of a particular sign you had.' He was jerking his thumb to the left of the stage. It was a sign currently out of his view, but clearly not out of his mind.

'*If you would be a real seeker after truth, then it is necessary that at least once in your life you doubt, as far as possible, all things. Descartes,* if I remember correctly. Well they say that doubt is the first step to gaining insight. So I hope our usual question and answer session allows me to remove any of your current doubts about God's word. But that's for later. First, you'll have to suffer my usual ramblings, I'm afraid.'

'What do you think to The Bible, Sal?' Phoebe asked her.

'I think it's a load of old rubbish. Page after page about who begets who. Half of it reads like a giant family tree. A Christmas Carol by Charles Dickens does it for me. Want something to make you think about behaving better? That's your book.'

'What about you, Yogi?'

'Up until an hour ago, I might have said the same. But having automatically quoted from it, to save Chloe's skin, I think I'd be a hypocrite to say it.'

Gabe was laughing.

'What?' Pete asked him.

'That name, Yogi. It cracks me up. You'll be asking Vic to rename the place Jellystone Park soon.'

'Ah, shut up, Boo Boo.'

'But before we get started, I've got an envelope to hand over,' Mike told them, pulling it out of his jacket pocket. 'As I was waiting to be let in, a chap came and asked me if I wouldn't mind delivering it. Must have thought I looked trustworthy.' He was smiling as he pulled in his chin to try look down at his own dog collar.

He held up the envelope to read out its front-named recipients.

'Do we have a Dan and Phoebe Saunders here with us?'

Dan immediately got to his feet, and with a look of intrigue, set off to collect it.

'Who's it from?' Sal asked as soon as he was back.

Dan slid into his chair, passing the envelope to Phoebe.

Phoebe opened it, eyes excited, and pulled out a 'With Sympathy' card.

It took her only seconds to read it, even less to drop it, push back her chair, and run. Dan immediately picked up the card. He read it, then he too left them in a hurry.

The others looked at each other with concern.

'What does it say?' Jude asked.

Sal had picked up the discarded card and was reading it. She didn't answer, she just passed it across. Jude read it, and passed it to Gabe. Gabe read it, and passed it to Pete. It had one cryptic line written in it: *Did you seriously think I wouldn't find you*?

'What does it mean?' Sal asked.

'It means they've got trouble in the shape of Dan's brother, at a guess,' said Pete.

'He's just got out of Wandsworth,' Gabe added, 'Dan told me. On the stag-night. Said he's the brother from hell.'

Jude's eyes widened with alarm.

'That is soooo scary. Getting a sorry for your death card from your psycho ex-con brother.'

Gabe took another look at the card.

'I happen to know a few in Wandsworth. I think I need to ask around and see what I can find out about him.'

Sal and Jude nodded, but Pete was more taken with the fact that Gabe knew a few jailbirds.

'The last time I was here,' Mike ventured, 'I discovered that a good many of you have had what we in the trade call an epiphany. And not just any old epiphany, but one that came after you'd been out in The Wilderness for a time. Or a dark, parallel universe as some of you have described it. Well, you're in good company. David, Elijah, Moses, John the Baptist, and even Christ himself went out into The Wilderness, always to return with a much greater sense of purpose. Christ spent forty days and forty nights there, and he —'

'Buddha spent six years!' Mo called out.

Mike smiled at him, but didn't care to engage.

'I dare say some of you spent less than forty days and nights in your own wilderness,' he continued, 'While others might have been lost out there for longer. But hopefully not as long as six years.'

Everyone was quiet. They probably didn't want to recollect how long, thought Pete. He certainly didn't.

'When some unexpected, catastrophic life event plunges us into a place we'd rather not be, we endure, and with God's grace, we survive. And when we come back from that dark, desolate place, we're never the same. We're born anew.'

Pete was listening intently, but he was frightened. Frightened of being pushed out into the wilderness again. Frightened of those deepest, darkest depressions and anxieties that had tormented him, night and day.

'Only by getting lost in The Wilderness do we find ourselves. Only in the midst of The Wilderness do we recognise that all we once strived for was meaningless. Only by emerging from The Wilderness do we get the chance to apply the rest of our lives to some higher spiritual purpose.

'When life turns bad, people always ask, is God testing me? And the answer to that is no. When Jesus was in The Wilderness he was sorely tested, but it was by the devil. Only the devil tests us and tempts us. The temptation towards avarice, towards power and status, is as strong for us now as it ever was. The temptation to wield the same power as God and to hold the same status. To have people idolise us and follow us, albeit on social media, has become a modern-day scourge.

'But knowing most of you as I do, I know that your wilderness wasn't one for a test of temptation. Far from it. Yours was a test of human spirit. But you survived, because you looked to the light to guide you through. Otherwise, you wouldn't be here now, listening to me. So, I want you to ask yourselves. Was that wilderness a curse? Or a blessing in disguise?

'There's a popular hymn that I'm sure most of you know. One of my favourites. It's all about being lost and being found. It was written after —'

Mike stopped short at the sound of singing.

'*Amazing Grace, how sweet the sound ...*'

Pete could see that it was one of The Swingers.

The rest of The Swingers joined in.

'*That saved a wretch like me. I once was lost, but now am found. Was blind but now I see.*'

Mick the Vic looked delighted, giving them instant applause.

'I need to go check on Dan and Phoebe,' Pete suddenly announced, picking up the abandoned card.

He didn't need to, but it was a good excuse. His need was simply to get away. He couldn't stay and listen to anymore. He'd survived the wilderness. He'd seen the light. He'd been lost and then found. He'd been blind and then saw. The thought of walking into that wilderness once again was too much to bear. He had to walk somewhere else.

He looked in every room of The Hub before he found them, sat outside on the patio, silent and stressed.

'What's with the sympathy card?' he asked, sitting down to slide it across the table to them.

Phoebe took one look at it and burst into tears, prompting Dan to reach out and put his arm around her.

'It's from my brother,' he said, 'to let us know that he's found us.'

'Because you hadn't told him?'

Dan nodded.

'Any reason why?'

'Lots.'

‘He did the burglary in Vic’s office,’ Phoebe blurted, ‘He did it just to spook us. We’re sure of it.’

Pete thought about the madman in the stolen van. He was enough to spook anyone.

‘If that’s the case, why don’t we call the police?’

‘Because it will only lead to him turning nasty,’ Dan replied.

Pete looked at them both, holding tight onto each other.

‘Is there something bad that happened between you and him?’

Dan nodded. ‘I refused to give him an alibi, in court. Which ultimately led to him being sent down.’

‘Ah,’ said Pete, ‘And now he’s out, he’s wanting to put the frighteners on you, in revenge.’

‘Something like that, yes.’

‘I tell you what. This time tomorrow, I’ll have round-the-clock security guarding the place. A team of lads I use up in Yorkshire. Hard as nails. The knock ‘em out first and ask questions later, sort.’

Phoebe reached out to squeeze his hand.

‘Thank you, Yogi. That’s really kind of you. That would make me feel so much better.’

At that, Pete immediately stood up.

‘Come on then, let’s get ourselves back in there before we miss the finale.’

They were just in time.

‘Tim? Why don’t you set us off with the question you asked last Sunday, in church?’

Pete looked across to Tugger Tim. Tugger who had recently started calling TC, JC. But it wouldn’t last. The year before he’d been a convert to Taoism and believed in The Tao, so TC had been TT.

Tugger stood up.

‘Do you think Covid is one of the seven plagues of the apocalypse?’ he asked.

Not a bad question thought Pete, if you were taken to believing The Bible, literally.

Mike gave Tim a thumbs up.

‘Covid. Something that’s clearly causing a lot of existential angst. Is it one of the seven plagues of Revelations? No, it most certainly is not. Revelations, the last book of The Bible, is seen as an apocalyptic text rather than didactic or historical. It was based more on visions, prophecies and allegory. People no doubt thought the Black Death was a biblical plague. And Typhoid. And Cholera. And AIDS. And the rest. I believe what is really meant, is that no matter the trial or trauma that befalls us, we must have faith that our death is not final. Faith is the one true way to salvation.'

Pete had read Revelations as a child. It had left him scarred.

'You alright, mate?' Gabe asked him, 'You look bleeding shocking tonight.'

For once, Sal didn't give him a SOL.

'Yes,' Jude agreed, 'you hardly ate any of your dinner?'

'I'm right enough,' Pete told them, 'Just got a bit of a bug.'

'Hope it's not Covid,' said Jude.

'Or the clap,' said Gabe.

Tamara put her hand up and Mike waved her onto her feet with both hands.

'What do you think, as a Christian, to Christ only ever preaching to Jews? And him telling his disciples that they could only ever preach to Jews, and never to Goyim. Non-Jews.'

Pete had forgotten that she and her twin were Jewish. Born Jewish, but obviously not practicing Jewish.

Mike had raised his eyebrows, clearly surprised by such a confrontational question.

'Sensible. All the non-Jews were worshipping false gods back then, so it would stand to reason. The Egyptians were worshipping the likes of Anubis and Horus. The Romans, Venus and Mars And the Canaanites, Baal, Ashtoreth and Molech. It was only the Jews who accepted monotheism.'

'No. It was because Jews were God's chosen people,' Tabitha stood to shout out.

Mike smiled. 'At the time, it would seem that they were, yes. They'd been blessed with laws that helped to keep them safe. Not to eat pork - full of worms. Or shellfish - full of effluent. To steer themselves clear of blood - being a carrier of diseases. And so on. So I'm sure it set them apart as the healthiest. But as for being chosen? I think they were only chosen to set an example to the rest.'

Tamara poked him again.

'The Old Testament is written by Jews, specifically for Jews. So why do Christians use it?'

Once again, Mike smiled, refusing to be goaded.

'You might say the same of Charles Dickens works. Written by an Englishman, for the English. But that's not to say those works haven't now been read right across the entire world.'

They all looked to Sal as she beamed proudly, seemingly having received confirmation that A Christmas Carol proved parity.

'And as for Jesus,' Mike went on, 'When he appeared to his disciples *after* his death, he told them, *Go and make disciples of all nations, baptizing them in the name of the Father and of the Son and of the Holy Spirit.* Which obviously paid off, considering none of us are currently worshipping Saturn, Horus or Molech.'

The Shining clearly remained unappeased but together they sat down, only for the current husband, James, to stand up.

'Times have changed. So why hasn't God given us an up-to-date version of The Bible? A Now Testament?' he asked. 'Or maybe it's time for us to create our own?' he suggested, pointing to the long sign above the kitchen doors. It was a new one.

Make your own Bible. Select and collect all the words and sentences that in all your reading have been to you like the blast of a trumpet – R W Emerson.

Mike shielded the overhead light from his eyes so he could read it, but the look on his face said he wasn't going to endorse it.

'Is James, Jewish?' Sal asked.

'Married to a Jew. Got to be,' Gabe replied.

Pete smiled and shook his head. Even though he was sat there, sick to his stomach with worry, some part of his brain was able to override it with an interlude of amusement.

The other three looked at him, questioning.

'Think of him as he normally is. Naked,' he told them.

They looked baffled, but then Gabe broke into a smile.

'No, I guess he's not.'

'Why?' Sal demanded.

‘Because he’s got a foreskin.’

‘Another question? Anybody?’ Mike asked them.

A less Shar Pei looking Shar Pei got to her feet.

‘Go ahead,’ Mike encouraged.

Shar Pei read from a slip of paper.

‘*And everything on which she lies during her menstrual impurity shall be unclean. And everything also on which she sits shall be unclean.* I think that’s a rather petty, misogynistic rule, don’t you?’

‘From Leviticus,’ Mike responded. ‘The blood thing again. I know it reads rather petty, but in that period — sorry for the pun — blood was seen as something rather bad. But if it’s not too personal a question, might I ask what you actually do in here? I mean, I know this is a nudist camp, so at that time of the month, do you ladies just sit yourselves down and hope for the best?’

There was a titter amongst them.

‘Most of us are past it,’ Mary shouted, ‘Apart from Phoebe. And she’s pregnant.’

As they always dressed for speakers’ evenings, Pete realised the village rector wasn’t aware of their club etiquette. That being, they normally took paper towels from the wall dispensers to sit upon, depositing them in the bin when they left. Periods or not.

Mike was now pointing to Mo.

‘If Jesus is the light and the way, and only through him can we be saved, what about all the people who believe in something else? What about all the people who have lived and died without ever having seen a bible, never mind read one? The Bible makes it very clear that there’s no other way to salvation.’

‘He’s right,’ Mac shouted out, ‘It’s not inclusive enough. The Hindus do it better. Hindus believe that there are many paths to finding God. They acknowledge the possibility of truth in all other religions.’

Pete could see Mike frantically thumbing through his bible.

‘Look to Romans,’ he told them. ‘*Since what may be known about God is plain to them, because God had made it plain to them. For since the creation of the world, God’s visible qualities, his eternal and divine nature, have been clearly seen, being understood from what has been made, so that people are without excuse.* What this is telling us, is that just by looking at the beauty of the world around us, it's plain for us to know that God exists. Everyone has the opportunity to acknowledge and to know God.'

Mo was smirking. 'If looking at the world around us is enough, then why do we need The Bible? And you?'

Tugger suddenly leapt to his feet.

'Because we need rules. We need to know what's expected of us. What's right and what's wrong. What we should be doing and what we shouldn't be doing,' he ranted, wagging his finger at Mo.

Mike immediately motioned for Tugger to calm down and to sit down.

'Christ came to us to set an example of how we should live. Buddhism provides similar guidelines to that. It's all about being the very best of ourselves. Unfortunately, as we now have Satan walking amongst us, he leads us to think this means being rich and famous, when all God really wants is for us to be kind and gracious.'

There was a moment of quiet thoughtfulness on that message, until Sal promptly shattered it.

'If you saw a man, masturbating, through a neighbouring window, should you knock and tell him he's a pervert?' she stood to ask, 'Or is it acceptable in The Bible?'

Sniggering and giggling ran around the room.

Once again Mike flicked through his bible.

'I'll read from Matthew. *You shall not commit adultery, but I tell you, that anyone who gazes at a woman to lust after her has committed adultery with her already in his heart.* Basically, I don't think the act itself is seen as a sin, it's more that someone might be tempted to view pornography while they're doing it. And I'd say that was a sin.'

A few more titters erupted and a lot of eyes darted across to The Swingers, but Pete could see that Sal's eyes were solely reserved for Tugger. She finally made eye contact with him, and in that brief moment, Tugger understood, and went pillar box red.

There was a sudden quiet amongst them. It created a space that was soon to be filled with Sugar and Spice. They were up on their feet, with Spice holding out his mobile to read from.

'God gave them over to shameful lusts. Even their women exchanged natural sexual relations for unnatural ones. In the same way the men also abandoned natural relations with women and were inflamed with lust for one another. Men committed shameful acts with other men, and received in themselves the due penalty for this. According to The Bible, gay people are condemned to hell. How are we supposed to live, knowing this?'

Mike had been thumbing through his bible as he'd listened.

'With that particular passage, we need to look at what comes after it. *They have become filled with every kind of wickedness, evil, greed and depravity. They are gossips, slanderers, God-haters, insolent, arrogant and boastful. Although they know God's righteous decree that those who do such things deserve death.* Pretty powerful words, wouldn't you say? And pretty powerful punishment to go with it. But think about some of those sins. Arrogance. Insolence. Gossip and slander.'

Everyone was suddenly looking at Chloe and now Chloe had flushed red.

'These sins,' Mike continued, 'are lumped together with homosexual acts. And yet we all know these things aren't worthy of a death penalty. We see them as all part of being human. And I think that's how you should take it. The Bible was written over a long period of time by a lot of different men, and although we believe they were inspired by God, God wasn't censuring their every word. No doubt there was an inclination to slant things toward the opinions of that time.'

Sugar and Spice sat down, looking unconvinced.

The Boar stood up.

'There's a lot in The Bible that talks about reward and punishment,' he began, 'And I'm with Einstein, one the best brains of our time, who said that he refused to believe in a God who rewarded good and punished evil. Which would seem rational, wouldn't it?'

Mike was quick to find the page he was looking for.

'*For although they knew God, they neither glorified him as God nor gave thanks to him, but their thinking became futile and their foolish hearts were darkened. Although they claimed to be wise, they became fools,*' he quoted to him.

'Are you saying Einstein was a fool?' The Boar bristled.

Gabe was sniggering. 'Mick the Vic's having a right old mare,' he whispered to Pete, 'They'll be nailing him to a cross soon.'

'No, of course not,' Mike replied, 'But no matter how intelligent we might be, God still wishes for us to acknowledge his existence. Consider how we raise our own children. You might not care to admit it, but reward and punishment are often the only way they heed what we say, turning them into decent adults, rather than not. As God's children, we surely benefit from exactly the same.'

Pete had drifted away from it all. He was no longer involved in the endless debate. He was thinking about heaven. Would Sal meet Pip? Would they get along? Was it okay to have two wives? The Bible was full of men who had umpteen wives, often with a sprinkling of concubines on the side, so maybe it was. He decided to ask.

'If a fella's been married twice. Does he have two wives when he gets to heaven?'

'Good question,' Mike told him. 'In Matthew, Jesus tells us, *At the resurrection, people will neither be married nor be given in marriage, but they will be like the angels in heaven.*'

Pete reached to squeeze Sal's knee beneath the table, but she'd suddenly stood up to shout out a question, herself.

'How sure are you that death isn't the end?'

Mike immediately came over to their side of the stage.

'Absolutely sure. One hundred percent sure,' he replied, quoting, '*He shall wipe away every tear from their eyes and death shall be no more, neither pain, mourning or crying, for the former things will have passed away.*'

As Sal sat down, Pete finally squeezed her knee, and she in turn squeezed his hand.

'Don't we have to get judged on our sins first? By Peter at the Pearly Gates?' Gabe shouted to ask.

'Yes. Why do we have to be judged,' Three Lugs called out, 'If Jesus died for our sins already?'

Mike smiled, but it was a pained smile.

'He did indeed die for our sins. But only those sins we repent of.'

‘Good job we all go to confession, then,’ Sheepteeth shouted out.

Mike’s eyes widened. He obviously didn’t know that they harboured some practices of Catholicism.

Pete wasn’t harboured. He was adrift. He was suddenly struck by a dreadful thought. Sal was the only person amongst them who didn’t subscribe to the confessional. Had her failure to repent been instrumental in her being smite with cancer?

‘What you have to remember,’ Mike told them, ‘Is that The Bible has been around for nigh on two thousand years. In that time, it’s led to a lot of believers.’

‘Buddhist teachings have been around twice as long,’ Mo shouted out, ‘So maybe we should believe in it twice as much?’

Mike chose to ignore him.

‘Before The Bible, people were sacrificing their children, alive, on open fires. They were lawless and anarchic. So, whatever you choose to believe about the good book, first consider that since we’ve had it, we’ve grown to live in an increasingly civilised society. Our laws are God’s laws. That’s why juries around the world still choose to swear an oath on it.’

Uncanny he should say that, thought Pete, with three of their own having just done exactly that.

‘As more and more people turn their back on God and his written word, the more we’ll return to heathen anarchy,’ Mike went on. ‘It won’t be long before people are just walking into shops and helping themselves. They’ll be stabbing each other, just for living on the opposite side of the street. Porn will become mainstream entertainment. And social media showboating will turn those observing to despair or hate. It’s coming. Mark my words. It’s coming.’

Adam had waved to catch the rector’s eye, before tapping at an invisible watch on his wrist.

‘Okay, you’ve asked me your questions, so now I’ve got one for you,’ Mike said to them. ‘Over the years I’ve been coming here, I’ve picked up on a custom you have. Quite a good one. Sol. You say it to someone when they curse. And then they nod or put their hand up, presumably to apologise. So, my question. What does it mean? Sol?’

Nobody said a word. They'd sworn an oath not to talk to about it, outside of The Fold.

'It's an acronym for Swearing Out Loud,' Pete told him.

Everyone was looking to Vic, to see if Pete had flouted their rules, but Vic was nodding.

'Ah,' said Mike, 'SOL. I think I might start using it at home. My wife's menopause has resulted in some very colourful language of late.'

They all tittered, she being a vicar's wife, but Pete was suddenly filled with guilt. The times he'd been incensed by Sal's colourful language was immeasurable. If it had been due to her menopause, then maybe it hadn't been her fault?

'Well thank you all for having me. It's certainly been an interesting night. And let my parting words to you be those you already have on a sign out in your car park. *If the only prayer you ever said was thank you, that would be enough.*'

Later that night, in the warmth of their bed, Pete held his wife closer than he had held her in years. Trying to capture the very essence of her so it would sustain him through the years he would be without her. He was awake every minute of the night, while she snored, soundly, in his arms.

CHAPTER THIRTEEN

ONE DAY IN OCTOBER

'Harry, I need you. I need you real bad.'

There was silence at the other end of the phone, and then, 'Is that you, Pete?'

'Yes. It's me. Only it's the old me, before you fixed me.'

'What's happened?'

'It's Sal. She's been diagnosed with terminal cancer. I found out four weeks ago and I haven't slept since. I'm walking around in the middle of the night having panic attacks and I'm sweating like a pig in a poncho, with that acrid smelling fear sweat under one armpit like before.'

'Shall I get you booked in for an appointment?'

'No, I need you now. Can I zoom you?'

'Pete, I'm in St Kitts. I'm on holiday with the wife. You'll have to wait till I get back.'

'I can't. Harry, please, I can't cope, I'm going under.'

He was ashamed to say it, but it was true. His wife was facing down death with a stoicism and pragmatism he would never have believed her capable of, and here he was, unable to deal with the resulting fallout.

'No, you're not. Come on Pete, you've got through this before, you'll get through it again.'

'Yes, but Sal won't be getting through it. It's déjà vu. It's like with Pip. I'm going to end up in that dark place again, I can feel it creeping up on me.'

'Pete. Stop hyperventilating. Remember your breathing techniques. Stop the shallow breathing, right here, right now. It's only the primordial part of your brain trying to protect you.'

'From what?

'The pain and grief of her forthcoming death.'

'Well, it's not protecting me. It's crucifying me.'

‘A death of someone near to us reminds our deep subconscious that we, too, are going to die. It’s something we bury deep inside ourselves, until one day, we’re forced to face it full on. And you faced it before, remember? So let it go, Pete, start where we left off. Face the fact that we’re all going to die. You. Me. The Queen. Everyone. Ever since Adam and Eve in the garden of Eden.’

If only Harry knew where he was right now. Pete would have laughed if his jaw hadn’t been so tightly clenched.

‘Remember the mantra, from Michel de Montaigne? *He who fears he will suffer, already suffers because he fears*. You’re fearful of fear. Pure and simply. Until I get back, I want you to do some TRE. Remember TRE? Trauma Release Exercises?’

‘Yes, I remember.’

‘Well get stuck into them. Try and get the shock out of your body. Last time, your breakdown was on the back of years of stored up stress, because you buried it. You popped like a pressure cooker. This time, just try and let the panic happen. It’s better out now than stored up for later, believe me.’

Pete stopped pacing and sat down. He vividly remembered the TRE tutorials that Harry had made him watch while on the couch of his Harley Street Practice, especially as they had started with the gazelle in the lion’s mouth. He needed to go and lay down somewhere and try and get himself into the release position.

‘Please TC, let me shake it all off,’ he murmured out loud, forgetting Harry was still on the phone.

‘Yes, go and shake it off,’ Harry told him. ‘I’ll be back before you know it and we’ll set up a meeting.’

‘Okay,’ Pete replied, ‘Thanks Harry. If anyone can get me through this, you can.’

‘No, Pete. *You* can.’

Sal had gone pony trekking with the girls and he knew she would be gone for a few hours. He paced and then he practiced TRE, without success, so he popped two diazepam that the local doctor had prescribed. He needed to sort himself out, he couldn’t let Sal see him like this. So far, he’d managed to keep secret the steady decline of his mental health. He hadn’t wanted to burden her with it. He wanted to be her rock. If he was going to go under, he wanted it to be afterwards, when she was gone.

As the diazepam began to kick in, he went outside and stepped into the freezing cold water of the hot-tub. Cold therapy had been another method Harry had recommended for his anxiety, but as he took a breath and sat down, he considered heart failure might cure it first.

Their hot-tub was normally hot, all year round, but Pete had convinced Sal it was good for tightening up their aging skin. She hadn't been convinced, but then she hardly used the hot-tub anyway, so she hadn't argued when he'd switched off its heating element.

As the cold bit into him he tried to hug his knees to his chest, but failed, due to his paunch getting in the way. Rather than pull his stomach in, he pushed it out, and began to count. Breathing in, breathing out. Belly breathing. He must stay calm. He must stay focused. Everyone dies. It was the cycle of life. He began to cry. He didn't want Sal to cycle and die.

There was a sharp woof and Pete looked over the edge of the tub to see Junior looking up at him. The small dog cocked his head to one side as if asking him what was wrong.

'I'm okay, son. Just feeling a bit maudlin. Come on, I'll order you a nice bit of steak, eh? No need for you to be miserable, too.'

Pete climbed out just in time to see Junior disappearing through the open hinged panel on the hot-tub's side.

He got down onto his knees to see if he could see him. He whistled. He called. Then he reached in to see if he could feel him. All he felt was a long flat box.

Pulling it out, he sat back onto his heels to put it onto his knee.

Inside was an Apple laptop. Why would Sal have hidden it out there? Why wasn't it in the top of their bedroom drawers where it normally was? It didn't make sense. Just then, Junior leapt out in front of him and scampered back indoors.

Putting on the kettle, Pete picked up his mobile to use the Starship delivery App, but before he could place his order, his phone battery went flat. He looked at Junior and Junior looked at him.

'No worries,' said Pete, taking the laptop out of the box.

The same App was also on that, and hopefully it wasn't flat.

As soon as he lifted its lid, he could see, top right, that it was three quarters charged. But bottom right, and bottom left, he could see that it wasn't their laptop. Top left, stuck on the screen, was a small post-it note, and on it was written: *Password – Victorious1.*

Thoughts suddenly filtered through Pete's mind like sand through a sieve, and try as he might, he couldn't plug the holes. This was Vic's laptop. Vic wasn't short for Victor, it was short for Victorious. Not a lot of people knew that, other than Pete. What was he to do?

He sat for five minutes just staring at the screen. Should he hand it back to him? But then how would he explain that his wife had stolen it? And why his wife had stolen it?

Eventually, he entered the password. Desk top icons of various gambling sites sprang up before him to fully confirm its ownership.

Pete tossed Junior a chew and then took his cup of tea and the laptop, to go sit at their small desk. He couldn't comprehend why Sal would want to steal it. And what had she done with Vic's precious collectables? It was as shocking as it was baffling. So much for Dan's brother being the likely culprit.

First off, he looked through Vic's calendar. There were various speakers' engagements, lorry deliveries, horse racing events, hospital appointments, birthdays belonging guests, accountant visits. Nothing out of the ordinary.

He then looked into his photo album but very quickly closed it down after seeing some very unsettling photos of emerging births. If that was porn, it was sick.

From there, he moved into his files. All listed alphabetically. Addresses. AGMs. Astral Events. Banking. Biblical Names. Bird watching. Calibrations. Confessions. Consultant – Hospital. Debts. Diagrams. Electrical. Health and Safety. None of them sparked an interest. Until he saw the one entitled POTs, and then he suddenly understood. This is what Sal had been looking for. Looking to find out who had been submitting so many POT shots against her. It had been her long term, ultimate quest to find out. He should have guessed.

He opened the file. It was just as it appeared on the weekly POTs results board. Spreadsheets showing names, totals of individual POTs, and sum totals. That was it. No breakdowns of who POT shotted who. It stood to reason. Vic would have had to list each and every one that was submitted. It would have taken him forever.

He came out of the POTs folder to take a look at the others. Observatory. Party Planners. Pippin Foundation. Regional Council. Resort Rules. Standard pricing. Again, nothing leapt out at him. He scrolled back up.

Biblical Names? What was that about?

The excel page was landscape, split into two columns. The left-hand column was headed up as Biblical Names, and the adjacent column, Members.

In alphabetical order, starting with Aaron on the left, there was a member's full name to the right of it. Aaron Cutler. Below Aaron, was Abigail, and to its right, Abigail Peters. And so it went on. There were three Andrews. One Benjamin. One Bethany. Two Chloes – was that really a biblical name? Two Daniels. Three Davids. One Deborah. Three Dianas. One Elizabeth. One Esther. One Gabriel. One Gideon. One Hannah. One James. One Jemima – no way was that biblical. Three Joannas. One Joel. Three Johns. One Jonathan. One Joseph. Two Joshuas. One Judith. Two Julias. One Leah. One Lisa. One Lucifer. One Luke. One Lydia. Two Marks. Three Marys. Two Matthews. Three Michaels. One Moses. Mo? Really? He'd thought he was simply a Mo. One Nathan. Two Naomis. One Noah. One Oprah – surely not Biblical? Three Pauls. Two Peters. He being one. Two Philips. Two Phoebes – absolutely no way. It was like Chloe, far too trendy. It was on a par with Kylie and Miley. One Priscilla. Two Rachels. Two Rebeccas. One Ruth. Three Sarahs. One Salome. Two Simons. Two Stephens. Two Susannas. One Tabitha. One Tamara. One Thomas. One Timothy. One Zoe.

He scrolled back up. One name had stood out in particular. To the left, Lucifer, to the right of it, Luci Ferranti. Vic had seen the opportunity to make it fit, just as he himself had seen the opportunity to make it her moniker.

On another tab there was a second spreadsheet, headed up as Applicants Non-Biblical. Here were listed other members; the members who Pete knew to have applied for the Covid lock-in.

These members had obviously failed to make the biblical grade that Vic had set as the bar to being accepted. Many of them did have Biblical names, as highlighted, but the difference being that it was only one out of the couple, rather than both. Pete suddenly had a thought. Vic's wife had been called Lilith. Was that a Biblical name? Had he chosen her based on name alone? Or possibly based on her having two children with biblical names? What the hell was wrong with him? Did the man have some sort of God complex?

Exiting the Biblical Names file he scrolled down to Confessions. Inside the file were individual folders, each one listed alphabetically by surname. He opened the first one. Attwood, David. He had to think. It was Ruthless.

Inside were dated pages with the most recent first, and under each date, a typed list of the confessions that had been made to Father Anthony. Pete read the latest with interest.

Still having lustful thoughts about Phoebe.

Not rung his mother for over a week.

Wanting to slap Salome Hardcastle for beating him again at tennis.

Pete immediately wanted to slap him.

He scrolled down to an earlier date.

Still dare not tell his mother that they're at a nudist resort.

Not been wholly truthful on his tax return.

Still upset with his sister and desperate that they should have separate cabins.

Sister? Ruth was his sister? Pete was flabbergasted. Was it incest? Or just a means to entering a couples only resort? Either way, it made him uneasy. He closed the folder and dropped down to the next, Attwood, Ruth.

It was pretty much the same thing, in date order.

Detests her brother, knows she shouldn't, but can't help herself.

Wishes brother would get Covid and leave.

Definitely not incest.

Slapped brother for eating her bacon.

Fantasises about shrinking brother and keeping him in a hamster cage.

Told mother that brother was a spendthrift and asked her to write him out of her will.

Pete was fascinated. Ruth had obviously never married, seeing as she had the same surname. And come to think of it, they did actually look alike. Maybe that was why they spent so much time apart, to stop people suspecting. Pete felt sorry for them. They were living a lie and Vic could easily have helped them, at least during the lock-in when so many cabins were sat empty.

He came out of Ruth's folder and scrolled down to Davies, Diana. Yakky.

Put terrible reviews on TripAdvisor of a hotel belonging old high school friend.

Still jealous of Oprah's bottom.

Still jealous of Phoebe's bosom.

Angry at husband for always telling her to shut up.

Still racked with guilt over the chalet in Gstaad.

It didn't say why, so Pete scrolled down through past months, looking for Gstaad to leap out at him.

Still feeling guilty over Gstaad chalet.

He scrolled back even further.

Racked with guilt over a chalet in Gstaad that isn't rightfully theirs. Belonged old lady they'd befriended. Found out no relatives and forged her will when dementia set in.

Pete was appalled. How could she live with herself? Didn't they have enough money already?

He came out of Diana's folder and scrolled down, passing his own, until he reached the last, Weiss-West, Tamara. He hesitated, but only until temptation got the better of him.

Same thing, the usual half dozen confessions in date order. He scanned through them until other names caught his eye.

Can't stop urge to laugh at Susanna Sutton's gigantic feet.

Pete realised he wasn't the only one. He scanned some more.

Can't stand 'Hardcastle woman' for being loud, coarse, and acting like she owns the place.

Lied that risotto was off when just had change of mind and wanted what sister was having.

Didn't help Starship when it got stuck on kerb, even though it kept asking.

Pete was rather beginning to enjoy himself, even though he was simmering with anger. Anger at Father Anthony, that he should be so willing to pass on all of their most personal and private revelations to Vic. And why would Vic want to know them? To the point of painstakingly recording them?

Still hates husband, for juggling her and her sister.

Sometimes fantasises about killing husband as life would be better for her and her sister.

Poor old James. Such a mild-mannered chap. But what was the juggling about? He closed Tamara's folder and opened her sister Tabitha's, directly above.

Sneaking in and putting hair removal cream in sister's shampoo.

Why would she do that? They were close. Closer than close. They even finished each other's sentences. He scrolled down through various confessions, mostly relating to unkind acts against her sister, but in-between, there were snippets as to why. Pre-Covid lock-in, there was one confession session in particular.

Sick of pretence of having to call James, Joe, when it's her turn to have him.

Sick of James sneaking back to be with her sister for half of the week.

Hates the photo-shopped prints they both have, making it look like there really is a Joe.

Pete was aghast. He scrolled back some more, not sure what he was looking for. And then there it was.

Feels trapped in the lie that she and her twin are married to twins, when they're not.

Ashamed at sharing same man with her sister.

Angry at James for feeling no shame at sharing himself.

Angry at sister for always having the lion's share of him.

Has bad thoughts of wishing James dead, so sister can't have him.

Pete could hardly believe it. They were sharing the same fella. The greedy bugger was a bigamist. He couldn't wait to tell Sal. And then, in an instant, he realised he couldn't. It would mean having to tell her that he'd found Vic's laptop.

Under normal circumstances, he wouldn't hesitate to have it out with her, to ask her why she'd stolen it, but their current circumstances weren't normal. Another thought struck Pete. Vic, having known about the twins' pretence, had allowed it to continue. Why hadn't he confronted them and kicked them out?

He closed down Tabitha's folder and scrolled up to Sutton, Susanna.

Still full of fury at Chloe Hughes.

This had to be back before the Congregational Court as Vic hadn't had his computer for at least a month at that point. It didn't say why she was furious, so Pete scrolled back in time until he spotted Chloe's name again.

Hates Chloe Hughes for coming to tell her she's seen husband going into one of spare cabins with staff member.

And at the following week's confession:

Thoughts of inflicting pain on Chloe Hughes, after she dropped by to warn her again. (Believes husband after his assurance it was for gynaecological advice only).

And week after:

Scratched Chloe's car in revenge for her smug sympathy.

(Believes Chloe is jealous of her good looking, professional husband).

And to think Vic had been blaming the staff for the vandalism. It was unbelievable. He'd known exactly who the culprit was. And poor Chloe. She'd said at the time that she felt victimised by having her car keyed. Although after the Congregational Court, Sal had said she was more a martyr than a victim, because no woman worth that amount of money would ever willingly submit herself to cleaning another woman's floors.

He closed down the Sutton, Susanna folder and continued to scroll up, pausing at his own. Did he really want to revisit all of the petty things he'd confessed to? No wonder Father Anthony had thought them so trivial. They were, in comparison to the rest.

He scrolled up to Fenton, Judith.

Her confessions mostly centred on Phoebe.

Jealous of Phoebe Saunders youth.

Jealous of Phoebe having such an attentive husband.

If only she knew that he was being equally attentive to Rin.

Jealous of Phoebe's pregnancy, having not been able to have children herself.

Really? So much for her saying she never wanted them, like Sal.

Angry at Phoebe for diluting her friendship with Salome.

It all made for uncomfortable reading. But scrolling back further, pre-Phoebe, he tapped into something even more so.

Still frightened that Gabriel will be found out.

Still worried that Gabriel will go to jail.

Worried that she might go to jail.

Worried that she will fall into a deep depression again due to stress and worry.

This wasn't just uncomfortable, it was disturbing. He came out of Judith and jumped straight into Fenton, Gabriel, next one up. It had to be the gambling that Jude was worried about. He had to be heavily in debt. Maybe he owed money to people he shouldn't? People in Wandsworth?

What constituted as Gabe's confessions were simply the number of cars that he'd bought each week, on-line. There was very little else. Certainly, no mention of gambling. But why would he confess to doing his everyday job? Since Covid, how else would he be gathering stock?

Pete kept scrolling back until he was almost at Gabe's very first confessions. And there it was. His confession to corruption. His entire business of sixteen second-hand car garages was just a front for money laundering. It was a complete and utter shock. Pete realised he was best friends with a common crook.

Was that why Vic had asked him if he knew what Gabe did for a living? Was he making sure he was innocent to it all, before he'd asked him to be club custodian?

Pete had looked at only a fraction of their folders but he was so totally upended by their admissions, that he was scared to open any more. He wasn't in The Garden of Eden at all. He was in a Den of Iniquity.

What was wrong with them all, that they should be prepared to offload their deepest, darkest secrets to a man who was impersonating a priest, badly. But although he remained shocked at all he'd discovered, he was still mostly affected by his initial discovery, of finding Sal capable of theft.

Had she really been so desperate to find out who'd been POT shotting her that she'd risk so much to do it? And why hadn't she told him? Confided in him? Had her terminal diagnosis made her indifferent to the consequences?

Just then, there was a voice. It was Sal, saying hello to Junior out on the front porch. Pete quickly shot out the back door, inserting the laptop into the box as he raced across the veranda to stash it back where he'd found it.

They met Gabe and Jude on The Dome's lower poolside terrace. Phoebe and Dan were meeting them later, after their massage.

'Here, Pete, come and take a butchers at this,' Gabe said to him as soon as they arrived.

Pete sat down on a chair and pulled it up alongside Gabe's, taking the mobile that was being offered to him.

'What am I looking at?' he asked.

'It's my search history, in Google. It's my family phone, not my work phone. It's the one I took with me on Prunie's stag-do, and it's the one Vic borrowed from me after his had gone flat.'

Pete had a look through the history. There was site after site of rare and valuable items. Rare books, rare coins, rare stamps, rare watches.

'I reckon as soon as Adam told him he'd been robbed, he was looking up stuff to make a claim for, on his insurance. Stuff he didn't really have.'

'Seriously?'

Gabe nodded.

'I could have told you that, already,' Sal piped up, absently flicking through a magazine that had been left on the table.

They all stared at her.

'How would you know?' Jude asked.

Sal looked up, and realising what she'd just said, stuttered a reason.

'Err, Eve told me.'

'Eve told you what?'

Sal shrugged. 'That she knew he didn't have any of that stuff. Said she'd been in his office enough times to know what he had and what he didn't have.'

Pete studied his wife. Was she lying? It was probably true, and Eve did know. But Sal already knew, based on the fact she was the actual burglar, whether Eve told her, or not.

'Why would he need to fiddle his insurance?' Jude asked, 'Isn't he's minted enough?'

Gabe shook his head. 'He's a gambler. Gamblers never have enough.'

Pete considered that statement to be probably the nearest he would ever get to an admission of corruption, from Gabe.

'Yogi! Yogi!' They all looked up to see Dan waving and beckoning from the far side of the pool.

'Off you lollop,' Gabe said to Pete, 'He's likely got a nice picnic hamper for you to break into.'

Pete smirked. He was growing accustomed to the bear jokes.

'Arek's waiting for you outside, Pete, but he said I'd not to tell you in front of Sal.'

Pete gave Dan's arm a quick squeeze, thanking him for his discretion.

'What shall I tell her?' he asked, as Pete headed off.

'Tell her …. you saw Junior, out wandering, and I've gone to look for him.'

Pete didn't like lying but he had to see Arek without Sal asking him why. She wouldn't be pleased to know he was picking up a bag of weed.

Pete hadn't smoked cigarettes in thirty-odd years, and marijuana, never. But since he'd visited Rosa in a state of panic and desperation, she'd rolled up a spliff and wouldn't let him leave until he'd partaken of it. It had been better than gin. Even better than diazepam. And in the middle of the night, when he was wont to pace up and down in a cold sweat, he now sat out on the veranda and lit up. Junior always sat beside him, chewing on a pig's ear, and together they pacified themselves with their little desiccated delights.

Arek was far left of the main doors, sat on a bench next to Rosa.

'How do?' said Pete, sitting down between them.

'Hello, Peter,' Rosa returned, while Arek simply nodded.

‘I came to tell you that Pippa has come through again. She’s definitely telling me you’re going to be free of it. She showed me the letter C again. This time she drew a cross through it.’

Pete pursed his lips and nodded. Last time Pip had shown Rosa the letter C, it had been drawn in sand, and then she’d shown her a wave, washing it away. He felt bad. He’d told Rosa that his mental state was due to him discovering that *he* had cancer, not Sal. He couldn’t tell her, not when he’d made a promise to Sal, not to tell anyone. And now, Pip, bless her, was making it clear to Rosa that he didn’t have it, not that he’d survive it, as Rosa was interpreting.

‘Let’s hope so,’ he replied, weakly, as he took the carrier bag from Arek.

It was blowing cold as he sped along the tarmac track that took him out alongside the river. The ponies weren’t there, but they’d left a lot of steaming evidence to show that they very recently had been.

Pete realised he was crying again. When he was on his own, he always cried, sometimes without even knowing it.

He took a short-cut that he very rarely used, reading the signs as they came fast toward him.

The meaning of life is that it stops – Franz Kafka

If only it didn’t.

I do not fear death. I have been dead for billions of years before I was born and not suffered the slightest inconvenience – Mark Twain

If only he could feel the same.

Memento Mori - Remember death.

If only he could stop remembering.

It might have been a while since he’d used the short-cut, but it would be a lifetime before he’d use it again. Vic had laid death right up to their door. Did he know that it was waiting there?

Back at the cabin, Pete pulled his golf clubs out of his bag and replenished the weed that was stashed at the bottom of it. It was the only place he knew that Sal would never look. Out on the veranda, he lit up the remains of the previous night’s joint, drawing on it, fast and furious, before flicking the roach end out into the undergrowth. In view of Junior still being laid on their bed, watching cartoons, he would say they'd left a door open, to validate Dan's lie.

As he set off back to The Dome, Pete heard singing. It was The Swingers. He decided upon a spur-of-the-moment detour to swing by their cabins. It annoyed him that they were all so near to his and Sal's. Numbers six, seven and eight. Eight being the nearest and the one they seemed to congregate in the most. Like now.

He pulled up behind a thicket of holly and went to peer around the edge of it. It would have been painful if he hadn't thought to put on his knee length, resort issue, fleece lined coat.

The singing was acapella style and it was emanating from the open veranda doors of their lounge. It was actually quite good. It reminded Pete of the American barber-shop singing his grandad always used to listen to. But without reaching a fitting end, the singing abruptly stopped. Pete crept further forward until he had a clear view inside.

There were two cameras set up on tripods either side of the room and one couple were kneeling on the floor in-between them, naked. Not that that meant anything, seeing as they usually were. Two others came into shot. They were dressed in studded leather, or maybe PVC, Pete wasn't quite sure. He braced himself. Their singing might be heavenly but what they were about to perform next, more likely wasn't. Past-it porn clearly had a marketable value. He quickly crept away.

Although he wasn't keen to witness it, Pete realised he couldn't wait to read about it, in their confessions, when next on Vic's laptop.

'What you doing here?' Pete asked Jake, as he approached the dry bar.

'The new guy had to leave.'

'Chlamydia?'

Jake shook his head. 'He couldn't hack it. Said he kept having nightmares about being naked in public places.'

'Understandable. I keep having nightmares about being dressed, in private places,' Pete returned, while concentrating on reading the sign at the back of the bar.

Do not associate with the fornicator, the gluttonous, the blasphemer, the drunkard or the swindler – Corinthians.

Well, that was The Swingers, Shar Pei, his wife, himself, and Gabe, all about to get the cold shoulder.

'What can I get you?' Jake asked.

'I'll have the usual round for the six of us, on a tray, please.'

Jake shook his head. 'Gabe's just this minute got them in. You sure you want another?'

'Aye, what the 'eck.'

Jake leaned forward. 'If I were you, I wouldn't. You'll regret it.'

'What d'you mean?' Pete asked him, surprised by Jake's unaccustomed front.

'You're stoned. You should stick to one or the other.'

'No, I'm not!'

'Your eyes are like flying saucers, mate. I know what stoned looks like. I appreciate you've found it helps with your arthritis, but you've got to stop spanking it or it'll spank you.'

Pete nodded, reminded of yet another lie he'd told someone in his subterfuge. He'd considered arthritis was easier for Jake to handle than cancer, but if he kept this up, he'd have a different affliction for everyone he knew. And he couldn't even confess his lies. Not anymore. Not now he knew Father Anthony wasn't to be trusted.

Jake filled a tray with snacks, instead.

'Full moon, tonight,' he stated, nodding skyward, 'Is the coven planning on doing anything special, with it being Halloween?'

Pete grinned at him. 'Nup. We'll be gathering naked around a huge erect symbol, just like we always do.'

'I think The Swingers are making porn movies,' Pete told them, as soon as he arrived back on the terrace.

Gabe burst out laughing.

'What makes you say that?' Jude asked.

'I dropped Junior back at ours and came back past theirs. Number eight. Their back doors were wide open and they were about to get down to it, in front of some cameras.'

'Are you sure?' Dan asked, grinning.

Pete nodded. 'They had professional lights set up and everything.'

'Christ Almighty,' said Gabe, 'How could anyone manage to crack one off while watching that lot?'

Sal began to cackle. Pete knew she would. She'd only recently found out that 'cracking one off' meant the same as 'having a tug', but it had become a term of infinite amusement.

'You'd think there'd be a POT for wife swapping,' Jude ventured, 'I wonder why Vic didn't create one? It's adultery, when all said and done.'

'Maybe he thought it would never happen?' Sal suggested.

Gabe was shaking his head. 'The temptation to sin in this Garden of Eden is probably just as strong as it was in the original.'

Pete didn't doubt it, he'd just read some of the evidence.

'You okay Pete?' Dan was asking him as the others debated the purpose of porn.

'Aye, lad, I'm champion. Just a bit off it today.'

'You said that on Monday. Maybe you should check in with a doctor?'

Pete shook his head. 'I'll be right. Just got a few factory troubles on my mind,' and then, turning to Gabe, 'Talking of work, how's things going in the car business?'

Gabe looked at him, clearly surprised that he'd asked.

'As well as can be expected, considering all the Covid restrictions.'

'Cars still flying off the forecourts, then?'

'Pretty much, yeh, why you asking?'

'No reason. Just thought I'd enquire. I've heard a lot of companies are having cash flow problems.'

Gabe went from surprise to suspicion.

'No cash flow problems at all,' he asserted.

'Definitely not,' Dan stepped in, 'He's just paid me out thirteen grand, pound notes, for my Audi.'

'The one in the car park?' Pete asked.

'Not anymore it isn't. It's on his website. And he's selling it same price as he paid me. How's that for mates' rates?'

Pete looked to Gabe. 'Very generous of you.'

Gabe smiled, but it was a smile that didn't sit well.

'He's more than generous,' Dan gushed, 'He's letting me have a Bentley, dirt cheap. An oldish one. But still, a Bentley.'

Pete rolled his eyes.

'It won't be cheap when it comes to servicing. Have you any idea how much new tyres are going to set you back?'

Dan shook his head, his smile suddenly flatlining.

'You're looking at five-hundred quid a corner.'

'Bloody hell,' said Dan.

'SOL,' said Sal.

'Five hundred quid?' Gabe scoffed, 'If that's what you've been paying for yours, you've been robbed. I'd be wanting the whole bleeding wheel for that.'

'SOL,' said Sal, and then, 'Oh my God! Have you seen her hair?' She was pointing at Tamara as she stepped down into the pool.

Pete lifted the peak of his cap to take a look.

The woman's hair was hanging in clumps, with bald patches showing in-between. It was like the mange his grandma's cat, Cockles, had once been struck down with.

'She thinks she's got alopecia,' Phoebe informed them.

They all watched as Tamara swam past.

'Maybe she just picked up some foreign written shampoo that was actually hair remover,' Pete put to them.

'Course she did,' Gabe scoffed, 'Next you'll be telling us that's why you're losing yours.'

They chatted and spatted until Tamara swam by again, this time with her sister.

'Shame,' said Jude, 'The pair of them had such beautiful long hair, and now only one of them has it.'

Yep, thought Pete, that was the plan. Tabitha's plan.

It was disturbing, seeing all their sins being played out in front of him. If he'd not read the Confessions file, he'd have been blithely unaware.

'Why don't we all go for a ring ride?' Sal suggested.

'Oh, yes, let's,' Phoebe enthused.

'Pete, go get Jake to turn up the current so we're all going around like the clappers,' Sal instructed him.

Pete did as he was told.

After four circuits, they'd all had enough, apart from Phoebe.

The sign above the massage suite door, was one Pete rarely read. But today, he read it twice.

Don't be anxious about anything, rather bring up all your requests to God in your prayers and petitions – Philippians.

He made a mental note.

'Sal not coming today?' Karina asked him, as he entered into the treatment room alone.

'No. She's gone for a nap.'

Chelsea immediately rushed to leave, grabbing the chance of an hour off before Karina could.

'You want neck and back, like I always do you?' Karina asked.

Pete nodded as he rolled himself onto the table, face down into its small built-in hole. He considered the hole an ideal place to hide his miserable face. Of late, Sal was always going back to their cabin for a nap. When she was fine, she was so completely herself that Pete forget she was actually ill, but then she'd suddenly become withdrawn and return to their cabin, leaving Pete to withdraw into his misery.

'This is third massage this week,' Karina said to him, 'And you more tense than each time before. Your musculs are like rocks from meteor.'

Pretty dense then. Pete couldn't help it. Sometimes he was so tense his thought his jaw was going to lock.

'Just do what you can with them,' he shouted through his funnel.

'Are you eating good food? Or shit food?' Karina asked, after a silent ten minutes of pummelling.

'The latter,' Pete replied, not wanting to repeat a SOL.

'Latter mean what? Late food?'

'No, it's the … shit food.' What the hell.

'Yes, I know this. You're growing fat in the skin and greasy in the hair.'

'Lovely. That's what chips three times a day does for you.' He was comforting eating and he knew it.

'No more shit chips,' she told him.

'No more shit chips,' he agreed.

His shoulders were next to be subjected to Karina's pincer like grip and he winced and grunted as she took him apart.

'We just had the twice come for massage. They very strange women.'

Pete smiled. The twice were the twins. Karina was like Sal, no matter how many times you corrected her, she stuck to what she preferred.

'They certainly are,' he agreed.

'My cousins are twice. Matching twice, same. They do crazy things. Like do whole time job, half-time each, with no one knowing. One time, they even dating with same man. And they use same driving licence after one is failed.'

'Clever,' said Pete.

'No. Stupid. They big stupid. They believe conspiracy everywhere. Like no man ever been on moon. And twice towers brought down by own government. Big stupid, huh?'

Pete didn't respond, he was still wondering how many other twins had dated the same fella. Was that what The Shining had done with James? Was that what had gotten them into such a mess?

Another fifteen minutes of deep tissue massage and Pete had reached the stage where he began to worry about internal haemorrhaging.

'Is Sal okay?' Karina asked him, 'She's no more talking, when before, she talk even through facials.'

Pete didn't respond. He suddenly couldn't speak. But then, he suddenly gave way to uncontrollable sobbing. With his face still wedged in the hole, it was hard for him to breath.

'Pete? What is it?' Karina asked, anxiously pulling his shoulders back to free his head out of the hole.

Pete lifted himself upright and then swung around to sit on the edge of the bed. Karina immediately hopped up beside him to take hold of his hand, but rather than be pacified, he began to worry that the bed might break. His worry only stopped when he heard her crying.

'Aw, don't get yourself upset on my account,' he told her, slinging an arm around her shoulders. 'My friend's just died, that's all,' he lied, 'But he was really old. And he'd had a wonderful life.'

Karina was dabbing at her eyes with the towel that had just been laid across his bum.

'My grandmother, also. Yesterday.' And then she began to heave with great, heart-rending sobs.

'Aw, sweetheart, I'm so sorry to hear that. That's terrible news. Especially when you've not seen her for so long.'

Saying that just made her worse, and Pete wished he hadn't.

'Shall I go get you a cup of tea? Or a brandy?'

Karina shook her head.

'How about a plane ticket home? To be with the rest of your family?'

'I can't go home. I haven't got passport, remember?'

Pete remembered. 'Okay, we can get you back the same way you came. Hidden in a camper van.'

She'd only recently told them about Arek, driving all the way to Ukraine to collect her. And how she'd sat inside a false fridge while going through border control.

'I can't. Rosa has too frightened me to go back to Mariupol. And all the time, I worry about them, my family, being where something bad is to happen.'

Pete sat mulling it over.

'Why don't they move to the west of Ukraine? Like Rosa suggested?'

Karina blew her nose on the towel.

'They have too much animals. They won't leave them. And the place they live now is for free, as long as they dig the harvest.'

Pete considered her plight, perversely grateful for the distraction from his own.

'Tomorrow, I'm going to bring my laptop, and we're going to look on the internet for a farm out to the west. One that's big enough for them and all the animals.'

Karina sobbed again. 'It's impossible. We have no money, like you.'

'Well hey-ho, there you go. Money, like me. I've got tons of the stuff. I can buy that farm. It'll be nothing more than a whistle out of my wallet.'

They smiled at each other. It was the phrase Sal had used after she'd given the girls a monkey, as a tip at Christmas, and they'd baulked at the magnitude of it.

But their smiles lasted all of five seconds before they both broke down again, arms flung around each other.

The door behind them had opened. They heard it, but with their backs to it, they couldn't see who had opened it.

'You lousy, cheating bastard!' a voice screeched.

Pete and Karina hopped off the bed and turned to see Sasquatch. She with the big feet. She with the indignant look on her face. She with the look that instantly turned from indignation to surprise, on seeing them both red eyed and tear stained.

They didn't speak. They just stood and stared at her.

'What happened?' she asked them.

Pete shrugged. 'You jumped to the wrong conclusion. That's what happened.'

'No, I mean, well, yes, I did. But I didn't realise you were upset.'

'Obviously,' Pete said to her, quickly gathering himself. 'But we'll forgive you. Even though you don't deserve it. Even though you didn't forgive Chloe.'

'What's she got to do with it?'

'She jumped to the wrong conclusion, like you just did. And now she's stuck with mopping your floors seven days a week. She'd be done with it now, if you'd agreed to it being just one month, like I said.'

Sasquatch glared at him, defiantly.

'Well that's just tough. If I hadn't let you coerce me into letting her stay, she'd be packed and gone.'

Pete gave her a wry smile.

'I tell you what. She's out there in the pool. You go and tell her that her time is up. One month, like I said. Which means she's done.'

'Not a chance,' Sasquatch shot back.

'Okay, have it your way. But let's just see if you feel the same way when everyone in here is unable to forgive you.'

'Forgive me for what?'

'For scratching Chloe's car, out in the car park. I think there could be quite a backlash when I tell everyone it was you that did it.'

Pete watched the colour slowly drain from her furious face. It was as if giant leeches were sucking on the end of her overly long toes, like they were straws into a milkshake.

'And what makes you think that was me?' she contested.

'I don't think. I know. Because my car was parked right opposite and it has a dashcam that operates twenty-four seven. All recorded and stored.'

'You're lying,' she challenged him, 'Nobody would bother putting a dashcam on that rusty old heap of shit.'

Pete raised his eyebrow at her. 'You sure about that?'

She squirmed and she licked her lips, but when she bit them, Pete knew he had her.

'Fine. Fucking fine. I'll go tell her.'

'Now?'

'Yes, now. And if you show that footage to anybody, I'll sue you for invasion of privacy.'

She stormed out, leaving Pete feeling strangely powerful. Having insider information on someone, to astonish them, or manipulate them, was remarkably thrilling. Maybe that was how Rosa felt. But maybe Rosa wasn't psychic at all. Maybe she'd just had access to the Confessions file.

'Did she really do scratchings on Chloe's car?' Karina asked him.

'She did. But best not tell anybody, because I don't really have any dashcam footage. It was just a lucky guess.'

CHAPTER FOURTEEN

NIGHT AFTER DAY

'Did you set the alarm clock?' Sal asked, as Pete shuffled sideways to give Junior more room in-between them.

'Nup.'

'Well don't fall asleep then.'

'I won't.'

Junior snarled as Sal rolled over onto him.

'Why aren't you sleeping?'

'You know why.'

'Stop making it sound like it's my fault.'

'It's not your fault. But why do you always have to ask me a million questions to do with the house as soon as I get my head down? I couldn't care less about the house. I don't understand why you couldn't either. You've got an incurable disease and yet all you want to talk about is what colour travertine you think we should have in the utility room, and should the driveway be blockwork, gravel, or tarmac? Who gives a shit?'

'SOL.'

'Aww, give it a rest, Sal. I get it. I get why you need to distract yourself.'

'No, you don't.'

'Don't I?'

'No. I'm just wanting to get it finished, so you don't have to worry about it when I'm gone.'

'Well trust me, I won't. It'll be the least of my worries.'

It was true. Reason being, he'd already signed the house over to his brother. He never wanted to set foot in it again. It was Sal's project. Sal's dream home. And knowing that, he wanted nothing to do with it. Whereas Andy and his wife had been coveting the house since its inception. They'd be selling up their three garden centres and retiring back to Yorkshire, soon as Sal had ceased to be. Not that Sal was aware of it, it was a secret he and his brother were both sworn to.

'I saw a rat this morning,' Sal told him, totally circuitous to previous.

'Oh, yeh. Whereabouts?'

'Down by the stables.'

The stables were new. Pete had overseen their building. The ponies would be sheltered for the winter because Phoebe had insisted on it. Arek had predicted they would become wilful and soft for it, so Phoebe had told Rosa to keep Arek out of the caravan, to keep him from going wilful and soft on her. Arek hadn't been amused.

'I'll get Arek and Hellmutt down there in the morning. Best to see them off before we get overrun.'

Sal sniffed and rolled away from him again.

'No need to bother, I rung him already. I needed him to bring me what he'd caught.'

'Rats?'

'Dead rats, yes.'

'What the hell for?'

Sal began to cackle.

'Come on? What did you want dead rats for?'

Sal cackled the more.

'I sent them out as deliveries to people. In the Starships. Soon as it got dark.'

Starships were programmed for anyone to use via their phone app, to deliver and to receive, so it was entirely possible.

'Anybody in particular?'

'As many as I had rats for,' Sal answered, 'For Halloween.'

Pete had forgotten about the day's auspicious date. And on a full moon. And a blue moon, by all accounts. A great night for Be-twitching. And a great night for delivering a load of dead rats to one and all.

'Brilliant. Absolutely brilliant.'

As usual, they'd slept in, hence they were the last to arrive. They left their clothes where they dropped them and scurried through the barrier shower into The Dome's vast open centre.

Everyone was gathered around the pool side, chatting and laughing, letting the temperate, tropical warmth envelop them.

'Can I have a word with you, Pete?' Adam asked, tapping him on the shoulder.

'Sure.'

Adam led him away to where nobody could hear.

'Vic isn't coming tonight. He thinks he's got Covid. He's asked if you could start without him and let everyone know why he's not here.'

Pete's eyes widened. 'Are you sure that's a good idea? When half the staff got Chlamydia, nobody cared a jot, but when two of them came down with Covid, they were a match away from burning them at the stake.'

'Fair enough,' said Adam, 'Just say he's not well, then.'

With a quick glance at the clock, Adam headed off to begin their midnight musical accompaniment.

At the first note, they all began to sing, and then they began to file down into the cerulean, underlit pool.

Pete remained on the side, waiting until they were all in.

'Evening all. I'm sorry to have to tell you this, but Vic won't be joining us tonight. He's got a bit of a stomach bug, so we'll have to —'

'Oh, come off it,' Gabe called out, 'Tell us the truth, why don't you.'

Typical of Gabe to know, thought Pete.

He opted to feign ignorance. 'And what would that be?'

'He's still down in the village. Trick or treating.'

Everyone laughed, including Pete.

It was getting harder for Phoebe to get through The Well's hidden opening. It was plenty wide enough to accommodate her bump, it was just that the bump didn't want to be accommodated. When submerged, it flipped her over onto her back, like an upended turtle, making it impossible for her to manoeuvre and making her reliant on others to push and to pull her through. Specifically, Pete did the pulling and Dan the pushing.

'Okay folks. Get ready to steady,' Adam shouted.

People who couldn't take hold of the outer circular bar, took hold of someone who could, and then Adam put into motion the raising of the floor. Once raised, they all spread out and sat down.

As The Vibration began, it brought with it the strange symphonic resonance that instantly shutdown their random thoughts. It was as if their brainwave frequency was instantly switched from Beta to Theta. Pete immediately peed himself. He used to be able to hold it in, to honour the sanctity of the place, but not anymore. Maybe he had prostate trouble? But more likely it was just how it was, for a man of his age. They were all probably peeing, as they were all of an age, apart from Dan and Phoebe, but then Phoebe admitted her pregnancy had her peeing on the back of a sneeze. No doubt they were all currently sitting in a soup of their own incontinence.

Pete looked for his new sign. A rarity for the well.

Don't seek, don't search, don't ask, don't knock, don't demand, relax. If you relax, it comes. If you relax, it is there. If you relax, you will start vibrating with it – Osho

It made the spacing of the original three uncomfortably uneven. He would have to get the ladders back in, to equal them all out.

Sat like small islands in a choppy sea, the water rose and fell around their shoulders in frenzied, pulsating ripples. The Vibration was travelling up Pete's spine and into the back of his head, making his teeth chatter. His jaw began to ache from an ever-increasing tension, but then it suddenly went slack and the chattering stopped. It was always the same.

He felt his right eyelid begin to flutter. And then his top lip began to quiver. This was it. Be-twitching had begun. It was like some unseen force had taken over his body. But tonight, instead of fighting it, like he normally did, he simply gave in. His relentless, all-consuming stress had taken him to rock bottom, and there was no longer any point in trying to stay in control.

Sal was floating. She was always one of the first, but others were soon to follow, hanging in suspension, limp and lifeless.

Pete closed his eyes and leaned back, frustrated that his ass stayed resolutely attached to the mosaic tiled base.

He decided to have another go at TRE, hoping to rediscover his trigger position. It had to be there somewhere. He'd managed it in the past, all he had to do was – Oh dear God – he was off. He was shaking, involuntarily. His entire body. If he hadn't had it explained to him – shown to him – he would have thought he was having a seizure. It felt primitive, but positive. Ravaging, yet restorative. He looked around. Nobody seemed to have noticed. The more he shook, the more The Vibration prolonged it. TRE was supposedly the ultimate tool for banishing the effects of trauma and here, in The Well, he'd found the perfect key to its release.

Several minutes later, when his shaking had stopped, a huge sense of lightness descended upon him, and for some unfathomable reason, he began to think of his grandmother. She was actually there, right before him, as luminous and warm as she was when he was a child. She was stood in the back yard of her one-up, one-down terrace house, with the tin bath hung out on the wall. The door to the outside lav was still hanging off its hinges, and if he'd gone inside, he knew he would have seen the squares of newspaper strung up there – having to wipe your backside on newsprint still remained the epitome of poverty, in Pete's mind.

His gran was giving him a little wave, nearly dropping Cockles in the process. Even the cat seemed to be smiling at him.

His grandad was now coming in through the back gate, wearing his flat cap and covered in coal dust from a day's work down the pit. Pete knew he must be nine years old. It was the year that the pit baths were being refurbished and put out of action. His grandad would wash at the kitchen sink, because it would be two years before they had their indoor shower and toilet fitted in the coal cellar, and the outside lav would become the coal-hole.

He'd been dreaming a lot about his childhood lately, at least for the few hours he did manage to sleep. The misery of living with his parents. The cruelty and neglect that they'd inflicted on him and his brother. The beatings they took from their unemployed, abusive father, and the meanness of their fat, lazy mother, who had them both cleaning and cooking from an unforgivably early age. But the hours of happiness that they'd spent with their grandparents had helped them to survive it. With them, they had been warm and fed and smothered in an abundance of love, and after all these years, the good memories were starting to win out over the bad.

He could now see that it was snowing and he and his brother were out on the old shale stacks, using dustbin lids as sleds. Why was he dreaming of snow while he was there in a tropical oasis? They were wearing coats that were too big for them. Always clothed in their parents' cast offs until Pete was old enough to work and to buy their own. He was trudging up the steep stack, pulling the lid that was tied with a piece of string, knee deep in snow and soaking wet. Up and up, climbing right to the very top, but when he turned to look back down, beneath him wasn't Barnsley's kith and kin, but The Well and the people now in it. He was back in the here and now, and he was looking down on everyone he knew.

Mary and Ginnel were floating, hand in hand. Three Lugs looked bored, sat with chin in hands and elbows on knees. Phoebe was trying to float on her back but her bump kept rolling her over. There was somebody doing a headstand, but who it was he wasn't sure as all he could see were their two legs. Gabe was sat with his eyes shut and Jude was floating with her head resting on his right shoulder. Sal was still floating. And so was he. At last, after all these years, he was finally floating.

But how could it be? That he was seeing himself? Should he be frightened? Was it possible to be in two places at the same time? Maybe he should stop smoking the weed? Maybe he should smoke more? Their oft spouted mantra came to mind. *Live in the world, but be not part of the world.* He didn't feel part of the world now. He knew that he was in it, but he certainly didn't feel part of it. He was dreaming, he had to be.

Turning himself over, he found that he was directly beneath The Dome's glass ceiling. Trapped, like a helium balloon. He could see cobwebs in the corners of each triangular panel and the tiny insects that were caught in them. He could feel the cold radiating off the surface of the glass and he could smell something akin to petrichor. Outside, the night sky was lit bright from the luminance of the full moon and he could now perfectly understand why it had been predicted as a blue moon. It had a beautiful cobalt blue tinge to it.

But then, something was amiss. He had a recollection of Dan saying it had nothing to do with colour. It was simply the name given to a rare, second full moon falling within any given month. Blue moon, as in once-in-a. So why was it blue? And why was it a pulsating blue? Pete spun himself around to see that the whole of the night sky, in the direction of The Hub, was awash with a blue strobing light. It could only be one thing. Plod. But then everything went black.

'Pete! Wake up, for goodness' sake!'

It was Sal. Shouting at him.

He floundered around in the water, landing on his knees beside her, totally baffled by the sudden eerie darkness.

'What's happened to the lights?' he immediately asked.

'We don't know. Adam thinks it's a power cut.'

Pete suddenly realised The Vibration and Sound were also absent. Everywhere was still and silent. Even the cicadas were dumbstruck.

'How are we going to get out?' Phoebe shouted to ask.

Pete immediately panicked. The escape hatch was inaccessible while ever the platform was raised. They were trapped.

'I'm sure the power will come back on soon,' Adam told her.

'But what if it doesn't?' shouted Three Lugs.

Adam didn't immediately answer. 'Then we could be here for some time.'

'Who knows we're in here?' Mary asked.

Again, Adam was slow to reply. 'Vic, but he's probably asleep.'

'Oh, isn't that bleeding marvellous,' shouted Gabe, 'We'll all be blanched by the time he gets up.'

'Arek knows we're in here,' Yakky shouted out. 'He's sat outside the front doors. When we don't come out at our usual time, he'll know something is wrong.'

'Yes. Arek. Our saviour, ' shouted Mary, 'He'll come and rescue us.'

'I'm sorry to tell you this,' Adam told them, 'But I've given him the night off. Once we were all in, I told him he could go to the Halloween party the kids were having.'

By kids, Pete knew Adam meant the staff. He also knew that Arek wouldn't have gone to party, he'd have gone to peddle his wares.

Everyone was suddenly full of chattering worry.

'The police are here,' Pete announced, loudly, surprising even himself, 'They'll be wanting to speak to somebody, other than the kids. All we have to do is sit tight and wait for them to come and look for us.'

Nobody spoke, and then too many spoke at once, all asking him the same thing. How did he know?

'I can't explain. I just know,' Pete told them. 'You'll see.'

'Oh, here we go,' shouted Gabe, 'You know what this is, don't you? A Halloween trick. We're being spook-spoofed by him. It's like the hog roast, when he convinced us all that Health and Safety would be dropping by.'

There was a sudden babble of conversation. Some people expressing grateful relief, some excited amusement, and the rest, utter indignation.

'I can assure you, I'm not,' Pete loudly declared, 'If we don't get out of here within the next half hour, I'm going up over the wall, even if it means breaking a leg. Being trapped in here, in the dark, is not my idea of fun, believe me.'

His comments were met by a barrage of disbelievers, and then somebody yelled, 'Shut up!'

Everyone shut up.

'Hello?' a voice was shouting out to them.

'Hello,' Adam shouted back, 'Who's that?'

'It's me. It's Jake. I'm here with Arek. Where are you, exactly?'

'We're in The Well,' Mary shouted out.

'The what?'

'Never mind,' shouted Adam, 'Do you know where the main power switch is? I think it must have tripped out.'

'Course I know. It was us that switched it off.'

'There you go!' Gabe declared, 'Hardcastle strikes again. No surprise that it just happens to be his little buddy out there. We need to watch ourselves. We don't want slipping another Mickey Finn potion again.'

Everyone gave noises of agreement.

Adam told Gabe to shut-up, and then shouted, 'Why did you turn it off, Jake? Is there a fire somewhere?'

'No. Worse. There's police. We've been looking all over for you. Shouting and bawling our heads off. Only thing I could think to do, was turn off all that humming racket so you could hear us.'

Pete's eyes had grown accustomed to the small light given by the distant moon and he could now see those around him, looking at him with wavering smiles of uncertainty.

'I need you to go switch it back on, quick as you can. We can't get out otherwise,' Adam shouted.

There was silence, and then they heard Jake's voice.

'Okay, Arek's gone to do it.'

As they waited, Gabe and Jude made their way over to Pete and Sal.

'What happens next?' Gabe asked Pete, as they sat back down in the rapidly cooling water.

'We get out, hopefully.'

Gabe grinned at him.

'And then what? We get met by a load of fake coppers? Cuffed, frisked and thrown in the back of a meat wagon?'

Pete just sighed and shook his head.

'And we know that the rat was from you, as well,' Jude told him.

'We got a rat delivered,' Ruthless immediately turned to tell them.

'Us too,' said Oprah.

Word quickly spread about their Halloween gifts, with those not having received one being the most disgruntled.

The lights, The Vibration and Sound, all jumped into being at once, with Adam promptly shutting down the latter and setting into motion the lowering of their raised platform.

'Okay, everyone, time to make an orderly exit,' he told them, 'And I don't want to appear rude, but Eve and myself will need to leave first. If there really are police out there, it's us they'll need to speak to.'

'There are no police,' Gabe assured him. 'And if there are, they're not going to be real. How could he have known about them, otherwise?' He was pointing at Pete, so pointedly, he had his finger poking into his chest.

While the others seemed to be in agreement, Adam seemed to be in shock. It was like the whole power cut thing had unnerved him. As the base touched down and the hydraulics ground to a halt, he was quick on the heels of his sister to dive out through the hole.

Pete hadn't been shy in pushing himself and Sal forward, allowing them to follow on next, with Gabe and Jude right behind.

'Well, well, well,' were the first words Pete heard on emergence. Plod words. Only it wasn't plod. It was Jake, wading ever nearer. Adam and Eve's miraculous appearance having disclosed the entrance to The Well.

'That was a well-kept secret, I must say,' Jake congratulated them.

'Yes, and we'd like it to stay that way,' Adam told him, 'So keep it to yourself.'

Jake just grinned.

More and more people began to emerge out of The Well, all clearly expecting to be met by further excitement, and visibly disappointed when they weren't. But not for long.

Two policemen came in through the revolving doors, soon to be followed by two more, all of them looking around, warily. When they saw the naked, middle-aged throng coming toward them, they were disarmed to the point of bemusement.

'Evening officers,' Gabe called out, already half way up the pool's steps to meet them. 'So nice of you to drop by. We've been expecting you.'

Pete closed his eyes in a horrified cringe and then opened them to see that plod had folded their arms in what appeared to be their first stage of defence.

'I'd like to be cuffed and frisked first, if that's alright with you?' Gabe said to them, turning to grin at his audience, while joining his wrists behind his back, in readiness. 'It's just that I've got a busy schedule of looting and shooting tomorrow.'

The police stared at him, and then they stared at the rest of them. Everyone stared back.

'What's got into Gabe?' Jake whispered over Pete's shoulder. 'He wants to be careful. That big guy in the middle is Inspector Halloran. He once nicked my mate for just looking at him the wrong way.'

Pete sighed. That was confirmation enough that the evening was going to end badly.

'How much are you lot getting paid for this?' Gabe felt licenced to go on, 'A pretty penny I should imagine, coming out at this time of night. But you've all got a look of the nightclub bouncer about you, so maybe these are your normal hours and you're just moonligh —'

'Alright, wise guy, your wish just came true. You can come for a little trip down the station. See how cocky you are after a night in the cells,' Halloran said to him. 'Get yourself off with Officer Dibble here, and find yourself some clothes to put on.'

Gabe threw his arms up in triumph.

'See! What did I tell you?' he said to his audience, 'Only Hardcastle could come up with that one. Officer Dibble. TC's nemesis. Maybe not our TC, but TC, nevertheless. It's a dead give-away.'

Everyone murmured in agreement.

'Oh, aren't we blessed,' Halloran sighed. 'I don't know what you lot have been on, and I sure as hell don't want to know what you've been up to, but as of now, it stops. You need to get yourselves back into your digs, pronto, and stay there.'

Everyone was looking at each other, amused, and Pete could see they were still disbelieving of the situation.

'Who's in charge of the place?' Halloran demanded.

Adam put his hand up, but then so did Pete.

'Alright, you two, get some clobber on and meet me out the front. And just in case anyone has any ideas about leaving the premises, don't. We're going to need to speak to each and every one of you over the next twenty-four hours.'

'Not this malarkey, again!' Mushette shouted out, 'We've been through all this before. You interviewed us over the two bodies that were dug up here. It was a complete waste of time, seeing as they turned out to be early Anglo Saxon.'

Halloran smirked, 'Yes, and now your little *time-team* has dug up another body.'

'Well bully for them,' Plucky shouted, 'And what makes you think this one isn't Anglo Saxon?'

'Because it's got fucking slacks on!' Halloran shouted back.

CHAPTER FIFTEEN

ONE DAY IN NOVEMBER

As Pete stood at the edge of the grave, he wondered at himself, that he should be so calm and composed in the circumstances. He hadn't expected it to happen so soon. And now, suddenly, he had so much to undertake and get to grips with.

It was cold, but the resort's members were all naked, apart from their black armbands. Over the years, Pete had become hardened to harsher weather, but he could see some of the others looking with envy at their staff, wrapped up in their hats and coats. But it was a small price for them to pay, to comply with the requested code of non-dress.

Death wasn't agreeable. He'd often asked TC why it had to happen. Going to all the effort of creating such unique and individual characters, watching them develop and progress, allowing them to love and be loved, and then simply extinguishing them. What was the point? He tried not to rail at the injustice of it, but it was hard.

He was stood at the head of the hole, looking down into it. The cardboard box that lay at the bottom was just like the one their fridge-freezer had arrived in. Was this how a green burial was? He'd known it was part of the plan, but it was still disconcerting.

Mick the Vic stepped forward and threw in a handful of earth. '*The Lord is my shepherd, I shall not want. He makes me lie down in green pastures. He leads me beside still waters. He restores my soul. He leads me in paths of righteousness for his name's sake. Even though I walk through the valley of the shadow of death, I will fear no evil, for you are with me, your rod and staff comfort me.*' He then stepped back.

Next, Genji, the Buddhist monk, came forward in his saffron robes. He threw a garland of white and yellow flowers down onto the box and then rang a little bell that was attached to his thumb. He began to chant a warbling nonsense, but a minute later, he stopped chanting and rang his little bell again.

'*A thousand candles can be lit from a single candle, and the life of the candle will not be shortened. Happiness never decreases by being shared.*' Genji then stepped back.

Rosa next came forward. She held out a crystal on a long chain and swung it above the hole. As it spun, it caught the light, and reflected an everchanging rainbow of colours. She was scanning all around, as if looking for someone, but not any of them.

'Spirit is all around. But I can't connect with anyone recently passed,' she told them.

They waited while she persevered, spinning her crystal and searching for someone hidden amongst them.

Then, suddenly, she yelled, 'Get out of that bloody hole, now! Do you hear me? Now!'

Everyone gasped.

Rosa was leaning forward, frantically shooing and shouting into the grave.

'That damn dog of yours is an absolute nightmare,' she turned to say to Sugar and Spice, 'If it wasn't already dead, I'd kill it.'

It was as shocking as it was amusing. The dog in question was a spaniel called Gordon. Named after their close friend. Unfortunately, the couple had lost him only three weeks earlier, when he'd run headlong into The Tree, chasing a squirrel.

Sugar immediately crouched down, 'Come here boy, come to mummy.'

Nobody was sure if the invisible dog had gone to mummy or not, least of all Sugar himself. Rosa just shook her head and stepped back from the grave.

It was Pete's turn.

He bowed his head and then he lifted it, to look at them all, solemnly.

'So, a vicar, a Buddhist monk and a clairvoyant walk into this bar,' he began.

There was an audible intake of breath and a sea of horrified faces staring at him, and Pete could only imagine what the three named stooges were thinking.

'Just joking,' he told them.

Nobody laughed, apart from Gabe.

'Firstly, I'd like to thank you all for turning out today. Funerals are never pleasant and people are apt to shy away. As for a eulogy, there's just too much to say. So, I'll leave you with a quote from one of our many signs. One of my favourites. *The Garden of Eden might be where we all started, but remind yourself daily, it could be from where you're departed.* A personal best from the great man himself.'

As Pete stepped back, Adam immediately switched on the Bose speaker and held it out like a lantern. The music of their honorary hymn began, and with it, their voices.

After the first verse, they repeated it, as was their wont, which immediately threw Mick the Vic into a confused consternation. While he was able to sing the whole hymn, they just stuck to that which they knew, nine times over.

As soon as they'd finished, Arek didn't even pause to reflect, or for respect, he plunged his shovel into the nearby mound of earth and began tossing it into the hole. They all backed away. Nobody wanted to chance witness the collapse of the cardboard box.

Pete suddenly sensed Three Lugs by his side.

'A stomach bug. That's what you'd said. And five days after that, he's damn well dead.'

Pete didn't deny it, but how was he to know that Vic had been at death's door, from Covid.

And now, Vic had undergone his funeral of choice. Green burial with a very short input from his three B religion. Bible, Buddhism and Beyond.

'I hear you're wanting a word?' Father Anthony said, tapping Pete on the shoulder.

Pete turned around.

'Yes, I am. Are you free for a confession this afternoon?'

Father Anthony consulted his watch. 'Two thirty do for you?'

Pete nodded, as just then, Sal arrived.

'As custodian, I thought the least you could do was give him a proper eulogy.'

Pete shrugged. 'Vic's written instructions. Each of us had three minutes max.'

Sal shook her head. 'Quickest damn funeral I've ever been to. You better come up with summat better than that for mine,' she told him, before heading off to speak to Phoebe.

Gabe sidled up to him. 'Rather ironic, don't you think? He's the one who wanted us all to be locked-in here, to avoid catching it, and after all that, he's the one who's gone and croaked from it.'

Pete nodded. 'Have you seen how many are wearing facemasks all of a sudden? I don't think any of them took it seriously, up until now. Some have even complained about Mick the Vic and Genji being allowed in.'

'Yeh, fucking Covid restrictions. Two of the bastards have cancelled the cars they were buying off me, thanks to nobody being allowed to bleeding go anywhere, anymore.'

Just lately, Gabe was swearing more than Sal. The money laundering business was obviously being hung out to dry.

'You staying for Vic's passing-over party, tonight?' Pete asked Genji.

'No, I don't think so. Think it's best that I get off. Saves me hanging around all day.'

'Shame. We've got some great facilities you could make use of. You name it, we've got it.'

'Yes, so I understand. It's just the nudity thing. I wasn't expecting it.'

Pete realised he'd not been forewarned. Speakers only ever saw them fully clothed and were never actually aware of their day-to-day state of undress, apart from Mick the Vic.

'The secret is, to join in. Once you're in the same state, you'll feel totally at ease. You should give it a go.'

Genji looked at him, doubtful, but just then, Pete heard his name being called. He turned to see Eeyore had picked up their golf buggy and was waving him over.

As soon as Pete climbed in, Eeyore floored it. It was like he couldn't wait to escape the emotionally charged atmosphere. As they hit the opposite kerb, they went airborne, and Pete reached into the back to hold onto his new clubs.

'So, a vicar, a Buddhist monk and a clairvoyant are walking down the road,' Eeyore began.

Pete guessed he was taking the mick, but then realised it was going to be a real joke. He smiled in anticipation.

'And a spaceship lands, right in front of them,' Eeyore went on. 'An alien gets out. It's human looking, but it's got enormous feet, like Susanna Sutton, and enormous teeth, like Simon Porter. The vicar immediately declares that it's the second coming and falls to his knees in reverence. The Buddhist monk bows his head to the alien and welcomes it as the new Dalai Lama. The clairvoyant tells the other two that it's just a departed spirit, projecting from the astral plane.'

Pete was grinning as he clung to his seat, while the buggy careered across the newly opened fairways.

'The alien walks toward them and asks, "How do you humans like your meat?" The three of them have a think about it. "I prefer mine well done" the Vicar tells it. "I like mine rare" says the monk. "I don't do meat. I'm a vegetarian" says the clairvoyant. The alien immediately pulls out his ray gun and ushers them up the spaceship's gangway. He shouts ahead, "Hey, Zyglob, I've got two for the barbeque, and one for the salad bowl".'

Pete shook his head. 'Not bad. But not great.'

'It's not meant to be great. It's meant to be thought provoking,' Eeyore told him. 'We can believe what we like about the afterlife, but the truth might be more horrific than we care to imagine.'

'Best not to imagine, then.'

'But what if aliens really did put us here? What if they're just waiting until the population reaches ten billion and then they come back and round us all up for their galactic deep freezer?'

Pete smiled. 'I think they'd have created us with a bit more meat on our bones.'

'Not necessarily,' Eeyore conjectured, 'I'd take partridge over pig any day of the week. You think about it. When a farmer drives past his field of cows, they're probably all looking at him, saying, "There's that nice human who put us into this lovely, lush field of grass. How kind he is? He must truly love us, seeing as all we do all day is shit and fart".'

Pete was laughing now, even though the premise wasn't funny.

‘Let’s just hope we both snuff it, then. Before we reach the ten billion mark.’

As they walked to the clubhouse, the heavens opened and hail stones as big as golf balls rained down upon them.

‘You got any neon balls?’ Eeyore asked, as they waited under the portico for it to abate.

‘Nup.’

‘Me neither.’

They both knew that trying to find their white balls, amongst all the ice balls, would be nigh on impossible.

‘You couldn’t make it up, could you?’ Pete murmured, ‘First day it’s reopened, and look at it.’

Eeyore smirked. ‘I reckon it’s Vic. Playing his last game against us, with half a million dropped balls.’

Pete liked the thought.

‘Same time tomorrow?’ Eeyore asked.

‘We can’t. We’ve got the DNA samples to give, remember?’

‘Blast. I forgot about that.’

They were all required to attend a police mobile unit, coming in the hope of matching one of them up with their Jane Doe. Previous enquiries having got plod nowhere.

‘Who do you think she was?’ Eeyore asked.

‘No idea. But Sal thinks it’s Eve Sutcliffe. Same as everyone else.’

‘Yeh, me too, but then where’s Adam?’ Eeyore asked, before adding, brightly, ‘Fancy a game of snooker instead? At least we’ll be playing with dry balls.’

‘Aye, why not,’ said Pete, ‘Saves them from getting chapped.’

Eeyore began to bray.

When Pete walked through the front door, he saw Sal sat at their small dining table, along with Eve. Eve immediately closed the lid of the laptop that was set before them.

‘Don’t worry. I’m not interested in who you’re swiping right or left,’ Pete said to her.

He knew she was man hunting. She’d been inviting Sal over for weeks, to help sort the wheat from the chaff. Sal always came back full of gratitude at having him for a husband, having seen so many ming-mongs on-line. Pete quite liked the gratitude.

Hence he quite liked Sal visiting Eve, and now, if Eve wanted to visit Sal, he didn't mind that either.

'What happened to your golf?' Sal asked him.

'Hail storm. Didn't you hear it?'

'You've played in the rain before?'

'Hail, Sal, hail. Balls the size of small children. And stop mithering me, I'm only back to grab my snooker cue. You guys crack on with match dot com cos I've got my own match to go to.'

And he had, now that they'd rounded up two more to play. Gabe and The Boar.

'The solicitor rang, Pete. He said he's going to be late,' Eve informed him.

Pete had forgotten all about it. As executor to Vic's will, he had been called upon to witness proceedings, but he imagined it wouldn't take long. Eve and Adam might have been his step-kids, but Vic had loved them like they were his own. As for Rin, she hadn't even turned up for his funeral. She obviously knew the kids were getting the lot.

'What time?'

'Three thirty. Is that okay?'

'Sure. It'll follow on nicely after my confessional.'

'He's also said that a tie's required.'

Seriously? A dress code for a will reading?

As Pete went past them, heading to the bedroom, he saw the yellow post-it note stuck at the side of Eve's mobile. On it was written: *Password – Victorious1.* His pulse quickened. That wasn't Eve's laptop, it was Vic's. It was the laptop he'd searched for every single day, since first finding it inside their hot-tub's electrics.

Pete perched on the end of the bed. Eve was in on it. The fake burglary hadn't just been faked by his errant wife; she'd had an accomplice. But why? What were the pair of them up to? Manhunting was obviously just a subterfuge, but a subterfuge for what? Should he go out there and confront them? Maybe not. Not when Eve had just buried her step-father.

He headed back into the lounge. They still hadn't lifted the lid on the laptop. Whatever they were looking at was clearly something they didn't want him to see.

'Don't forget I'm at the hairdressers,' Sal told him as he headed out the door. 'I won't be back till half six, so mek sure Junior gets his tea.'

Pete gave her a thumbs up. Vic's pass-over party had no doubt led to another twelve-hour shift for their two hairdressers.

In the snooker hub, Pete found his three opponents ready and waiting, snacking on the lunch buffet that had just been delivered. He took off his resort issue, fleece-lined coat and hung it next to theirs. Then he helped himself to a growler.

The snooker hub had four tables, set out facing north, east, south, and west, all from a central, round score table. One of the four tables was already in use and Pete was pleasantly surprised to find that it was taken by Genji and Mo.

Mo and Oprah being Buddhist, it wasn't such a surprise that Genji had sought him out. But that Genji was naked was a revelation Pete hadn't expected.

'We're playing for the usual,' Gabe informed him.

No surprises there. The only snooker matches that had bets placed upon them were the ones that Gabe was part of. He being something of a pool shark had lent itself well to the gentleman's game, and where Pete reigned as golf king, Gabe held the snooker crown.

Pete pointed to the sign on the back wall.

Do not wear yourself out trying to get rich, be wise enough to know when to desist – Proverbs.

'I'll not be wearing myself out, it'll be a doddle,' Gabe assured him.

As Pete opened his wooden case and began to screw together the two pieces of his cue, Gabe sidled up to the table in play.

'Fancy joining us for a round-robin tournament?' he asked.

Mo nodded, but Genji looked across at them, warily.

'I'm not sure. Looks like you're all keen players.'

'What makes you say that?'

'You bring your own cues, for starters,' Genji pointed out.

'No, we don't,' said Eeyore, pointing to Mo, who was now weighing up a straighter cue from those available in the wall rack.

'Yes, we do,' Gabe agreed, pointing to the length that was hanging between Mo's legs.

They all sniggered.

'What?' Mo asked.

Nobody replied.

Lighting up two more tables, they laid the green baize with balls.

'You alright putting up a monkey?' Gabe asked Genji.

Genji shrugged and smiled, clearly thinking it was some sort of trick question.

'Here,' Pete called to him, tossing him a metal disc from out of his cue case.

They all placed their monkeys into the glass beaker that Gabe was holding out, then duly paired up over three tables.

'What made Vic want to be buried beneath The Tree?' The Boar asked Pete as they played against each other.

'Because he was a Man United fan,' Gabe threw out from the adjacent table.

The Boar looked to Pete for explanation.

'The red and white strips. Colours of Man United. But seeing as he detested football, that would be a no.'

'Didn't stop him from doing the score draws every week though, did it?' Gabe scoffed.

'Am I correct in guessing the red strips are Buddhist prayer ribbons?' Genji asked.

'Of a sort, yes,' Pete confirmed.

'What about the white ones? With there being so few in comparison?'

Pete stood back from the table. Genji was right, the ratio was probably the same as in snooker balls, fifteen red to one white.

'The white ones are the reason for all the red ones,' he told him.

Genji looked intrigued, but didn't pursue it.

Pete beat The Boar. Genji beat Eeyore. Gabe beat Mo. And then they swapped tables and played again with different opponents.

‘I never knew Mo was short for Moses,’ Pete said to him, as they played against each other.

‘And I never knew Sal was short for Salome,’ Mo returned.

Pete potted a red and lined up for the green.

‘You know, I was thinking about it just the other night. You do realise, we’ve all got biblical names in here, don’t you?’

‘Have we?’ Eeyore stopped to ask.

‘Aye, every one of us. Look ‘em up,’ Pete told him. ‘What are the chances of that?’

Mo beat Pete. Gabe beat Eeyore. Genji beat The Boar. And then they swapped tables and opponents.

‘When did you become a Buddhist, then? Pete asked Genji as they squared up.

‘When my four-year old son told me he used to be my father,’ Genji replied, chalking his cue tip.

They all stopped to stare at him.

‘Are you winding us up?’ Eeyore asked.

‘No word of a lie,’ said Genji, ‘My dad died the week before my son was born. That’s why we gave him the same name, Max. But when Max turned four, he casually told me that I was his son. He also told me how he’d died. Where he’d died. The age he’d died. And that he was cross because I’d buried him in his old suit, rather than his Sunday best. All of which was true. If something like that happens to you, you’re pretty much sold on reincarnation.’

They were all still staring at him.

‘Is that how it works?’ The Boar asked, ‘You pop off one week and arrive back the next?’

Genji shook his head. ‘That happens rarely. It normally takes years before you make your way back. It’s only the Dalai Lama that comes back the instant he goes.’

Pete had always thought there’d been a succession of individual Dalai Lamas, not one continuous one.

‘But there’s other religions that believe in reincarnation. What made you pick Buddhism?’ he asked.

‘Because I don’t believe there’s a God, or gods, ruling over us. Because I don’t think we should eat animals. Because I’d had déjà vu moments myself that made me think I’d lived here before. Because the guidance Buddha left us with made perfect sense. Because, because, because. When do you want me to stop?'

'When I've managed to distract you long enough to win,' Pete told him.

They laughed and went back to their game.

'What about you Mo? What made you become Buddhist?' Eeyore asked him.

'The wife,' Mo replied.

Eeyore beat Mo. Gabe beat The Boar. Genji beat Pete. And then they swapped tables and opponents.

'Since you've been in charge of counting up the POTs, everyone thinks you're fixing it. Did you know?' Eeyore asked Pete.

Pete was bent over the table, ready to pot pink. He straightened back up.

'Is this a distraction ploy?'

Eeyore shook his head and looked across to Mo for confirmation. Mo nodded.

'And why would they think that?' Pete asked.

'Because Sal was always top. And now she's not even half way up.'

'And she still swears like a bricklayer with PMT,' Gabe threw out.

Pete grinned. 'Have you considered that whoever was POT shotting her, now knows that it's me who's collecting them all up? And that I might possibly tell her? Do you think they'd risk a bricklayer with PMT finding out it was them, all along?'

They all laughed, apart from Genji who smiled in the absence of knowing.

Pete beat Eeyore. The Bore beat Mo. Gabe beat Genji. And then they swapped tables and opponents for the final time.

Nobody spoke.

Genji beat Mo. Gabe beat Pete. Eeyore beat The Boar. Then they tallied the score.

The Boar had won only one of his five games. Pete, Eeyore and Mo had each won two. Gabe and Genji had each won four.

‘Three tokens apiece,’ Pete declared, shaking them out of the beaker and handing them over.

‘All or nothing?’ Gabe immediately suggested to Genji.

Genji shrugged and put his tokens back into the beaker. Although he seemed keen enough to win, he clearly wasn’t bothered about a few bits of monkey headed metal.

‘As much as I’d love to stay and watch, I’ve got a confessional to go to,’ Pete told them, ‘But shouldn’t be long. I’ve only got the one thing to get off my chest.’

As he began to unscrew his cue, he hesitated.

‘Here,’ he said to Genji, ‘use mine, for luck.’

Genji didn’t hesitate, the communal ones being as bowed as bananas.

‘Bless me father for I have sinned. Yesterday, Plucky pulled out in front of me on his scooter and nearly took me out, so I called him a big, fat, goofy, gormless, lump of lard.’

He could hear Father Anthony draw back a laugh.

‘Did he hear you, my son?’

‘Probably.’

‘It’s not like you, Pete, to be so unkind. Apart from some of your pet names, of course.’

‘Don’t get started on those, Father. I’ve repented them enough already.’

‘Okay. A penance for it,’ he told him, ‘Anything else, my son?’

‘Yes. I called you a dishonourable, sneaky, leaking sieve that deserved a thick ear.’

There was complete silence.

Pete waited. ‘Are you still there?’

‘Yes, I’m still here,’ Father Anthony replied. ‘Am I to gather you think I’ve repeated something that you’ve told me?’

‘Think? I absolutely, one-hundred percent know.’

‘And I also know, that you’re very much mistaken.’

‘Okay, then show me your notebook.’

Father Anthony lifted the confessional grille and passed through his notebook. Pete immediately flicked through it. On each page was a name, and beneath it, simple crosses in circles.

Beneath the crosses, a numbered total. The sins weren't written out as he expected, they were simply noted by a cross.

'Where's your mobile?' Pete barked at him.

'It's in my jacket pocket,' Father Anthony replied.

'Well hand it over,' Pete demanded, certain it would be set to record.

'I can't. It's in the back of my car,' Father Anthony replied. 'Do you want to come around and frisk me? I don't mind. If it helps alleviate your suspicions.'

Pete immediately left his side of the booth and went around to the other. Father Anthony had stood up and put his hands on his head.

Pete couldn't do it. It was suddenly all too ridiculous.

'You swear on your life that you've not been recording these sessions and passing it all on to Vic?'

'Vic's dead.'

'I know he's dead. But he wasn't always dead. And before he *was* dead, he typed out all of our confessions on his computer. Which means that you must have passed them on to him.'

'I can assure you I did no such thing.'

The two men stared at each other, and then, at the same moment, they both began searching the confessional booth. Pete on his side, Father Anthony on his. It didn't take them long.

'There's a microphone hooked under my seat,' Pete announced, wrenching it out. It was the old-fashioned type, with the bulbous head, and it had a thick cable stemming from it that they both set about following.

It went out through the floor of the antique wooden booth and ran beneath a piece of old carpet until it reached the cabinet on the back wall. Pete pulled open both doors at once, and there it was. A vintage, reel to reel tape recorder.

'You'd need to be Vic's age to know how to operate it,' Pete surmised, picking up the headset and listening.

'I think it has to be revolving for you to hear anything,' Father Anthony told him. 'My guess is, Vic set it to recording before I even came in. Probably left it running the entire day.'

Pete guessed his guess was correct.

'Did he ever mention it to you? That he was taping your sessions?'

Father Anthony shook his head.

'I think he'd have known I wouldn't agree to it. It's one thing letting people off-load their sins on you, but to let someone else use those sins for their own personal entertainment, is another,' he told him, and then, more concerned, 'He wasn't using them to blackmail people, was he?'

'I've no idea. Why would you think that?'

Father Anthony looked pensive. 'I'm not one to speak ill of the dead, but there might have been somebody. Just the one. It was something they once said, in confession.'

'About being blackmailed?'

Father Anthony nodded.

'Who was it?'

'I'm not prepared to say. I've never told anybody anything about anybody, and I'm not about to start now, whatever you might think.'

Pete reached out and squeezed his arm.

'I believe you. I'm sorry that I didn't. It's just so bizarre that Vic should do this. But what I find even more bizarre, is that people have been willing to tell you such shocking things. Things that would get them into all sorts of trouble if they were ever found out.'

Father Anthony nodded. 'I've often wondered the same thing. But maybe now Vic's gone, I stop coming? As custodian, you could pull the plug on the whole thing,' he suggested, clearly contrite.

Pete thought about it. Maybe he should. But people obviously had a compelling need to off-load their guilty secrets, and as his gran always used to say, better out than in, although she'd mostly said it to mean her wind.

'Nup. You just keep on coming. And keeping it to yourself.'

Father Anthony smiled and patted Pete on the back.

Leaving the confessional hub, Pete headed straight back to the snooker hub. He was just in time to see Genji pot the final black, and win. There were hoots and cheers from those watching, which were many, due to word having quickly spread throughout The Hub.

As Eeyore tipped the contents of the beaker into Genji's hand, Genji in turn handed them over to Pete.

'Not much use to me,' he said.

Pete handed them straight back.

'Oh, I think you'll find that they are,' he told him. 'Do you know what a monkey is in cockney speak?'

Genji shook his head.

'You toddle off through to reception and tell Katie that you want to cash these babies in,' Pete told him, 'And then you'll find out.'

Genji toddled.

'Have you heard the good news about the planning application for across the road?' Mo was asking. 'The housing estate got quashed. And then replaced with an eighteen-hole golf course. I've had a quick look. Best course architect in the UK has designed it. It's going to be outstanding. And, get this, it's just been passed. What do you think of that? No more whining that we've only got nine holes to play on. We can just nip over the road for another eighteen. Provided we all get in as members, of course.'

'And it's been passed?' Pete queried.

'Yes, Mick the Vic sent me a text, half an hour ago. Passed in record time.'

'Then it's definitely good news,' Pete agreed. 'As soon as it's built, we need to get ours remodelled, thanks to the Shovelbums decimating it.'

'It's not that bad. The main thing is we're able to play on it again,' said The Boar. 'And at least they didn't find any more bodies. At one point, I thought we were going to have to change our name to The Garden of Rest.'

'Have they found out who she is yet?' Mo asked.

'Have they hell,' said Gabe, 'Useless bleeding coppers. You'd think they'd have got somebody banged up by rights for it by now.'

'It's a miracle it's not you they banged up,' Mo returned, 'Especially after you frisked Officer Dibble.'

They all began to snigger. The memory of it was priceless.

‘I blame Vic,’ Gabe countered, ‘If he hadn’t given The Bums notice to quit, they wouldn’t have been working nights to wrap things up. And then we wouldn’t have had the Old Bill here at some unbelievable hour.’

‘They use dental records these days,’ The Boar imparted, ‘But her false teeth were missing, so they couldn’t.’

‘Who told you that?’ Mo asked.

‘Shovelbums, before they left. They also said she’d not been dead for more than fifteen or sixteen years. So if you ask me, somebody here knows who she is.’

They all looked at each other.

‘Can’t wait for the DNA sampling tomorrow,’ said Eeyore, ‘Can you imagine? If it turns out Chloe was right all along?’

‘DNA doesn’t prove you were somebody’s wife. You have to be blood related,’ Gabe pointed out.

‘Yes, but they might have scraped under her finger nails. If she tried to defend herself, there’d be blood or skin.’

‘After sixteen years, she probably doesn’t have any bloody finger nails,’ Gabe volleyed back.

A mobile phone was suddenly ringing and they all went to check their coat pockets. It was Pete’s, and for once, he answered it.

He listened, and then he replied, ‘Yes, I just heard. I don’t know whose palms you had to grease, but it certainly worked. You’ve earned your bonus, fair and square.’

Whatever was their response, Pete laughed at it, and then, ‘How about you get the next set of plans submitted while their palms are still greasy? We could really do with getting that tunnel, otherwise we’re stuck with having to get the buggies across the road.’

Pete nodded to the response, and then, ‘Okay, Arthur. Thanks again. Speak soon.’ And he rung off.

They were all staring at him.

‘You bought the bleeding land, didn’t you?’ Gabe said to him.

Pete grinned. ‘Everyone has their price.’

‘How much?’

Pete shrugged. ‘Let’s just say, I had to round up a menagerie of monkeys.’

He'd been told the will reading was to take place under The Tree, near to where Vic had been buried. It was presumably due to Covid restrictions, insisting people meet outdoors.

As he approached, he could see that there were six people present, one of which was sat to a small fold-out table. Nearer still, he could see that it was a typical solicitor. Slicked, grey hair, parted to the left. Pinstripe suit. Pinprick eyes that instantly weighed up what hourly charge you might be able to afford — not so easy to do when someone was naked, except for a tie. But bearing in mind how cold it was, Pete suddenly wished he hadn't given in to devilment and come suitably dressed.

'Mr Hardcastle?'

'That's me.'

It was only then that Pete took in the other five people in the imaginary room. Eve and Adam were sat to the right. Rin to the back. Dan and Phoebe to the left. What were they doing there?

'Please take a seat,' the solicitor instructed him, pointing to the chair, centre front of his desk. Pete suddenly felt like he was about to be interviewed.

'I'm Mr Carmichael, from Carmichael, Mayhew and Merryweather. Mr Dawson's solicitors.'

Pete gave him an elbow bump and then took his seat.

'Very well,' the solicitor began, 'Now that we're all gathered, let's press right ahead, shall we?'

He lifted a large, heavily embossed envelope from his open briefcase and unwound the ribbon from its studded disk. It was obviously meant to make the thing look official, just in case there was any doubt.

'*This is the last will and testament of I, Victorious Dawson, on the date of nineteenth September, two thousand and twenty. I hereby revoke all former wills and testamentary dispositions made by me. I appoint as my executors, Mr Peter Hardcastle, temporary residence being, The Garden of Eden, and my solicitors, Carmichael, Mayhew and ....*'

Pete zoned out. He hated all the legal jargon and pompous terminology. What was the point of it in this day and age? He made a mental note to alter his own will. As it stood, Salome Hardcastle was to inherit everything, in its entirety, but with her imminent demise, it seemed prudent to alter it. The beneficiaries he had in mind, so far, had amounted to his brother, Andy, and Barnsley Rovers. He really needed to spread it further.

'Are you agreed to being an executor, Mr Hardcastle?'

What exactly was an executor? He was just there to see that Eve and Adam got their rightful inheritance, wasn't he?

'Mr Hardcastle?'

'Yes, sorry, yes, I'm agreed.'

'*In this will, where the context so admits, my estate shall mean all of my property, of every kind wherever located, the money, investments and property from time to time representing all such property. For the administration of my estate, my trustees shall pay my debts and testamentary expenses and inheritance tax on all property which vests in them.*'

Pete tried not to yawn. Due to lack of sleep, he was always tired these days. He wanted to get back to his cabin and have a nap. Junior was probably still where he'd left him, watching television. Pete always left the television on for him. He liked cartoons best.

'Now we come to specific pecuniary legacies,' Carmichael continued. '*I wish to leave specific legacies as follows. To my step-son, Adam Turner, I leave the sum of one million pounds. To my step-daughter, Eve Mitford, I leave the sum of one million pounds.*'

Pete looked at them both. They were totally unresponsive. Why? It was a nice slice of cash to add to their sharing of The Garden. Had they been expecting more?

'*To Rin Yamaguchi, I leave the sum of two million pounds, to be given for the undertaking of that which is set out in our contract, as stipulated in accordance with the attached codicil belonging this will. An additional amount of one hundred thousand pounds, is to be paid each subsequent year that she remains resident in The Garden of Eden.*'

Rather than being pleased, Rin looked slightly agitated. Was she hoping for more? And what was she expected to undertake within their contract?

'*To Daniel and Phoebe Saunders, I leave the sum of three million pounds, to be given on fulfilment of our contract, as stipulated in accordance with the attached codicil belonging this will.*'

Pete stared at Dan and Phoebe. They too looked impassive. Why would Vic leave them such a large amount? So much more than Eve and Adam? And what were they expected to fulfil in *their* contract?

He stared at Eve and Adam. Why weren't they shocked? Outraged even? What was going on?

Carmichael cleared his throat. '*I leave my entire residuary estate, to the following. One hundred percent, to Mr Peter Hardcastle.*'

Pete stared at the solicitor, and he at him.

'Does that mean what I think it means?' Pete asked.

'Yes. Barring his legacies, he's left you his entire estate. You've just taken possession of The Garden of Eden Resort and Spa, Mr Hardcastle. Congratulations.'

Pete stared at Eve and Adam, and they at him.

'Why aren't you angry?' he asked them.

They didn't speak.

'Look, I don't think Vic was right in his head before he died. Probably not even when he wrote this will. I'll have it all signed back to you as soon as I can get my lawyers on it,' he told them.

Eve put her hand up, to stop him.

'There's a reason he left it to you, Pete. And if you don't accept it, then I'm not sure we'll actually get the money that's been left to us. Any of us.'

Pete looked at her, puzzling over what she'd just said.

'You heard that bit in the will, where it said *my trustees shall pay my debts, my testamentary expenses and inheritance tax on all property which vests in them?*'

Was he expected to nod? He nodded.

'If you take a look at what's in this envelope, you'll understand.' She passed over a white envelope.

Pete took out the paperwork. It was bank statements.

'As of yesterday, that's Vic's current debt, secured against The Garden. With leaving it to you, there was the chance you might want to keep it and be willing to pay off those debts and inheritance tax. If you decide not to accept it, it's likely the banks will foreclose on the place by March of next year, and sell it off to developers. Probably the same developers that have put in for the housing estate across the road.'

She obviously hadn't kept up with the times, Pete realised, as he looked through the statements. The debt was hefty. Heftier than hefty.

'And there was me, thinking he saw me as the most enlightened. When what the old bugger really saw, was that I was the most enriched'

'He knew what he was doing, that's for sure,' Adam remarked, 'But you're not obliged to accept, Pete.'

Pete would have to give it some thought. He'd only just bought a new golf course. But without The Garden, what use would that be?

'Copies of the contracts mentioned in the codicil,' Carmichael interrupted, taking out two ancillary envelopes. 'I understand the originals are already in the possession of Miss Yamaguchi and Mr and Mrs Saunders, so these are here under instruction of being passed to Mr Hardcastle, for him to now read and to then keep in his possession.' He passed the envelopes to Pete.

Pete put down Eve's envelope and took the others. The top one had Mr & Mrs Saunders handwritten across it, and *Open First*. So that's what he did.

It was one page, neatly typed and signed at the bottom by Vic himself. Beneath Vic's signature were the signatures of Daniel and Phoebe Saunders. He began to read.

It took him a good five minutes, but once it was read, he folded it and put it back into the envelope. Then he opened the one bearing the name Rin Yamaguchi, and *Read Second*.

It was in the same format and took Pete the same amount of time to read.

When he'd finished, Carmichael took it as his cue to continue.

'I now have one last task to perform,' he told them. 'Mr Dawson came to visit me the day before he died — which I still find rather disconcerting. It was to personally hand me a letter. This letter.' He was holding it up for them all to see.

'It came with the strict instructions that it was to be opened immediately after the will reading. To be read to those present, and in front of a police representative.'

As soon as he'd told them that, he stood up, waving in the direction of The Hub.

From out of nowhere, a uniformed officer stepped out and strode toward them.

Pete wondered what was in the letter, that required plod to hear it.

As the officer approached, Pete instantly recognised him from their Halloween Be-twitching night.

'I'm led to believe that you've already met with Inspector Halloran, so I'll dispense with any introductions,' Carmichael told them, as the Inspector came to stand beside his makeshift desk.

Pete caught a glimpse of Adam and Eve suddenly looking worried. More than worried. They'd reached out to take hold of each other's hand and Eve's face looked like it had just been slapped.

'The letter has been signed across its seal. If you'd care to take a look, Inspector? You'll also note that it has *police* written as ultimate recipient.'

It was duly inspected. And then it was opened.

As Carmichael scanned it, he gave way to a subtle, but noticeable flinch before he began to read.

'*I, Victorious Dawson, wish to confess to the compassionate ending of a life. That of my wife, Lilith Dawson.*'

They all looked to Eve as she let out a small strangled gasp.

'*Due to her advanced cancer causing severe and relentless pain, it was her wish that I undertake the merciful act by means of suffocation. The story that she took her own life was a complete fabrication. After abandoning her car on the beach in Cornwall, she actually returned to The Garden of Eden with me in my car, rather than going out to drown at sea which is what we wished people to believe. This was solely for the purpose of keeping me from criminal charges.*

'*The reason I am now compelled to reveal this to you is that the body recently found beneath the golf course, and as yet unidentified, will prove to be that of my wife, Lilith Dawson. DNA taken from either of her children, Eve Mitford and Adam Turner, will substantiate this. Yours in perpetuity.*' Carmichael paused briefly, to look around at them.

'The letter is signed and dated, and again, there's a note to say that it's to be handed directly to the police.'

The letter was handed over accordingly.

Pete felt numb. He could see why Vic had chosen to keep it secret. Mercy killings still carried a substantial prison sentence in the UK. And yet, something didn't sit right. Vic's biggest regret, the whole time Pete had known him, was that he hadn't been able to follow through with his wife's request for an assisted death. Why had he perpetuated that lie with him?

'Now that was something I wasn't expecting,' Inspector Halloran stated, as he slipped the envelope into one of his many jacket pockets. Turning to Adam and Eve, he added, 'In view of what's been disclosed here, I'd appreciate you both coming down to the station to provide the requisite DNA samples.'

'Of course. We'll be there first thing tomorrow,' Adam told him. 'And what about everyone else?'

Halloran looked puzzled. 'What about them?'

'Tomorrow, there's a bus coming to site, for a mass sample taking. Is that still going to go ahead?'

Halloran shook his head. 'We can dispense with that, now that we know what we know.'

Pete felt relieved. He didn't know why, he wasn't guilty of anything, but anything out of the ordinary unnerved him these days.

Carmichael closed his briefcase and stood to leave.

'If ever you should require the services of Carmichael, Mayhew and Merryweather, for whatever legal services you see fit, please don't hesitate to contact me,' he told them, leaving his business card on the table.

As Carmichael left, Adam went to talk with the Inspector, and Dan came to talk with Pete.

'Are you alright?' Dan asked him.

'I'm not rightly sure. It's a lot to take in.'

Dan nodded. 'Well at least you know why me and Phoebe are here, now.'

A gust of November wind brought down a sudden swirl of withered leaves and Pete looked up into The Tree. It would soon be as naked as he was.

Pete fed Junior, suspecting Sal had already done so, but knowing Junior wasn't one to turn down a meal. Not that he ever put on weight. He just defecated like a dinosaur. Where ShamPoo couldn't, Junior couldn't stop.

He then headed straight for the veranda and the hot-tub. He instinctively knew that the laptop was going to be there, even though it hadn't been since its initial discovery, not there or anywhere else. The side panel was wide open, just like before, because Sal could never tell a latch from a catch.

He reached beyond the inner mechanics of the tub and put his hand straight on it. It had probably been with Eve in the interim, but now it was back and he had until six thirty to make the most of it.

He poured himself a whisky and sat to the study table. The post-it note was gone, but Pete remembered. *Victorious1*. And he was in.

He went straight to the Confessions file. Pondering upon a choice of folders.

It had been his intention to look first at Saunders, Daniel and Phoebe, but owing to what he'd just read, he no longer had a need to.

Second up, he'd intended to look at Sutcliffe, David and Lydia, but owing to what he'd just heard, he no longer had a need to.

It now fell to a choice of six. Swingerdy-do, swingerdy-dah, he chose Carr, Benjamin.

Eating too much junk food.

Upsetting the wife by forgetting to flush the toilet.

Not exercising enough.

What about the wife-swapping-swinging? What about the past-it-porn movies?

Stood on a spider instead of putting it outside.

Really? Was that something worthy of confessing?

Left etiquette paper towel on dining room chair instead of binning it.

Oh, get a life why don't you. Pete was frustrated. He'd been expecting something deliciously debauched. Maybe Ben was in denial of his real sins?

Pete checked out the folder of his wife, Carr, Rachel.

Feeling too full of pride after huge success of latest video.

This was more like it.

Resents Asian market being their largest. Thinks fame in foreign country is pointless.

Pete would have thought it better to remain unknown on home turf. What if their neighbours were to see it? How embarrassing would that be?

Angry at husband for getting his timings out and exposing her right nipple.

Odd. Upset at exposure of a nipple didn't speak to Pete of porn. There was a highlighted website link attached, proving Vic must have been curious enough to want to look. Pete was curious too. He clicked on it.

It took him directly to the *Cor-blimey Choristers*. What kind of title was that? Maybe they swung from church bells rather than chandeliers.

Their website had a photo of the six of them, smiling, in the hot-tub, looking like they'd just met up for cocktails rather than cock. There was a menu on the righthand side and Pete clicked into it. *Blow Jobs* was top of the list. Pete took a breath. He was either going to be aroused or disgusted, hopefully, the latter.

The video was taken inside their cabin. He recognised it straight away. Two of the women were kneeling on the shag pile rug, somewhat portentously. They had small wooden stands in front of them which held various musical instruments, two of which covered from view their pubic regions. And they were holding song sheets, just at the right height to cover their thre'pennies. Their heads precisely covered the genitals of the two men who were stood behind them.

Within seconds, the four of them had begun to sing. Really good singing. Really clever singing. The barber-shop thing again. Their voices dipping in and out of each other, taking on different pitches and rhythms. And then they began to move. The man on the right dropped his song sheet, clearly on purpose, and as he ventured to get it, the woman in front of him reached out to take up a trombone. With perfect comic timing, her arm, and then the instrument, strategically covered the man's genitals. As he came back into position, the woman on the left leaned forward to pick up a saxophone, exposing the man behind her, if not for the random arm of someone out of shot reaching in to offer him a tuba. It was a perfectly timed work of art. They were constantly moving, but with such precise choreography that nothing that might upset the children was ever seen. And all the while, the singing continued. It was fabulous to listen to, while funny to watch. Pete was reminded of an old-fashioned fan dance he'd once seen, and more recently, a similar thing done with balloons. But this talented act were using props that they could actually play, and as they moved them around, front to back, left to right, swapping them as a means to keeping things covered, it was clear that they could all play each instrument, even if only for a short riff between singing their acapella. Wind instruments – *Blow Jobs*.

So, this was their past-it porn. Not porn at all. Definitely more cor blimey than hardcore. They weren't swingers. They were singers. And obviously making a good living from their on-line subscriptions, seeing as a screen pop-up had just reminded Vic that his was due for renewal.

Pete considered subscribing. They were good. So good he had to wonder why they hadn't advertised themselves to the club. He shut down *Blow Jobs* and had another look at the menu. *Hanky-Spanky*. What was that going to be? Sadomasochism hidden behind handkerchiefs? *Forest Fornication.* A woodland frolic with strategically placed flora and fauna? *Hot-Tubbing-Rubbing*. Possibly just cleaning it while passing around chamois leathers and sponges. Pete sniggered. The titles hinted at things that could be aptly misconstrued; the fun being in guessing how they'd pull it off, so to speak.

Pete had other confessions he wanted to look at, so shutting down the link, he came out of Rachel's folder, and scrolled down to that of Sutton, David. DoLittle.

Having previously checked out his wife, he'd regretted not having had a peek at his at the same time. He liked him, of course he liked him, he'd given him their dog. But as Sal had declared after Chloe's Congregational Court, there was never smoke without fire.

The folder was the largest yet at seventy-eight pages. DoLittle might not do a lot, but he certainly had a lot to confess.

Still can't stop even though it's getting riskier by the week.

Found another cabin with door unlocked, but feels guilty as he personally knows the owners.

Smoke, for sure, but who was lighting his fire?

Pete skipped back two dozen pages.

Lottie still threatening to end it unless he gets a divorce, but as wife is the one with the 'protected' wealth, he's not prepared to give that up for a 'mouthy little tart'.

So that was who he was tup-scuttling. Hey-ho, there you go. DoLittle wasn't doing little, he was doing Lottie. He would have to be DoLottie from now on.

Pete scrolled forward.

Furious at being blackmailed but considers he has no choice due to risk of divorce.

Blackmailed? DoLottie was obviously the person Father Anthony had mentioned.

But why would Vic want to blackmail him? And who was to say his wife wouldn't forgive him? She had him on a very high pedestal. More likely she'd throw Lottie under the bus, or at least scratch all around her new Fiat 500.

Pete scrolled forward a page.

Feels he's being held over a barrel. Desperately doesn't want wife to find out he was struck off. (Wife believes he's a 'retired' Consultant Obstetrician)

This was more like it. This was worthy of blackmail. But then, Vic had heard the confessions. He knew it was the wife that had all the money. Maybe it was someone else doing the blackmailing. Someone who was aware of his past.

Pete scrolled back in time, stopping sporadically within the dated confessions.

Lives with regret at having had an affair with two patients at the same time, especially as they found out about each other and reported him to the GMC.

Still angry at himself - wishes he'd denied everything at the board of enquiry.

The man was a serial womaniser. Wasn't he sick of vaginas by the end of his working day?

He came out of Sutton, David, and went into the folder of Morgan, Joanna. Aka Shar Pei.

Had three cream cakes delivered in three different Starship deliveries.

Had fish and chips, twice, for lunch.

Ate husband's leftovers, again.

No wonder she expanded so rapidly.

Had no exercise for five days.

Lied to husband at poolside, telling him going to visit friend when going back to cabin to visit fridge.

Pete realised all her sins were food related, which wasn't what he was looking for, but then:

Cheated again at coffee morning quiz.

This was exactly what he'd been looking for. He scrolled down further. It was always the same. Overindulgence and cheating at the quiz. But how did she cheat? He kept scrolling, and looking, until finally, he found out.

Wore spy glasses and hidden earpiece again. Michael enjoying the spying part, she enjoying the kudos. Feels guilty, but can't stop.

Michael? Michael Morgan. Secret Squirrel. He who bragged of being ex-MI5. With equipment like that, maybe he actually was, rather than the Walter Mitty they thought he was. There was a website link attached. Vic had obviously looked into it further. And Pete didn't hesitate to do the same.

It took him directly to a publicly available 'exam cheating' shopping site. Anyone could buy these spy glasses. They sent a clear video of all that you could see to a nearby accomplice; one who could use a speedy internet connection to look up, and then relay, all of the answers. Shar Pei must have jotted down each question on her paper so Secret Squirrel could see it. Same as he jotted them down, when he didn't immediately know the answer.

What fun he was going to have, turning off the resort's Wi-fi for the duration of their quizzing hour. There was no other signal available in their deep sided valley, so the pair of them would be totally scuppered.

CHAPTER SIXTEEN

NIGHT AFTER DAY

Pete went to let Junior out for another poo and porch inspection, leaving the door ajar for his return. Hearing the acapella of The Singers, in the distance, he smiled to himself. Out of all the resort's members, he had thought them the most immoral and as it was turning out, they were the least.

Back at the laptop, Pete clicked open the Debts file. It was all down to gambling. Vic owed money to every bookie in the county by the look of things. It was sad to read.

He pondered upon what he was going to do. Should he sell The Garden and pay off the debt? Or should he pay off the debt himself and keep The Garden? He would have asked Sal, but that seemed like a cruelty when she wouldn't be there to be part of it, and he knew she would definitely have wanted to keep it. He would need to think on it some more, but not now; now he needed to investigate further. It was already six o'clock.

He exited Debts and entered The Vibration and Sound file. It was a dull read.

The tuning fork is kept vibrating at its resonant frequency by a piezoelectric device. Amplitude of oscillation goes down when it comes into contact with solids, so it can be used as a switching parameter for detecting point level for solids. But the resonant frequency of a tuning fork changes when coming into contact with liquids ....

He quickly exited and went into Observatory.

There were various sub-folders. He opened Key. All that was inside was a single line.

Key hidden under the donkey's water trough.

He'd try to remember that. It would be interesting to take a look when he was next up there. He considered the other sub-folders. *Operating Manual. Constellations. Maintenance.*

The folder that had been the most recently read, presumably by Vic, was *The Great Conjunction*. He opened it. Inside were snapshots of newspaper clippings, all of which were related. He chose to read just one of them, headed, *The Great Conjunction of 2020.*

On the evening of December 21st, Jupiter and Saturn will move together until they appear as one. The last time this happened was 1226, when Francis of Assisi died and Thomas Aquinas was born - two of the world's most prominent visionaries and theologians. But before that, it occurred at round 5 BC, which is when most historians are agreed on being the more likely time of Christ's birth. The Great Conjunction will give the cruciform shape that many believe the Magi to have followed, making it their Star of Bethlehem. Our Christmas Star. Look south-west on the winter solstice, just after 6.30 pm, and you will see it with your naked eye. If you have a telescope, be sure to also look out for Jupiter's four Galilean moons.

Pete made another mental note, to go up there on the winter solstice, with a compass.

He came out of Observatory and went into Consultant – Hospital. Vic's pee-bag had always struck him as a bit severe for a mere UTI. And surely UTIs were beneath the pay grade of a consultant.

The file contained letters, all noted as having been attached to e-mails, in date order. He opened one at midway point and scanned through it. *Prognosis not good - Treatment to begin straight away*. He opened the last. *Advanced, stage four, terminal cancer - How to manage it, going forward - Palliative care*. Poor Vic. It had more likely been the cancer that had seen him off than the Covid. Covid had probably been the final straw. Terminal cancer. Just like Sal. What were the chances of that? Was there something in the water there? He read through the letters once again. They were extremely sad. And they were extremely familiar. They were from the same hospital and the same Consultant that Sal had, he was sure of it. Was that possible?

He went into the bedroom and found Sal's hospital letters in her bedside drawer, bringing them back, to compare. They weren't just from the same hospital and the same Consultant, they had the same headings, the same paragraphs, the same specific details, and exactly the same signatures. The only difference being, Sal's were relating to breast cancer and Vic's were for bone. Pete was suddenly unnerved. The more he looked at them, and the more he compared them, the more unnerved he became.

'You look busy,' Sal said to him as she breezed through the open door.

Pete looked to the time at the top right of the screen. Six-thirty. Shit. But hey-ho, there you go. No time like the present.

'I need to talk to you,' he told her.

Sal's smile evaporated as she ascertained it was something serious. When she saw the letters and the laptop, the colour drained away from her rosy, incredibly healthy-looking cheeks.

'Pour yourself a whisky,' Pete instructed her.

She did as she was told and then went to sit down on the arm of the sofa, opposite him.

'I'm going to ask you one question,' he told her, 'And you're going to give me a simple yes or no. Do you understand?'

She nodded.

'Have you got cancer? Or not?'

She squirmed. She sipped her drink. She scratched her leg. And then she replied. 'Not.'

Pete felt winded, almost as much as when the roles had been reversed and it had been him sat there, whisky in hand, receiving her bad news.

'You stupid fucking cow!' he levelled at her.

'SOL,' she said.

'What the fuck possessed you?'

'SOL,' she said.

'Were you out of your fucking mind?'

'SOL' she said.

'Is that it? Is that all you can say? Fucking SOL?'

'SOL,' she said.

Pete wanted to get up and punch her, but he resisted. He went instead to pour himself a whisky.

'Do you have any idea what you've put me through? I've been zooming with Harry. I've been smoking weed. I've been having middle of the night panic attacks, while you've been sleeping like a woman who hadn't a fucking care in the world.'

Sal went to open her mouth but he cut her off.

'If you say SOL one more fucking time, I'll throw you straight out that fucking window!'

Sal sipped her drink, and stared at him. She didn't seem the least remorseful.

'Have you finished?' she asked him.

'No. I want to know why? I want to know why you did this to me? What have I ever done to you to deserve what you've just done to me?'

Sal smiled at him, but it was a cold smile.

'You really want to know?'

'Of course I want to fucking know!'

She got up from the sofa and went to stand behind him. Reaching down to Vic's laptop, she clicked out of the Consultant – Hospital file and into the Confessions file. Inside of that, she scrolled down through its folders until she came to the one named Hardcastle, Peter. And then she opened it, and went to sit back down.

'The last few months you couldn't even bring yourself to say it, could you? It was just, *Still doing that thing I know I shouldn't.* But before then, right back at the beginning of our lock-in, you confessed it, loud and proud. You said you were sick of me being called the northern fishwife and the potty mouthed harpy. It needed to be done. And then after that, you actually confessed to finding it entertaining. It was a laugh. It was only over your last few sessions that you actually felt any kind of guilt over it.'

As she stared at him, Pete didn't respond, he was still trying to compute.

'And all those times I was furious. When I was desperate to find out. All those times when I begged you to help me find out. You devious, spiteful, nasty, evil bastard. It was you POT shotting me all along.'

'Oh shit,' said Pete.

'Oh shit. Oh shit. Too fucking right, oh shit,' Sal said to him. 'So I lied to you. So I made you feel some pain. So what? You deserved it. And let's not forget how easily you lied to me those first six months we were together. Having me believe you lived in that pokey little shithole flat, just in case I turned out to be a gold-digger. You're not averse to doing some pretty serious lying yourself, Peter Hardcastle.'

Pete looked down at the keypad. He didn't know what to say.

'But you want to know why I really did it?' Sal fulminated, standing up to lean over the desk, into his face, 'No, it wasn't for retribution. It was to put you to the test. To see how much you really loved me. Because if you could do something like that to me, I thought you must detest me. And you obviously do. Because this whole time, after the initial shock of me telling you, you've carried on just as normal. Like it meant nothing to you. Like my dying meant absolutely nothing. Life just carried on the same. Swingerdy-do, swingerdy-dah.' With hands clasped together, she was swinging them like she had hold of an imaginary golf club.

'Sal. It meant everything. Believe me. I've been to hell and back. I've had another AGM. I just didn't want to burden you with it. I've been keeping it all to myself. Speak to Harry, he'll tell you. Look at the bottom of my golf bag and you'll find the bag of weed I've been using. I'm also back on the Amitriptyline and Diazepam. I'm a fucking wreck, I'm telling you.'

Pete didn't know whether to cry from relief or dribble with rage. His emotions felt like they were belonging two different people.

They stared at each other for what seemed like five whole minutes.

'And Eve knows you nicked it?' Pete asked, nodding down at that which was nicked.

Sal nodded. 'She was the one who helped me do it. She wanted to help me find out who was POT shotting me. But it was on one condition. That once I had, I was to pass the laptop to you, for you to look at the accounts and see that Vic was in trouble, financially. She hoped you'd step in and do something about it. Only Vic didn't keep records of individual POT shotters, so I had to look a little deeper. And there you were, in Confessions, guilty by your own admission.'

Pete realised he had been as lax as the rest of them, only too eager to divest himself of his guilty misdeeds. As he shut down the laptop, to hide away his sin, the Apple logo on its lid struck him as highly ironic. The apple. Being the temptation of Eve. In The Garden of Eden.

'Anyway, I didn't keep my end of the bargain,' Sal went on, 'Once I found out it was you, there was no way I was going to hand it over to show you the accounts. Not until I'd punished you. So Eve took it back. Up until today. When she said I'd punished you enough and that you needed to know the truth.'

'And you agreed?'

'I said I did. Just so I could get the laptop back. But I'd no intention of telling you until I was forced to. Until I failed to die.'

Pete was shaking his head.

'Nice to know that Eve was willing to forgive me, when you weren't. But that's okay, you can also never forgive me for signing over your house to our Andy.'

'What do you mean, signed over?'

'I've given it to him. I believed — no, you led me to believe — that you wouldn't be seeing this side of spring. And what would I want with it after you'd gone? So now it's his.'

Sal was wide eyed with defiance.

'Well you can just go and sign it right back,' she told him.

'Not a chance. What's done is done. And don't you go getting onto him, either. He wept for days when I confided in him that you were a gonner. He deserves to keep it.'

Sal slid off the sofa arm into the seat.

They stared at each other, again, for what seemed like five whole minutes.

'What do you want to do now?' Pete asked her, 'Put it all behind us? Or get divorced?'

Sal shrugged. 'What do you want to do?'

Pete shrugged. 'I'll go along with whatever you want. It's up to you.'

'Alright then, we'll get divorced.'

'Fine. I'll get a pair of lawyers sorted out for the both of us.'

Sal leapt off the sofa to throw her arms around his neck, clinging to him like a groupie on a rockstar.

'No divorce. I couldn't bear it.'

'Me neither. No fucking way.'

'SOL,' she whispered.

They were late for the pass-over party, but only because Junior had gone AWOL, and as he'd got a new bowtie for the event it was only right that he attend.

'You've missed a corker!' Gabe told them as soon as they reached their dining table.

Pete could see Phoebe, instantly taking hold of her undercarriage as she began to laugh.

'Go on?' Pete told him.

'Mick the Vic walked in, starkers apart from his dog collar. He obviously thought he'd make one in and come dressed like the natives, like we were this morning. Only the natives turned out to be dressed.'

'Aw, bless him,' said Sal. 'He must have felt a right chump. Where is he?'

'He's gone home,' said Phoebe, 'To get his tux on.'

They sat to the table, allowing Junior to head off in the direction of Hellmutt.

'Who's serving the drinks?' Pete asked, seeing the others all had one in front of them.

'Nobody,' Jude told him. 'Staff have been given the night off. But it's champagne only, so just go grab yourself a bottle.' She was nodding to the two ice buckets centre of table.

'And get us another while you're at it. It's going down like pop,' Gabe told him.

As Pete walked over to the bar, he passed the buffet that was already laid out. It had four dogs sat staring up at it. His own included.

Adam came in through the kitchen doors, and as soon as he caught sight of Pete, he headed straight toward him.

'Have you made a decision?'

Pete nodded. 'Is that mic working?' he asked, nodding up toward the stage.

Adam looked across to it. 'Yes. If you give me five minutes to go turn it on.'

Pete gave him a thumbs up.

No sooner had Adam gone, than Jake and Karina intercepted him.

‘Pete. Thank you. Thank you so much,’ Karina said to him, taking both his hands and kissing his knuckles. ‘I never knew somebody be so kind.’

‘No worries. I’m just glad it went through alright. My lawyers aren’t that great when it comes to dealing with anything outside the UK. It looks like a pretty big place, though. Plenty of additional bungalows and buildings. Maybe they should consider taking in other families and making some rent out of it?’

Karina nodded and smiled, her eyes glassy and emotional.

‘Okay. My turn,’ Jake said to him, offering out his hand to shake.

Pete ignored it. ‘Your turn for what?’

‘Don’t give me any of that. You know what.’

‘Do I?’

‘Course you do. Who else do I know, who would buy a row of cottages and then just sign them over to their occupants? Not to mention arranging for new bathrooms and log burners to be put in.’

‘Ginnel?’

‘Ginnel, my arse. He doesn’t even know where I live. Even his shares turned out to be not worth a toss.’

‘So I heard,’ said Pete, finally offering out his hand, ‘But at least with the new stove and lav, you’ve got a choice of burning them or wiping your backside with them.’

No sooner had Pete poured two glasses and sat down, than Adam was out on stage, inviting him up.

Pete pushed back his chair and put back on his jacket.

‘Evening all,’ he said to them, taking the mic being passed to him by Adam.

Some shouted evening back, some waved, some gave him a thumbs up.

‘I’m not sure about you, but I’ve never been to a wake before. Certainly not a champagne wake. But from what I’m to understand, we’re expected to do at least two bottles each and stay up dancing till dawn. So good luck with that one. Anyroad, the reason I’m actually up here, is to let you know that as of today, I’m the new owner of The Garden of Eden.’

There was an immediate breaking out of applause and hoots and cheers.

'So being from Yorkshire, I'll be doubling your annual fees straight off,' he told them, as soon as they'd quietened down. The quiet was suddenly deafening.

'I'm just joking with yer, yer daft apeths,' he told them, laughing at their reaction. 'The annual fees will stay just as they are now, up until you park me out there under that tree, next to Vic.'

Another breaking out of applause and hoots and cheers.

Pete smiled as he looked around at their warm, appreciative faces, not least Sal's, who like everyone else, had been none the wiser up until that moment.

'I know you were probably expecting Eve and Adam to be taking over as the new owners,' Pete continued, 'But it's an enormous enterprise to commit to, and I dare say the prospect of managing to keep it afloat was daunting.'

To anyone astute enough, he knew they might recognise the possibility that the place had been near to sinking.

'That being said, they're both planning on staying here with us for the foreseeable future. Which is fantastic news. I mean, what would The Garden of Eden be without its very own Adam and Eve?'

Again, there was immediate applause, to which Adam and Eve stood up so they could give acknowledgement with a reciprocal hand clap.

'So, there you have it. Not much else to say really, except tonight, in honour of Vic, let's all get absolutely shit-faced.'

There were immediate joyous shouts of SOL.

As Pete came off stage, Adam climbed back onto it.

'We weren't intending to have anyone speak tonight,' he told them, 'But Rosa would just like to say a few words, if that's okay.'

He turned to look into the wings and beckon her forward.

Rosa strode out to stand in front of the mic. Her long skirt was caked with sand all around the hem, as if she'd gone via every golf course bunker to get to them.

'Hello. Glad you're having a good party,' she told them, waving like she was on a departing ship.

'Today, at the funeral of Victor, I didn't see him and I didn't hear him. Which is sad for you, I know. But now I think you'll be pleased that I've seen him this afternoon. He came through very strong, which is impressive for a first time. I'm sure he'll soon be sending me his voice as well as his vision.'

Everyone fell silent and Pete realised that they didn't know whether to be pained or pleased.

'So maybe there is something you would like for me to be saying to Victor?' Rosa asked them.

Quiet again, and then, 'Tell him he still owes me a pony from the Epsom Derby sweepstake,' Gabe shouted.

They all laughed. They knew what Gabe and Vic got up to.

'What did he look like?' Three Lugs called out to ask. 'Did he look okay?'

Rosa smiled and nodded as she came centre front of stage.

'He looked like Victor. He came as an apparition through the mist of the lake. He waved and then he vanished. Next time, he'll come nearer and he'll speak, for sure.'

Holding her pipe in one hand and scratching her broad, prominent chin with the other, she reminded Pete of Popeye.

'But I have something else,' she told them. 'Since they knew I was coming to you, your people have been flooding me with messages. In the end, I told them, "You're too many. Only one word each. I have to be back in time for Coronation Street".'

Everyone laughed.

'And they did good,' Rosa went on, after taking a few puffs on her pipe. 'They went away and they came back with the one word. And now, of course, I will bring that word to you. Not everybody, but I think nearly half.'

A murmur of excitement ran around the room.

'But remember what I always tell you. These messages are only to bring confirmation of life after death. Nothing more. This word is their gift to you, for Christmas. They know something that is happening now, that you don't. Which will be your proof. The word will mean nothing. Not yet. But it will. Maybe tomorrow, maybe next week, but definitely before Christmas. Maybe good. Maybe bad. Have you been naughty? Or nice?'

She came off stage and began to move amongst the tables, consulting a long strand of toilet paper that she'd opted to make her list on.

'One word? Is that it?' Sal bemoaned.

'I'll take that. It's ages since we've had anything,' Jude responded.

They sat, waiting and watching, until Rosa arrived at a nearby table, and then they strained to listen.

Rosa put a hand on Yakky's shoulder.

'Avalanche,' she told her.

As Yakky looked perplexed and slightly worried, Pete thought of their stolen chalet in Gstaad.

Rosa went to put her hand on Secret Squirrel.

'Clueless,' she gave him.

Pete smiled. He could have delivered that one himself. He could even have told Squirrel when it would come to pass. The next coffee morning quiz.

Rosa came to their table. She put her hand on Gabe's shoulder.

'Pryvit,' she told him.

Gabe and Jude looked at each other, totally bemused.

Rosa took a step toward Pete. She nipped his arm, causing him to swing around and face her.

'Seventeen,' she said to him, looking hard into his eyes. And then she blinked, smiled, and left the room.

Pete looked to Sal. Sal simply shrugged.

Once they'd had their first attack at the buffet, everyone was starting to wander through to The Ballroom hub, where Jake was making the most of the two disco decks.

'Did you buy it off them?' Gabe was asking.

'Eh?'

'Did you buy the place off Adam and Eve?'

Pete shook his head. 'Vic left it to me.'

'Bleeding hell. Didn't he think you had enough coin, already?' Gabe squawked, 'You're a jammy git, Hardcastle.'

'No, he's not,' Phoebe declared, 'This place is on the verge of going bankrupt. Vic left him it because he knew that he'd bail it out.'

Gabe, Jude, and Sal, all stared at Pete.

Gabe smirked, 'So you inherited a pile of gambling debts?'

'Pretty much.'

'You must be mad,' Jude told him.

'As a hatter,' Pete agreed.

Pete looked to Sal, who was as yet to comment. She just gave him a glowing smile and a tiddly wink.

'What were you two doing at the will reading, anyway?' Jude turned to ask Dan and Phoebe.

Neither of them replied.

'Don't deny you were there. We saw you,' Jude pursued.

'They were there for the same reason plod was there,' Pete informed her.

'Oh, shit, yeh, we couldn't believe it when Halloran showed up,' said Gabe, 'What was that all about?'

Dan and Phoebe were now looking to Pete, clearly wondering what he was going to say.

'Vic left a letter, admitting he'd bumped Lilith off. To put an end to her suffering. It was basically to inform plod that the body The Shovelbums dug up, is her. Dan and Phoebe were just invited as impartial witnesses, to relay the news to everyone, afterwards.'

It was weak, but it would have to do.

'Lilith didn't drown at sea, then?' Jude immediately asked.

Pete shook his head. 'That was just a ploy to save Vic from going to jail.'

'But how can they be certain that it's Lilith?' Sal quizzed, 'It could be just a red heron, to throw them off track?'

'Because tomorrow, they're going to take Adam and Eve's DNA. And nobody else's.'

'Christ almighty. Vic's got to be the happiest ghost going,' said Gabe, 'He died just in time to avoid bankruptcy. And just in time to avoid going to jail.'

'Well good for him. At least that means the sampling thing is now off. I didn't fancy having my DNA taken,' said Jude.

'Me neither,' said Sal.

'It's not painful,' Dan told them, 'Me and Phoeb had it done. It's no big deal.'

'What did you want to do that for?' Sal asked.

As Dan suddenly looked lost for an answer, Adam appeared, looking flustered and alarmed.

'Pete, your security guys are saying the police are here. And not just local police either, they've got some plain clothed from The Met with them.'

'What the hell do they want?' Pete asked.

Adam shrugged.

'Maybe they've caught whoever broke in to steal Vic's rare collections,' Phoebe suggested, casting an anxious look at her husband.

The others shared a knowing look. They knew there hadn't been any rare collections to steal.

Pete pushed back his chair, slipping away from the party that was now in full swing.

'Take off your jacket and bowtie,' Adam told him, once they were out in the corridor.

'What for?'

'Just in case. We don't want them thinking we're living it up when we're supposed to be in another lock-down.'

'Chuffin' hell. You don't think they're here because of that, do you?'

'Who knows,' said Adam, throwing his tie and jacket over their resident statue of the current Dalai Lama.

There were three of them, stood outside the doors of The Hub's reception.

'Inspector Halloran, no less. We weren't expecting to see you again so soon,' Pete said to him.

'No, me neither,' Halloran replied. 'But I'm glad to see you've finally dressed, especially as I've got DCI Devlin and DCI Rutherford here with me, from The Met.'

The two plain clothed DCIs nodded at Pete and he nodded back.

'You might remember that I recently arrested one of your residents,' Halloran reminded him, 'A gentleman who refused to give us his name and address. Resulting in the taking of his fingerprints. And low and behold, those prints have now been flagged up on The Met's database.'

Pete looked to Adam, and they both shrugged.

'Do you have a Mr Gabriel Fenton residing on your premises?' DCI Devlin asked Pete.

'We did have, yes.'

'When you say, did, you mean he's no longer here?'

'Correct. He had some urgent business he needed to attend to. Spain, I think he said it was. Left us early November. Not long after his unfortunate misunderstanding with your colleague here.'

Devlin stared at him, coolly, 'And Mrs Fenton, did she leave with him? Or is she still here?'

'Judith? She went with him, obviously. Very close couple, Mr and Mrs Fenton. Do you mind me asking what this is all about? You weren't hoping to deliver some bad news to them, were you? I hope there's not been an accident in the family?'

'We have a warrant for Mr Fenton's arrest.'

'Oh, my goodness. That's quite … shocking.'

'Indeed,' Devlin agreed, 'Might I suggest that should Mr Fenton return, or get in touch for any reason, you immediately contact us.'

'Of course,' Pete replied, taking the card that Devlin was holding out.

The two detectives immediately headed off to their unmarked car, leaving Halloran and his squad car behind.

'After you asked me, this afternoon, I made some enquires,' Halloran said to Adam. 'It turns out we received an anonymous tip off about a known criminal by the name of Scott Saunders. He's apparently got form for this sort of thing. And as there was CCTV of him, in the village, both prior to and after the robbery, I'm pleased to inform you he's now in police custody, pending trial.'

'Did they recover any of our stolen property?' Adam asked.

Halloran shook his head. 'There's an underground network for the specialist stuff. They often use the Dark Web. Which means it's very rarely recovered.'

'Not to worry,' said Adam, 'The insurance is due to pay out any day, so it would only complicate things.'

'What'll happen to Saunders?' Pete asked.

'Depends on the judge,' Halloran told him, 'Most likely, he'll get banged up in Wandsworth again.'

‘What are you going to do now?’ Adam asked Pete, as soon as Halloran had driven away.

‘I’m going to tell Gabe and Jude to get the hell out of here. And believe it or not, I’ve just bought the perfect place for them to hide up in. Providing they’re prepared to squeeze into a false fridge and freezer to get there.

‘And then tomorrow, Dan is going to give his brother the alibi he always wanted. Saying he was solely hereabouts to visit him and his pregnant wife.’

‘Wouldn’t he be better off with him back inside?’ Adam asked, knowing Dan’s brother was the reason for their new cameras and security guards.

Pete shook his head. ‘With a fella like that, it’s better that he’s forever beholden than forever begrudging.’

CHAPTER SEVENTEEN

ONE NIGHT IN DECEMBER

'Where d'you think you're going?' Sal asked, as Pete zipped up his jacket and put on his flat cap.

'Stargazing.'

'Stark raving what? Bonkers?'

'Star gazing. Looking at the stars,' he reiterated.

'At this time of night?'

'I'm hardly going to be seeing them during the day, am I? And it's not night. It might be dark, but it's only gone half four.'

Sal huffed as she lifted Junior onto the kitchen worktop. Since he'd scared them with his veterinary emergency of chicken bone lodged in intestine, she'd taken to feeding him by the spoonful, like a baby.

'If you're off up to that blinking observatory, you're definitely bonkers, it's bitter outside.'

'Then be thankful I'm going out stark raving and not stark naked.'

As Sal tutted to herself, Pete smiled to himself. He was always smiling of late. A matter of weeks ago, he'd been on the verge of his second nervous breakdown, but now, he was brimming over with happiness. Sal was back to her old self, apart from one single thing, she was no longer in the habit of swearing. After their major meltdown session, she'd actually seen fit to drop the F, the S, the B and the P words. Blinking was her go to exclamation word of late. Which pleased him no end. Unfortunately, he now couldn't stop swearing, it just fell out of him at every verse end.

'I'll be back before you know it,' he told her, checking he had his torch and compass before setting out.

It had been raining for most of the day and the steadily rising track, up through the wooded valley side, was like a series of rapids. It wasn't long before Pete's feet were squelching in their boots.

Sal was probably right. He was bonkers. Would he be able to find the key? Would he be able to operate the telescope? Would *The Great Conjunction* actually be visible? He'd been looking through the on-line newspapers for the past few days and they'd been full of promise at the sightings of the once in a lifetime phenomenon. The Bethlehem Star. On the Winter Solstice. A possible portent, they were saying, of something eventful, just as it had been before Christ's birth.

Pete had spoken to Mick the Vic about it, to air the possibility of a second coming. When the rector had stopped laughing, he'd promised Pete that he'd ring him if he chanced upon three gift bearing, camel riding kings.

The torch had a strong beam and it was illuminating every drip that dropped from the bare branches hanging overhead. It reflected in the eyes of the many deer that peered out at him from deep within the woodland thicket, and it shone like a laser beam into the patches of night sky that appeared between the trees.

At the top of the climb, Pete came out onto the wide path that led around the valley head. He followed it, keeping a sharp lookout for where the new track branched away.

The sky had finally cleared itself of clouds and the half moon was now wholly visible, along with myriad stars.

'Are you there, TC?' Pete asked, aloud, 'Is this something you've put together? Maybe a sign of something monumental about to happen?'

He came to the narrow track and followed it left, weaving between the gorse, the holly and the rhododendron, until he came to the neatly cut hole in the high wire fence.

The white stones lay just beyond and his torch beam bounced off them, brightly, as he forged ahead. He should have brought Dan. Dan would have enjoyed the adventure and would have known how to operate the telescope, considering he knew how to operate pretty much everything else.

Pete followed the trail until the black dome of the remote observatory appeared straight ahead of him, bringing a surge of adrenalin. He wasn't sure if he was excited or scared.

After the day-long downpour, the water trough was full to the brim, and on seeing it, Pete had a minor panic. Was the key under the trough? Or at the bottom of the trough? He couldn't remember what the one-line instruction had said. If he reached under, it meant blindly searching between the two bricks that held it off the ground, chancing to meet a hidden rodent. Reaching into the bottom of it, meant a freezing cold arm and a possible encounter with a hibernating amphibian. Neither option appealed.

Getting down onto his knees, Pete reached beneath. Rubble and wet grass, but no key. He took off his jacket and jumper, then plunged his hand deep into the trough. Not the best place to hide a metal key, even if he found it, it might be so rusty as to prove useless. Either way, his search proved fruitless.

He couldn't believe that he'd come all that way on the strength of something written months ago by a man since deceased.

Putting on his jumper and jacket, he picked up his torch and headed off in reverse of the stone trail. Sal would be pleased at his early return, if nothing else, but he was bitterly disappointed. Although, maybe, there was still one more option. He returned to the observatory and stood before its door. It was worth a try.

Taking firm hold of the handle, he levered, and pushed.

Much to his surprise, it opened. There was a lamp, lit, off to one side. And there was someone sat, silent, beneath the enormous telescope centre space. Their head was tilted up to its lens, but that head immediately turned around to stare into the full beam of Pete's torch.

'Aaargghh. Aaaargghh,' Pete screamed.

He dropped his torch as he fell backwards out of the doorway, his heart pumping faster than Tugger's right hand, screaming so much he forgot to breathe. He grappled through the grass for his torch and then with it, stumbled toward the white stones. He was beside himself with shock and horror, pushing his way through the branches that seemed hell bent on holding him back. He was six stones away when he heard a voice calling out to him.

'Peter! Peter! It's me! Come back! I'm not a ghost! I'm alive!'

Pete sank onto his knees. Did he trust it? Was it alive? Or was it just wanting to communicate with him, from the other side? He stayed stock still, and listened.

'Are you still there?' the voice shouted to ask.

Pete's heart was now down below two hundred beats per minute and he took a breath.

'Yes,' he managed to shout back.

'I'm sorry I gave you a fright. If I'd known you were coming, I'd have got Rin to warn you,' it called out. 'Don't be angry with me. It was all part of the plan. Come back and I'll tell you about it.'

Pete couldn't believe what he was hearing. Was faking your own death that easy? It obviously wasn't hard. First Sal, faking her future death, and now Vic, faking his recent.

He got to his feet and headed back.

Vic was stood in the doorway waiting for him, giving him a meek little wave.

'What the fuck are you playing at?' Pete asked, as he approached him.

Vic shrugged. 'Come on inside. I'll explain.'

Pete followed him into the small domed space that was filled with the giant telescope and perched on the only seat other than that beneath the ocular lens.

'Am I dreaming this?' Pete asked, slapping his own face, left hand, right hand, left hand.

'Stop it. It's no dream,' Vic told him.

'No, it's a fucking nightmare.'

Vic grinned at him. 'Aren't you pleased? That I'm alive?'

Pete stared at him. 'No. I'm not. It's going to upset a lot of people.'

'People are never going to know. I'll be dead soon enough, so what's a little extension going to matter?'

'Extension? Is that what this is? Has the cancer gotten into your brain?'

Vic raised his eyebrows. 'When did she tell you I had cancer? She wasn't supposed to tell anyone.'

'It wasn't Rin. I just bumped into someone in the village, that works at the hospital.'

He couldn't say that he'd seen the Consultant's letters on his stolen laptop, so it was the best lie he could throw out, but he could see Vic looked suspicious of it.

'Never mind any of that,' Pete told him. 'What are you doing, hiding out here?'

Vic sniffed and then wiped his nose on the sleeve of his pullover.

'I've not been hiding here. I've been in my cabin. This is only the second time I've been out. First time, I got seen, and had to fling myself into the bracken and crawl back.'

'By Rosa?'

Vic nodded. 'Can you believe? I was at the far side of the lake and I actually waved at her before it dawned on me.'

'It's okay, she thought you were a vision.'

'I guessed she would. Good that it was her that saw me and nobody else, eh?'

Pete shook his head, amazed at how lightly Vic was treating it.

'And you thought you'd chance it again, today? To come and see the star?'

Vic nodded. 'Rin brought me up on the donkey before first light. I've been here all day.'

He pointed to the half-eaten food and flask and cup.

Pete reached out to take one of the remaining biscuits and then stood to walk around the telescope.

'Have you come to see the star of Bethlehem?' Vic asked.

'Yes, it's been on the news. There's quite a lot of interest in it.'

'I know, I've seen it. But I've been interested in it for years.'

'You don't look well,' Pete told him, ignoring the rest.

'I'm not. I'm done for, well and truly. The only thing keeping me going is the steroids and the morphine. But not for much longer. I'm going to be doing euthanasia soon.'

'You mean suicide?'

'No. I mean euthanasia. You don't say you're going to put your old cancer riddled dog down by suicide, do you?'

Pete guessed not. 'When?'

'Just before Phoebe gives birth to my baby. Which you obviously know about, having read the contracts.'

Pete sighed as he sat down. He did know, but he'd had trouble accepting it.

'Why would you want a surrogate child at your age? Especially when you knew you were on your way out? And why commit su — euthanasia, before you get a chance to see it?'

'I don't want to see it. I never intended to see it. I'm going to die just as it's about to be born. Because I'm going to reincarnate into it.'

The morphine. It had to be the morphine. It was making him delusional.

'You can't really believe that?' Pete scoffed.

'Why not? If the Dalai Lama can do it, then why can't I? Rin is going to help me with a lethal injection just before the actual birth. It's been the plan all along.'

Thanks to Genji, Pete was aware of the Dalai Lama's instant rebirth, but that wasn't to say he believed it.

'Fucking hell, Vic, I know you're a big believer, but this has got to be a bit of a stretch, even for you.'

'Why are you swearing? You never used to swear. What's happened to you?'

'A lot,' Pete replied, but refused to be diverted. 'Go on, then. When's she due?'

'She was artificially inseminated on the twenty-fifth of March, because I want it to arrive on the twenty-fifth of December.'

Pete smirked. Vic had never had children, otherwise he'd have known these things didn't happen exactly nine months to the day.

'And you planned it that way because, what? You want to come back as Jesus? Is that what you want this star to be all about?'

'If I wanted to be Jesus, I'd have left instructions to be christened Jesus, instead of Victorious.'

Pete began to laugh. The whole thing was absolutely, mind-blowingly ludicrous.

'You sure it's going to be a boy?'

'It's definitely a boy. But if it hadn't been, I'd have accepted being a girl.'

'And being called Victoria?'

Vic shook his head. 'Bernice. It's a biblical name that means the same thing. Victorious.'

'Bernice is alright, but what lad would want a name like Victorious, these days?'

'A lad like me. I'd want the same name. It will be familiar. And it will remind me of the life I had before, hopefully.'

'And you don't think it's a bit creepy, coming back as your own son?'

'Not in the slightest. Ask any Buddhist monk and he'll tell you that we often reincarnate back into our own families.'

Pete was finding it extremely tenuous.

'Bit of a gamble, wasn't it? Expecting your sperm to attach itself on the exact date you wanted it to?'

'It was the one thing I wasn't prepared to gamble on. I took Clomid. It turns those bad boys into Olympic swimmers.'

Pete had to smile, it was funny, even though it was twisted.

'But I did edge my bets. I had two other couples here, doing the same thing, at the same time,' Vic cared to divulge, 'Only you never saw them, because they didn't have any success.'

Pete gave it some thought.

'So that's why Dan and Phoebe came out of quarantine bouncing around like spring lambs? Because she'd done a positive pregnancy test and won a golden ticket to stay on. For three million quid.'

'You're catching on well. Almost as well as my sperm,' said Vic, dryly, and then, 'You know what's expected of you, don't you? It wasn't a lot to ask, bearing in mind I've left the entire place to you.'

'Are you taking the piss? What you left me, was a place that had umpteen-million quid's worth of gambling debts secured against it, you devious old bastard. You only gave it me because you knew I could pay it off.'

'No. I gave it you because you love the place as much as I do. And I knew you wouldn't let such a paradise slip through your fingers.'

Pete was shaking his head, but it was pointless to argue. Vic was right, he wouldn't.

'So? Are you going to carry out my one request? In view of how simple it is?' Vic asked.

Pete took a breath and sighed.

'Yes, I'll carry out your cuckoo request,' he assured him, 'But why me? Why not Adam? He's the one who normally operates The Well.'

'Because I knew he wouldn't agree to it, and if he did, he'd only be ringing for an ambulance the first time she let out a moan or a groan. This thing has to go according to plan. And aren't you forgetting? Eve and Adam know nothing about this. They didn't get to see a copy of those contracts, like you did. Though I dare say they must be wondering why I left so much more to the Saunders than to them.'

'The Saunders *and* Rin.'

'Rin's money is for staying here and raising me. Two million to bank. And a hundred thousand every year, until I'm old enough for her to leave and go back home to Japan.'

'Which means we're stuck with you for what? Another fifteen, sixteen years?' said Pete, thinking it best to humour him, in light of him having gone quite mad.

Vic smiled and reached out to fist bump Pete's shoulder, but as he did, Pete grabbed him around the wrist.

'I've a bone to pick with you,' he told him.

'A bone?'

'Yes. Lots of bones. A whole skeleton of bones.'

'Ah. You mean Lilith.'

'Yes, Lilith. Why didn't you ever admit to me that you'd helped see her off? Why did you keep up that pained pretence of having let her down, when you hadn't?'

'It wasn't a pretence. Because it wasn't me who helped her on her way. It was Adam and Eve.'

Pete stared at him, trying to figure it out.

'I'd no idea. Not a clue,' Vic told him, 'Not until after she'd accidently been dug up and the kids came to tell me what they'd done. Their mother had begged them. And the pair of them obviously had the guts to do what I couldn't. They dug the hole. They did the deed. They took out her teeth. And they buried her. Is it any wonder Adam was in a state of flux, at me letting the archaeologists loose on the place.'

Pete immediately recollected Gabe, telling him about Adam and Vic almost coming to blows over it, on their journey back from London.

'And they didn't just have the guts, they had the brains,' Vic went on. 'As soon as they'd got the job done, Eve dressed in her mother's hat and coat and drove her car to Cornwall to abandon it on that beach. With Adam half an hour behind, to bring her back. I'd never have thought of that. That there'd be cameras all along the route, helping to prove her suicide and save them both from going to jail.'

Pete was still staring at him. Still trying to work it out.

'And after they came to tell you all this? You told them you'd fake your own death and take the rap for it?'

'I didn't tell them anything. I'm sure they believe I've died of Covid, just like everyone else. But I'd like to think my letter, confessing to it, gave them a lot of relief.'

'I'm sure it did,' said Pete, 'After they got over the first ten minutes of heart failure.'

'How do you mean?'

Pete grinned at the memory of it.

'When Carmichael produced your letter, and invited plod over to hear its contents, Eve looked set to run for the hills. I reckon they thought it was going to reveal the truth about what they'd done.'

'Oh dear,' said Vic, 'I never considered that.'

'Well I wouldn't worry about it. What's ten minutes of heart failure, compared to the relief of a lifetime?'

Vic nodded, but just then, a small alarm clock started beeping, loudly.

'Conjunction time!'

He swung beneath the telescope and popped his eye to the lens.

'Do you know whereabouts it is?' Pete asked, coming to hover at his shoulder.

'Of course. I've got it trained on the exact coordinates.'

Pete was hopeful of getting a glimpse of it, although he appreciated it was Vic's baby, in every sense of the word.

'They've been pretty much joined together for hours, but this is supposedly their optimal moment. And I would agree. It really is something to behold. Truly amazing. Can you believe that this was exactly what the three wise men would have seen all those years ago.'

No, thought Pete, he couldn't. But he could imagine.

Vic had a minute of mesmerisation before he lifted from his chair and urged Pete into his vacated position.

'It's bright,' Pete commented. 'And it's just like they said it would be, in the shape of a cross. Which is rather sad.'

'Is it?'

'Yes. If this really was the star, hanging over Christ's birthplace, then it wasn't just showing where he was going to be born, it was also showing how he was going to die.'

'That's a humdinger of an observation. I never even considered that.'

Pete moved out of the chair to allow Vic a further sighting. He guessed the observatory had been built for this one sole purpose, so it was only right that Vic should make the most of it.

'I understand the police came to my wake?' Vic asked, while still glued to the lens.

Rin had obviously told him.

'They did, yes. I thought we were about to get shutdown for breaking Covid rules but it was just news about the break-in.'

It was the truth, but not the whole truth.

Vic gave it twelve seconds, and then, 'I hear Gabriel and Judith have left us?'

'Yes. Gone to live abroad.'

'That was sudden. Was it anything to do with the police visit?'

He'd clearly put two and two together. He'd heard Gabe's confessions; he knew he was a crook. But Pete couldn't let on that he knew, that he knew.

'As a matter of fact, they —' There was a noise outside that prompted Pete to stop. 'Is that your donkey?' he asked.

'That or Joel Ferranti,' Vic replied, wryly.

The braying stopped as soon as it had started and then the door opened and in walked Rin.

Rin looked to Vic, and then looked to Pete, and then back to Vic. She was plainly surprised to find he had a visitor and equally surprised that the visitor seemed calmly accepting of Vic's resurrection.

'Phoebe's gone into labour,' she announced, 'You need to come. It's time.'

'She can't be,' said Vic, 'It's not due till Christmas Day. This is only the Solstice.'

Pete coughed out a laugh. 'You didn't actually believe it would arrive nine months to the day, did you?'

Vic looked stunned that there was a possibility it might not.

'Oh, for heaven's sake! If I can manage to hang on to life up until Christmas, why can't she can do the same?'

Rin threw her arms up. 'No time to complain. If this is how you want it to be, you've got to hurry.'

Vic looked to Pete.

'Don't look at me, mate, I'd be clinging to life till it took me out squealing. I figure this is the only one we get.'

Vic grabbed his jacket. 'Oh, ye of little faith,' he said to him.

'I've got plenty of faith, it's just not in having been here once as a chicken.'

As they helped Vic onto the donkey, Vic passed Pete the key for the observatory.

'All yours,' he said to him.

Pete had a sharp intake of breath as he realised the significance of it. This would be the last visit Vic would be making to the place. To any place.

There was another route that Pete hadn't known about. It was wider and smoother and they were able to go at a faster, steadier pace. Rin held the reins while Vic just held on.

As they reached the rim of the valley head, Pete's torch lit up a sign at the start of their descent.

With three people walking together, there is always a teacher among them – Confucius.

It felt like a significant coincidence, with there being the three of them. But as to who was the teacher?

Halfway down the valley side, Pete began to sing.

'*We three kings of Orient are ....*'

Vic and Rin immediately joined in.

'Bearing gifts we travel so far, field and fountain, moor and mountain, following yonder star. Oh-oh, star of wonder, star of light, star of royal beauty bright. Westward leading, still proceeding, guide us to thy perfect light.'

They sang it, same verse and chorus, over and over, until they reached the open meadow that surrounded the lake.

'They weren't kings,' Vic summarily announced. 'They were never kings. They were Magi. Magicians. Wise men. Seers. They had the gift, same as Rosa.'

Pete immediately looked across the water, to Rosa's caravan. It was warmly lit, with smoke billowing from its ever-more-crooked chimney pipe. He hoped that she and Arek were deeply engrossed in Coronation Street. Vic, alone, might be considered an apparition, but not alongside himself, Rin, and a donkey.

The Dome stood ominously black against the starlit sky as they made their way toward it. While ahead of them, their resident barn owl swooped long and low as if to say a final farewell to the man who had always shown such an avid interest in it.

'Have you considered how Rin's going to get your body into the box that you *didn't* get buried in?' Pete had a sudden thought to ask.

'She's not. We were never going to do it that way. Not even before I brought my funeral forward, to help the kids. The box was always going to be filled with sandbags. Just as the doctor ordered.'

'So what's going to happen to your body?'

Vic didn't reply.

'Aren't you going to tell me?'

Vic clearly didn't want to, but, 'You know the panels on The Dome's roof? The three that are metal and not glass?'

'The air-conditioning panels?'

'Yes, them. You can get out through one of them, for maintenance. And as those units were decommissioned, since getting the new ground-level ones, that's where I'm going to be making my exit, literally. And that's where I'll be staying, because Rin's going to throw away the key.'

'Out on the fucking roof?'

'Yes, out on the roof. And stop swearing why don't you.'

Pete couldn't believe it. It was grotesque.

'I tried it out with a dead deer that I got Arek to put up there,' Vic told him.

'You're telling me Arek knows about all this?'

'Of course not. There's only us three. And you wouldn't have known if you hadn't decided to gate-crash my Conjunction. I told him it was to encourage red kites to the site.'

'And he believed you?'

'Yes. Because it did. And that deer carcass was gone in no time.'

Pete seriously couldn't believe it. It was beyond grotesque.

'Okay, so I get why you have to do it this way now, with your funeral been and gone. But why plan on doing it this way before? Before you had to? Why not plan to get buried under the tree for real?'

'Like I said, doctor's orders. He'd only issue my death certificate if there was no possibility of it being proved false. If I was found to have a lethal drug in my veins, there was every chance he would get struck off. No body, no chance.'

'Alright, but why put the cause of death as Covid? Why not the obvious? Cancer?'

'Cancer was what it was going to be, but with me contracting Covid, it was considered a more feasible option.'

Pete was still incredulous of it all.

'Is it really that easy to get a false death certificate?'

'Too easy. Especially when you've got terminal cancer and you're being prescribed drugs that can just as easily kill you. The coroner's not going to give it a second thought. But it helps if you know a dodgy GP.'

Pete wondered if it was the same village GP he'd used. The one who'd been willing to give him enough Diazepam to flatten an elephant.

'What about the announcement on Christmas Day? Are you still wanting me to go ahead with it?' he asked.

It had been the final paragraph in both Rin's and the Saunders' contracts. An announcement was to be made:

Congratulations to Vic and Rin on the birth of their healthy boy, Vic Junior, with many grateful thanks to Phoebe Saunders for being surrogate mother.

It had brought a tear to his eye when he'd read it, believing as he did, that Vic was already dead.

Vic sighed, 'There was going to be a follow-up announcement to that. An hour later. Telling everyone I'd died from over excitement. But that had to go, obviously. Maybe the first should, too. Just tell everyone yourself, Peter, if you wouldn't mind. Once Dan and Phoebe have gone. Tell them all why they left their baby behind, with Rin.'

Pete nodded. He could do that. As long as he didn't have to tell them it was Vic, reborn.

They entered The Dome by the side door; the one used only by the staff. Rin relit her torch and led them up the rear stairs.

'Are you sure you want to go ahead with this?' Pete asked, 'You could have months left yet?'

'Yes, months on drugs that are killing me quicker than the cancer. I'm shedding skin and shit like an incontinent leper. I'm doing it. And I've never been more excited in my entire life. I'll be closing one door behind me and stepping straight out through another, with a whole new healthy life ahead of me.'

Pete decided not to argue. Better that Vic had such great faith, than not. Better to be looking through a lens to the stars than down the barrel of a gun.

As they came out into the rafters of the roof, they traversed its long narrow gantry, looking down upon the lush tropical vegetation beneath them. The only lights were Christmas lights. White and gold. Making the place looked magical. And yet it was a magic tinged with the surreal. A man was soon to be injected with a lethal drug, and die, while a woman close by, having been injected with his sperm, was about to give birth to his baby.

Phoebe was there. Pete could see her. They were entering into The Well down below. Dan was helping her, as were two others. A man and a woman.

'Their contract said they'd have a doctor and a nurse there with them?' Pete queried in a whisper to Vic, not trusting The Dome's constantly tumbling water to provide soundproofing enough.

'They have.'

'DoLottie and Sasquatch?'

As Vic grinned at him, Pete realised his name slip, but Vic obviously knew who he meant.

'Like their contract says. A doctor and a nurse. Who I hope you can show some respect to by using their real names, for once.'

Pete considered he would try, but since their little faceoff in the massage suite, he and Sasquatch were beyond name calling.

'And they volunteered for this?'

Vic shook his head. 'I gave them a little something, for doing it.'

Pete knew he was lying. They didn't need the money, for starters. This was what DoLottie had been blackmailed into, he was certain of it. But how had Sasquatch got involved?

'What if it goes wrong and she can't deliver naturally?'

'He'll have to do a Caesarean.'

'What? In the fucking Well?'

'Okay, Rin will ring for an ambulance,' Vic snapped, 'They're getting three million pounds for doing this, she needs to do it the way I want it. Anyway, it's time you went. They can't get started without you.'

With one hand, Pete wiped down over his face, trying to clear away the craziness.

'Come here,' said Vic, 'We didn't get chance to say goodbye before my first death, but we can do it before my second.'

They hugged, long and hard, and Pete might have been sad if not for seeing how physically frail and tortured Vic was. It helped that Vic himself was genuinely excited, like he was on his way to a fabulous foreign holiday.

'I'll be seeing you soon,' Vic said, as he pushed Pete to go, 'And I'll be talking to you in a couple of years. I'll try and remember you, Peter, but I can't guarantee it.'

Pete smiled and shook his head at the preposterous possibility and then he was on his way. He had a job to do.

'We thought you weren't coming,' Dan said to him as he emerged into The Well.

'I was out of range of a signal,' Pete told him, truthfully.

Phoebe's moaning suddenly became agonising groaning.

‘You were supposed to be on-call. I’d have thought that meant staying well within range,’ Sasquatch remarked, snidely.

Pete was instantly irked. Irked at being challenged and irked that they knew he was due to attend, while he hadn’t known they were. And how competent were they after all this time? Doc might be an obstetrician, but he was a struck-off obstetrician. Good job Dan and Phoebe didn’t know that.

A protracted yodel from Phoebe brought Pete sharply back into focus and he went to Adam’s usual position by the operating panel. Since reading their contract, and knowing what was expected of him, he’d made it his business to get accustomed to the controls, beforehand.

He started up the hydraulics that lifted the base and then, without waiting, he switched on The Vibration and Sound. The giant tuning fork began resonating, and then the water started shimmering and shuddering. Pete loved The Sound. It reminded him of the singing bowls he’d heard Rin playing during his many visits to Vic. It was instantly soothing. But the next time he would be flicking its switch, it would be to turn it off, and he was already dreading it.

With the platform raised and the water level lowered, Phoebe was able to sit down; with the others hovering beside her. It was only then that Pete spotted the paraphernalia floating all around them. Various plastic tubs. A rubber-ring. A foil blanket. Sun-lounger cushions. Snorkel and mask. It was like a cruise liner had sunk directly beneath them.

‘Remember your breathing techniques,’ Susanna was telling Phoebe.

‘How long ago did her waters break?’ Doc was asking Dan.

Phoebe breathed as Dan shrugged.

Pete settled down for the duration, relieved that everything seemed to be going swimmingly. But not for long.

‘Noooooo, I can’t do this. Turn the fucking pain off!’ Phoebe bellowed.

‘Come on Phoebs, breath through it, you can do it,’ Dan coaxed.

'It's alright for you, you aren't — Aarrgghhhhhh — You aren't the one having to do it. I want pain relief! And I want it now!'

Pete wondered if he should lower the base and go ring for an ambulance. Sod Vic and his deluded ideas. What difference did it make where she gave birth? Why was being in The Well so essential?

'We're going to help you,' Susanna was saying to Phoebe, 'I know we're not supposed to, but we decided it was the right thing to do. Vic isn't with us anymore, he's not going to know, so we brought something in with us.'

'Oh, thank God,' Phoebe gasped.

'Pete?' Susanna called out, 'Over near you, on top of the magnetic rail, you'll see a canister with Entonox written on the side. There's also a carrier bag. Do you think you could bring them to me?'

Pete was floored by her sudden conciliatory tones. He wanted to ignore her, but for Phoebe's sake, he was forced into a truce. He retrieved the goods, and then passing them to Susanna, stood to watch as she attached a tube and mouthpiece to the canister.

'When the next contraction begins, breathe it in, slow and deep,' Susanna told Phoebe, placing the tube into her mouth.

Pete wondered why Vic hadn't wanted Phoebe to have pain relief. Was it all part of his unhinged beliefs? Was it due to what God had inflicted on Eve, as punishment for eating the apple?

I will multiply your pain in childbearing and in pain you shall bring forth children.

Had Vic not wanted to go against the biblical decree?

He waded to the far side of the orb to avoid further involvement, sitting down to submerge himself in the warm water. He knew from Pip's three births that Phoebe still had some time to go.

He thought of those births. And of their three sons, out in Brazil. It would be the fourth Christmas in a row that he hadn't seen them. Pip would be heartbroken that it had come to such a prolonged estrangement.

To pass the time, Pete began to aimlessly swim around, using all the flotsam and jetsam as an obstacle course.

The Saunders' contract had stated that if Phoebe went into labour during the day, the fire alarms would be used to empty The Dome, with an electrical fault being the excuse for keeping everyone away. But as the place closed nightly, at eight, they'd timed it to perfection, arriving as they had, at half past. He could only hope they'd be done by eight in the morning, when it reopened.

Pete was trying to blank out the screaming. Entonox obviously wasn't the perfect panacea.

He wondered why the Suttons hadn't pulled out of the whole thing. Vic was dead, at least to them, so why had they opted to go through with it? Why not tell Phoebe to draft in another birthing team? Come to think of it, why were Phoebe and Dan going through with it? Why hadn't they just gone straight to the hospital? He began to wonder if his own purpose for being there was more than just to flick the switches. Had they all been told that he was there to witness things being carried out to the letter?

Should he tell them? That he didn't give a shit? Probably too late now. And what would happen if he did? What would Vic do, marooned on the roof, watching them all leave?

Pete thought of the roof. Of Vic and Rin. Ready to climb out through the maintenance panel and administer the lethal injection.

If he had known that morning how things would turn out that evening, he would have stayed in bed. And what would he tell Sal when he got back? He'd told her about the contract and Vic's surrogate child. He'd also told her about his own minor role in Phoebe's water birth. A simple operating of the mechanics. But now, it was more than that. Now, he could never tell her. Certainly not about Vic's extended life. She'd only freak out every time she saw a kite coming to land between the air-con units.

Pete was getting bored. Hours had passed and if he stayed sat on the floor any longer, he felt certain of acquiring Vibration White Testicle.

As he patiently waited, he pondered upon the possibility of having another out-of-body experience. He lay back, hoping to float, surprising himself that he immediately did. He could see the halfmoon framed through one of the glass panels, and across to one side, he could just make out Rin through the hanging vines. But no sign of Vic.

For no reason at all, his body suddenly decided to roll over and he found himself floating face down with his eyes wide open.

On the blue, mosaic tiled floor, Pete saw something he'd never seen before. Letters. Made out in an ever-so-slightly darker shade and barely discernible. The letters formed words and the words formed another of their customary adages and aphorisms.

He paddled up and down to read the subliminal message.

THINGS THAT ARE HIDDEN ARE OFTEN JUST BENEATH THE SURFACE. WHEN WATER IS IN OUR EYES, WE GET A GLIMPSE OF THEM.

As Pete pondered on it, he was yanked out of his reverie by Phoebe's shrill and sudden shouting.

'This is total fucking agony. I'm never having sex again. You stay away from me, Daniel Saunders. You keep that evil penis of yours to yourself from now on, do you hear me?'

Pete could see Dan, half smiling, half anxious. He was holding his wife with his arms hooked under her armpits as he knelt behind her. Pete felt sorry for him. He wanted to shout: 'It was a syringe that got you into this darling, not his penis.' But the time obviously wasn't right.

Pete commandeered the rubber-ring to sit in. He began to think about The Vibration and Sound. Railing at himself for being so blasé about it. For not gaining some in-depth understanding of it before Vic went. And now he'd never know.

'Aarrgghhhhhh,' Phoebe screamed, 'Holy fucking cow! So much for the magical experience. That birthing book is sooooo full of shit. I'm going to sue the fucking author once I'm through with this.'

Pete was smiling to himself, and then, he had a sudden eureka moment. The Book. Vic's book. On Vic's laptop. What was it he'd said? A guide for future Custodians. Explaining everything intrinsic to, The Fold, The Well, The Fork, The Vibration and Sound. The Garden of Eden in its entirety. A summary short of being finished before it was stolen. But he could get by without a summary. He could even do a summary himself, once he'd digested the detail. All he had to do was find the book on the laptop.

Phoebe had gone quiet, so Pete took a swim to the other side of the orb to see what was going on. Doc had donned the snorkel and mask and had gone down to ogle between Phoebe's legs. Was she fully dilated? If she was, what was to stop the water from going in? Would the baby drown before it was born? And then came another bloodcurdling scream.

'That's it. Start to pant. Deep breath. Pant. Pant. Pant,' Susanna instructed.

'Come on Phoebs, you got this,' Dan was saying, 'Not long now.'

Phoebe just howled, and in-between howling, she panted.

Pete wondered what it was like, giving birth. Gabe said he'd imagined it was like passing a bowling ball while you had piles. Pete remembered that Pip had developed piles toward the end of each pregnancy. It was the weight, apparently. He wondered if Phoebe had developed piles. He wondered if she thought it had been worth it, the pain and the piles. Three million was probably a fortune to them. He knew a lot of women did it for less. Some even did it for free, for their sisters or friends. Pete wished he hadn't had kids. They were a huge disappointment to him. He wondered if Rin would find Vic Junior a disappointment.

According to her contract, she was to stay in The Garden to raise their surrogate child, which had left him with the impression she was infertile and the baby was for mainly for her. But now he knew it wasn't, it was entirely for Vic.

'You need to get ready, Pete,' Susanna shouted to him.

Bloody hell, he was expecting it to take another few hours; their first had taken Pip over twelve. He hoped they'd heard, up above, and were readying themselves. He went to stand by the operating panel.

Why in TC's name was Rin willing to administer this fatal drug? When Vic had first met her, she'd been working as a croupier in a casino, which hardly qualified her for the job in hand. Dealing cards wasn't the same as dealing death. And where had they got the lethal dose from? Not something you could go and buy over the counter in Boots. Maybe they'd got it from the dodgy doctor who'd pronounced Vic as dead?

'Okay. The baby's on its way,' Doc was saying, 'At the next contraction, I want you to push as hard as you can.'

Pete had his hand, hovering by the switch.

'Aarrgghhh. Aarrgghhhhhh,' Phoebe screamed.

'Nearly there,' said Doc, 'Two more pushes and it's over.'

Pete could see Phoebe's face was purple from the strain as she screwed up her eyes and clenched her jaw.

'Okay, Pete, we're here,' Susanna told him, 'For whatever reason you need to know, this baby is going to be with us within minutes.'

Pete suddenly panicked. He was going to be instrumental in ending someone's life. Should he ? Or should he not? What the fuck was he to do? There was no way out. Vic would never forgive him if he didn't. He flicked the switch – and The Vibration and Sound immediately ceased.

He almost collapsed from the sudden, overwhelming, unexpected stress.

Up until that evening, he'd known only that he was to turn off The Vibration and Sound immediately prior to the baby's appearance. A bizarre request, but the only one Vic had required of him. He hadn't known that it would be the signal for Vic to make his exit — and anticipated re-entry.

He looked at the other four in the pool. If they knew what he knew, what would they say? Probably nothing. They were too absorbed with life right now to give a thought to death. Two minutes later, there was the unmistakable cry of a baby and Pete immediately burst into tears.

'You soft git,' he found himself saying aloud. He waded across to take a look.

The Suttons were using implements from their floating plastic tubs. They were clamping the umbilical cord. They were clearing the baby's nostrils. They were inspecting him, all over. They were weighing him with a hanging scales and sling. They were cutting the umbilical cord. And then Phoebe was helped into the rubber-ring and the baby was placed onto her belly.

She and Dan looked smitten.

Pete hoped not too smitten, seeing as it wasn't long to be theirs.

He had spotted the bottle of champagne next to the Entonox canister, and now he spotted the small stack of plastic cups alongside it. This was clearly the final piece of the birthing kit.

They were all elated. But it was an elation borne of relief. Pete passed Dan the bottle and the cork was duly popped, shooting out to land in the crook of The Fork's tines, on top of the staghorn fern.

'Does anyone know how we're going to get the baby out of here, without it drowning?' Pete thought to ask, as soon as he'd drained his glass in a single gulp.

Phoebe and Dan looked instantly alarmed.

'Don't worry,' Doc told them, 'Babies up to six months have a diving reflex. It's called the Bradycardic response. It's a survival technique that means they naturally hold their breath when under water.'

The relief on the young couple's faces was plain to see, but what was also plain, was that they would be very reluctant to hand this baby over. Pete was aware that surrogates often changed their minds when it came to it. But what they both had to remember, was that in the not too dim and distant future, this child would develop an uncanny resemblance to one Victorious Dawson. And they wouldn't be so enamoured of it then, he was sure.

CHAPTER EIGHTEEN

DAY AFTER NIGHT

Rin was already waiting for them outside of The Well. Clearly keen to take delivery of the new-born baby. Pete wondered if she actually believed it was Vic, reborn, or if she thought it was a load of old tosh, like he did.

'Congratulations,' she offered to the young couple.

As Phoebe waded toward her, babe in arms, smiling, Pete gave a sigh of relief. She was going to hand it over, no problem.

After kissing Phoebe on both cheeks, Rin took a look, but nothing more.

Pete suddenly felt a hand upon his shoulder.

'We need to talk to you, while they're still in there,' Dan told him, throwing his eyes over the wall to where Doc and Susanna had remained to gather up.

Hey-ho, here we go, thought Pete. He pointed toward the wide, shallow steps of the pool and they all waded across to sit on them.

'It's our baby and we're keeping it,' Dan told him, bluntly.

Pete looked to Rin, but Rin didn't react. She just sat expressionless and inscrutable, with her long black hair floating around her like an oil-slick.

'We decided to take a prenatal paternity test, as soon as the restrictions made it available,' Dan continued. 'It's not Vic's. It's ours. One hundred percent ours. And we don't want the money. We just want our baby.'

Pete looked to Phoebe, and then to Rin, and then back to Dan, while all three of them just stared at him.

'Did Vic not get a paternity test done?' Pete asked.

Dan and Phoebe both shook their heads.

'The only thing he seemed bothered about, was finding out what sex it was,' Dan replied, 'Phoebe had to eat bananas and broccoli every day, because he wanted a boy.'

Pete raised an eyebrow. Was that an actual fact? Was that what Pip had unwittingly done, having developed a craving for both?

'We had sex,' Phoebe suddenly blurted, 'A couple of days before the insemination. I know we weren't supposed to. We'd been really good up until then. We'd abstained for three whole months like we were supposed to, but it was just … it just happened. Just the once. We didn't think it would come to anything.'

'And you didn't think to tell Vic that it was in no part his?' Pete asked them.

Dan shook his head. 'We were still going to hand it over, according to plan. We thought we'd be able to. For us, three million is a life changing amount of money. But as the baby grew we realised we couldn't, so we confided in Rin because we didn't want to disappoint her.'

'But she wasn't disappointed at all,' Phoebe was quick to add, 'She didn't even want it in the first place.'

Pete looked to Rin, who was nodding, frenziedly.

'And then when she told us Vic hadn't got long to live, we all decided, for his sake, to pretend to go through with it, for however long he had. Once he was gone, we'd just take the baby back,' Dan expanded.

Pete looked to Rin and Rin nodded, frenziedly.

'The whole thing has been so stressful. For all three of us. Me and Rin kept meeting up, over and over, having endless discussions about what we should do. And then, when Vic suddenly died of Covid, it complicated things even further.'

Pete immediately looked to Rin. This time, she was wide eyed and subtly shaking her head. They didn't know. She hadn't told them that he hadn't died. Thankfully, Dan and Phoebe weren't aware that their child was meant to be nothing more than a vessel for Vic's transmigrating soul. He subtly nodded back to Rin. He would gladly withhold the truth of it.

Dan was now wringing his hands, nervously.

'Rin suggested that all we had to do, was go through with having the birth here in The Well, as per Vic's plan, and then we would get our money. We would get ours and she would get hers, all set to be automatically transferred on Christmas Day.'

'And then we'd leave and go our separate ways, right after the announcement,' Phoebe added.

Pete thought of the cancelled announcement, telling everyone of Vic's surrogate child. Enough to put anyone off their pigs in blankets.

'But they would keep baby. And I would go back Japan,' Rin finally voiced.

Pete studied the three of them.

'So why are you telling me all this? Why aren't you heading off to pack your bags?'

'Because you've been so kind to us. From the very start,' said Dan, 'And especially after what you did with sorting out my brother. And then knowing the place had been left to you so heavily in debt, it didn't seem right to add another five million to it. Plus, Rin was worried that Vic might come back to haunt us if we took the money without sticking to the contracts. That's why we decided to tell you the truth before the money was transferred, so you could stop it. Then we could all leave with a clear conscience.'

Pete stared at them. He was at a loss what to say. But what a relief, on so many levels. Rin and Dan had been meeting only for discussions. The baby wasn't Vic's. And he wouldn't be waiting and worrying that its first words were going to be, 'Hello, Peter, it's me.'

All he could think to do was put out his hand for each of them to shake.

'Now I go back Japan?' Rin asked him.

Pete shrugged. 'Absolutely. The baby isn't Vic's. The contracts are null and void as far as I'm concerned.'

'And money nil and void?' Rin asked, 'Or maybe we get some smaller, for stress compensation?'

Pete thought about it. Five million, between them. Rightfully, it should go back to Vic's estate and reduce his debt. He knew from having looked through the accounts that the money had already been placed into a separate holding account, in readiness, but he could easily move it back. But then, hadn't Rin just earned her two million? He imagined it took a lot to euthanise someone. She could be scarred for life. And as for Dan and Phoebe? What the hell. Three million would give their little family a great start in life.

He looked at them, the three of them. Staring back, like their lives depended on him.

'The announcement won't be going ahead, on the twenty-fifth,' he told them, 'But the bank transfers will. You can have it. All of it. Merry Christmas.'

Rin immediately flung her arms around his neck and hugged him, while Phoebe and Dan just dropped their jaws, and hugged their baby.

This had to be the best part of being stinking rich, thought Pete.

Rin was up onto her feet. 'Okay. Tomorrow. I'm gone,' she told them, backing out of the pool, as if turning her back might allow Pete the chance to change his mind.

Pete only had chance to do one thing, and that was to let his own jaw drop.

Rin. Vic's petite personal assistant and live-in lover. The one who had been prepared to raise Vic in his second coming. The one who Pete had always believed to be a woman. Had a penis. She was a ladyboy.

'Will you be the baby's godfather?' Dan was asking him.

Pete was too shocked to speak.

'Pete?'

Pete just pointed at Rin, who was now scurrying away.

'She's a man,' he mouthed.

Dan smirked. 'Didn't you know? Why else would they need a surrogate?'

Pete shrugged.

'So would you like to be the baby's godfather?' Phoebe repeated.

Pete realised he was being remiss.

'Of course I bloody would. It would be an absolute pleasure.'

In the absence of any grandkids, it would be the next best thing.

‘And we don’t have to call him Victorious, like in the contract?’ Phoebe queried.

‘You most certainly do not.’

‘Oh, thank God for that!’

Her relief was understandable.

‘Why not go and get yourselves dressed,’ he said to them, ‘I’ll stay here and wait for the Suttons.’

He didn’t have to wait long. The sealed plastic tubs burst out onto the pool’s surface like pent-up geyser bubbles, soon to be followed by Susanna, with the carrier bag tight in her hand, and then Doc, with the Entonox canister.

‘We’ve gathered up most of the afterbirth,’ Doc told him. ‘We’ll chuck it somewhere out off the track for the kites to polish off.’

Pete nodded. It could be an appetiser before their main course, up on the roof.

‘Thanks for everything you did in there,’ he told them, holding out his hand.

Doc took it and shook it.

‘If that was what Dan and Phoebe wanted, then we’re happy to have obliged. And it was evidently important to Vic, too. He absolutely insisted on me doing it.’

Insisted? Well, he could hardly say he’d been blackmailed into it, Pete supposed.

‘Are they related in some way?’ Susanna asked.

Pete smiled. ‘Almost, but not quite,’ he replied, enigmatically,

They looked baffled, but they didn’t ask.

Rounding up the floating plastic tubs, they made their way toward the steps.

‘Is it alright if we come for the key straight after breakfast?’ Doc asked him.

‘Sure. But what key would that be?’

‘Number sixteen. The Lawsons cabin. Vic said it was ours, if we did what we just did.’

The Lawsons? Ah, The Prunuptials.

‘Vic never told me,’ Pete replied, ‘And I’m afraid I’ve just let it go to Dave Attwood and his sister — like wife, because they are, like brother and sister now, instead of husband and wife. That's why they wanted a cabin to themselves, each.'

The truth would come out eventually, about Ruth and Ruthless, but he didn't intend it to come from him.

'That's hugely disappointing,' said Doc, looking hugely disappointed. 'What with you scrapping the couples only rule, and that being the only vacant cabin. We're like the Attwoods, you see, we're now wanting to live separately.'

'Then you can have ours. When we've moved out,' Pete told them.

'Nooooo,' Susanna screeched, 'You can't. We need you here. Please don't be an absent owner.'

Bloody hell, thought Pete, it wasn't that long ago she'd been ready to castrate him with her bare teeth.

'Yes, please think again,' Doc added, 'When you took over as the new owner, everyone was absolutely delighted. You're fair. You're genuine. You're a straightforward, straight-talking Yorkshireman. We couldn't have asked for better.'

'I'm right chuffed to hear it. But we're only moving out so we can move into Vic's place. Rin's leaving as of tomorrow, and Sal's always loved the view from up there.'

Susanna's eyes lit up. 'And we can have yours? Are you sure?'

'Sure, I'm sure. Shake on it. Seeing as I'm a straightforward, straight-talking Yorkshireman.'

Doc shook his hand and then so did Susanna. Pete thought his wrist would snap, but no wonder, her hands looked as big as her feet.

As the Suttons headed off to the changing rooms, Pete headed towards the pool's revolving doors. His clothes were still in a trail where he'd dropped them, in his haste, and he struggled to get them back on with still being wet.

Out in the main foyer, he saw Eve and Adam coming hastily toward him across the other side of the barrier shower. They had two paramedics with them and the blue flashing lights of an ambulance were right outside.

'We'd no idea,' Adam told him, breathlessly.

'Oh my God, they've got a baby!' Eve squealed, swinging left to point at Phoebe as she and Dan appeared at that very second.

Pete realised Rin must have rung for an ambulance as soon as Vic had passed away. He was grateful. There had been moments when he would have rung himself if he'd had his mobile with him.

The paramedics immediately led Phoebe and her baby out to the waiting ambulance, with Dan, Eve and Adam following on. It was time for Pete to make his exit.

He hopped into one of the golf buggies and headed for home along the riverside track. At the far side of The Bridge, he smiled as his tiny headlights lit up his latest sign.

We are not human beings having a spiritual experience. We are spiritual beings having a human experience.

Approaching The Hub, he could see people in their dressing gowns gathering on the front steps. Mary immediately stepped out into the road to flag him down.

'The ambulances woke us all up. Has Eden arrived?' she eagerly enquired.

'Who?'

'Eden. The baby. That's what they wanted to call him. Eden Saunders.'

'Yes, he's safely arrived.'

'The baby's been born!' Mary turned and shouted to everyone.

A huge cheer went up with ensuing applause.

'If you hang around, the ambulance will be coming up with them. Why not have yourselves a look?' Pete suggested, 'There's only the one.'

'One? Were they expecting twins?'

'Ambulance. You said ambulances. But there's just one.'

'Haven't you heard?' Mary asked him, before covering her mouth at the shock he was about to receive.

Pete stared at her for a second. He had doubts as to even ask after the night he'd just had.

'Heard what?'

'The other ambulance. It was for James. He's dead. People are saying he might have taken his own life.'

Pete's eyes widened in disbelief.

‘It must be a terrible shock for the twins,’ said Mary, ‘Not to mention his own twin, Joe. What a miserable Christmas they’re all going to have.’

Not really, thought Pete. If anyone had taken James’ life, it was The Shining. And as for Joe, he didn’t exist. Not that he could tell Mary that.

‘They always say that when one goes, another one comes,’ Mary continued, ‘Looks like that’s been proved right tonight.’

Pete nodded. But the truth of it was, two had gone.

‘You’ve been a long time looking at them there stars,’ Sal said to him, as he slid into bed beside her.

‘I’ve been in The Well. I got the call and had to make a dash for it.’

Sal immediately turned on the bedside light and put some effort into sitting upright.

‘Did it go alright?’

‘It did. Seeing as our resident doctor and nurse did themselves proud.’

‘You’re joking? You mean DoLottie and Sasquatch?’

‘Yup. We never expected it to be them in attendance, did we? He’s been retired for God knows how long.’

‘He’s been struck off, that’s what he’s been.’

Pete smiled. He kept forgetting that she too had read their confessions. He sat up, to join her. It was pointless trying to sleep now, it was already half past five and his stomach was gearing up for breakfast.

‘I hope he hasn’t got any of that venereal disease left in him. He might have passed it on through the water.’

‘Jake?’

‘Nooo. DoLottie.’

“The Doc had Chlamydia?’ Pete asked, incredulous.

‘Didn’t you know? He was the one that gave it them all. Picked it up when he was away with you lot on Prunie’s stag-do. He had a bit of a skirmish with one of the barmaids on the boat, and then brought it back and passed it to Lottie. Then she passed it to Jake. And then he passed it to Chelsea. And then seeing as Chelsea can’t keep her knickers on. Wipe out.’

Pete was shaking his head. ‘How do you know all this?’

‘The nurse.’

‘Susanna?’

‘Noooo, yer chump. Our nurse. Father Anthony’s squeeze. She had to needle them all with the antibiotics and then take their bloods after.’

Pete was casting his mind back to the riverboat on the Thames, to where the original transmission had taken place. Doc, doing his utmost to hold onto his trousers, to save them from going overboard, except, obviously, when he’d been all too keen to part with them.

‘And did they hand it over?’ Sal asked.

‘What?’

‘The baby. Did they hand it over to Rin? Or did Phoebe refuse, like I said she would?’

When Pete had told Sal about the bizarre contracts, it had been the first thing she’d said, “She’ll never part with it.”

‘The contracts turned out to be worthless. The baby wasn’t Vic’s. It was Dan’s. Stupid old sod never got a paternity test done. Bit of a crazy gamble, expecting them to go without sex for three months, at their age.’

Sal huffed. ‘Well, he was, wasn’t he? A gambler. Serves him right. Why would anyone want a baby at that age?’

Pete was about to tell her, but thought better of it.

‘Did you ever wonder why they couldn’t have a baby themselves? Vic and Rin?’

Sal shrugged. ‘She must be infertile, seeing as his sperm was good to go.’

Pete nodded. He’d tell her, one day.

‘Have you heard about James?’ he asked.

‘Heard? I’ve done nothing but. I must have had eight people come knocking the door down to tell me. And he’s another one that got what he deserved That’s what you get for juggling two women. As soon as you cancelled the couples only rule, I knew it was just a matter of time before they did him in. And I bet they get away with it too. The cops around here are blinking useless. Which I suppose is no bad thing, otherwise Gabe and Jude wouldn’t have gotten away so easily.’

Pete smiled as he rolled out of bed to go for a pee.

‘Have you seen your e-mails today?’ Sal shouted to him in the en-suite.

‘Don’t think I’ve looked at them for over a week,’ he shouted back.

‘Why not?’ she asked, when he returned to climb into bed.

‘Because I know that you’re always reading them, and if there was anything interesting, you’d holler.’

‘Well I’m hollering,’ she told him, reaching to her bedside table for the two Apple Macs that were stacked there.

She passed him the top one and he opened it up. It was theirs, so he tapped his way into his e-mails.

‘Ignore the rest. Just take a look at the one that came last night, from your Andy,’ she told him.

‘What’s he e-mailing me for? He never e-mails me.’

‘Be quiet and just take a look at it.’

The e-mail heading was: *You need to see this!!!*

He’d have to take his brother’s word for it. He opened it.

The mail had no actual message, just a website link. He clicked on it and it took him straight to the Barnsley Chronicle, October 2020. Two months old.

It was a full-page article headed: *Barnsley Boys Do Good.* Surely not another story of his rags to riches success? It was old hat now. But, boys? Maybe this time it included his brother. Three garden centres weren’t to be sniffed at. He settled back to read. If it was important to his brother, then it was important to him.

He scrolled down beyond the headline.

Brothers, Connor, Kyle and Jeremy Hardcastle, Barnsley born and bred, have just been awarded OBEs in the Queen’s recent Honours List.

Was this a joke? A very bad joke?

Now based in Brazil, Connor took time out of their incredibly busy schedule to grant a short interview.

Incredibly busy schedule? It was definitely a bad joke.

They are the three sons of another of Barnsley’s best, our very own, Peter Hardcastle – on whom this journal has run many a story — and it is with the same gritty attitude as their father, that they have achieved something undeniably deserving of the public recognition. They have created a charitable foundation that has looked to save the lives of countless abandoned and neglected children surviving in abject poverty on the streets of Brazil.

Connor spoke for all three when he told us: "For years, we struggled to make our father proud. Trying to emulate his monumental success. But his shoes were just too big for us to fill and after too many failed business ventures, we were pretty much at rock bottom. It was at that point, that Jeremy happened to see a newsreel on the street children of Brazil. The Meninos de rua. He was so fired up about it that he insisted both me and Kyle watch it. It was heartrending. So much so, that the three of us felt compelled to do something about it. We'd no children of our own, as we'd also failed in our marriages, but that wasn't to say we didn't have some latent paternal instincts. And there's no doubt that it was those instincts that led us to sell everything we owned and set off to Rio.

"It wasn't easy. We had a lot of obstacles to overcome, not least the fact we couldn't speak Spanish. But necessity as they say, made the three of us get a grasp of it pretty damn quick. We now have a dozen children's homes spread right across Brazil, and for each, we've sourced access to free medical care and dedicated teachers willing to donate their time. We even managed to get some of Brazil's famous footballers onboard to give free places within their soccer training foundation. This is what led to us setting up our own foundation. The Pippin Foundation. We decided to name it after our late mother, Pippa, remembering how she used to call us her three Pippins.

"After years of chasing entrepreneurial goals, believing that was the only way for us to feel successful, we can honestly say that those goals wouldn't have given us a fraction of the satisfaction we feel right now. We might not have the business acumen of our father, but we have his drive, determination and resourcefulness, and that's what's made The Pippin Foundation such a monumental success."

It's not clear who nominated the three brothers for their OBE awards, but it's believed it could be from high-ranking officials in Brazil as well as from the UK's own senior politicians.

The Chronicle aims to run a follow up story when the three of them return to England for their investiture.

Pete stared at the photograph. It showed his three boys. Tanned and smiling and surrounded by dozens of tanned and smiling kids.

'Proud, or what?' Sal said to him, grinning.

Pete was speechless. He was stunned. He was overwhelmed. He was incredulous. And yes, he was proud. Too damn right he was proud.

'The Pippin Foundation? I've seen that somewhere?' he said, trying desperately to think.

Sal opened up Vic's laptop and tapped her way in, driving down through his alphabetically listed files. She turned to show it to Pete, and there it was. Pippin Foundation. She swapped over laptops.

Pete opened up the file, to find himself looking at an excel spreadsheet. It showed, for near enough the past two years, that Vic had been transferring a sum of ten thousand pounds, each and every month, direct from The Garden of Eden's bank account to that of The Pippin Foundation. He was flabbergasted.

'How did Vic know about it?' he asked.

'He knew because he liked nothing more than to pry into all of our lives. If you google Hardcastle, Rio de Janeiro, The Pippin Foundation comes up top of the list.'

'But why would he send them money?'

'Because you weren't. And he probably knew that one day you'd regret it.'

Pete slumped back into his pillows.

'All those calls from them, that I refused to take,' he reflected, 'I could have been helping them, every step of the way. I bet they think I'm a right tight-arsed twat.'

'You're not getting it, are you?'

'Getting what?'

'Vic. It was all part of his plan. He knew you'd find out eventually. When you'd inherited the place and looked into its accounts. He's spared you the guilt. All you have to do is send an e-mail to them, via The Garden of Eden website to The Pippin Foundation website, and they'll believe it's been you sending the payments all along.'

Pete was suddenly excited. 'Shall I write to them?'

'Definitely.'

Pete pondered what to put, and then he typed: *Congratulations on your OBEs. If you're free today, we could zoom you. Dad x.*

'What about that?'

'That'll do. Fire it off.'

Pete fired.

'What time do you think it is, over there?' he asked.

Sal immediately googled it.

'I think it might be two in the morning. We probably won't get a reply until this afternoon.'

'No, I guess not. I'll go put the kettle on.'

Pete got out of bed and followed Junior to their lounge kitchenette, but before he'd even opened the dog biscuits, Sal shouted to him.

'You've got one back!'

Pete rushed back into the bedroom to share the laptop with her.

The top inbox message said: *Congratulations right back at you!*

Pete just stared at it.

'Open it, then!' Sal shouted at him.

He opened it.

Great to hear from you dad. Yes to the zoom. 18:00 your time. And congratulations on becoming grandad to the seventeen kids we've adopted between us.

There were seventeen smiling emojis and then a gap followed by three laughing emojis.

Sal stared at Pete, and then she cracked up. She was cackling like the wicked step-grandmother she intended to be. Wicked in the way Jake always meant it.

Pete was dumbfounded. He was a grandad. Just like that. Seventeen times over.

'Seventeen!' Sal screeched, 'That's the word that Rosa gave you!'

They stared at each other, wide-eyed in wonder.

While Pete mashed a pot of tea, Sal put in an order for a celebratory champagne breakfast.

'Has Derek got much work on, since he finished your house?' Pete asked, carrying the tea tray back to bed.

'You mean, your brother's house?'

'Aye, sorry.'

'Well don't be. I was honestly starting to loathe it. It was just one big bling box. We would never have felt at home in it, you and me. I'm glad it's gone.'

'Truthfully?'

'Truthfully. When have I ever lied to you?'

They both burst out laughing.

Fifteen minutes later, a Starship was outside, shouting its arrival, and Pete hurried to respond.

'What the?'

He couldn't get to the Starship for the large wooden crate that sat directly outside their front door.

'Have you ordered something off Amazon?' he shouted over his shoulder to Sal.

Sal came to take a look.

'I think it must be for somebody else,' she told him, climbing over it to get to their breakfast delivery.

Pete pulled it inside. 'It's bloody heavy, whatever it is.'

'Aren't you going to open it?' she asked, passing him a croissant. 'It's got, *For the new Owner,* written on this side. That's you.'

The only tools they had in the cabin were a pair of plyers and a lump hammer, but they did the job well enough. The wooden box was soon in pieces.

Inside, was another box, gift wrapped, and Sal wasted no time in unwrapping it, leaving them staring at a boxed Toshiba microwave.

'Is ours broken?' Pete asked.

Sal shook her head.

'Then why would someone think we needed a new one?'

'It's not new. Look, it's already been opened.'

The box had been badly sealed with masking tape, which Sal easily peeled away. And then opening the flaps, they found themselves staring into a nest of straw which had two large, marble eggs laid in it.

'Huh,' Sal grunted, 'I think we need to get Christmas out of the way, before we start on Easter.'

Pete lifted out one of the eggs and turned it around, resulting in a high-pitched squawk from Sal.

Pete immediately reached in to rotate the other egg.

'You know where these belong, don't you?'

Sal nodded, reaching out to stroke the marble face of Eve.

'On our headless statues.'

An envelope sat inside the nest and Sal took it and opened it. It was a Christmas card.

'Who's it from?' Pete asked.

Sal began to read: '*We're very sorry for vandalising your statues but we didn't like having a nudist camp so close to our village. Although it no longer said it on the front gates, we still didn't want anyone guessing by you having Adam and Eve stuck there.*

'A chap by the name of Nigel Nolan will be getting in touch with you. He's a stone mason and an expert in fixing this sort of thing. We've already paid him, so all you have to do is give him a time.

'We're genuinely sorry, especially as you've managed to do what we couldn't in getting rid of the proposed housing development. The golf course plans look beautiful and we're all delighted with it. We understand the council have put in a clause saying clothing must be worn at all times, but please feel free to ignore it and play in the nude. We've all made a pact to stop being so prudish, so you can rest assured that there will be no complaints from any of us.

'Apologies once again and Merry Christmas.'

Pete began to laugh.

'After all these years. Who'd have thought it was the locals?'

'I wonder if Jake, or Mick the Vic knew?' Sal mused.

'If they did, they did a good job of not letting on.'

He opened the champagne. The second bottle of the day and it wasn't yet nine o'clock.

'I think you should e-mail Derek and ask him if he's busy,' he suggested, as he filled two flutes.

'Why? What you up to? Are you renovating somewhere?'

‘No. You are,’ Pete told her. ‘We’re flitting into Vic’s cabin. You’ve always said you’d love to have it, if ever you had the chance, and now you have. Rin’s leaving. She’s off back to Japan. So I suggest you get it how you want it before we move in.’

Sal immediately took two handfuls of straw and threw it high into the air, in celebration.

‘Would you ever consider living here permanently?’ Sal asked him, as they tucked into their salmon mousse breakfast.

‘I would. But wouldn’t you miss home?’

‘This is home.’

‘You mean to say, that of all the sodding mansions we could afford to buy, you’d chose to live here in a five-room cabin?’

‘A cabin with an amazing view, yes. And our house back home is enormous for just the two of us.’

‘Are you suggesting we sell it off?’

‘Of course not. We need to get a fix of God’s country every now and then. And besides, we’ll be needing all those bedrooms for when the grandkids come to visit.’

Pete smiled and nodded.

‘And that double-decker bus is going to come in handy, too,’ she told him, ‘It’ll be ideal for taking them all on trips to the seaside.’

Pete’s heart was suddenly bursting with love for her. She wasn’t the brightest but what did that matter when she was the warmest and the kindest.

As Sal e-mailed Derek, Pete swept up the straw that Junior had spread far and wide.

‘Remember when the kites kept landing on the roof of The Dome?’ he asked her.

‘Hmmm, you said it was because they liked the heat,’ she replied, as she typed.

‘Well, I think they’ll be coming back soon.’

‘I’m sure they will. Mary says it’s going to drop really cold next week. They’ll be wanting to get warm.’

‘And fat,’ Pete added.

There was a moment’s lull while Sal finished off her e-mail.

‘Talking of fat, Shar Pei’s putting some timber on again. You’re going to have to change her name until she gets another gastric band fitted.’

Pete shook his head. ‘I’m going to quit the name calling. I’ve decided they’re too fucking cruel.’

‘Cruel would be alright, if they weren’t so ridiculously childish.’

‘Well, either way, from now on, no more names.’

‘Good. Then while you’re at it, you can stop the swearing. It’s not becoming of a new club owner. You could end up being top of the POTs.’

‘No, I won’t,’ Pete assured her.

‘Oh yes, you will,’ she told him, ‘Because I’ll make absolutely goddamn sure of it.’

Of the twenty-five Personally Observed Transgressions (POTs) relevant to The Garden, only twelve are mentioned and used. As below:

BAB = Bragging And Boasting
EAC = Excessive Alcohol Consumption
EVE = Excessive Vanity Evidenced
GBH = Grievous Bodily Harm
JOE = Jealousy Or Envy
PIP = Personal Imperfections Parodied
POG = Pointless Overindulgent Greed
ROY = Rude Or Yobbish
SAC = Self-Absorbed Conversation
SIC = Sarcastically Intrusive Conversation
SOL = Swearing Out Loud
TIT = Too Immoderately Togged

Many thanks to Karina Kuraian
for the front cover painting.
Your dreams are now my dreams.

Slava Ukraini!

Слава Україні!

Also by this Author

Burning Belief

If you remembered who you were in a previous life, would it alter who you were in this? Might you be wiser? Maybe kinder? Or scarred, scared and embittered?

What if you came back with a memory of a place that held something rare and precious? Would you dedicate your life to finding it? Or what if that precious thing could be found within yourself? A rare innate talent? Might it be a blessing or a curse?

As a consultant archaeologist, Bethany Craven has taken a private commission on a remote Scottish estate. A place found to be inherently rare and precious, where the wise are scarred, the embittered unkind, and the famous and the fortunate as cursed as they are blessed.

Exposing layer after layer of their well-hidden secrets, Beth finally uncovers proof enough to believe they all have a past life cross to bear.

www.ingramcontent.com/pod-product-compliance
Lightning Source LLC
Chambersburg PA
CBHW070432170726
48291CB00002B/459